# CRITICAL PRAISE FOR
## *EYES OF THE HAMMER*!

"THE READER HAD BETTER HANG ON, BECAUSE HE'S IN FOR A HELL OF A RIDE! An exciting look into the world of America's fighting elite, the Green Berets, Delta Forces, the Air Commandos, and the CIA's direct action elements. The story is as hot as it can be . . . Mayer knows the details of special operations, and he can tell you how it all works—and why."

—Daniel Bolger, author of
*Feast of Bones*

"A first novel by a former Green Beret, this is NOT TO BE MISSED . . . A thriller that delivers in all areas—plot, suspense, pace and authenticity. The climax will have the reader yearning for more nails to bite."

—*Library Journal*

"LOTS OF GUTS, LOTS OF ACTION."　　　—*Kirkus*

"General Norman Schwarzkopf singled out the U.S. Army's Special Forces for special praise following the Persian Gulf War—now you'll understand why."

—John J. Duffy, U.S. Army
Special Forces (Ret.)

# EYES OF THE HAMMER

## BOB MAYER

ST. MARTIN'S PAPERBACKS

Published by arrangement with Presidio Press

EYES OF THE HAMMER

Copyright © 1991 by Bob Mayer.

Library of Congress Catalog Card Number: 91-6683

ISBN: 0-312-92862-9

Printed in the United States of America

Lyford Books hardcover edition published 1991
St. Martin's Paperbacks edition / October 1992

10  9  8  7  6  5  4  3  2  1

**To My Parents**

# GLOSSARY

**AC-130**   See Spectre.

**AH-64**   See Apache.

**AK-47**   Standard Soviet automatic rifle. 7.62mm caliber.

**AO**   Area of operations.

**Apache**   Newest army attack helicopter (AH-64). Armed with cannon, rockets, and missiles.

**A-Team**   Basic operating unit of Special Forces.

**AWACS**   Airborne early warning and command system.

**Blackhawk**   Newest army transport helicopter (UH-60). Dual-engined, with greater power than the Huey. MH-60 version is the special operations model with better navigational systems built in.

**Boltz rig**   Series of straps designed to hold a rubber boat against the belly of a Blackhawk helicopter, allowing the helicopter to fly at full speed with the boat ready for immediate use. Named after the team sergeant in 5th Special Forces Group who invented it. Also known as the external air transport (EAT) system.

**Briefback**   Briefing given at the end of isolation period by the A-Team to show the commander the plan and prove that the team is ready to execute the mission.

**CARP**   Computed air release point.

**Chem light**   Chemical light that when cracked will emit low-level light for several hours.

**CIA**   Central Intelligence Agency.

**Claymore**   Crescent-shaped antipersonnel mine that shoots out hundreds of ball-bearing projectiles in an arc.

**C-130**   Hercules four-engine turboprop plane; can hold up to 64 parachutists. May be jumped from either rear two doors or off the ramp.

**Combat Talon**   Modified Hercules (MC-130) used by Air Special Operations to infiltrate denied air space at low altitude under almost all weather and light conditions to conduct airdrop, airland, or surface-to-air recovery methods.

**DCSOP-SO**   Deputy Chief of Staff Operations-Special Operations.

**DEA**   Drug Enforcement Agency.

**Delta**   Army's elite counterterrorist force.

**Det cord**   Detonator cord. A line of explosive that burns almost instantaneously. Used as a fuse to detonate nonelectrical blasting caps.

**DOD**   Department of Defense.

**DZ**   Drop zone.

**E&E**   Escape and evasion.

**1st SOW**   1st Special Operations Wing. Air Force's special operations aircraft (AC-130, MC-130, HH-53) are all in this unit.

**550 cord**   Nylon cord used for parachute suspension line.

**G-1**   Administrative section of a headquarters, responsible for personnel actions.

**G-2**   Intelligence section of a headquarters.

**G-3**   Operations section of a headquarters.

**HAHO**   High altitude, high opening parachute operation.

**HALO**   High altitude, low opening parachute operation.

**HARP**   High altitude release point.

**HH-53**   See Pave Low.

**Huey**   Utility helicopter (UH-1, Iroquois). An older model transport helicopter, primary Vietnam-era helicopter.

**Intel**   Intelligence.

**IR**   Infrared. Anything IR (chem light, strobe, light) cannot be seen with the naked eye but appears as regular light when seen through night-vision goggles.

**Isolation**   The time period prior to a mission when an A-team is kept isolated to do mission preparation. Ends when briefback is accepted by the commander and the team departs for the mission.

**KC-10**   Modified DC-10, used by the air force as an aerial tanker for in-flight refueling.

**Klick**   Kilometer.

**LLLTV**   Low light level television.

**LZ**   Landing zone.

**MAC-10**   Ingram submachine gun used by drug runners.

**MANPADS**    Man portable position azimuth direction system. A portable computer system that can pinpoint present location and direction and azimuth to another location.

**MC-130**    See Combat Talon.

**MH-60**    See Blackhawk.

**MILES**    Multiple integrated laser engagement system, used to record "hits" during training exercises.

**MOS**    Military occupation specialty. A soldier's job title.

**M-203**    M16 rifle with a 40mm grenade launcher built in under the rifle barrel.

**M60**    Medium machine gun. 7.62mm caliber. Belt-fed.

**MTT**    Mobile training team.

**NCO**    Noncommissioned officer.

**NVG**    Night-vision goggles.

**NSA**    National Security Agency.

**ODA**    Operations Detachment Alpha. See A-Team.

**OP**    Observation point. Position from which surveillance is conducted.

**OPORD**    Operations order.

**Ops**    Operations.

**Pave Low**    Two engine, single rotor, heavy lift helicopter (HH-53) designed to operate in Special Operations missions at low altitudes under nearly any weather or light condition. Modified from CH-53 cargo helicopter.

**PIC**    Pilot in command.

**PZ**    Pick up zone.

**PVS-5**    See NVG.

**Q-course**    Qualification course conducted at Fort Bragg for all soldiers who want to be in Special Forces.

**Recon**    Reconnaissance.

**RPG**    Rocket propelled grenade. Consists of a launcher and separate rounds for firing, like a bazooka.

**SAW**    Squad automatic weapon. Light machine gun, 5.56mm caliber.

**SF**    U.S. Army Special Forces.

**SFOD-D**    Special Forces Operations Detachment-Delta. See Delta.

**SOCOM**    Special Operations Command.

**SOP**    Standard operating procedure.

**Spectre**   Modified Hercules (AC-130) used for direct fire support of ground forces. Has two 7.62 miniguns, two 40mm automatic cannons, and one 105mm autoloading howitzer.

**Task Force 160**   Army's special operations helicopter unit.

**Thermals**   Thermal sight. Uses the spectrum of light to discern radiating heat.

**TOW**   Tube-launched, optically-guided, wire-command-linked missile. Heavy antitank missile system.

**UH-1**   See Huey.

**UH-60**   See Blackhawk.

**Zodiac**   Inflatable rubber boat.

# WEDNESDAY, 21 AUGUST

## SPRINGFIELD, VIRGINIA
## 8:12 A.M.

The convoy was caught in the tail end of the morning traffic crush pouring out of the suburbs and cascading into Washington, D.C. The three four-door Chevys with tinted windows were sandwiched in a long string of cars rolling east along Keene Mill Road. Another mile and a half along the two-lane road that bisected Springfield, Virginia, and they'd reach the Beltway girdling the nation's capital.

The morning sun was low on the horizon, its slanting rays a harbinger of the broiling heat to come later in the day. Penetrating the dark windshield of the second car, the bright sun caused the occupant of the right front seat to squint as he scanned the road ahead. Although the sun hurt his eyes, Jenkins resisted the temptation to put his sunglasses on, knowing that the combination of dark glasses and a tinted windshield would effectively blind him to the shaded areas along the sides of the road, which he was methodically scanning.

Conscious of his responsibilities as the agent in charge of the convoy, Jenkins twisted in the seat and glanced over his shoulder. Car Three was lagging behind. Before another car could slip into the gap, he picked up the radio microphone and keyed it. "Three, close it up."

"Roger, Two."

Jenkins shook his head in slight irritation as he put down the mike. There was never enough time to train his men correctly.

1

He glanced over his left shoulder again to ensure that the third car had closed the gap sufficiently. Satisfied, he continued his forward surveillance of the right side of the busy two-lane road.

Jenkins checked to make sure that his own driver was maintaining the proper interval behind the lead security car. He wished he could roll down his window. Smoke from the cigar in the backseat was overpowering the air-conditioning. The cigar smoke from their charge was just one of several things Jenkins didn't like about this assignment. He envisioned himself as a man of action, and bodyguard details bored him. In his opinion they were usually a waste of personnel. Six U.S. marshals to guard one person wasn't what Jenkins considered an efficient use of manpower.

He returned his attention to the route. They were driving along a section of road bordered on both sides by expensive houses. Fifty meters ahead of the lead car, a group of about twenty high school students waited for their bus along the right side of the road. Jenkins briefly considered them as a source of danger, then rejected the possibility.

He shifted his gaze twenty-five feet farther down the sidewalk and raked his eyes over two men walking toward the students. Two men carrying gym bags and wearing dark glasses. Two Latino men. The last note started a little alarm pinging in Jenkins's mind as the first car began to pass the school bus stop.

Jenkins was already grabbing for the mike as he watched the two men stop and pull submachine guns out of their bags. He keyed the mike as they began firing at the youngsters. Seeing the young bodies getting bowled over by the fusillade, Jenkins was stunned for a split second. The lead car was already turning toward the firing.

Jenkins's training was screaming for him to order his driver to accelerate away. His reaction as a human being conflicted with that. Already the sidewalk was littered with young bodies. Fleeing children were crossing the street in front of the convoy. Jenkins whipped his gaze back to the right. The lead car had stopped. Its doors were swinging open.

"No! Keep going!" Jenkins screamed futilely into the radio.

The two marshals from the front car leapt out, one from each door, their Uzi's at the ready. Jenkins was shocked as a machine gun, hidden in a culvert on the left side of the street, opened fire. The two exposed marshals wilted under the fire.

An explosion from behind caught Jenkins's attention. The trail security car was a ball of flame. "Go! Go!" Jenkins yelled at his driver, Parker.

Parker needed little prompting as he spun the wheel and attempted to get around the stopped lead car. But to do so, Parker would have to run over the bodies of some of the students who had been gunned down in the street. He couldn't bring himself to run over the youngsters, some of whom were still alive and crawling away from their attackers.

Jenkins grabbed Parker's shoulder. "Go! You've got to go!"

Jenkins flinched as the car's windshield crackled under the impact of the machine gun that had shifted its fire to his car. The bulletproof glass was designed to stop a sniper rifle, not the pounding of a heavy-caliber machine gun. Jenkins ducked just before the glass finally gave in and rounds crashed into the interior of the car. Blood splattered the front seat as a round sheared off the top of Parker's head. The engine died as armor-piercing rounds tore through the engine block.

A ricochet ripped into Jenkins's chest and slammed him further down on the seat. The right side of his chest initially felt numb, then little sparks of pain started flaring.

The chatter of the machine gun ceased. Dimly, Jenkins could hear the screams of the wounded. Gasping with pain, he drew his mini Uzi submachine gun from its scabbard on the right side of his seat. He reached up and pushed his door open, but before he had completed a roll into the street, he was hit with four more rounds fired by men approaching the car from the rear. The rounds hammered him to the ground, half beneath the car.

As darkness filled his mind, Jenkins heard the crunching of approaching shoes. His legs were kicked out of the way as the back door was swung open. From a distance, he heard an accented voice.

"Is it him?"

"*Sí.*"

The darkness finally enveloped Jenkins as a submachine gun roared.

# THURSDAY,
# 22 AUGUST

## LANGLEY, VIRGINIA
## 8:00 A.M.

The director of the CIA, Bill Hanks, turned his baleful gaze on the man seated across from him. Hanks didn't like the nattily dressed man, but the elderly director had long ago learned to respect and use talent wherever he found it and in whatever form it appeared. Peter Strom embodied some of what Hanks felt was wrong with the "new CIA," yet the young man also was a shining example of many of the qualities needed in the modern world of intelligence. Strom could compile and summarize information better than anyone Hanks had ever worked with. Hanks also knew that Strom's meteoric rise to deputy director at the relatively young age of thirty-four had been largely due to his ability to ingratiate himself with the people in power. Strom had been a particular favorite of the previous director, and Hanks had inherited the man. He detested Strom's two-faced behavior—sucking up to his superiors and lording over his subordinates. Yet, not liking someone's personality was not a good enough reason, in Hanks's book, to demote the man. Being honest with himself, the director also had to admit that his deputy did excellent work, and that was one of the reasons Strom was present in his office this morning.

The director waved a hand, indicating that he was ready for the briefing to start, then swiveled his chair to gaze out his window. He knew it irritated Strom not to be looked at while he briefed. "Give me the background on why Santia was here, so I'm up to date. The Old Man is screaming bloody murder across the river, and he's probably going to hit me up for something about the whole Springfield thing when I see him later this morning."

Strom snapped open a folder and started speaking in a rich, cultured voice that Hanks was sure he practiced. "Judge Santia was one of the twenty-four Supreme Court justices in Colombia. Using diplomatic pressure, the State Department finally got Santia and two other judges to sign extradition papers on several members of the Colombian drug cartel, most specifically members of the Rameriz family from the Cartagena branch, one of the most powerful drug families in Colombia. The Justice Department presently has three members of the Rameriz family here in the United States awaiting arraignment for drug trafficking.

"In exchange for signing the extradition order, State agreed to bring Santia and the other two judges here to the United States for protection. They've done this several times in the past, ever since '85, when eleven members of the Supreme Court in Bogota were massacred for allowing extradition of some drug traffickers."

Strom glanced up as Hanks mused out loud. "I remember that. They torched the damn Supreme Court building, didn't they? Held out for a couple of days there until the government ordered the army in?"

Strom nodded. "Yes, sir."

Hanks indicated for him to continue with the briefing.

"Santia was to finish testifying before a congressional subcommittee on drug trafficking on Friday and then he was to disappear into the Federal Witness Protection Program."

Hanks cut in. "Obviously that isn't what happened."

Strom glanced up from his notes. "No, sir."

"What did happen then?" Hanks swung his chair around and faced Strom. "What has the FBI turned up on the actual attack?"

"I've got an eyes-only copy of their initial report." Strom slid some pictures across the desk. Hanks didn't bother to ask where Strom had gotten hold of the highly classified internal FBI report. Obtaining useful information was another of Strom's assets. Hanks pulled his chair up to the desk to look at the pictures as Strom briefed.

"The final tally from yesterday's attack was seventeen killed. That includes Judge Santia, six U.S. marshals, and ten bystanders. There are six youngsters still in the hospital, two in critical condition.

"As best as the FBI can reconstruct, the sequence of events was as follows: The attack began with two unidentified males opening fire with 9-millimeter Ingram MAC-10 submachine guns on a group of twenty high school students waiting for the school bus." Strom pointed at one of the pictures. "Right about there. This was apparently done to lure in the lead car and stop the convoy."

The director of the CIA looked up. "Weren't those men properly trained to ignore a diversion like that?"

"I imagine that the killing of the school kids made them forget what they were supposed to do. That was just one of several mistakes they made," Strom sniffed, apparently feeling that the U.S. marshals had committed some personal affront to him.

Hanks didn't bother to hide his irritation. Strom had never seen a shot fired in anger. "Well, I guess they won't make any more mistakes, will they? Continue."

Strom pointed at another picture. "The lead car pulled up to the bus stop and the two marshals inside exited. As they did so, an M60 machine gun opened fire on them from across the street, located here in this culvert. The FBI believes that the machine gun and its firer had been hidden in there since dawn, because they have not been able to find any witnesses who remember seeing anything suspicious earlier that morning. They believe that the firer most likely stayed hidden well back in the culvert until the attack started.

"The initial M60 firing killed the two marshals from the lead car who had stopped to engage the men firing at the students. At about the same time that the M60 was taking out the first car, a Soviet-style RPG antitank rocket was fired from a van behind the trail car. This rocket destroyed that car, killing both marshals in it."

Hanks shook his head. "Jesus. Those boys sure had a shitload of firepower."

Strom ignored the interruption. "After the destruction of the trail car, the car carrying Santia attempted to go around the lead car and escape forward. Apparently, the driver hesitated when he saw the bodies of the youngsters lying in the street in front of him. The rearward route was blocked by the destroyed trail car and the van."

"It looks like they deliberately used those school kids to stop the car. Probably would make me stop, too," Hanks mused out loud.

"They did, sir. Use the youngsters, I mean." Strom pointed at another picture. "Although they killed several students in their initial burst to draw attention to themselves, the two gunmen literally herded the surviving kids out into the street with bullets and then cut them down to block the road.

"The M60 then engaged Santia's car. Although the car was armored and had bulletproof glass, the protection was not designed to stand up to concentrated heavy machine-gun fire. The 7.62-millimeter bullets from the machine gun broke through the windshield. The driver was killed by a round through the head. The agent in the front right attempted to roll out his door and fire back. Apparently he was immediately shot down by gunmen advancing from the van."

Strom looked up. "At this point, the assassins went up to the center car to confirm that Santia was inside. He was killed, torn apart really, when they emptied two magazines from MAC-10 submachine guns into him.

"The attackers escaped using the van. It was found abandoned near Fredericksburg, Virginia. The van had been stolen the previous night from the Springfield area. It was wiped clean of prints. The FBI's forensic people haven't been able to turn up any leads from the van.

"Quite frankly, that's as much as they've got. Tracing the spent cartridges has turned up nothing useful. Standard 9-millimeter parabellum for the MAC-10s. The ammunition for the M60 has been traced to a lot sent to the Contras over four years ago. The Contras have no way of tracking down that ammunition after all this time." Strom summed up the situation as he snapped shut the file folder. "The FBI investigation is at a dead end unless they get a break."

Hanks pointed at the folder on the desk. "What do your people have to say based on this information?"

"We really don't have enough yet to be able to speculate anything," Strom said evenly.

Hanks shook his head. The president wasn't going to buy that. Although the FBI was catching the heat over this, Hanks knew that sooner or later his agency would get drawn in because of the high probability that foreigners were involved. He wanted to be able to give the Old Man something if asked this morning.

"I know you don't have anything that you can go to a court of law with, Strom, but I want your professional opinion. Surely after working on this for the past twenty-four hours you have some idea."

Strom realized he wasn't going to be able to skate out on this one. "Yes, sir. I have some theories. My best guess is that Santia was killed on orders from someone in the Colombian drug cartel. Everything points to that. Santia had struck a powerful blow against one of the most influential drug families down there with his extradition orders. One of the weapons used in the attack, the Ingram MAC-10, is a favorite of the Colombians. The descriptions of the two men firing on the kids match that of Latinos. The brutality of the attack and the disregard for bystanders is indicative of the way the Colombians do business in their own country.

"Additionally, whoever shot Santia spaced the rounds in a T pattern on the body. This is a trademark of the Bogota branch of the drug cartel, the Terminators I believe they call themselves, although that may have been done to mislead us. The Terminators are under control of the Ahate branch of the cartel, not the Rameriz's branch."

Hanks nodded. "It's good to see that you agree with the newspapers, Strom. What do you think the chances are of catching the people who did this?"

"Truthfully, sir, I think the gunmen are already back in Colombia. I doubt the FBI will turn up anything here, stateside."

"Which means there's a good chance we'll get involved," Hanks mused.

"Yes, sir."

Hanks switched to another tack. "I imagine the FBI is

examining how the attackers learned where Judge Santia was and when he would be traveling?"

Strom nodded glumly. "Yes, sir. Unfortunately, they have no leads on that angle either."

"Anything from the State Department side?"

"Yes, sir. With the media really jumping on this Colombian angle, their government has been getting nervous. As you know, their ambassador has been making all sorts of public exclamations of shock and outrage. On the private side, though, he requested a meeting with the secretary of state to discuss the situation."

Strom consulted his notes. "They met last night, and the Colombian ambassador still denies any knowledge of the people behind this crime. But he's smart enough to realize that something has to be done. He flew back to Bogota after the meeting to confer with President Alegre. There's another meeting set up between the secretary of state and the Colombian ambassador tomorrow morning at 6 A.M. to find out what they've decided."

Hanks assimilated the new information. "OK, Strom. I want you to let me know immediately what's happening with that. Tell our source in State that this is top priority. I want to know what comes out of that meeting."

"Yes, sir."

Hanks peered at the ceiling. "What about the DEA?"

Strom flipped through his files. "I've got a summary of the DEA's report to the president. They take the old party line in it."

Hanks reached out. "Let me see it." He scanned the document. He was only slightly surprised at the bluntness of the language. Cory Mullins, the acidic new director of the Drug Enforcement Agency (DEA), must have had a hand in the writing.

The Colombian government can deny it all they want, but cocaine is their primary export and a mainstay of their economy. They've pretended all along that the drug trade was something they were against and trying to eradicate. Quite frankly, they've been presenting us with a smoke screen.

The conclusions drawn in this report are based on years of DEA field experience in country. Without the tacit support of the Colombian government, the drug cartel would never be able to do the amount of business it presently conducts. Corruption and graft are an accepted part of the culture in South and Central America. Judge Santia was threatening the drug cartel with his extradition order on the three members of the Rameriz family. Santia was a problem and the cartel got rid of that "problem" the only way it knew how. Subtlety is not a trademark of its operations.

We are not saying that the government was behind the assassination; we believe the drug cartel was. But in Colombia the line between those two institutions is very vague. Drugs, money, power, and politics all go together down there. Colombia's economy relies more heavily on the drug trade than on the coffee business. We estimate an approximately 50 billion dollar a year business in the cocaine and marijuana export field and we believe that estimate is on the low side. Any political movement against the drug trade is a self-inflicted economic wound for the Colombian government.

Admittedly, President Alegre has been making some progress in the war against drugs. However, the progress has been mostly cosmetic rather than real. Since the summit in Cartagena the Colombian government's efforts have at best cut the export of cocaine by approximately 10 percent, a rather insignificant dent in the torrent of drugs flowing out of that country.

There is no doubt in this agency's mind that the Colombian drug cartel was behind the events last Friday in Springfield, Virginia.

Hanks shook his head in disbelief as he finished the brief summary. "Mullins actually sent this forward to the president?"

Strom nodded.

Hanks laughed. "Since when does the DEA have a collective mind?" He threw the report down. "I would like to come up with some tentative courses of action in response to this assassination. I need your people to give me options to go on if the president hits me up."

Strom made a note on his pad. Hanks gestured toward his subordinate's folder. "Anything else I should know? What about the Department of Defense? What's their stand?"

"Secretary of Defense Terrance is still against using active forces in the drug war. He sticks to the legality of it. The old 'it would be illegal if they were used domestically' argument.

Also, the same old 'it would deteriorate the state of readiness of our forces' argument."

Hanks shook his head. Terrance better get off his ass, he thought to himself. The Old Man wasn't going to buy those lines much longer. The sooner the Department of Defense (DOD) got behind the president's policies, the better.

Strom found a note he had buried in the back of the folder. "Even though the secretary of defense isn't too thrilled about using the military in the drug war, I have information that General Macksey is war-gaming various military options for retaliation."

Hanks sighed. "They have to have a target to retaliate against and they don't. Is that it?"

Strom nodded.

Hanks stood up. "Whatever comes down on this, you're going to be responsible, so I want you to stay on top of everything and keep me up to date."

"Yes, sir."

# PENTAGON
# 1:30 P.M.

"I'm not sure what form any action would take, even if we are asked to do something, so I want to be prepared with a wide range of options." General Macksey, the chairman of the Joint Chiefs of Staff, fixed Lieutenant General Linders, his deputy chief of staff operations for Special Operations (DCSOP-SO), with his dark eyes.

"The conventional boys are shaking the dust off their plans for a sea and air blockade of Colombia. The president is pretty pissed about the Springfield attack yesterday and he wants to be able to put the heat on the government down there to gain some cooperation in finding the killers."

Macksey leaned back in his chair. "What I want you to do, Pete, is get your people working on contingency plans using the Special Operations folks. I want a plan for sending some of your people to Colombia to react if we find out who was behind the attack."

Macksey trusted Linders. Although relatively young, the DCSOP-SO had done an excellent job in an unenviable position. Linders had worked hard over the past six months to build up the strength of the military's Special Operations Forces in spite of fierce opposition from the tradition-bound, conventional infrastructure of the various services. Over the years, the Special Operations branch of the Pentagon had been handed a lot of dirty missions to plan, such as this one. Fortunately, or unfortunately depending on the perspective, they had been authorized to actually implement only a few of the plans. Nevertheless, Macksey wanted to be prepared, just in case.

Linders had taken a few notes and looked up from his notepad. "Anything else, sir?"

Macksey shook his head. "No. Whatever we do, if anything, depends on what the State Department uncovers and how the president decides to react. Most likely, we won't be doing anything down south. The Colombian government would have a fit if they knew we were even war-gaming some military action. I think this whole mess is one the politicians are going to have to play with. Maybe the FBI can come up with some solid evidence, but even then, State will have a hell of a time extraditing anyone."

Macksey dismissed his subordinate. "Get your people thinking about it, and I'll get back to you if anything comes up."

Linders stood up and saluted. "Yes, sir." Then he spun on his heel and left for his office. As he wove his way through the Pentagon's labyrinth of corridors, he considered the tasking. As an air force officer, Linders still felt uncomfortable dealing with his army and navy Special Operations counterparts. He knew any sort of mission into Colombia was going to require ground forces from the army. As he entered his office, he brusquely shot an order at his secretary. "Get Colonel Pike up here ASAP."

Linders settled down behind his desk and used the time before the colonel arrived to consider his position. He viewed his job as the Pentagon's highest ranking Special Operations staff officer as a political one. Budgets and lobbying at cocktail parties with senators were his forte. He usually left the actual operations to his more experienced subordinates. So far, in the six months he had held this position, that philosophy had worked well.

Linders was idly twirling a pencil when his secretary buzzed the intercom to tell him that Colonel Pike was outside. Linders told her to send him in. The door swung open and an army colonel wearing camouflage fatigues limped in. A worn green beret was stuck in the cargo pocket of the man's pants. The name tag over the right breast pocket read PIKE. Over the left pocket was sewn a pair of master parachutist wings topped by a Combat Infantryman's Badge.

Pike had the appearance of an old man, after twenty-nine hard years in the army. He was almost six feet tall and thin as a rail. His face was lined and weather-beaten and his head was topped with hair that had turned completely gray.

As Linders returned Pike's salute and told him to sit down, he wondered why he always felt a little funny when dealing with the colonel. Some of it, he knew, stemmed from the fact that Pike had been in the military a year longer than Linders had, yet Linders greatly outranked the colonel. Part of it also, Linders had to admit to himself, was that whereas the closest he had come to combat was in a B-52 thirty-five thousand feet over North Vietnam, Pike held a reputation as one of the most combat-tested officers in the army. Pike exuded a sense of toughness and competence that overshadowed Linders's political charisma.

Linders decided not to waste any time. He had a meeting across the river with some congressmen in thirty minutes. The sooner he passed the monkey onto Pike's back, the better.

"I just finished talking to the chairman. He wants us to prepare contingency plans in case we get tasked to send some people down to Colombia in response to the attack in Springfield yesterday."

Pike sat down. "Has that been traced back down there already, sir?"

"No, but it's pretty much assumed that the drug cartel was behind the attack. If the FBI or CIA gets good evidence and can finger who did it, there's the possibility we might have to send some people down south."

Pike shook his head slightly. "Snatch or snuff?"

Linders frowned at the terminology. "Plan for extraction of indicated personnel."

"Sir, with all due respect, we've got people who are ready to do that, but if all I can give them is a country but no names or locations, there isn't much they can do as far as planning goes. Delta's been sitting on several OPLANs for hitting the people behind the kidnappings in Lebanon for over four years now."

Linders had to agree with Pike's reasoning. "I know it isn't likely that we'll do anything, but I want to be able to tell the chairman, if he asks, that we're working on it."

Pike bowed to the inevitable. "Yes, sir. I'll take care of it. Anything else?"

Linders was glad to be rid of the responsibility. "No, that's it. How long do you think it will take?"

Pike shrugged. "Without more specific intelligence, the boys down at Bragg will simply pull out their country area study on Colombia and do some figuring on aircraft ranges and stuff like that. That's about all they can do, sir. I'll alert them today and they should have all that ready in two days. I'm going up to Plattsburgh Air Force Base tonight for one of the nuke testing missions. I'll be back tomorrow evening and I'll check back in with Bragg then."

Linders dismissed Pike. "All right. I'll assume it's taken care of, then."

Pike saluted and left to make his way down to his less elaborate office. He was used to getting such vague taskings. He didn't enjoy the thought of passing this one on to the Delta Force operations people at Bragg. Pike had spent several years with Delta and he knew that this sort of "prepare to do something but we're not sure what, yet" tasking was viewed as a pain in the ass.

Since coming to the Pentagon a year ago, Pike had grown more and more discontented. In all his previous twenty-eight years, he had never seen as many dumb decisions being made as he had in this building. Pike considered himself a warrior. He had never married, the army being his first and only love. Here, though, Pike was seeing a side to his love that he had not been forced to deal with before. He understood that he couldn't spend all his time with soldiers, preparing for combat, but he was sure that the time and energy he wasted every day in the Pentagon could be put to better use.

Over the course of the last six months, Pike had watched the different services scramble to protect their slices of the shrinking budget pie. The incident that had lit the match under Pike's discontent had occurred only two months ago. He had written a position paper for the DCSOP-SO relating to the relative budgetary importance each service placed on its Special Operations Forces (SOF). He had pointed out that over the course of the past five years, the combined budget for SOF in all three services had amounted to less than one tenth of one percent of the total defense budget. Yet, in that time period, SOF had conducted over 50 percent of all real world military missions conducted by Department of Defense forces. Those missions ranged from numerous military training teams spread across the world working with other countries' military forces, to covert operations by units such as Delta. Pike felt that the disparity between the SOF units' budget and their production output was ridiculous. He had argued in the report that funding for Special Operations units be somewhat more commensurate with their present contribution. He had been dismayed when his report was sent back by the Pentagon's deputy chief of staff for operations with a "nonconcur" written in red ink on the cover.

Pike didn't need to be a genius to see the handwriting on the wall as well as on his report. He'd tried to get a transfer out of the Pentagon, back to a post where real soldiers did real things. The Special Forces branch representative at personnel headquarters had been blunt: With Pike's mandatory retirement looming less than a year away, they weren't going to move him anywhere. Pike still loved those soldiers he knew were out in the woods training hard, but he no longer felt the same about the big green machine. He was just a cog, an old one at that, and the machine was getting ready to throw him out on the scrap heap.

Because of that, Pike had started spending as much time as possible away from the Pentagon on any sort of trip he could possibly justify, such as the one to Plattsburgh this evening. There was no real need for Pike to be there, but since his office was responsible for coordinating the nuclear security testing missions, observing one of those missions was justifiable. The bottom line was that he wanted to get the hell away from this building and see the real Special Forces in action.

# NIGHT OF THURSDAY, 22 AUGUST

## PLATTSBURGH, NEW YORK
## 11:00 P.M.

The battered van rumbled up the ramp off the Northway. Fifty feet from the exit it pulled into the parking lot of a used-motorcycle shop. The headlights illuminated the gate in the chain link fence that surrounded the shop's motorcycle graveyard. The driver, a large, bearded man wearing a denim jacket emblazoned across the back with Harley-Davidson, stopped the van, got out, and walked over to unlock the gate. He returned to his van, drove into the yard, and parked in the dark shadows behind the shop.

After resecuring the gate, he opened the back of the van. Ten dark figures, bristling with weapons, slipped out. The leader of the group, a short, slim man, shook the driver's hand. The driver got back in the van and settled in to wait.

The ten silhouettes moved to the rear of the yard. The fence there was slightly different from the one that enclosed the other three sides of the shop's parking lot. It was chain link topped with barbwire. An old, rusted sign hung on it. After years of neglect in the harsh Adirondack winter, the sign was barely legible: "U.S. Government Property, Keep Out."

The leader of the band, identified as Riley in the few whispered conversations, gave a command. One of the figures detached himself from the group. Weapon slung over his back, he opened the fence with bolt cutters. Quickly the ten men squirmed through. The last man laced the cut links back together using parachute cord. In the dim light the fence appeared whole again.

Riley nodded to himself. So far, so good. He tapped the man behind him and, as the signal was passed back, moved out, leading the way. The group crossed the dirt road that ran the perimeter of Plattsburgh Air Force Base, and entered the blackness of the four square miles of forest that bordered the runway on its western side. Their target was nestled in those woods.

Riley switched on his night-vision goggles. Through them he immediately spotted the previously unseen infrared chem light that marked their designated path. Riley led his men to the first chem light, sliding through the trees and underbrush with the skill of a man used to such nighttime forays. Approaching the glowing dot that indicated the light, he spotted another one beckoning him onward through the woods to the northeast.

Following the trail of lights, the group of armed men moved like wraiths through the dark forest. Nine hundred meters from the fence, at the last chem light, Riley spotted to his right front the on-off flickering of an infrared (IR) light, indicating someone flicking the IR switch on a pair of goggles as a signal.

Riley moved forward to the man wearing the goggles. Reaching the guide, he turned and, touching the man behind him, signaled the group to move into a tight defensive perimeter. The signal was silently passed back, and after a brief rustling of leaves the entire team was settled down, weapons pointing outward.

Riley put his head next to the guide's and whispered. "What you got, Partusi?"

"Same as the photos. Nothing much has changed. Leave these guys here and I'll show you."

Riley signaled the rest of his party to stay in place, then he moved forward with Partusi another seventy-five meters. He didn't need the night-vision goggles as the ambient light grew brighter. Reaching the edge of the woods, he peered out. The compound was big—larger than he had expected from the pictures—almost three hundred meters by one hundred. It was completely enclosed by a chain link fence topped with barbwire. Riley was studying it from the woods that paralleled the south side, looking longways through the compound.

Every hundred meters along the fence stood a guard shack. It was obvious to Riley that the shacks were designed more as places for the guards to stay out of the weather than as defensive positions. Riley could make out movement in the nearest one.

On the right side of the compound, the eastern side, Riley saw the lone tall guard tower reaching fifty feet into the night sky. In the glow of the arc lights that illuminated the compound, he could discern the muzzle of an M60 machine gun poking over the sandbags on top. His eyes continued their inspection.

"Damn," he hissed to Partusi. "When did that thing get moved in?" Riley indicated a four-wheeled armored vehicle inside the fence, underneath the tower. "I thought that stayed over by the main post with the reaction force."

Partusi shrugged and whispered back, "Our asset said sometimes it do and sometimes it don't. Tonight's a don't."

Riley nodded. They had prepared for this possibility anyway, along with many other contingencies. Across the center of the compound Riley counted the massive berms. Each over sixteen feet high, they squatted in two rows of five, with a road between them running north to south. From their asset's briefing, Riley knew that the side of each berm facing the road consisted of a massive iron door ten feet high by twelve feet wide. The other sides and top were covered in earth, masking the six feet of steel-reinforced concrete underneath, which protected the contents.

Riley turned back to Partusi. "Give me the rundown on your surveillance."

Partusi pointed as he quietly briefed. "Got a man in each guard shack. That's eight guards to start off with. Six have M16s. Two are armed with M203 grenade launchers—the one there in the southeast corner and the third one up on the west side. The tower's got an M60 machine gun with two men up there. The Avenger, that's what that armored thing under the tower is called, got a crew of three. An M60 is in the turret as its main weapon.

"We also got a Chevy Blazer, with two air force police in it, driving the compound perimeter road about every thirty to forty-five minutes. They really ain't checking too carefully. The guard changed at 2000 so we got this crew until 0400. Nothing much else."

Riley nodded. Everything was just as the civilian base worker they had recruited as an intelligence asset had told them it would be. Thirteen guards on target. Possibly two more in the Blazer. A reaction force of thirty men over at the main airfield that could be on target in six minutes, give or take a couple.

Partusi continued. "The ground sensors are there. Just before dark the air police in the Blazer drove off the dirt road and onto that grassy strip between the road and the fence to check them. They seem to be working. No remote cameras, but the sensors must be relayed back to the reaction force. There's a phone and radio in the tower. The Avenger probably got a radio too; you can see the antenna on the turret. I'm not sure about the guard shacks. Probably landline to the tower, but they haven't been doing any checks that I could tell.

"No air activity since a quarter to ten. Had two F-111s land then. You can't see the runway from here but it's over to the northeast, beyond those trees up there."

"What about the grating?"

"All taken care of."

Riley considered the situation. He looked at the glowing dial of his watch. The team still had four hours before they did the job. After giving Partusi some final instructions, he went back to the rest of the team. Gathering them in close, he briefed them on the information that Partusi had imparted. Finishing that, he updated the tactical situation.

"Everything stays as planned. Except I want you, Haley, to take out that armored vehicle under the tower right away. Miller, you hit the guard with the M203 in the southeast corner with your first shot. I've already detailed Partusi to take out the other 203 on the west side with his first shot."

He looked around at the faces darkened with burned cork. "Any questions? Now you all know that the air force takes this nuclear stuff real serious. So when the time comes, let's do what we came here for and get the hell out before they even know what hit them."

## 1:15 A.M.

An army two-and-a-half-ton truck with New York National Guard stenciled on the front bumper rumbled up to the main gate of Plattsburgh Air Force Base. The air policeman on duty stopped it, checking the ID cards of the two men in the front. As he matched the pictures on the cards to the two faces in the front seat, he queried the driver, "Where you heading?"

The driver gestured toward the back of the truck. "We're dropping off unused field rations at your warehouse from our annual training."

The guard waved the truck through. He glanced at the back as it went by. The canvas covering was down and he couldn't see in. He was a little curious as to why they were dropping off rations so early in the morning. The guard shrugged as he turned his attention back to the road. Part-time soldiers, he thought. Probably had to be back at their regular jobs in a couple of hours. He felt a little sorry for them having to be up so late.

## 1:20 A.M.

Riley signaled the six men forward. They slithered into a dirt drainage ditch that linked up with a creek farther back in the woods. Riley led the way in the opposite direction, crawling through the mud in the bottom of the fold in the earth toward the fence. After passing through the culvert under the perimeter security road and coming out the other side, Riley peered ahead to where the drainage ditch passed under the fence.

This potential weak spot in the perimeter had not been overlooked by the designers of the compound. A metal grating allowed water to drain out but blocked entry to anything bigger than a small squirrel.

However, this avenue of approach had an additional advantage besides being out of the line of sight of the guards. The security specialist they had consulted had given them an 80 percent chance that the bottom of the ditch wouldn't be lined with sensors as was the rest of the perimeter, since the type of ground sensors used here by the air force tended to short out when constantly wet. The fact that Partusi had successfully completed his task the previous night confirmed that the ditch wasn't wired.

Riley crawled up to the grating, ignoring the mud that soaked the front of his shirt and pants. He reached up to the iron bars and carefully pulled on them. Partusi had done a good job. The hacksawed metal parted under his tugging. He glanced over the lip of the ditch toward the nearest guard shack twenty feet away. There was no indication that anything was amiss. Placing the grating aside, Riley led the way in, taking the left fork as the ditch split around the end of the road.

## 1:22 A.M.

Powers, sitting next to the driver of the army National Guard truck, checked his watch. The truck was parked next to the ready building for the pilots of the squadron on alert—or where the pilots would be if there was an alert. Presently, the building should be empty except for a duty officer.

Peering ahead, Powers could see the raised, corrugated tin roof covering the four F-111 fighter bombers that were parked in the alert ready area. Fueled and armed, the aircraft were ready to fly in the event of an alert. From the asset's briefing, Powers knew that the pilots were not in the building but on a fifteen-minute recall confined to the limits of the air base.

Powers could also see two air police Chevy Blazers parked at opposite corners of the ready area with their engines running and lights on. Two more guards on foot patrolled the area.

Off to his left, three hundred meters away, Powers could see the airfield's control tower piercing the night sky. Below it, to the right, stood the short, squat building that housed the airfield defense reaction force. Several vehicles were parked outside.

Powers calmly checked his watch again. Only a few more minutes.

## 1:25 A.M.

They'd made it inside without being spotted. That in itself was a major accomplishment. Like a snake, with Riley as the head, they low-crawled in the knee-high grass toward the second bunker up on the west side. That was their target.

As he edged forward, Riley felt the seconds go by, willing each one to last a little longer. Every inch they managed to crawl forward undetected was that much less they'd have to make under fire. He slid up to the first berm, shivering in the surprisingly cool August night air. He had never expected to make it this far without being spotted. He glanced at his watch. Any second now.

Shots ripped through the calm. The initial crack of the sniper rifles was lost in the roar of a machine gun spitting flame into the compound from the darkened tree line.

Riley and his comrades leapt to their feet and ran toward the next bunker. They still hadn't been spotted as the incoming rifle and machine-gun fire riveted the guards' attention to the outside of the compound. Already, six of the perimeter guards were out of action. The attacking forces' machine gun in the wood line was dueling with the one in the tower. A roar and flash seared the night sky in the vicinity of the eastern wood line. Riley knew that indicated Haley had fired the Viper antitank rocket. The armored vehicle was out of commission.

Riley made it to the target bunker. Quickly, three of his men went into the routine they had rigorously practiced for the last three days. One taped detonation cord, known as det cord, along the seams of the doors, taking care to keep the cord from crossing itself. The other two men followed along, hooking in charges at premeasured points and priming them.

Riley and the three others fanned outward, ten feet from the massive doors to provide security. They were in position just as a reinforcing guard came running down the road between the berms from his northern guard post. The hapless air policeman was shot before he even realized there were intruders on the inside of the compound.

The M60 in the tree line won the battle with the tower as the gun up there went silent. An air policeman ran out of the immobilized Avenger with an M60 on his hip, blasting away at the tree line. Another started climbing up the tower to try to put that gun back into action.

Riley shook his head. Too many John Wayne movies. He raised his AK-47 and fired, picking off the man climbing the tower. The supporting fire from the wood line raked the hero with the machine gun on his waist, who tumbled forward to the ground. Riley was impressed. Nice performance.

The men rigging the demolitions were done. The det cord was tied into a short section of time fuse, which in turn was attached to a fuse igniter. The man with the igniter glanced at Riley, who nodded. The man pulled the ring and the fuse was lit.

"Let's go!" Riley yelled and gestured toward the southern fence. He pulled up the rear as the men ran for the hole. The outgoing fire from the compound was diminishing, with just a few surviving guards still returning fire. As Riley and his crew were spotted heading for the fence, two of the guards shifted fire. One of Riley's men was hit. The man didn't even notice and kept running until Riley stopped him and had two others carry him.

As Riley slid back through the hole, the time fuse finished burning and the explosives behind them went off with a bang.

## 1:30 A.M.

The firing to the south had started two minutes ago. Powers patiently watched as the reaction force poured out of the building next to the tower. The air police jumped into three Blazers and two trucks and headed across the runway less than three minutes after the first shot. Both the Blazers at the aircraft ready site turned on their sirens and roared off to join the procession.

Powers pounded on the wall of the truck behind him, then opened the right door and hopped out. Men tumbled out of the back of the truck. Quickly, Powers counted heads. Fourteen. All present.

"Let's do it." He gave a thumbs-up to the driver and turned toward the aircraft. His men spread out behind him. At a slow jog they moved across the open tarmac, closing the distance between themselves and the F-111s. The truck slowly followed behind them.

The two air police on foot patrol watched the approaching men warily. They'd heard the firing off to the south and were confused by the two unexpected developments. One policeman tentatively raised his M16 to his shoulder and called out, "Halt!"

The reply was a roar of gunfire from the approaching men.

### 1:34 A.M.

Riley experienced a slight feeling of relief. They were in the wood line and running, but two men had been shot. Carrying them slowed down the entire procession. Riley could hear the sirens of the reaction force behind him. He wasn't sure if the air police would chase them through the woods. He doubted it. Once the air police figured things out, they would probably try to circle around using the base perimeter road to beat the intruders to the fence. Riley was confident that his team could make it to the motorcycle shop before the air police were aware of what was going on and made it to the point where they'd entered the air base.

Another six hundred meters and they'd be at the fence.

### 1:40 A.M.

Powers guided the truck as it backed up to the F-111. He nodded to himself as he checked his watch. With six men they could easily remove one of the bombs slung under the aircraft and heave it into the back of the truck.

## 1:42 A.M.

Riley piled his men into the van and ran around to the front. He threw his web gear onto the floor and slammed the door shut. "Let's hit the road."

The driver roared out of the parking lot and turned toward the Northway.

Riley held up a hand. "Whoa! Slow down, man. We don't want to get stopped by cops."

As if that was the cue, the flashing lights of a state police patrol car came on a hundred meters behind the van. The big man turned to Riley. "What do I do now?"

"We stop."

## 1:43 A.M.

The two-and-a-half-ton truck pulled off the flight line and onto the road heading toward the main gate. Powers allowed himself a brief smile, but it was wiped off his face as the driver slammed on his brakes and Powers's head barely missed the dashboard.

"Shit!" Powers looked up. Two air police cars with lights flashing were straddling the road in front of the truck. With drawn pistols, the drivers stood behind the vehicles, aiming at the truck's windshield.

## 1:44 A.M.

Riley watched the state trooper approach the van warily. The driver rolled down his window. Riley slouched in his seat trying to appear inconspicuous—a hard task considering his darkened face and dirty camouflage fatigues. He crammed his AK-47 under the seat and tried wiping some of the burned cork off his face with his shirt sleeve.

"Would you step out, please?"

The driver obliged. Riley slid lower in his seat.

"You, too, over there on the right."

Riley sighed. He opened his door, got out, and walked around the van. The policeman stared hard at his appearance. The trooper's right hand unclipped the tie-down on his pistol. His fingers rested warily on the butt. "Open the back."

The driver shot a pleading look at Riley. Riley shrugged and nodded. Shaking his head, the big man led the state trooper around to the back. He unlocked the door and swung it wide open.

# FRIDAY, 23 AUGUST

## LANGLEY, VIRGINIA
## 8:00 A.M.

Hanks didn't say a word as Strom entered and took a seat across from him. He simply leaned forward, putting his chin in his hand, and waited for his deputy director to speak.

Strom flipped open his ever-present file folder and studied his notes for a second before beginning. Hanks felt it was all part of an established little performance. He wanted to see how good this one was.

"The secretary of state met with the Colombian ambassador this morning for approximately forty-five minutes. The ambassador again denied any knowledge of who the people might be behind the assassination of Judge Santia. Nothing new there." Strom flipped a page. "The FBI's investigation is—"

"Hold your horses for a second." Hanks sat back in his chair. He was going to enjoy putting Strom in his place. "That's all you got out of that meeting?"

Strom sensed something was amiss and used the time-honored defense of removing himself one step from the information. "That's all my source relayed."

Hanks smiled. "There was quite a bit more to that meeting than protestations of innocence by the Colombian ambassador. In fact, a deal was offered. A deal that we are probably going to be very involved in if the president buys off on it."

Strom frowned, obviously wondering how Hanks could be privy to information that he wasn't aware of. "What kind of deal, sir?"

"President Alegre is offering a way for our two countries to meet mutual goals. We get to strike back at the drug cartel and reduce their production. Alegre has a dangerous internal problem in the form of a powerful criminal element attacked."

"Strike back how, sir?"

Hanks decided he would play with Strom a little longer before dropping the bombshell. He liked watching Strom dangle in ignorance. "That hasn't exactly been spelled out yet. Some of it has to do with a matter before the United Nations that comes up for preliminary vote at the beginning of next week."

Hanks watched as Strom processed that. "The sea-bottom rights issue?"

The director was impressed. "That's part of it."

"What are they offering?"

Hanks couldn't resist the barb. "I thought you could tell me that."

Strom had to admit defeat. "I haven't heard anything, sir."

Hanks was satisfied. "That's good, because this whole thing has got to be kept in real tight. Even if the offer isn't accepted, the very fact that Alegre has made it puts him in a precarious position. If word of this deal leaked, the government down there wouldn't last a week. The cartel would go to war.

"We can't afford to have Alegre fall. He's not the greatest, but at least he's loyal and we can count on him in the crunch. We don't need any loose cannons in power down there."

Hanks could tell he had Strom totally mystified and also extremely interested. Alegre's offer was presently known by only four people in the United States: the president, the secretary of state, the secretary of defense, and Hanks, who had been informed of the proposed deal just twenty minutes earlier over the secure phone line by the secretary of state himself.

Hanks leaned back in his chair. Enough games. "All right. Here's the deal that Alegre presented through the ambassador this morning. Basically the Colombians are offering to allow the United States to conduct covert, unilateral military raids into their country to destroy cocaine processing laboratories."

Strom sat quiet for a few seconds digesting that. "What are the president's feelings on that, sir?"

"The president bought off on it. As you can imagine, Defense wasn't too happy about it, since they're the ones stuck with the dirty work, but the president's so upset over this Springfield thing that he's lost a lot of his patience. The fact that Alegre was the one to offer this deal made the president very inclined to take it up. There still is no solid evidence on who was behind the Springfield attack, but everything points to the drug cartel."

Strom's mind was obviously leaping to some of the implications for the CIA. "How are they going to know where to target?"

"As part of this deal, the Colombian government will provide, through a contact to one of our agents already in country, locations for processing labs they know about."

Hanks looked up. "You know Jameson in Bogota?" Strom vaguely nodded. "Well, he's going to be the one getting the intelligence. Once we get a location, we verify it using satellite imagery. That way we can be sure they aren't leading us on a wild goose chase."

Strom shook his head. "We already did something like that several years ago and it didn't work. In 1986 the army sent some helicopters with pilots down to Colombia on a mission they called Operation Blast Furnace. Basically it involved using our helicopters with their troops. It was pretty much a failure." Strom obviously decided to temper the comparison. "However, this proposal does sound somewhat different."

"It is," Hanks noted dryly. "They're offering to allow our people to hit the processing labs without any Colombian involvement. We have carte blanche. As far as Alegre is concerned we can use anything we want against the designated targets. The ambassador's exact words were that we could 'wipe them off the face of the earth.' They're not talking about arrests here. They're talking direct military action."

Hanks continued. "Our forces are authorized to violate Colombian air, water, and land space whenever and however they need to, to conduct these missions. All that Alegre asks is that we do it covertly. If word leaked that the government down there was allowing us to do this, he wouldn't last twelve hours before being toppled—both by the drug dealers and by the people. We all know how sensitive Latin American countries are to the presence of American forces."

Hanks decided to let Strom know where he stood on the concept. "It's a good idea. It helps them out by reducing the power of the drug cartel. It helps us out by allowing us to strike right at the source."

Strom's mind was working in overdrive. "With all due respect, sir, I think there might be a problem. How do we know what the Colombians will target for us?"

"Because, like I said, we'll check the information they give us with imagery, which we'll provide to the people doing the mission. Also, the president directed the secretary of defense to have his people verify the target before destroying it."

"Verify? That means they're going to have to put people on the ground. I thought the original concept was to do this covertly." Strom considered the situation. "That means they won't be able to just run in and bomb like we did in Libya. And once DOD puts people on the ground they run the risk of compromise. There are a lot of angles to this that need to be considered before rushing into it."

Hanks shook his head. "Secretary of Defense Terrance raised those objections this morning and the president has already considered them. This is past the debating stage and has reached the action level. That's the main reason I'm telling you all this. You're going to be my case officer for this operation. The Department of Defense will have overall control, but we're going to be relaying the intelligence from Bogota and providing any other kind of intelligence support the DOD people ask for."

"Sir, when did you say we'd get the first location?"

"Within two days Jameson should be getting some information. I've already personally alerted him to be prepared. He'll set up the meet with the contact. From here on out you handle Jameson."

Hanks waited a minute while Strom made a few notes in his file folder. He was interested to see what Strom's reactions were to the whole thing. "Well, Strom, what do you think? If we can hit some of the processing labs in Colombia, what effect will that have?"

Hanks watched as Strom composed his answer. As always the

man had his facts. "Sir, eighty percent of the cocaine that comes into this country goes through those labs. However, there are a lot of variables here. It depends on how many and how large the labs are that we hit. The last intelligence estimate I saw from the DEA was that four to six major labs operating down there process approximately eighty-five percent of the cocaine coming out of Colombia that goes to the United States. The other fifteen percent comes out of the numerous smaller labs operated by free-lancers. Each of the three main drug families operates one or two major processing labs. Hitting a major lab, especially if they catch it with a good stockpile, will severely hurt that faction of the drug cartel. Taking down a couple will reduce the flow of cocaine by a considerable degree, at least temporarily."

Strom's mind was already two steps ahead. "We have to consider the aftereffect. What are the other dealers going to think after one or two labs get blown away? I'm sure the Colombian government will deny everything. If they've kept this tight enough in their government they just might get away with the denial."

Hanks interjected. "Their ambassador said this came direct from President Alegre to him personally. No one else is in on it."

"If that's the case," responded Strom, "then the drug dealers will probably believe them. The cartel has bribed so many people in the government and military that they'll know their own government didn't do it. What then? They'll eventually figure out we're doing it. But initially they'll probably think it was one of their own. They have some pretty fierce intrafighting going on all the time between rival groups."

Strom started warming to the idea as he realized it was a good chance to make a name for himself. "We could probably take down a few of the factories before they even begin to suspect it was us. Even destroying just one or two of the major labs would significantly reduce the flow of cocaine for a short while.

"Blast Furnace was a failure because our people had to work with the local Colombian authorities. The drug dealers knew where the helicopters were going to hit almost before our pilots did. Also, the only labs targeted were those operated by small-time people, putting out maybe a few kilos a week.

Even then there were so many leaks, when the helicopters with the Colombian troops went in, all they found were abandoned labs. If we can operate unilaterally, without having to notify the Colombians of when and where we're going to hit, we could really do some damage. Especially if they target labs operated by the members of the cartel."

Strom frowned as he considered that aspect. "We'll hold the advantage of timing, but they'll still know the where. If there's a leak, the labs could be moved."

"Yes, but according to the ambassador only the president and the contact will know the locations."

Strom shook his head. "The question I have is how is that contact going to get the locations? It's not good to trust intelligence when we don't know its source."

Hanks agreed. "Nothing's a hundred percent certain. All we can do is verify, both with the imagery and on the ground. If the information is wrong, the military does nothing. If it's right, they slam them. That's one of the reasons I'm putting you on this. It's part of your responsibility to try to make sure the intel is as accurate as possible.

"I agree with the president's reasoning on this. It's a great opportunity to take some positive action. We've been on the defensive against drugs all along. Finally we get a chance to go after these guys."

Strom was considering other potential pitfalls. "What if the press gets a hold of this? 'U.S. Forces Attack Colombian Targets.' What do you think the effect will be, sir?"

Hanks shrugged. "The press better not get a hold of it. But if they do I think the effect will be positive. No one thinks drugs are good. After what happened in Springfield last week, I don't think we need to worry about how the press will react to our striking back at the people behind the massacre, especially if we've been invited to do so by the president of Colombia himself. Look at all the positive press we received when we went into Panama a year and a half ago.

"State has been trying to get the Colombian government to do something for years. Now it looks like some of their pressure has worked. The president feels that if we don't take Alegre up on this offer, we'll probably never get another chance."

Hanks glanced at his watch. He had another meeting coming up shortly. "Defense is currently trying to figure out how they're going to verify and destroy these labs. I imagine Terrance has dumped this on General Macksey's lap. The Department of Defense is also going to have overall control of the actual operation. I want you to be prepared to relay the intelligence you get to whatever organization they set up. I also want you to assign a liaison officer from the Latin American section to work full-time with the military task force on this."

Hanks stood up, indicating the meeting was over. He'd handed off the ball and now Strom had to run with it. "By the way, do your people have anything further on the Springfield massacre?"

"Nothing significant, sir. I think all the suspects are back home in Colombia. The FBI is stymied."

Hanks slapped Strom on the back. "All right then. Let's go out and get some results with this."

# PLATTSBURGH
# AIR FORCE BASE, NEW YORK
# 9:00 A.M.

"Damn, I just about peed in my pants when that state trooper whipped out his .357 magnum and started waving it."

Riley glanced up as the briefing room echoed with laughter at Miller's comment. "Hell, how do you think *he* felt, opening up the back of the van and there he's eyeball to eyeball with ten guys armed with automatic weapons and machine guns?"

Powers looked at Riley sourly. "Laugh all you want, guys. You're just damn lucky that one of those National Guardsmen was a Plattsburgh city cop and knew that state trooper. Otherwise, you might have spent the night in the local lockup until they got it straightened out."

Partusi shook his head. "I thought the air force police were supposed to notify the local cops and state police of the exercise."

Powers snorted. "They said they did. You know how that goes. Somebody always doesn't get the word."

Riley stood up from where he had been reviewing his notes. "All right, let's get our act together. We have to brief their colonel in a minute or so. I want you all to remember not to throw stones or drop dimes. Let's keep this thing professional."

Powers looked at the team leader. "I tell you what, Chief. I'm still kind of pissed off about the way they stopped my truck going off post. Those asshole toy cops had live rounds in their guns. Somebody could have gotten hurt. And that somebody could have been me."

Riley sympathized with his senior noncommissioned officer. Powers looked like a not-so-gentle teddy bear sitting on top of a table in the back of the briefing room. "I know that, Top. I've already talked to Colonel Pike about it. But they didn't expect us to hit them in two places. Those guys who stopped you didn't know what was going on. We'll let the air police talk first and see what they have to say."

Powers shook his head, still irritated with the whole thing. He was glad Riley was doing the briefing on this one. Not only could the team leader speak quite well, but his name and appearance always surprised people when they first met him, and Powers liked watching the reaction. Riley himself was used to the surprise. His last name conjured up visions of a freckle-faced Irishman. At the very least, it was difficult to connect that name with the short, wiry Puerto Rican wearing the silver bar with two black dots indicating U.S. Army chief warrant officer.

Another strength of Riley's was that he exuded competence during briefings. It was hard to attribute to any one aspect of his appearance; it was the complete picture—the finely honed face, the piercing black eyes, the slim body that suggested a lot of power per pound. Most importantly, just the way he held himself.

Riley's demeanor was carefully cultivated. Standing only five foot seven inches and weighing a lean 145 pounds, Riley had learned long ago the importance of first impressions. The product of a brief marriage between a long-forgotten Irish father and a Puerto Rican mother, Riley had learned his lessons at an early age on the streets of the South Bronx. He'd discovered that if he looked tough, then most often he didn't have to actually prove it was true. But Riley also knew how to follow through when it was necessary.

Riley looked up as the door to the room swung open and Partusi called out "Attention!"

The air base commander, Colonel Albright, walked in, followed by his staff and the major in charge of the air police on post. Trailing the party limped Colonel Pike. The old-looking army officer was in charge of the Department of Defense's nuclear facility testing team in addition to the many other jobs he did as army assistant to the DCSOP-SO. Pike presently had four Special Forces teams working for him on the project, one from each of the active army Special Forces groups. The teams traveled to every Department of Defense installation that held nuclear weapons and tested how well the weapons were safeguarded. Pike made it a point to attend every team's outbriefing at the installations they had tested. Riley had never met a senior officer he respected more than Pike.

Pike was a legend in the Special Forces community. At the beginning of his army career, he'd been an enlisted man and served two tours with Special Forces in Vietnam. Because of the high quality of his performance of duty, he'd been recommended for officer candidate school (OCS) during his second tour. Passing the four-month "shake and bake" OCS course at Fort Benning, he'd been commissioned in the infantry and found himself back in Vietnam for a third tour, this time as a platoon leader with the 173d Airborne.

As soon as possible, Pike had worked a transfer back to Special Forces. As commander of a recon team doing cross border operations into Laos, Pike had picked up his limp. During a difficult extraction he had been pulled out on the end of a rope hung below a Huey helicopter, a common practice when the terrain lacked suitable landing zones. During that particular mission, the inexperienced pilot had misjudged how far the Special Forces man was hanging underneath the aircraft and had run Pike into a stand of trees. Slamming into limbs and trunks, Pike had suffered several cracked bones, and his back had never been the same. Over the years the injury had become progressively worse. It hadn't, however, stopped him from becoming more involved in the cutting edge of Special Operations.

After Vietnam, Pike had continued on in his beloved Special Forces, eventually rising to command a battalion in the 10th Special Forces Group at Bad Tolz, Germany.

After that tour, he'd been with Charlie Beckwith during the birth pains of Delta Force. Riley had heard rumors that Pike had entered Tehran prior to the aborted raid to free the hostages, to relay intelligence out before the strike, and to be on the ground to help guide the force when it came. Pike's connections with some of the original members of Delta ran deep, and despite the years that had gone by since he'd last served with Delta, Pike still enjoyed a good working relationship with the men at Fort Bragg.

Pike's degenerating health, combined with an unwillingness to keep his mouth shut when he felt something needed to be said, had led to his failure to be selected for a Special Forces group command. Lacking that career ticket punch, he'd been passed over for promotion to brigadier general. Being the army gofer for the DCSOP-SO was Pike's last hurrah before being shuffled off to mandatory retirement. Riley felt it was a crappy way to treat a man who had given so much to the army and who was one of the most experienced and caring leaders he had ever worked under.

Pike gave a covert wink to Riley as the wrinkled old colonel lowered himself stiffly into a chair. Riley answered with a brief nod and a smile.

Riley turned his attention to the air force base commander, who was looking over the nine dirty Special Forces soldiers standing at attention in front of their chairs. "Haven't you gentlemen had a chance to get cleaned up and changed?" asked Colonel Albright.

Riley answered for his team. "No, sir. We needed the last couple of hours to get our notes together for this briefing. We'll take care of all that when we're done here."

The colonel nodded. "All right. Who's this Mister Riley Colonel Pike has been telling me about?"

Riley stepped forward. "I am, sir." Albright managed to hide his surprise at Riley's appearance.

The colonel moved to his seat and opened the proceedings. "Let's get on with it then. Major Baley, you first. Everyone else please take your seats."

Riley sat down as the cleanly dressed air force police major walked up to the podium.

The major cleared his throat. "Good morning, sir. I'll be briefing you on the results of the security test of our nuclear safeguards that was conducted last night. I'll start off with a brief description of the scenario that was set up. I'll then describe what happened and finish by giving you our recommendations for improving security. I'll be followed by Warrant Officer Riley from the 7th Special Forces Group, who will brief you on events from their perspective.

"The exercise was set up to be as realistic as possible. To help accomplish this we borrowed eighty sets of MILES equipment from the army at Fort Drum. MILES stands for multiple integrated laser engagement system. Basically what it is, sir, is a laser emitter that is attached to all the weapon systems. When each system is fired using blank rounds, a laser beam is sent out wherever the weapon is aimed. All our personnel and vehicles involved in the exercise had harnesses on that could pick up these laser beams. A hit on a person is indicated by a loud beeper going off on the harness. A hit on a vehicle sufficient to disable it is represented by a flashing yellow light going off on top of the vehicle and a loud tone being sounded on the intercom system inside. We had all our personnel at the weapons storage facility and ready line equipped with this gear.

"Our first indication of trouble came at 0126 . . . "

Riley tuned out the major and mentally reviewed his own presentation. The man was doing his best to make his organization look good, which was to be expected. Riley tuned back in as the major wrapped up his presentation.

"Sir, overall I feel our men did a good job. We do have some areas we need to work on. First, we are going to revise our reaction SOP to cover the possibility of multiple attacks. However, I must point out, sir, in all fairness to the lieutenant in charge of the reaction platoon, that it is extremely unlikely that a terrorist organization would be able to mount two attacks on the scale we experienced last night.

"Additionally, the attackers used army ID cards and a military vehicle to gain admission onto post. Again, this would be very difficult for a terrorist organization to accomplish.

"As a further recommendation, we are going to increase the number of surveillance checks we do on both the post perimeter road and the storage facility perimeter road. Sir, pending your questions that concludes my briefing."

Colonel Albright looked at his air police commander in surprise. "That's all you have, Major?"

Major Baley shifted his feet nervously. "Yes, sir."

"All right, Major. You can sit down. Mister Riley, let's hear what you have to say."

Riley walked over to the podium. Typical briefing for the air force, he thought to himself. Try to make things look as good as possible. It didn't look as though the post commander had bought off on it, though. But the colonel would have to decide for himself.

Riley sorted out his notes while Partusi pulled out a schematic of the air base mounted on cardboard and placed it on an easel. Partusi extended a collapsible pointer and stood at parade rest next to the easel, prepared to point during Riley's presentation.

"Sir, I will first brief you on our perspective of the operation as it was conducted. Then I will highlight some areas, with our recommendations, that we believe your people ought to focus on to help improve weapons security.

"To conduct this mission we recruited eighteen members of the local army National Guard to act as guerrillas for us. We recognize we used a larger force than expected but our instructions from the Department of Defense were to create a worst-case scenario. Due to your post's proximity to the Canadian border, we feel it is quite possible that a terrorist organization may be able to infiltrate by vehicle across the border and attack here, so the number of personnel that participated last night is not improbable.

"We trained our guerrillas for two days in the Adirondack State Forest near Meacham Lake. We received intelligence regarding the physical layout of the post and guard activities from a civilian worker who has access to all areas of the post. She provided us with detailed descriptions of everything we asked for. We drew up our plan based on this intelligence and on building information we found in the Plattsburgh Chamber of Commerce."

Riley looked up. "I don't know why they're there, but a complete layout of the nuclear weapons storage facility is on record in the Plattsburgh County clerk's office. Although it doesn't detail the security setup, it does greatly facilitate planning a mission. Anyway, to continue. We recruited the civilian who owns the Harley-Davidson dealership that is adjacent to your south fence to assist us. Utilizing his van, the diversion force arrived at the . . ."

Riley proceeded to factually relate the events of the target hit. He'd done many briefings like this before. He could see that his audience was listening carefully. They usually did. Commanders' ears tended to perk up when anything regarding nuclear weapons was discussed. In all truthfulness Riley had to admit that the Plattsburgh Air Police had done a pretty decent job and had a good setup. Unfortunately, they had to realize that decent and good didn't cut it when you could get a nuke stolen. Riley finished his narration of events with both raiding parties being stopped.

"You may have noticed some difference in our account of events and the air police's account. Most of that is due to the excitement and the darkness. However, it is important to note that your guards were not aware we were inside the storage facility until we were departing. We were not driven off. Rather, we were leaving of our own volition, having completed what we set out to do. That team's mission was to draw in your reaction force. It succeeded in doing that.

"We did have some trouble with a couple of the National Guardsmen playing the game with the MILES equipment. Two of them were hit and their indicators went off as we departed the storage facility. Both failed to 'play dead or wounded' until I forced them to. I apologize for that. However, we were fortunate to have these men give up their free time to participate in the exercise.

"None of the attacking personnel at the flight line were hit. Those people stayed long enough at the aircraft to simulate the amount of time they would have needed to remove one of the nuclear warheads there. We—"

"Excuse me." An air force lieutenant colonel in a flight suit raised his hand. "I hate to burst your bubble, mister, but I believe that would have been much more difficult than you think. I'm the squadron commander for those aircraft that were on the flight line. I had my head crew chief brief me this morning on how long it would take to safely remove one of those bombs. It was quite a bit longer than the amount of time you spent there. Almost twice as long."

Riley nodded. "Sir, the key word there is *safely*. I believe your crew chief was giving you data regarding how his crews remove the warheads without damaging the aircraft. The method we would have used, had we done so, would have involved some damage to the aircraft."

The squadron commander wasn't going to give up so easily. "I know you probably don't understand all the technicalities, but you just can't mess around with one of those warheads. You go indiscriminately cutting some of the umbilicals to the aircraft and you could damage the warhead also. There are certain safety devices installed to prevent such a removal."

God, how I love pilots, Riley thought. Able to fly above it all and never get their hands dirty. Know everything there is to know, too. This guy probably watches *Top Gun* every night, he thought sourly. He patiently replied, "Yes, sir. I understand that. However—"

"Mister Riley does understand the technicalities." Colonel Pike's soft voice interrupted the proceedings. Pike swiveled in his seat to look at the lower ranking air force officer. "You didn't receive the briefing on his background, and the team's. Every member of this team has gone through the navy's nuclear weapon surety program—the same program from which all of your pilots received their knowledge about nuclear weapons.

"This team has been doing this for over a year now, traveling around the world testing security at installations that have nuclear weapons. I don't believe the Department of Defense would choose incompetents to do such a sensitive mission, do you? So I believe we can assume that they are qualified and do know what they're talking about. Wouldn't you agree?"

The squadron commander fidgeted uncomfortably. "Yes, sir."

Pike turned to the base commander, who had remained aloof from the conversation. "Sorry to have interrupted. It's just that

I wanted the record to be straight. If Mister Riley said Master Sergeant Powers could take a bomb off your plane in the time he said, I for one believe him."

The post commander nodded weakly. "Yes. I imagine so." He turned back to the front of the room. "You may continue, Mister Riley."

Riley figured it was time to quit while the quitting was good. The briefing was only a formality anyway; the important thing was the stuff in black and white. "Sir, we'll be leaving a written report with our recommendations. In all we have thirty-one recommendations on how to improve security."

Riley briefly reviewed a few of the most significant recommendations. He was tired. Tired from not having slept the night before. Tired from people treating him like the enemy when all he was trying to do was help them. But even more, he was tired from traveling around the world for the past year. Living out of bachelor officers' quarters on permanent temporary duty was getting to him. This was their last nuke mission. Riley wanted to go back to Fort Bragg and finally relax.

He wrapped things up. "Sergeant First Class Partusi and I will remain here for another day working with Major Baley and his people. The rest of my team is departing for Fort Bragg this afternoon. We've appreciated working with everyone here and hope our visit has been worthwhile."

As the meeting broke up, Colonel Pike shuffled over to the team. He waited until all the air force people were out, then he waved them into seats. "Gentlemen, this is the last mission you run for me. Your year is up and your replacement team is rotating in from 1st Battalion. I've appreciated working with you all and want to tell you that you've done a super job.

"There aren't many 'atta-boys' in this job. Nobody congratulates you when nothing happens, but that's the only way to judge the success of this program. No nuclear weapon has yet been stolen from a U.S. military facility and hopefully your efforts over the past year will help things stay that way.

"There's one more thing I want to say. You often hear bullshit speeches by commanders, saying you're the best and all that crap. Well, I'm going to tell you all something I haven't told any of the other teams: This detachment, 055 from 2d Battalion, 7th

Special Forces Group, is indeed the best team that has worked for me in this program."

Pike looked at all the team members. "I think that's due to a lot of reasons, not the least of which is your team leader, Mister Riley, and your team sergeant, Master Sergeant Powers. And just as important is the work each of you soldiers has done as an individual and a member of the team.

"I wish you all the best of luck as you go back to Bragg. I wish I was going with you instead of warming a desk in the basement of the Pentagon. Best of luck, men."

Riley led the way as each member of the team walked up and shook the colonel's hand. Not many officers could make a speech like the one Pike had just made and have people truly believe it. Although Riley was glad to be done with this assignment, he knew he was going to miss the colonel. There weren't many officers like him left in the army.

# PENTAGON
# 11:00 A.M.

General Macksey quickly sketched out to Lieutenant General Linders the tasking he'd been handed by the secretary of defense. Macksey wasn't happy about the mission but he was loyal to the secretary and wanted to have a good plan of action ready in case the president really did decide to give the final go-ahead with the Colombian mission. He concluded his presentation by asking Linders's opinion on how they should proceed with the tasking.

Linders pondered the situation for a minute and then started jotting his ideas on a notepad as he spoke. "OK, sir. First we're going to have to get a ground unit to go in and do the verifying. They'll also probably do the final targeting. We don't need a lot of folks. Probably no more than ten to twenty. They've got to be good soldiers, because we damn sure don't want them to get caught." Linders circled the number 10 on his pad.

"They've got to be good at infiltration, exfiltration, and surveillance. I'd say we take them from either the Rangers, Special Forces, or Delta. Delta would probably be the best, but I'm not sure we want to use that asset. As you know they've got other things they're tied up with right now and they're stretched pretty thin just maintaining their counterterrorist reaction force. The Rangers are damn fine soldiers and—"

Macksey interrupted. Linders was air force and sometimes didn't quite understand Macksey's own service—the army. "Rangers are damn fine soldiers but surveillance isn't their mode of operation." Macksey pointed at the black-and-gold Ranger tab on his own left shoulder. "Rangers like killing things. Asking them to go look at something and not do anything is like asking a kid to go into a candy store with a dollar and not buy anything."

Linders nodded in agreement and underlined Special Forces. "If I remember rightly, most of the Special Forces guys have worked a surveillance mission under various proposed wartime scenarios. They're trained on laser designating and electronic beacons, which we're probably going to have to use. They've got the radio equipment and long-range communications ability we'll need to talk to them in country. Also, they're proficient in the infiltration and exfiltration techniques that could be used down there: parachuting, helicopter infil, maritime operations."

Linders's reasoning made sense. Macksey nodded. "I want you to get with the Special Operations Command at Bragg and get us some people. Enough to run two surveillance missions at the same time. One A-Team in split team mode ought to be able to do that."

"Yes, sir." Linders looked at his notepad. "Another thing, sir. I'd recommend we pick a senior officer with some experience to head this thing up. This task force is going to be working with the CIA and DEA, so we need someone who can handle that."

"You have any recommendations?"

"He ought to be of flag rank at least. That limits us. Every general is slotted against a billet somewhere and we just can't pull one out of the woodwork. Plus the guy ought to have some Special Operations experience, and you know how few of those we've got with flag rank."

"How about we pull some colonel and brevet him to briga-dier?"

"That would work, sir," said Linders. A thought struck him: "I think I have just the man we need. Colonel Pike. He's got considerable Special Operations experience with both Special Forces and Delta, and he works in my office. He'll be back tonight from Plattsburgh Air Force Base. I'll also get a hold of General Slaight over at SOCOM to OK the requisition of the bodies.

"Initially, we can base these people out of Fort Belvoir. There's plenty of room there since the army engineer school was moved over to Fort Leonard Wood. That puts them close to the intelligence base here in the D.C. area and also close to us. Once the task force is operational we can move them down to Fort Gulick in Panama."

Macksey shook his head. "I don't think Panama is such a great idea. It's still too much in the press. Maybe the aircraft, but not the ground people. Let's keep them based out of Belvoir so we can keep an eye on things and keep it quiet."

Macksey checked his desk calendar. "I've got to go to Fort Monroe for a TRADOC meeting this afternoon and I won't be back until tomorrow evening. I want to see Pike then." Macksey penciled in the meeting. "1800 sharp. I want to brief him personally. We'll run this with Pike as the officer in charge. He'll go to you only for help. Your job will be to provide Pike with whatever support he requests from the Special Operations community. Most particularly aircraft."

Linders stood up and saluted. "Yes, sir."

# SATURDAY, 24 AUGUST

## FAYETTEVILLE, NORTH CAROLINA
### 1:43 P.M.

The wheels of the 707 hit the ground with a bounce. Riley turned to Partusi with a nod out the small window. "Home, sweet home."

"I can deal with it."

"Bet you can't wait to meet your old lady."

Partusi smiled at the thought. "Yeah. She's been pissed as hell with all the temporary duty this past year. She'll be glad to have me at home for a little while."

Partusi nudged Riley. "Last time I talked to her on the phone she said she had a girlfriend from work she wants you to meet. You'll have to come over for dinner soon. But not too soon. Me and Gina got some lost time to make up for."

Riley rolled his eyes in mock dismay. "Not another one of Gina's real estate girlfriends. I'd rather do a blind night drop into Panama than go through that again."

"I'll tell Gina you said that," Partusi threatened playfully.

"You do and I'll jumpmaster your next jump and forget to check your static line. I like Gina but I can't deal with those friends she sets me up with." Riley waited until the plane rolled to a stop and then stood up. "Let's go."

He led the way through the aisles, down the stairs, and across the tarmac to the small terminal that served Fayetteville. Entering the building he spotted the back of a figure encased in camouflage fatigues and topped with a green beret. "Our ride's here."

Riley snuck up behind his team sergeant and grabbed him around the neck. "Man, you'd get run over by a bulldozer, you're so unobservant."

Powers didn't turn. "Seems some sort of insect is hanging off my back. Probably be best if that bug lets go before I squash it."

Riley released his grip, laughing. "I'm too fast for you, Dan. You'd have a heart attack trying to catch me before you could squash me."

Powers finally turned. "Yeah, right, Dave. I didn't see you come in 'cause you're such a miniature human being it would have required binoculars to spot you."

Riley nodded. "Sure. You missed Partusi, too." Leading the way to the baggage claim, Riley tried to get up to speed. "What's going on back at group? What's the team doing?"

Powers grabbed Riley's duffel bag off the carousel. "Not much. Most teams in the battalion are down in Panama doing the police MTT. Nobody has said much of anything to me. I gave the guys Monday and Tuesday of next week off. Only reason I'm in uniform is to pick you up. You all can sign in and I'll drop you off at home. The colonel said not to show up until Wednesday."

Riley smiled. "Sounds like things are finally going to slow down. Maybe they've got a good deal lined up for us."

Powers turned and shook his head. "When you've been in the army as long as me you don't believe in good deals. It's like in combat: Just when you think things are quieting down is when you get hit the hardest."

## PENTAGON
## 6:00 P.M.

Colonel Pike eyeballed Macksey's aide warily. Meeting the chairman of the Joint Chiefs of Staff on a Saturday evening in the Pentagon was most unusual. Meeting him *anytime* would be unusual for Pike, since he was just one of hundreds of colonels running around the Pentagon. Certainly his job was involved in a sensitive area but not one that had ever gained such high-level notice before.

In addition to the time and place, not knowing the purpose of the meeting put an extra edge on Pike's unease. He doubted very much that he had been called to the Pentagon on this Saturday evening to be congratulated for doing such a "fine job" on the nuclear security mission. On the other hand, Pike couldn't think of anything from his job, unless it was the Colombian thing Linders had mentioned, that would require the involvement of the chairman. Pike smiled wryly to himself. Nor could he remember mouthing off to anybody lately, either. So that left a whole bunch of in-between reasons for the meeting.

The general's aide put down the phone and indicated for Pike to go in. Pike knocked on the chairman's door and entered. Behind a massive desk, flanked by flags, the chairman looked up from a file he had been reading. Pike crossed the room stiffly, stopped three feet in front of the desk, and snapped a salute. Macksey returned the salute smartly and indicated the chair he wished Pike to sit in. He then continued to read the file, occasionally glancing up at his visitor. Great leadership technique, Pike thought to himself. Macksey was what Pike termed a "political officer." The chairman had risen so high that in Pike's opinion he'd forgotten what it was like to be a soldier and real leader.

After several minutes Macksey put down the file. "Very interesting." He looked Pike in the eyes. "You and your people are doing a fine job on the nuclear testing. Very good job."

"Thank you, sir." And? Pike thought.

"There's another job, actually you'd call it a mission, that has come up. Based on the last mission, and your record, I want you to head it up. As far as personnel goes, I want you to pick whoever you want out of the Special Forces community. I've already talked it over with Slaight at SOCOM and told him to give you whatever A-Team you want." Macksey looked at Pike, searching for a reaction.

Pike was noncommittal. How the hell could he know what A-Team he would want if he didn't know what the job was? Whatever happened to mission statement up front? "Yes, sir."

The whole thing was typical of the army, he thought. Do a good job and your reward is another, most likely tougher, job. The chairman probably wants to deploy me to some godforsaken place where I'll work seven days a week, around the clock, Pike thought. Screw up and the punishment is a quiet eight-to-four job on a nice backwater post waiting for retirement.

"It's a very sensitive matter. In a nutshell, I want you to head a task force that's going to conduct unilateral strike missions into Colombia to destroy cocaine processing laboratories. This mission comes from the highest level of our government and it must remain covert."

Pike's mind shifted into overdrive as he assimilated the information. He didn't need the chairman to tell him that this was going to be sensitive. And it sure as hell was a lot more exciting than fighting with air force pilots over what could and couldn't be done with a nuke.

"The president of Colombia has sanctioned this operation, so it's not as if you're invading the country. However, he most likely won't acknowledge the sanction if your people get caught."

Macksey passed a folder with a top secret/eyes only cover on it across his desk. "In there you'll find everything you need. On the first page are the points of contact here in the Pentagon from each service. This mission has top priority. If the person listed there doesn't give you what you want, you call me and I'll get it for you. My private numbers are there on the bottom of the first page.

"The key man for a lot of the coordination you'll be doing here in the Pentagon is your boss, Lieutenant General Linders. He can do the tasking of Special Operations units through the people down at MacDill. I've already given him a heads-up on this and he's ready to help you out. Other than him, no one else is authorized to know about these missions.

"Also you'll need these." Macksey reached in his desk and pulled out two shoulder boards with a star on each. "You've been breveted by the president. It'll be approved by Congress Monday."

Pike wasn't overly impressed with the stars. Breveting meant that when the mission was over he'd have to give the stars back.

He *was* impressed with the mission, though.

Macksey pointed at the folder in Pike's hands. "On page two you'll notice that you'll be getting a CIA and DEA liaison. They'll both be at the meeting tomorrow at Fort Belvoir along with the team you choose. Now you and I both know that those two will be briefed to pay lip service to you and report back to their own bosses. That's OK as long as they do what you need them to do. If they give you a hard time, or become uncooperative, let me know right away. I'll relay that to Secretary Terrance and he'll grab the CIA director and get some action. As you can tell this is being watched at the highest levels. I know you can handle it."

Sensing he was dismissed, Pike stood up and saluted the chairman. So much for any time off, he thought as he left the room and worked his way to his basement office. Pike leafed through the folder. Nowhere in there was a written order spelling out the operation. He was struck with a peculiar sense of déjà vu. He'd had some experience running missions without written orders.

Pike entered his office and threw the file down on his desk. He stretched his back, trying to ease the constant ache. That discomfort was a reminder of one such official "unofficial" mission almost twenty years ago.

Pike pulled out a notepad and started sketching the framework for operational support for this mission. Most other officers would have picked up the phone and immediately alerted 1st SOCOM to get a Special Forces team moving. Pike had long ago learned the value of patience and careful review of options before action. He wouldn't start the wheels turning until he figured out where the wheels were going.

# SUNDAY,
# 25 AUGUST

## FORT BRAGG,
## NORTH CAROLINA
## 10:00 A.M.

Riley was methodically kicking the heavy bag that hung in the corner of the team room. Ten turn kicks left leg, ten right leg, ten back kicks left, ten right. He pressed on as he felt the sweat pour off his body and the pleasant pain of exertion flood his limbs.

The team room for 055 consisted of the top floor of a renovated World War II barracks. It was essentially a large bay, almost sixty feet by twenty-five feet. The dominant feature in the room was a large T-shaped table in the center. Wall lockers holding the members' field gear stretched along one wall.

The corner in which Riley was working out held both a heavy and a light punching bag, a lifting bench, and assorted weights that team members had deposited over the years. The floor of the room was tiled in an ugly shade of red in which some long-forgotten team member had taken the time to cut and emplace white tiles to spell out the detachment's number, 055, and the motto of Special Forces—*De Oppresso Liber*: to free the oppressed.

A refrigerator sat against another wall, flanked by two large padlocked boxes that contained the team's radio and engineer equipment. The refrigerator was technically used to store batteries for the radios. In reality the batteries took up only the bottom shelf; cases of beer and soda filled the rest of the shelves. The soda was for the duty day and the beer for after hours when most of the unmarried team members would hang around until the early morning. In extremes, the team room became home for members who had had too much to drink.

Enjoying one of those cold beers, M. Sgt. Dan Powers sat with his feet on his beat-up desk and watched Riley from across the team room. "Damn, compadre, don't you ever get tired? I mean it's hot out and everything, and it's Sunday. The good Lord designated today as a day of rest. Why don't you take a break and grab a brew?"

Riley paused. "I can see you're resting enough for both of us. Dan, one of these days that beer belly of yours is going to get you in trouble." He stepped back. With a yell he leapt and hit high on the bag with a flying side kick. The bag lurched, then settled back, rattling the chains that connected it to a beam in the ceiling.

Powers burped. "Yeah, Dave, it might at that. But I'll die happy. Guess you little greasers need to work out to be tough, not being a natural-born stud like me." He scratched his belly under the worn-out green T-shirt that made up his off-duty garb. "Hey, you hear we might be getting a team leader? A real live commissioned officer? Not like you make-believe warrant officers."

"Keep it up, redneck." Riley started working his arms. His hand strikes rattled the bag only slightly less than his kicks had. "Any idea who? Somebody from inside group, or is it a new guy from the qualification course?"

"Don't know. Just heard a rumor there're two officers coming into battalion. But, hell, with four teams that need captains we probably won't get one. The colonel likes you too much. You ain't raped nobody lately or created any international incidents. Besides, I like you as team leader and I don't need to be breaking in no new captain."

Riley smiled as he continued punishing the bag. He and Powers had been running the team together for over a year. Their initial mutual respect for each other's competence had grown into a genuine friendship. That friendship was a critical ingredient in making the team one of the best in the battalion, which is why they'd been picked to join the nuclear facility testing team. Riley was glad that mission was over.

Riley felt the team deserved a break. Everyone had been frozen in the assignment for the year, as the team traveled around the world. Now people could move, and three of the nine team members were leaving in the next week. That left the team with only six of its twelve authorized slots filled. Hopefully, they would get some time off. One of the greatest banes of Special Forces duty was the time spent away from home.

Riley knew he'd get in some replacement people, but he wasn't sure he wanted a captain. He'd never worked under a team leader since he'd gotten his warrant over a year ago and he wasn't sure how he'd like it. He figured it'd be nice to have someone else get all the ass-chewings but not at the expense of losing control of the team. It would upset the benevolent dictatorship under which Powers and he ran things.

Riley also wasn't sure what the team's next assignment would be. In 7th Group, almost everyone spent at least half the year down south in Central America training local military and police forces. The 2d Battalion operations officer had told him before the Plattsburgh trip that 055 wasn't going anywhere for the next couple of months at least. Which was just fine with Riley.

Riley started working the striking edges of his hands on a two-by-four wrapped in hemp rope to toughen the calluses. We'll probably be pulling post police call for the next couple of months, he figured, since most everyone else in the battalion was deployed. As near as he could tell by looking at the battalion training board, when he'd gone up to talk to the ops officer, eleven of the fifteen operational teams were gone. One of the four remaining was the Gabriel demonstration team, which did all the shows for the "Great American Public" at Fort Bragg and as requested around the region.

Riley could do simple army math as well as anyone. That left three teams to pull all the crap details that came down from group headquarters. The thought of picking up pinecones at Fort Bragg didn't thrill Riley but it beat traveling around constantly. At least for a week or two. Then Riley knew he'd be anxious to be on the move again, doing something. Hitting the singles' bars in Fayetteville, North Carolina, wasn't his idea of a fun time.

Finished punishing his hands, Riley turned to his team sergeant. "Hey, Dan, let's go over to the sports club range and do some shooting. I got about three hundred rounds of 9-millimeter in my trunk I want to burn up. Let's go get your H and K submachine gun and pop some rounds out of that."

Powers burped amiably. "It's hot out there, man. I know you dark-skinned folks like the heat, but us fair-skinned people gots to be careful. Don't you ever sit still and just enjoy yourself?"

Powers crushed his empty beer can with a massive paw. "Yeah, all right. I got nothing else to do. Bought me a new shotgun yesterday that I need to break in anyway. Wait'll you check it out—a twelve gauge with a ten-round box magazine that can be fired on semi-automatic."

Riley laughed. "What the hell are you going to use that on? You have hordes of deer attacking you on your hunting trips?"

"Never know, my friend, when you might need a lot of firepower." The phone in the hall outside rang. Powers got up and headed toward the door to answer it. "Who the hell could that be on a Sunday morning?"

Riley was toweling himself off when he heard Powers start cursing. "Goddamnit! Goddamnit! I knew I should'a took off for the mountains for the weekend to get away from the freaking phones."

Riley poked his head out the door. "What's the matter?"

"A goddamn alert! You believe it? We've only been back a couple of days and they have to alert us! Sometimes I get sick and tired of these goddamn army games."

# DEA HEADQUARTERS, WASHINGTON, D.C.
# 6:00 P.M.

Rich Stevens nervously dashed out his fourth cigarette in the last ten minutes and lit his fifth. He got up and paced around the executive conference room. Stevens didn't know the reason he had been ordered to fly to Washington this morning from Bogota. Whatever it was, it couldn't be good.

For once Stevens thought he had wrangled himself a "get-over" job down in Colombia. His official designation was DEA embassy liaison. The job was supposed to entail being the DEA's man in the U.S. embassy in Bogota, coordinating DEA operations in country with both the State Department and the Central Intelligence Agency. In reality, due to the high profile of DEA operations in Colombia, the DEA station chief did most of the coordinating personally. Stevens's role had been reduced to one of glorified paper pusher at the embassy, working on the routine traffic and paperwork the DEA processed through.

Stevens had been quite happy with the arrangement. He was normally able to finish off the few papers in his in box by lunch and that allowed him the rest of the day off. He had kept a low profile, not wishing to have anyone at the embassy notice that he really wasn't employed productively. But someone must have noticed something, he thought nervously, or else why was he back here in D.C.? The DEA station chief had been evasive in response to Stevens's questions about why he was going back, claiming he didn't know.

Stevens briefly wondered if it was because of his drinking. The fact that he went to the aptly named Embassy Cafe across the street from the U.S. embassy and got blasted almost every night wasn't exactly a secret. There wasn't a whole lot else to do in that godforsaken city.

Why he'd volunteered to go down there in the first place he couldn't immediately remember, preoccupied as he was with the sudden recall. Then he did. He cringed as he pictured his wife's bloated face in his mind. That bitch. It was worth being in Colombia to get away from her and the three screaming kids. If everyone was entitled to one big mistake in their lives, Rich had made his thirteen years ago when he married Norma.

And, boy, had she turned out to be big, Rich mumbled to himself. He couldn't remember the last time he'd gotten laid. How could you want to with that tub? She was fine where she was—back in Boston. Being in Colombia and working with the beaners sucked, but it was better than being with her. Stevens just hoped that this recall to the States wasn't permanent.

Thinking of getting laid brought a vision of another face into his mind. Just two nights ago, he'd been sitting on his usual stool in the cafe drinking his normal combination of shots of tequila chased with a mug of beer, when he noticed a new woman bartender come on duty. The new girl was one of the most beautiful women Stevens had ever seen. He had talked to her briefly and found out that her name was Maria. He had also learned that she was working at the bar to learn English so she could go to college in the United States. Stevens hoped he would have a chance to go back to Bogota and talk with Maria again. She'd sure been friendly enough to him. He'd be more than willing to teach her some English and a lot more.

Stevens was startled as the door opened. Thoughts of the bar girl disappeared in smoke as he saw the director of the DEA come in alone. Stevens's fears and concerns returned, now even stronger. Whatever was going to happen had to be extremely important for the director himself to be here. This was the first time Stevens had ever met Director Mullins.

"Evening, sir."

"Hello, Richard. Or may I call you Rich?"

You can call me anything you want, thought Stevens. "Rich is fine, sir."

Mullins sat at the end of the conference table and indicated for Stevens to sit. "You're probably wondering what's so important that you had to fly back up here."

No shit, Stevens thought. I've just about got an ulcer from worrying. "Yes, sir."

"How would you rate the Colombian government's efforts to eradicate the processing laboratories?"

Stevens sighed inwardly with relief. Same old crap. At least it wasn't an ass-chewing. "On a scale of one to ten, with ten being doing all they can and one being doing nothing, I'd have to give them a negative five. If anything they're helping them. I've seen reports of army troops being used to guard some of the shipments and air force planes carrying the stuff. Behind coffee, cocaine's their second leading export. In terms of U.S. dollars it's got to be ahead by now.

"Since the heat's been on the past year they've tightened up some, and I've got to admit that President Alegre has shown real guts with some of the steps he's taken, but in the field the situation's pretty much the same."

Mullins nodded. "That's interesting. Nothing much has changed down there, has it?"

"No, sir. They talk a better line of denial now, but it's business as usual. Alegre wouldn't stay in power five minutes if he really tried cracking down on the cartel. He's on the edge right now with the steps he has taken. A lot of people's livelihoods down there depend on the cocaine industry, and they don't like anyone screwing with that."

Something clicked in Stevens's mind. "This meeting wouldn't have anything to do with Santia getting gunned down, would it?"

Mullins knew Stevens was an alcoholic and a burn-out, but the man wasn't stupid. "Yes, it does in a way. What would you say if I told you the Colombian government has told us they want the United States to conduct unilateral military strikes against the processing labs in their country?"

Stevens stared at his boss to see if he was joking. "I'd find that real hard to believe, sir. Once word got out, the parliament in Bogota would be in flames. Alegre wouldn't last a day. Remember what happened in November '85? When their Supreme Court decided to allow the extradition of drug people we had outstanding warrants on? The Supreme Court building in downtown Bogota was attacked and eleven of the twenty-four justices were massacred. The guerrillas were actually the ones who conducted the attack, but it's felt that the drug cartel played a strong instigating role, particularly in the execution of those judges.

"Hell, some of their judges are here in the States under our witness protection program for the rest of their lives just because they handed down an indictment or extradition order against someone associated with the cartel. That's why Santia was up here in the first place. If those judges had stayed in Colombia, they wouldn't have lasted a month.

"As far as U.S. military involvement goes, the Colombians just about went through the ceiling when the president mentioned putting that carrier task force off the coast to help interdict traffickers. And the invasion of Panama hasn't reassured anyone down there either."

Mullins nodded. "I agree with everything you say. However,

the theory is that word of this won't get out. The entire operation is to be done covertly. That's why I've brought you up here. You're going to be working with the military and CIA on this operation."

Stevens considered this change in his job role. If it's not one thing it's another, he thought. Time for him to start working for a living. "How are we going to know where to hit, sir?"

"The Colombians have agreed to give us locations through a contact with the CIA."

Stevens shook his head. "I hate to say it, sir, but this is probably going to be a waste of time. They'll most likely give us abandoned locations or at best the location of one of the small-time free-lancers. There's no way they'll target one of the big boys from the cartel."

Mullins held up his hand. "The Colombian ambassador promises that we'll get information on the cartel. Alegre's goal is to break the cartel."

I'll believe it when I see it, Stevens thought. "Sounds good, sir. When do I start?"

"Tomorrow at ten at Fort Belvoir."

## PRESIDENTIAL PALACE, BOGOTA, COLOMBIA
## 6:45 P.M.

President Alegre looked across the table at the finely dressed man seated there. "More coffee?"

"No, thank you." The Ring Man leaned back his chair and pulled out a cigar. "So, it is all going as planned?"

Alegre nodded. "Yes. The Americans have agreed."

"Good. Excellent."

Alegre wasn't entirely sure if the man was referring to the international situation or his cigar. The president shifted uncomfortably in his high-backed chair. He didn't like dealing with this man. The Ring Man had burst upon the cartel with devastating ruthlessness a little over four months ago, assassinating his boss, Ahate, in Bogota and taking over the operation. No one even knew his real name. The drug dealer took his name from the gold rings that adorned every finger. Shoulder-length hair, tied behind his head, framed the hatchetlike face. Alegre worried whenever he looked into the eyes that burned out of that face. They didn't seem totally sane.

"Do you have the targeting information for me?"

Ring Man passed a piece of paper across the table. "The map coordinates of two labs. One of Suarez's and one of Rameriz's. The timing is rather fortuitous, since my informants tell me both of these labs also hold major stockpiles of produce."

Alegre fingered the paper. "I hope this will get the Americans off our backs."

The Ring Man smiled benevolently at the president. "I have some other actions being developed as, shall we say, safeguards." He paused and his benevolence disappeared. "In fact, I am myself trying to find the people who were behind the unfortunate incident last week in America. Such foolish business practices could hurt my operation."

Alegre looked at the man across from him. His best guess was that Rameriz was responsible for the American massacre, but he wouldn't put it past the Ring Man to have done it himself to put more heat on him to get the Americans involved in this plan and put the pressure of suspicion on the Rameriz family.

Alegre knew he was playing a dangerous game with the Ring Man. Their goals were different, but for now the paths to their goals remained the same. Alegre wondered what would happen when their paths diverged and Ring Man found out.

The fact that the Ring Man sat brazenly in his office with impunity was a sign of the drug lord's power, Alegre knew. There was no way Alegre could touch him right now, legally or otherwise. To do so would be tantamount to committing suicide. Ring Man wielded too much power and had legally insulated himself from the dirty end of his business through numerous cutouts and subsidiaries. The man may appear insane but he had a mind of startling cunning. Even if Alegre had enough hard evidence on Ring Man, he seriously doubted he could get a judge to issue a warrant. It would be asking that judge to sign a suicide note.

The purpose of the meeting accomplished, Alegre stood up

and escorted the Ring Man to the door. "I will relay the information through my contact to the Americans."

The Ring Man smiled coldly at the shorter man. "I hope we can continue to do business together in such an amiable fashion."

Alegre smiled thinly. "I hope so also."

## CIA HEADQUARTERS, LANGLEY, VIRGINIA 7:20 P.M.

Strom surveyed the agent seated across the desk from him. He spoke slowly, making sure every word got across.

"Agent Westland, you're going to be our representative on the task force that's being formed." He passed a folder across his desk. "This contains your instructions on how to maintain contact with Jameson so he can give you information from Bogota. You're going to be the one relaying that intelligence to the military.

"It's essential that you check out the information as carefully as possible. Since you'll be operating out of Fort Belvoir you'll have access to the air force imagery unit over there. You can also use anything you need from here. You're authorized to go up to level six on the data you can show the army people. That ought to be more than sufficient. You know Patterson down in graphics?"

Westland nodded. "Yes, sir. We worked together on the Panama invasion intelligence the year before last."

Strom steepled his fingers. "Hmm. Yes, that's right. You all did a good job on that operation. The DEA is also going to have their embassy liaison from Colombia attached to the task force. From what I have found out, he might not be too much help. The man's an alcoholic and hasn't done anything worthwhile since he got posted down there. His name is Rich Stevens.

"The whole operation is going to be run by some army general. Technically he'll be in charge of you, but in reality you report back to me. This whole thing is going to be real tricky, but whatever happens we don't want the cover blown. We've worked hard to keep Alegre in power and we bloody well want to keep him there. I'm sure you're up to date on all that's going on down there and how precarious his situation is.

"I've ordered Norton, your section chief, to give you an update briefing anyway, just in case. However, he's not to know what you're working on. As of now you're relieved of all your normal duties and responsibilities. The director and I are the only ones, besides you, who are cleared for information on this mission and I want it to stay that way."

"Yes, sir."

Strom smiled benevolently at the agent. "This is a great opportunity for you to show us what you can do. I'm sure you won't let us down."

"No, sir."

"You need to get over to Norton's office right now. The first targeting information should be coming in tonight and I want you to be ready tomorrow when you meet the rest of the task force over at Belvoir."

"Yes, sir."

Strom stood up. "Good luck and keep me informed."

# MONDAY,
# 26 AUGUST

## FORT BELVOIR, VIRGINIA
## 9:00 A.M.

Bern Holder, the team's junior engineer, drove the van while Riley sat next to him navigating. Scrunched into the back were the other ten members of the team, along with all their gear. It would have made a great commercial for Chevy carryalls, Riley thought to himself.

Arriving an hour ago at the post airfield, after flying in from Bragg, the team had picked up the van that was waiting for them there. The sergeant who signed the vehicle over to Riley had handed him a map of the post with a building circled in red. Go there, he told them. The man had shrugged when questioned further. He was just a gofer. He didn't know anything. Riley felt empathy with the man on that score. Since the alert yesterday, all he'd gotten from the group duty officer was information on where to go and when, but no whys.

"Turn right here." Riley started counting building numbers.

"We there yet, Mister Riley?"

Riley shook his head. He felt like a parent on a long car trip with children whining in the backseat: "We there yet?" Except it sounded a lot worse coming from a captain in the army. During the hustle of getting the team ready to move out yesterday, the team had been assigned six additional bodies to fill out Operational Detachment Alpha (ODA) 055, as the team was formally called, to its authorized strength of twelve. One of those new bodies was Captain Vaughn, who had nominally taken over as team leader. Riley hadn't had the chance to really talk with the new captain yet. It had been enough hassle just loading out and getting everyone up here to Belvoir. So far, Captain Vaughn had left Riley particularly unimpressed.

Riley spotted what he was looking for according to the map. "That's it there. Turn in."

Holder turned the van and they rolled through the gates into a fenced compound. The van pulled up to the front of a two-story brick building that looked as though it had once been some sort of unit headquarters. A sedan with government plates was parked outside.

Riley turned to Powers, seated behind him. "Let everybody out to stretch their legs but don't unload the gear yet. I'm not sure if we'll be staying here or not. I'll take the captain in and see what we can find out."

Powers tapped his forehead with two fingers. "Roger that."

Riley turned to Captain Vaughn. "Let's go in and see what we've got, sir."

The captain nodded and put his beret on his head. "Let's go." Watching Vaughn struggle to get his new beret adjusted correctly, Riley quietly sighed. A Q-course cherry. Why'd he have to get saddled with that?

Riley followed the captain through the front door. Standing in the hallway a slender figure was waiting. Riley smiled with genuine delight in recognition. "Congratulations, sir! I didn't know you were on the promotion list."

Pike shook his head. "I wasn't. It's just temporary for this mission we're going to be running." He looked at the captain. "I'm Mike Pike," he gave a dry laugh, "and you can call me General Pike. I'll be your commander for the duration of this mission."

Vaughn didn't know whether to salute the general or shake the offered hand. So he quickly snapped to attention and popped off a salute that Pike indulgently returned, and then they shook hands.

"We aren't going to be busting into nuclear power plants are we?" Riley asked hopefully as the general ushered them into a large room that took up the majority of the first floor of the building.

"No. This one's a little bit different, Dave. I want to brief you two before the others get here."

"Others, sir?" Riley asked.

"Come on in my office and I'll fill you in. This here's the isolation area, and I'm set up in that office to the left," he said, pointing to the first of a series of three doors on the far side of the room.

Riley hesitated. "Sir, should I tell Powers to have the guys unload their gear?"

"Yep." Pike pointed. "Up those stairs and to the right are eight rooms with bunks in them. The work area is down here. Might as well get your team settled in."

Riley went outside and told Powers to have the men move the gear inside. Then he invited Powers to the meeting with the general. Pike hadn't specified bringing Powers in, but the general knew how the team worked. Of course, now that they had a commissioned officer as team leader, things might be changed, but until Vaughn said something different, Riley would keep things the same. Leaving the rest of the team at work, the two walked across the iso area into the small office where Vaughn was trying to exchange small talk with Pike.

Pike sat behind a standard army-issue desk with several plastic chairs surrounding it. He stood up, seeing the newcomers. "Master Sergeant Powers. Good to see they dragged you along for this trip." Pike came forward with his hand extended. Pike was one of the few senior Special Forces officers whom Powers liked and respected.

Powers shook the hand. "Didn't have much choice, sir. If I'd have known it was an alert I'd have never answered the phone."

Pike laughed. "That's the way it goes. I figured you'd be getting bored sitting around at Bragg doing nothing for two whole days, so I thought I'd liven things up for you."

He gestured around the office. "You all grab chairs and let me tell you what's going on." He waited until they were settled. "I just moved into this building last night, which was also when I got picked for this job. So I've only got a twelve-hour head start on this thing."

Pike steepled his fingers and placed his elbows on the desktop. "Our mission is to conduct unilateral interdiction missions into

Colombia against cocaine processing laboratories."

Riley's heartbeat kicked up its pace for a few seconds and then settled down.

Pike continued. "These missions are sanctioned by the Colombian government; in fact, they're the ones who will be supplying the information we'll use to find our targets. However, the timing and method will be completely up to us and we'll receive no assistance from the Colombian government or military. I'm not sure how many of these missions we'll be conducting or the duration of this task force.

"We'll be getting a CIA and a DEA liaison here in about a half hour who will support this operation. The CIA rep will be bringing the first couple of potential targets and will provide us with CIA and NSA intelligence and imagery. I've got contacts in the Department of Defense from each of the services providing us with whatever support we request. The DEA man is the DEA embassy liaison from Colombia and can give us firsthand information on the in-country situation."

It was all sinking in slowly. Riley processed each piece of information separately, trying to come up with the whole picture. "Who else from the military, sir?"

Pike indicated the building about them. "We're it right now. Whatever specific support we need, we request on a case by case basis. This task force is supposed to be kept quiet to the max. I received a personal briefing from the chairman of the Joint Chiefs of Staff last night on the political sensitivity of these missions. Each one has to get personally approved by the chairman himself before it can go.

"In reality, you're the verifying and targeting team. We need somebody on the ground to make sure the right target gets hit and that it is legitimate. We've got the resources of the entire Department of Defense to make the hit with—that's the hammer. You could say that you men and your team are the eyes of the hammer. And when I say hammer, I mean it. The targets are going to be a free-fire zone. Once you verify, everything and everybody in it is expendable."

"You mean we kill everybody," Powers clarified. Riley smiled. That was one reason he brought Powers to meetings. The burly team sergeant reduced the bureaucratic jargon to terms everyone understood.

Pike nodded. "Everybody. This administration means business about drugs. You want facts and figures, they gave me a whole book full last night—about the number of Americans who die each year from drugs and drug-related crime, and all that. After what happened in Springfield, Virginia, this past week, there are a lot of pissed-off people in the government. General Macksey told me that as far as this administration is concerned, it's war."

Riley shook his head. "Yes, sir, but even in war we couldn't just waste everybody in a certain area. What if there are women and kids there? What if the drug people are forcing peasants to do their work?"

"Technically, Dave, if it's a processing laboratory, it gets blasted. In reality, that decision is up to you on the ground." Pike looked them in the eyes. "That's why I picked 055. I trust your judgment and I'll back you up on whatever you do."

Riley glanced over at his new team leader, who seemed a little overwhelmed with all that had been said. They didn't teach situations like this in the Special Forces qualification course, Riley thought to himself. This was the real thing.

Riley turned back to Pike. "Do we have anything in writing, sir? Or are we going to do all this on a promise from the chairman of the Joint Chiefs that we'll be taken care of? I'm concerned that if this leaks to the media we'll get fingered as murderers or some crap like that. I don't want to be left hanging in the wind, particularly if something goes wrong down south and someone gets stuck there."

Pike let out a deep breath. "To be honest I don't know how much support you'd get if this thing blew up. I haven't seen anything in writing other than this authorization order from the chairman to alert and use DOD forces. It doesn't specify for what purpose or where those forces would be used. You know I'll back you up, but as far as official reaction goes, you know as well as I do that it's going to depend on the circumstances. All I can do is guarantee you that if your ass is in the wind, mine will be right out there next to yours."

Figures, Riley thought. It really didn't matter. Promises were only worth the paper they were printed on. If this thing blew up, there'd be elbows flying all over D.C. as the politicos tried to cover their butts. Pike's word was worth more than any paper they'd ever get.

Riley sorted the pieces out again and examined his initial feelings. It was a good, worthwhile mission. One that most experienced men in 7th Group had figured would come along sooner or later in one form or another. Riley had heard rumors that Task Force 160 and Delta Force were doing some drug interdicting off the coast of Florida. No arrests or any of that legalese. The law of the bullet on the high seas, out of everyone's jurisdiction.

Riley didn't need to look at Pike's book of figures to know about drugs. He'd grown up on the streets of the South Bronx, where he'd seen firsthand the effects of drugs. It wasn't an abstract thing that he read about in the papers or saw on TV and thought: "How awful." Riley had lost boyhood friends to drugs. He'd seen the bodies and the families torn apart. He also knew that, but for the army and Special Forces, there was a damn good chance he'd have been one of those statistics. Fighting drugs was a cause that could make a man feel good about himself and his job.

Riley briefly remembered China—a little over two years ago now. There he'd given his blood, and half a year recovering in a hospital, on a mission that had ultimately meant little, except to the men and women who had participated. The lines had been blurred there—here the lines seemed crystal clear.

The question Riley now pondered was: how effective would all this be? Even if they shut down some labs, the addicts would still get their stuff one way or another. The price may go up, but as long as the demand existed, and people were willing to pay a lot of money, someone would always be willing to take the risks to meet the demand. On the other hand, Riley reasoned, doing nothing was tantamount to throwing your hands up and saying, "I'm defeated." That was something Riley had never said in his life and he wasn't about to start now.

Riley turned to the new team leader. He figured he'd done enough of the talking so far. It was time for the captain to earn his pay. "What do you think, sir?"

Vaughn looked slightly startled but quickly regained his composure. "I didn't hear the general asking us if we wanted to do this mission, Mister Riley. I do what I'm ordered to do. Sounds like a good mission."

Riley smiled to himself. Good answer. Nobody had asked them. Sure, they could make a big stink, but the bottom line was that they really didn't have much choice. That was part of being in the army.

Pike stood up. "You all have about twenty minutes to get settled in. The DEA and CIA will be arriving then. We'll meet across the hall in the main isolation room. We don't have much of anything in there except office supplies and furniture. The CIA is supposed to be bringing all the maps and intelligence you'll need to start planning."

## 9:45 A.M.

Riley dumped his rucksack and duffel bag in the small room he would share with Dan Powers. Glancing out the window he saw another government sedan pulling into the compound. He grabbed Powers and they went down the stairs and out into the lobby. The sedan pulled up in front of the door. A woman got out of the passenger side and a man out of the driver's. Riley watched as they opened the trunk of the car and started unloading cardboard filing boxes. Riley opened the door as they came in with the first load. He stood in front of them. "CIA or DEA?"

"CIA."

Powers stepped in front of the man, his bulk completely blocking the door. Riley knew Powers didn't like the CIA. "Don't mind if I see some credentials, do you?"

The man looked irritated. He set the box down, pulled out his wallet, and showed his ID card. Powers nodded. "You and your secretary can dump all that stuff in the room there to the left."

Powers turned and looked into the isolation area. He spotted two figures. "Marzan and Partusi! Get over here." The two came out. "Give these people a hand unloading the car," Powers directed them.

The woman called over her shoulder as she went back out for another load. "There's more in the backseat."

"Yes, ma'am."

Two trips later the car was unloaded. The two CIA agents shook hands, and one got in the car and drove off. The other turned to Powers. "My associate won't be working with us. I'm Agent Kate Westland. I'll be your liaison from the agency for the duration of the mission."

Riley almost laughed out loud as Powers blushed and stammered. "I'm sorry, ma'am. I just thought, well, I don't know. I didn't mean nothing. It's just that, well—"

Riley interceded. "Master Sergeant Powers has never worked with a woman before, so he made the wrong assumption. I'm Chief Warrant Officer Riley, the detachment's executive officer. General Pike should be back here shortly. He just went over to see the post commander to get some military police support to secure this compound."

The woman took the offered hand, then turned and went into the isolation area. Riley looked at her as she walked away, cataloging her as he did all people he met. She was of medium height, actually tall for a woman, about five foot nine, which made Riley look up at her slightly. She had somewhat broad shoulders, which seemed incongruous on an otherwise slender build. Looking at her bare arms Riley could see the muscles twist and ripple as she moved some of the file boxes. He nodded to himself approvingly, using a somewhat different scale than most men. She definitely took care of herself physically. She had dark hair, cut short in a more functional than fashionable manner. Her skin tone was almost as dark as Riley's. She looked younger, but judging by the lines around her eyes, Riley estimated she was probably in her late twenties to early thirties.

Another car drove into the lot. Pike got out with difficulty and came inside. Riley pointed out their new teammate. "There's the CIA."

Pike walked over and introduced himself. As he was doing so, a third car rolled in. An overweight man got out. Peering around he walked up to the door.

Riley inspected the new arrival. Old to be a field agent. Looked to be in his fifties. Riley examined more closely. Most likely he was in his early forties. A red-veined nose and a beer belly suggested that alcohol had aged him. Riley cursed to himself—they didn't need a rummy, if the man was one. He checked the man's ID card and then let him into the planning room. The DEA had arrived.

Riley sent Powers out to round up the team. Time to start the fun and games.

## 10:00 A.M.

The fifteen task force members were seated on folding chairs in a rough circle, facing each other. General Pike started the meeting. Riley knew that the general would keep it somewhat informal. Pike believed that people thought better that way and would contribute important ideas they might not otherwise convey.

"Good morning. I think the first order of business is introductions and a little background information on each of us. I'm General Pike and I'm the officer in charge of this task force. Prior to this assignment I was the army Special Operations staff officer in the office of the DCSOP-SO in the Pentagon. As part of that job I supervised the nuclear facility testing team project. Six of the members of the detachment here were on one of those teams. Prior to that assignment, I spent a few years doing various army things, most of them in the Special Operations arena." That was an understatement if Riley had ever heard one.

Pike looked at Captain Vaughn. "Captain, I'd like Mister Riley to introduce your team if you don't mind, since he's worked with them longer than you have. Dave, I'd like you to include a brief description of each man's skills."

Riley wished the general had let Vaughn introduce the team. The captain was getting his ego damaged enough as it was with all the constant referrals to Riley instead of him. However, the general also knew that Vaughn didn't even know all the members of the team and probably wasn't clear on their responsibilities and capabilities, having never worked with an SF A-Team outside of a school environment.

Riley stood up. "I'm Chief Warrant Officer Riley, the detachment executive officer. I'm responsible for all intelligence matters and am the second in command of the team."

He circled behind each team member's chair as he introduced them, starting with the captain. "This is Captain Vaughn, the detachment commander. He's responsible for everything the detachment does and fails to do." Vaughn stood up briefly as he was introduced, as did each succeeding team member. The captain, standing only five foot five, was the only person on the team Riley could look down upon. The captain's clipped red hair and pug nose made him look even younger than his twenty-seven years.

"Master Sergeant Powers is the team sergeant. He's the senior noncommissioned officer on the team and also the operations sergeant. He is responsible for the detachment's training and is the primary tactical planner for the team."

Powers was the only true combat veteran on 055, although Riley had been on several classified missions involving live fire. Powers was physically the strongest member of the team, but he was also slightly overweight. Nevertheless, Riley knew that the senior NCO could hold his own in the field. Riley had never seen his team sergeant falter because of his weight. Powers was a calming influence on some of the younger members, and his hard-earned combat experience from Vietnam made him invaluable. Riley circled behind the bulk of the team sergeant standing easily in front of his chair.

"Sergeant Lane is a weapons sergeant." Gus Lane, the weapons man, was young and inexperienced. But he made up for that with an intense dedication to his job. Lane had light skin and a head topped with short, crew-cut blond hair. He boasted a compact, muscular body and stood three inches taller than Riley at five foot ten inches.

"Staff Sergeant Marzan is a communications sergeant." Hosea Marzan could easily pass for a native in most South and Central American countries. His dark skin and Spanish looks had hooked him more than enough girls out in Fayetteville, the local town off Fort Bragg. Riley appreciated Marzan's steadiness and maturity. On top of that, he was an experienced communications man and could be relied on to do the job.

"Sergeant Holder is an engineer." Bern Holder, the engineer/demolitions man, was relatively inexperienced. He'd joined Special Forces two years ago, coming over from the engineer battalion in the 82d Airborne. Riley liked the young man because he was so earnest. He always tried hard, even though he often failed—not out of any lack of trying but because, as Riley reluctantly had to admit to himself, the man was a few slices short of a full loaf upstairs. Holder had made it through the qualification course on sheer guts and fortitude. Riley figured a man could break his way through any wall with his head if he hit the wall enough times and didn't mind the pain. That's what he thought of when he considered Holder. Not too bright but willing to try hard.

"Staff Sergeant Partusi is the medic." The last member of the old team present, Frank Partusi had been on 055 longer than Riley. Partusi was as swift as Holder was slow. The man was a damn genius as a medic. Riley had watched him perform minor surgery and been extremely impressed. Partusi had spent two years in medical school before coming to Special Forces and had joined up because he enjoyed the challenge of being a Special Forces medic. He was planning on getting out when his present hitch was up next year and going back to medical school.

Riley introduced the first enlisted member attachment to the team. "This is Sergeant First Class Alexander. He is the detachment's intelligence sergeant and works with me on intelligence matters." Alexander came to the team with a relatively good reputation after a stint as an instructor with the Operations and Intelligence School staff at the Special Warfare Center. Or at least that was what Powers had told Riley. Riley would reserve judgment until he had some evidence.

"This is Sergeant First Class Paulson. He's another weapons man. The weapons men are responsible for all individual and crew-served weapons the detachment may use or train indigenous forces on." Paulson was a thickset man who looked as though he had some SF experience. But all the new men were unknown quantities as far as Riley was concerned. The only way to really tell how good they were was to do something for real and see how they reacted.

"This is Sergeant Atwaters, the detachment's junior communications sergeant. He and Sergeant Marzan are responsible for maintaining a secure communication link between the detachment and our support base and for all aspects of communications planning." Atwaters had rubbed Riley the wrong way at their first meeting the previous day. The young E-5 was the caricature of the southern redneck. He was of medium height, sported stringy black hair just shy of being too long for regulations, and had a loud, obnoxious manner.

"This is Sergeant Hale, the senior engineer. The engineers are responsible for target assessment and demolitions planning." Hale seemed competent. He was a skinny, black six-footer. He had talked little in the last twenty-four hours but Riley sensed he was observing everything. Riley liked that in a man.

"Staff Sergeant Colden, the junior medic. The medics are responsible for the health of the detachment." Colden seemed to be Atwaters's running buddy. The two had graduated from the same Q-course. Colden was a lean man, given to chewing tobacco, a habit Riley hated.

Riley turned to the two guests. "Both of you are probably unfamiliar with working with army, never mind Special Forces troops. In Special Forces we tend to be a bit more relaxed about rank and all that than the rest of the army is. We also try to use everyone's brainpower to the utmost. That's why all twelve of us are sitting in on this meeting and not just the commander and executive officer."

Or at least that's the way it's supposed to be, Riley thought to himself. With a new detachment commander things might change. However, Riley didn't think Pike would let anything too outrageous happen. Pike had been around Special Operations even longer than Powers and had forgotten more things about running missions than Riley had ever known.

"From what we've been told so far, we'll be operating in a split team mode for this operation. That means we split each pair of specialists and make two teams out of the one you see before you." Riley returned to his seat.

"Thanks, Dave." Pike turned to the other two people attending. "Why don't you introduce yourselves."

The CIA led off. "I'm Agent Westland. I'm from the Latin American section. My area of specialty is Colombia and Panama and I have traveled to both countries several times. I speak Spanish and Portuguese fluently.

"Basically, until now I've been an intelligence analyst collating and summarizing raw information about those two countries into intelligence." In other words, Riley thought to himself, she was a desk jockey and not a field agent. In his opinion that was probably an asset. They sure didn't need one of the field heroes with an ego the size of a 747 whom he had met on other missions.

Westland continued. "I'm here to provide you targeting intelligence and logistics support. I'll be working with you for the duration of this project. I've brought with me as much information on Colombia as I could track down in the short amount of time I had. I also have the first two potential target locations along with supporting imagery." She sat back down.

Stevens got up. "I'm Rich Stevens. I am . . . was . . . the Drug Enforcement Agency's embassy liaison in Colombia. I've been brought up here to assist you in any way you desire. I've been in Colombia seven months on this tour. Four years ago I did a two-year stint there. I can give you some background on the drug situation down there whenever you want. Also, I've brought pictures of drug labs that were raided during Operation Blast Furnace, to give you an idea of what you'll be looking for." Stevens returned to his chair.

Pike nodded. "All right. Now that we know each other, let's get to work." He turned to Vaughn. "Captain, I'll let you work out a schedule for the isolation. I will need at least a brief concept of operations from you by tomorrow night. The key things I'll need are infiltration and exfiltration means and how you propose the target be destroyed. I'll be able to give you some potential weapons systems and means of target destruction when I get back from the Pentagon early this afternoon, but for now basically consider every system in the armed forces at your disposal." Pike collected his briefcase and left the room.

Riley turned and looked at the captain along with the rest of the remaining occupants in the room. It was an early test for the new leader. Riley knew that Vaughn had, at best, a vague idea of how to organize the isolation. If he was smart he'd ask for help from Riley and Powers, to whom the whole procedure was old hat.

Vaughn seemed unsure of what to do. Riley decided to ease

the burden for the young man and take him off the spot. In training, Riley might have kept quiet until asked, but this was the real thing; it was no time to make a point. "Sir," he said, standing up and getting the captain's attention. "If I might make some suggestions?" Vaughn nodded.

Riley grabbed a marker and went up to an easel with butcher block paper on it. He split the page in half with a line. On the left he divided responsibilities. On the right he worked out a time line as he spoke.

"Frank," he said, turning to the senior medic, "I want you and Colden to secure this isolation area. Cover the windows, get an access roster going, and all that. Basic S-2 stuff.

"Paulson, you and Lane and Holder hang the maps and set this room up according to team SOP."

Riley looked around. "For those of you who just joined the team, there are some copies of the 055 standard operating procedures (SOP) in the isolation footlocker we brought up here. Take a quick look through at the section on isolation procedures to get up to speed. The SOP pretty much breaks out your responsibilities by MOS and how we conduct isolation. I think each of you will have plenty to do for a while after you read that."

He turned to Vaughn. "Sir, you and I and Powers and Alexander should look at the locations of the targets and try to war-game it as far as what General Pike wants. Try to get some basic ideas." Again Vaughn nodded.

Riley turned to Westland. "Could you give us all a thumbnail sketch on Colombia? You know, culture, geography, current events. Whatever you feel we need to know as background, minus specific info on the drug people, which I'm sure," he turned to the DEA agent, "Mister Stevens can give us."

Westland held a pencil over her notepad. "When do you want it?"

Riley checked the time line. "Can you be ready by noon?" She nodded and he marked it in.

He looked at Stevens. "How about you go right after her?"

Stevens nodded glumly. Riley marked in a few more events on his tentative time line and then capped the marker. "Let's get going."

# 12:00 NOON

"All right. Let's pay attention." Riley counted heads and then turned his gaze to the CIA agent standing next to the podium.

Westland clicked the remote in her hand and a slide came on the screen behind her as she started. Riley noted that she spoke with confidence. It was apparent that she had either given this briefing before or had spent a lot of time working over the material.

"The Republic of Colombia is located here at the northern end of the South American continent. It's the only South American country with both a Pacific and an Atlantic shoreline. It is also the land gateway into South America from Panama.

"Colombia has an area of roughly half a million square miles, about slightly less than twice the size of Texas. With a population of about thirty million, it is the fourth largest nation in South America. The official language is Spanish, with some isolated Indian dialects spoken.

"The currency is the peso and the economy is based on agriculture and the export—besides cocaine, of course—of coffee and other agricultural products. It is estimated that anywhere from ten to twenty-five percent of the population is directly or indirectly involved in the cocaine industry."

Westland glanced back at the map of Colombia lit on the screen behind her. "I'll now cover the geography in a little more detail. Colombia is a land of great geographical and climatical contrasts. Depending on where you are in the country, you could be standing in a tropical rain forest, an open savannah, a temperate forest, or near-arctic conditions in the higher elevations.

"The terrain features that dominate the country are the Andes mountains and its various smaller ranges. The second-largest feature lies to the east of the mountains and is called the Llanos, or area of plains. For the purposes of this mission we can basically ignore that part of the country, since it stretches off into the jungles of the Amazon basin. It's sparsely populated and undeveloped. The places we are concerned with will either be in the mountains, such as in the vicinity of Medellin or

Bogota, or down on the Caribbean seacoast, where Cartagena and Barranquilla are located.

"Medellin and Bogota are located in the central highlands, on plateaus between the mountain ranges. Bogota, the capital city, is at an elevation of 8,660 feet above sea level; Medellin is at 5,000 feet. This makes for a temperate climate despite the proximity to the equator.

"Not far out of each city you can find yourself on steep, vegetated mountainsides. I don't mean to steal any of Mister Stevens's spiel, but I believe that this is the terrain where you will find some of your targets. Of the two initial targets I've brought, one is located in the hills just outside Medellin. The second is near Cartagena, which is located here."

Westland looked over her audience. "The Caribbean coast outside of the cities is swampy and tropical, crisscrossed with streams and lakes. Most people think of jungle when they talk of Colombia, but the terrain you will be concerned with will be either lowland swamps or temperate highlands. The areas you will be working in are not like the jungles you might be used to from your missions in Panama, although there may be a little of that along the coast, depending on where exactly you go.

"A quick sketch of recent history may give you an idea of the kind of social climate you'll be working in. Due to various reasons there has been a strong guerrilla movement in the country for many years. The two largest of these groups are known as the M-19 movement and the FARC. However, there are a total of almost a hundred splinter guerrilla organizations operating there."

Riley shook his head in amazement. What kind of screwed-up country were they going into? "What's the relationship between the guerrillas and the drug cartel?"

Westland shrugged. "Off again, on again. Mostly off. One of the reasons the cartel has the military so infiltrated with informers, and also receives a lot of tacit support from the armed forces, is because the cartel often helps in the war against the guerrillas, who have been a threat to their business operations at times.

"However, the guerrillas and the cartel have been known to cooperate when mutual goals have coincided. For example, the attack on the Supreme Court in late 1985 was actually the work of the M-19 group. This took place right after the Court took the step of allowing extradition of cartel members to the U.S. for prosecution, so saying that the executions were coincidence is kind of hard to do. It took us almost five years to recover from that blow to the point where they allowed extradition again.

"The government's recent efforts against the cartel have placed it in the unenviable position of having to fight two separate enemies—the cartel and the guerrillas. The military appears to feel, with some justification, that the guerrillas are the worse of the two evils.

"As a whole, the country of Colombia is perhaps the most lawless in the world. In many areas the only law is the power of the drug gangs. They employ people they call *sicarios,* which means *paid assassins.* Comparing the Mafia to the Colombians is like comparing Snow White and the Seven Dwarfs to Attila the Hun and his army. The Springfield massacre was a typical example of how the sicarios operate.

"Over the past decade, the drug cartel has made several different offers to the government, ranging from asking to be legalized to threatening to take over the country. They have even offered to erase the country's approximately sixteen-billion-dollar foreign debt if the government would formally recognize them."

Riley considered this information. It was all very interesting but, hopefully, would not come into play in the upcoming missions. His war-gaming with the other senior team members had sketched tentative plans that would have the recon element on the ground less than twelve hours for each mission. Nonetheless, it was a tenet of Special Forces operations to have a working knowledge of the area of operations. You never knew when such information might be useful. Riley wished they had more time to do a proper area study of Colombia, but he knew that wouldn't be possible under the present compressed schedule. He stood up, since Westland seemed to be done. "Anything else?"

She shrugged. "I could go on for hours but I'm not really sure you need more detail from me. I think Mister Stevens is going to give you more specific information concerning the drug cartel that might be more along the lines of what you need."

Riley appreciated her conciseness and ability to see what was needed. It was a trait not many people possessed. "Thanks for the briefing. I'm sure we'll be hitting you up over the next couple of days for more specific information as we find out we need it." He turned to Stevens. "All yours."

Stevens took Westland's spot, replacing her slide tray with his own. He cleared his throat and started. "I'm going to give you a quick briefing on the drug network that you'll be attacking. This information should allow you to better understand what you're up against.

"The drug we're primarily concerned with is cocaine. It's estimated that there are ten to twenty million users in the United States. We're not exactly sure of the number because people don't line up and answer polls on that sort of thing. Suffice it to say there's a whole bunch of folks snorting the stuff. You also have to add in the rapidly growing number of crack users, since crack is a derivative of cocaine.

"The cocaine network begins in the Andes mountains of South America, where the coca plant is grown. The majority of the coca crop is cultivated in the countries of Bolivia and Peru. We roughly estimate there are over 400,000 acres presently under cultivation, producing well over 100,000 metric tons of leaf annually. The leaves, when mature, are harvested and taken to initial processing labs in the immediate area. Leaves are sold for ten to fourteen dollars a kilo. Leaves have a cocaine content of about one half to one percent by weight.

"At this initial lab, the leaves are ground up, soaked in alcohol laced with benzol, and mixed. The alcohol is drained and sulfuric acid is then added and the mixture is stirred. Then sodium carbonate is added. The whole thing is washed with kerosene and chilled, leaving crystals of cocaine behind. These crystals, called coca paste, have a cocaine content of anywhere from thirty-five to eighty percent, usually near the lower end of those two numbers. It takes approximately two hundred kilos of coca leaf to produce one kilo of crude coca paste.

"The paste is then taken to several cities in South America where buyers congregate—places such as Tingo Maria in Peru, Santa Cruz in Bolivia, Iquitos in Peru, and Leticia in Colombia. There the paste is purchased and shipped to processing laboratories. The majority goes to Colombia, where it is further refined into base.

"In Colombia there are four main locations for the final processing labs that we are concerned with." Stevens turned and pointed at the map on the wall. "They are in the areas around the cities of Bogota, Medellin, Cartagena, and Barranquilla. I'd say there are about twenty labs operating at any one time in the country. Over half of these are relatively small time when compared to a lab operated by one of the three lords of the drug cartel."

Stevens turned and looked at the team. "A key factor to our success in this task force will be which labs are targeted for us. If we hit a couple of the big-time ones, we'll make a strong impact on the entire network.

"At these labs the coca paste is turned into base, using ether. It takes approximately two and a half kilograms of paste to make one kilo of base. The base is then turned into cocaine hydrochloride. This is done on a one-to-one scale." Stevens turned to the view screen behind him and hit the switch for the slide projector. "These are examples of what you're looking for. The key signs are the drums of ether or hydrochloric acid, which are used for the last two steps."

Holder, the junior engineer, observed, "That place is an explosion waiting to happen. All that ether."

Stevens nodded. "It has been known to happen. Somebody gets a little careless and the place ceases to exist. The chemists who work there get paid enough to make the risk worthwhile."

The chemicals would compound the effect of the firing platform, Riley thought. He watched as the pictures continued to flash across the screen.

Stevens went on. "I have hard copies of all these photos and will leave them here. Also, I'm leaving some intelligence reports on the makeup of some of the drug organizations."

Powers raised his hand. "What about security at these labs?"

"Security is heavy. It's not unknown for one drug lord to try to rip off another. Like I said, there are three main lords down there right now. Combined they are called the cartel, but that doesn't necessarily mean they work together. One is based in Medellin. That's Suarez. Another controls Bogota and Barranquilla.

That's Ahate's people, although there have been rumors there's been a coup in that gang and a man known only as the Ring Man is presently in charge. He used to be one of Ahate's top sicarios. The last, Rameriz, also known as The Shark, works the coast out of Cartagena.

"At a typical major lab I'd say you have anywhere from twenty to thirty men for security. They're armed with the latest automatic weapons and machine guns. I've heard that some of them have black market Redeye antiaircraft missiles for use against helicopters, and with the amount of money these people have, I could well believe it.

"Let me tell you something about the wealth you're dealing with. Let's back the whole process up. For one kilo of cocaine hydrochloride you need over a thousand kilos of leaves. That costs $700 to $800 in Bolivia. That initial investment, when turned into a kilo of cocaine hydrochloride, becomes worth a lot, because when it reaches the States the kilo is stepped on several times; that is, it's diluted with a neutral substance, such as lactose. That's done maybe three times, making that initial kilo into eight kilos. Each of those eight kilos can sell for let's say at least $15,000. So we're talking a total sale of $120,000. And that's not street value. On the street the kilos are further broken down and sold as grams for a higher per unit price."

Stevens looked at the men in front of him. "With that kind of money you can afford protection. There've been reports of foreign mercenaries working for some of the factions, running training camps for the sicarios and in some cases actually doing some of their dirty work. I've heard of some Americans there but it mainly seems to be German and Israeli ex-military.

"Each branch of the cartel has its little army of sicarios. For example, Rameriz's sicarios call themselves the Terminator gang and mark their victims with a T pattern of bullet holes. You've also got the Rambos, the Hernan Botero gang, the Black Flag gang, and several others. They use women extensively as assassins."

Stevens clicked off his projector. "The entire drug cartel in Colombia is a highly organized and ruthless bunch. If the government down there tried to stand toe to toe with the cartel and fight it out, I'd put my money on the cartel."

## 2:00 P.M.

Riley felt that the isolation was going well so far. Most of the team members were wading through the information Westland and Stevens had brought with them, sorting out those facts they needed for both their area of expertise and as background for the overall mission. All the maps were posted and the isolation area was internally secure. Pike had arranged with the post commander to secure the outside of the compound with military police.

Riley glanced around the isolation area a little nervously, steeling himself to go over and talk to the new detachment commander. Riley disliked personal confrontations. He'd spent his childhood avoiding conflict, and even the possibility of having to argue with someone made him nervous.

Riley hadn't had a chance to talk with Captain Vaughn one-on-one so far. Too much had happened, and Riley had been kept busy trying to get the team on track to start mission planning. Now he knew he'd have to make the time. The whole operation was moving much faster than he had originally expected. Based on the intelligence and targeting information, the first split team was projected to go on a mission in two or three days.

Riley knew it was time to start making some hard decisions regarding mission planning and organization—decisions that were technically the captain's to make. Equally important, he also wanted to get an idea of what the captain thought and felt about the whole mission.

With a sigh, Riley got up and wandered across the room in the general direction of Captain Vaughn. He hovered near the captain's desk until Vaughn glanced up and noticed him. "Excuse me, sir, but I thought we might sit down and discuss some things privately."

Vaughn nodded. "That's a good idea. I've been wanting to talk to you about the way things are going."

Riley pointed. "We can use the general's office. He's over at the Pentagon trying to coordinate some of the support we need." Riley led the way into the small room and closed the door. He figured he needed to be the one to begin things. He perched on the edge of the general's desk while the captain took a chair.

"Sir, first off, you need to know that I'm not used to working under a team leader. I've been the commander of this team since I got my warrant, going on a little over a year. Before that I was an E-7 team sergeant, so I was in control on the enlisted side then. This situation, with you in command and me being the XO, is as new to me as it is to you. I think we can work together to make the transition for the two of us and the team as smooth as possible."

Riley was trying to be nice. Although having a commissioned officer as detachment commander was new to him as a warrant officer, being in Special Forces wasn't. It was all new to the young captain. Riley was hoping that Vaughn would want to utilize his experience; in return, Riley was willing to teach and support the captain.

Vaughn's reply indicated to Riley that either he hadn't quite understood what Riley was offering or wasn't interested. "I hear what you're saying. I can understand that it might be hard for you to accept that I'm in command. But that's the way it is. I know I don't have any Special Forces experience, but I spent four years in the 82d Airborne Division and had a successful company command there. So I know what's going on. Also, I did well in the qualification course. I was the top officer graduate in my class."

Riley looked the captain in the eyes. "Sir, you're going to find things are a bit different over here than they were in the 82d. I spent two years in the eighty-deuce when I was enlisted and I know what it's like. We operate differently here in SF, and the Q-course doesn't teach you everything you need to know."

Vaughn shook his head. "I don't see the need to operate differently on this mission. It looks very straightforward to me. Just like a mission out of Ranger school. We go in, verify the target, and then call in some firepower to blast."

Riley rubbed his forehead. I'm glad my mother taught me patience, he thought. Of all the people to get saddled with—a former member of the 82d Airborne gang. Riley had found an amazing consistency among the officers from that unit. A frontal lobotomy must be part of the in-processing when a new officer reported to the division. On the other hand, the enlisted soldiers were super. They would do damn near anything they were asked. Which was part of the problem. They didn't question it when their officers told them to do something stupid. And Riley had seen a lot of stupid things ordered by the officers of the neighboring 82d Airborne Division in his seven years at Fort Bragg.

"Sir, to be frank, the first difference between here and at division is that this team operates alone. It's just you and the eleven of us. Second, things are never as clear-cut as they appear. This mission appears straightforward, but I have bad feelings about it."

Riley could see Vaughn trying to decide whether the eleven-to-one thing had been a veiled threat. Apparently he couldn't figure it out because he latched onto the second remark. "What kind of bad feelings are you talking about?"

"Sir, I tend to wonder *why* about things. Like in this case, I wonder why the Colombian government is fingering some cocaine labs. The intel that CIA woman, Westland, brought seems to check out with the imagery. It looks like we've got two good targets. But all the background stuff we've studied in the last couple of hours on Colombia says that the government and the drug cartel are in a sort of alliance. Kind of a 'you don't bother me and I won't bother you' arrangement. So why the change all of a sudden?"

Vaughn pondered that for a few moments. Riley expected to see smoke pouring out of the captain's ears any second. "You've got a point. But I also don't think it's likely that we'll find out. Obviously there are some internal maneuverings going on down there that we don't know about. The key thing to be worried about as far as we're concerned is getting ambushed. The first mission is going to be key. If it's a setup, that's the one that will tell."

Riley's estimation of his new team leader went up slightly. The man had hit the nail on the head. "That's exactly what's been bugging me, sir. The first one is going to be critical. Since we're going in split team I suggest we stagger these first two hits. Hold off on sending the second team in until the first one is out successfully."

Vaughn concurred. "That's a good idea. No sense in endangering all of us at the start. Kind of like sending a recon element across a danger area, like I was taught in Ranger school. I agree."

Riley nodded. "I recommend that I take in the first split team and you take the second, sir. We can work out the makeup of the split teams later today."

Vaughn agreed. "OK. When the general gets back I'll see what he thinks about it."

# BOGOTA
## 4:20 P.M.

President Alegre, throughout the bustle of the day's business, had kept one thought in the back of his mind—the situation with the Ring Man. He considered the recent developments. The Americans had the locations of the first two targets by now. They had to act quickly. Laboratories moved occasionally. The facilities were just a collection of shacks. Keeping drugs worth many millions of dollars in one location too long was a risky proposition in Colombia. The country had the highest crime rate per capita in the world.

Alegre shook his head as he considered the larger picture. He truly believed the drugs were the Americans' fault. It was their organized crime that controlled the overseas market, and the American people who created the demand. Alegre felt his people were just trying to make a living. Unfortunately, the use of drugs among Colombians was growing at an alarming rate. The international political fallout was also damaging. The Americans had never stopped putting the pressure on his administration to do something. Alegre knew he could have ignored the American pressure and nothing significant would have happened, but he had other factors to consider.

In four days the United Nations was going to vote on the border dispute with Venezuela over the Gulf of Venezuela. Although the gulf was almost entirely enclosed by Venezuelan land, Colombia still maintained a claim on a third of it by nature of Colombian territory on La Guajira peninsula. The potential oil and mineral rights from the ocean bottom there were forecast to be in the billions. With the backing of the United States, Colombia might be able to ram its claim through the United Nations.

With the economic boom that claim would bring, Alegre felt

that Colombia could finally throw off the money leash the drug cartel held on the people. Without the carrot of mining rights in the Gulf of Venezuela to offer the economy, he knew he would never be able to fully destroy the cartel.

Another factor, of a more personal nature, was the fact that if the cartel was willing to gun down schoolchildren in America, they wouldn't hesitate to kill a president in Colombia. Alegre knew he was in office only at the tolerance of the drug cartel. He didn't like that setup. He believed the best defense was a good offense. Since being elected, he had bided his time until the situation was right, placating the cartel. The time to fight back appeared to be now.

For the present, Alegre would work with the Ring Man. Their immediate goals were the same. Alegre shivered briefly. If the Ring Man knew Alegre's ultimate objective, there would be blood spilled in the presidential palace.

Alegre sighed. It was all so complicated. Playing people against each other. Trying to manipulate the situation for the country's good. There was a price to be paid for everything.

# FORT BELVOIR, VIRGINIA
# 6:30 P.M.

Alone in the small, two-man room they shared, Powers sat on his bunk unperturbed by his friend's agitation. "It's his neck. Let him hang himself."

Riley shook his head in exasperation. "Come on, compadre. That isn't the way it's supposed to work."

Powers leaned back on his bunk contentedly. "Listen, Dave. Stop worrying about everyone else's problems for a minute. If the little Napoleon wants to split the team up into the new and old guys, that makes sense to me. I'd rather go in with you than with him."

Riley had had a feeling that Powers wasn't going to be too upset with Vaughn's proclamation on the makeup of the split teams. Vaughn had split the twelve-man team in half. The six old members of 055 would go together under Riley's command on the first mission. The six new additions would assume the second mission under the captain's command. What really irked Riley was that the captain hadn't even consulted him. He thought they had had an understanding after their conversation earlier this afternoon. Obviously, he'd been wrong about that.

Riley knew that Powers was also less than pleased with the captain's leadership technique, or rather lack of it. In Special Forces the team sergeant as a minimum should have been consulted before such a decision was made. Riley and Powers had always worked together, bouncing ideas off of each other, consulting the rest of the team where feasible. The idea was to maximize the considerable brainpower every team possessed. With his solo decision Vaughn had acted as though he was still in the 82d Airborne.

Powers continued. "It splits the MOSs exactly. Each split team got one medic, one commo man, one engineer, and one weapons man." Powers sat up and looked at his old friend. "And one officer."

"You know that the team sergeant is supposed to go with the team leader," Riley retorted.

Powers began getting irritated. "Bullshit. That's not written anywhere. Technically, the team sergeant always takes the other half of the team from the captain."

"That's before we had warrants, and the XO was just a lieutenant who couldn't find his ass with both hands."

Powers slammed his hand on the desk next to his bed. "Goddamnit, Dave! Listen. Alexander is a good man. He can take care of the captain. This gives our split team a much better survival chance. We got the guys we worked with all year. Everyone knows the SOPs."

"What about the other guys going with the captain?"

"So what do you want to do? Reduce the survivability of both split teams?"

Riley paused and reconsidered. Powers did have a point there. Riley sighed. What was he getting so worked up about? Deep inside he was happy to have people he knew and trusted on his part of the split team. Plus it opened up more possibilities for infiltration.

Powers wasn't through and was obviously thinking along the same lines. "The bottom line on it is the infiltration. You seem to be forgetting that. Alexander's the only free-fall parachutist out of all the new guys. And he's not free-fall jumpmaster qualified. I'm the only free-fall jumpmaster you got and, since we're thinking of going in from thirty thousand feet on the first mission, I think you're going to need me. The second mission just about calls for going in by Combat Talon with their ass in the grass at two hundred fifty feet. All the new guys can handle that, but they sure as hell ain't going to be able to HAHO in on the first one. Anyway, you ain't got no choice, partner. It's got to be the way the captain set it up."

Powers reconsidered. "Well, maybe it doesn't have to be that way and I don't like the way he did it either, but the end result would have been the same even if he did consult with you or me."

Riley nodded reluctantly. Looking at it from that perspective he realized he was more pissed at the lack of respect the captain had shown him than at the actual decision. He decided to put this one in the past and drive on.

"Screw it. Get the guys on our split team together. I want to do a practice briefback."

Powers grinned. "Now you're getting smart."

# TUESDAY,
# 27 AUGUST

## FORT BELVOIR, VIRGINIA
## 1:00 P.M.

General Pike gestured toward the maps on the wall of the isolation room. "Give us an update, Captain Vaughn."

Riley half expected Vaughn to tell him to get up and do it. But the captain stood up and walked over to the maps. He turned and faced the general and the two civilians.

Riley glanced over at the two agents. Stevens was slouched in his chair trying to pay attention. Probably couldn't wait for the briefing to be over so he could sneak his afternoon pick-me-up, Riley thought. His original suspicion about the DEA agent's drinking had been confirmed the previous afternoon when he had detected the unmistakable scent of alcohol on the man's breath. He had complained to the general about the agent's drinking, but the general had been unwilling to rock the boat too far with the DEA. Besides, Pike had reluctantly admitted, it was too close to the first mission to replace Stevens now.

Westland was sitting straight in her chair, a notepad on her legs. She was wearing a gore-tex running suit and looked as though she had just finished a hard workout, which Riley knew she had. The previous hour he had occasionally glanced out the back window at the woman working out. He'd been surprised that she apparently had some martial arts background as she did some basic kicks in her calisthenics. Riley idly wondered if she had done that to prove to the team that she could hold her own physically. He shrugged. He didn't care. Just as long as she gave them good intelligence. It wasn't as if she was going on the ground with them.

Vaughn cleared his throat and Riley shifted his attention to the front of the room. "Sir, our analysis of the data we've been provided has led us to the following tentative plan. We have two potential targets that were provided to the CIA by a source representing President Alegre. Checking both against satellite imagery provided by the National Security Agency indicates that there appear to be buildings and materials in both areas that conform to what a processing laboratory would have. Most particularly important is the presence of large numbers of steel barrels in both areas. As you know, they are used to hold the vast amount of chemicals that are used in cocaine processing.

"We have designated this one here," pointing at the map, "as Nail One and this one here as Nail Two." Riley smiled wanly. The captain had come up with the code names. After all, they had decided to call themselves Task Force Hammer.

"We propose sending in a surveillance team, Eyes One, Thursday evening to verify Nail One. Once verification is radioed back, we propose that the target site be hit the same evening, or actually early in the morning on Friday. That's pending coordination of the actual hit force this afternoon by you, sir.

"We propose the split team be pulled out the same morning. Then the second team, Eyes Two, be sent in against Nail Two on Friday night, with that target hit occurring early Saturday morning and that team being pulled out the same morning."

Vaughn paused to check the reactions. Pike was nodding in affirmation. The general knew all of this already. He'd spent most of the morning coordinating aircraft and firepower to support the proposed missions. This update was for the benefit of the civilians.

Westland raised her hand. "Can you mount the first mission that quickly and still be safe? That doesn't give you much time."

Vaughn glanced at Riley, who stood up as the captain yielded the floor to the leader of the first mission. "Yes, ma'am. It's not much time but the mission is pretty straightforward. We'll fly direct from here to Colombia and jump in almost on top of the target. Scope it out. If it's a valid target we'll call in the firepower to level it. Once we verify destruction, we'll get pulled out by a helicopter coming in from Panama. It will fly us back to Panama, where we cross-load back onto a C-130. We'll be back here hopefully within twenty-four hours.

"The only things we're waiting for now are confirmation of the Hammer force and exfiltration and infiltration aircraft. Also, we're still waiting for the sterile equipment the agency is supposed to provide us."

Westland fielded the implied question. "The equipment will be here this afternoon."

Riley continued. "We'll be spending the rest of today and tomorrow finalizing our plans and familiarizing ourselves with the equipment. Also, we'll be doing contingency planning for any unexpected occurrences."

General Pike turned toward the DEA agent. "Everything good to go on your end?"

Stevens sat up. "I'll be flying down to Bogota tomorrow. I've got the codes to talk back to you all here at the agreed upon time every day. I'll also be set to monitor the SATCOM from the embassy for all the missions. Like we discussed, I think I can do you all a lot more good down there. Get an idea of what the reaction to the raids is and also let you know the scope of the damage and who you hit."

Pike nodded. "All right. Sounds like everything is rolling. I'll be getting confirmation of our Department of Defense support later this afternoon from General Linders."

Riley was impressed in spite of his misgivings about the mission. They were definitely getting fast action on requests for support for this operation. That was a rare event, based on his experience in past dealings with military bureaucracy.

Pike continued. "You'll be briefing the chairman tomorrow morning to get his approval. Once we have that, Task Force Hammer will be ready to go."

## 5:00 P.M.

Kate Westland sat in the small office they had given her just off the isolation area. She leafed listlessly through the documents she had brought with her on the drug cartel. She knew that the Special Forces people were still planning in the main room. The equipment had been delivered two hours ago from Langley. Some of those Green Berets had acted like little kids at Christmas, oohing and aahing over the weapons and other gear.

Kate put aside the papers and sighed. Her job for the first mission was pretty much done, and now it was in the hands of the men in the next room. She wasn't happy about that. All her seven years with the agency had been spent at Langley as an analyst. She knew she was damn good at it but she wanted to do more. She had never had the chance to go on a field mission. She felt she had to get some experience in the field in order to round out her career. It wasn't just that she wanted to punch her ticket with some time as a field agent. She wanted to do the job she felt she could. She wanted to be out on the cutting edge instead of always back at the hilt. That was the reason she had joined the agency in the first place.

Thinking about her career reminded Kate of her ex-husband. They'd met while going through the basic agents' course at Langley. In retrospect, it was easy to see that she had mistaken his tolerance of her career as acceptance. It had finally come to a head two years ago. He'd received an offer to move to Berlin and do fieldwork. He'd been shocked when she refused to leave her field of expertise, Latin America, in order to follow him. She had been equally shocked to find out how little he thought of her career. He had never seemed to understand when she told him her job was as important to her as his was to him. He'd filed for divorce two weeks after her refusal. She'd picked up the pieces of her life, pouring her passion into her work. Her proficiency at that work had led her to where she was now.

Strom had said this was an important assignment. She knew that from the simple fact that he had personally given her the mission briefing. But it still wasn't really a field assignment. She'd be sitting here on her butt in Virginia while these soldiers went down and did the dirty work. Maybe if this operation turned out well she would get the transfer to a field site that she had been requesting the last five years.

Kate cleared her mind of this cloud of thoughts and went over to the door. She figured she might as well see what was happening, and find out if the soldiers had any problems with the equipment. She opened the door and stopped as she heard voices raised loud in banter.

" . . . she could probably kick your butt."

"Yeah, she probably thinks she's hot shit." The soldier's voice went shrill: " 'I'm Agent Westland of the CIA and I'm a bad ass. Do you think you men can do the mission in that short amount of time?' " There was some laughter.

The soldier continued. "Remember those stupid equal opportunity classes we had at Bragg? I wonder if she wants to be called a 'woman CIA agent' or a 'female CIA agent'?"

Westland glanced around the room. They hadn't seen her yet. Three of the soldiers, the ones laughing, were gathered around the maps to her right. She saw the intense-looking Puerto Rican soldier, the warrant officer named Riley, raise his head and stare at them.

"Hey, smackheads. If you don't have anything better to do . . . ," he glanced over at her and paused. The three soldiers turned and noticed her for the first time. One of them blushed under his stringy black hair.

She walked over and stood in front of the soldier who had been doing the talking. She remembered he'd been introduced as Atwaters. "Which would you like to be called?" She paused while the soldier frowned in confusion and then she continued. "Butthole or asshole?"

There was silence in the room as she turned and walked back to her office. She heard a few muffled chuckles break out in the room as she shut her door.

Westland sighed as she sat back behind the desk. She'd had to put up with stuff like that ever since she joined the agency. She was so tired of it. No matter what she did, no matter how good she was, it still happened. But she was damned if she'd put up with it, or turn and run away. That's what they expected women to do.

There was a knock on the door. "Come in."

Riley came in. She sensed he was uncomfortable, as though he didn't know what to say. "What can I do for you, Mister Riley?"

"Listen. I apologize for what was said out there. These guys aren't used to working with a woman. Sometimes they say stupid stuff. They didn't mean anything by what they said." He let a small smile lighten his dark face. "I like the way you handled it."

Kate wasn't buying it. "I think they did mean something. You might not understand but I've faced crap like that my entire career."

Riley looked her in the eyes. "Let me tell you something about not understanding. You're right. I don't understand what you've had to face as a woman trying to make it. But I do understand what it's like to have people look at you and judge you on what you look like rather than who you are. I don't know which is worse or harder: being a woman or being half Puerto Rican from the South Bronx. Probably neither. They're just different. But I've had my share of the bullshit, too."

Kate backed off. She didn't need to antagonize the one person who seemed to care. "I'm sorry. It's just that it caught me off guard."

Riley seemed to relax and laughed. "If you're going to deal with these people you can't let your guard down and you can't back off. They respect strength and competence. They're like vultures, though, if they sense any weakness. I don't think you're going to have any problem."

She nodded. She knew she could hold her own. She'd done it for seven years in the male-dominated corridors at Langley. It was just that having to be constantly on guard was draining. She couldn't concentrate on just the job. "Thanks. I appreciate it." She felt slightly uncomfortable talking about herself and decided to change the subject. "All the equipment satisfactory?"

Riley led her back into the planning room. "Yeah. Everything looks good to go. We'll run some more rehearsals and do a couple of internal briefbacks to make sure everybody knows what they need to do, then we'll be ready to go." He looked at his watch. "We're going to do a practice briefback tonight at 1900 after we meet with Pike. You're welcome to sit in on it. Probably learn something."

"I'll do that. See you then."

Kate turned and walked out into the hallway. She wanted to head over to the imagery people at Langley and get the latest satellite photos before the evening meeting with General Pike.

Before going out of the building, she stopped in the lone bathroom on the first floor. Someone had hung a cardboard sign on the door. She flipped it over to occupied and went in. The first sight that greeted her was a centerfold from some men's magazine hanging on the wall. Her immediate reaction was to tear it down, or go back and tell Riley to have them take it down. Then she reconsidered. That would be just what they wanted. There were better ways to handle things.

# WEDNESDAY, 28 AUGUST

## FORT BELVOIR, VIRGINIA
## 8:00 A.M.

"Attention!"

Riley popped to his feet as Powers's voice boomed through the isolation area. Riley stood in front of a folding metal chair, with the other members of Eyes One stretched off to his left along the cinder-block wall that made up one side of the room. Across from Riley, the windows facing the parking lot were covered with butcher block paper to prevent anyone from seeing in. Seated in front of the windows, facing him, were the members of Eyes Two.

Separating and perpendicular to the two teams, a dozen chairs were set up. It was to these chairs that General Pike was leading the two people to whom the upcoming briefing was to be given. The "briefback" was a tenet of Special Forces operations that was unique in the army. Most army units issued operations orders for missions and even briefed the plan, but few took the time, or had the expertise at such a low unit level, to prepare a briefback comparable to what Special Forces A-Teams put together.

Riley studied the newcomers out of the corners of his eyes as he stood at a rigid position of attention. The chairman of the Joint Chiefs of Staff, General Macksey, led the way and took the center chair facing the front of the room, where the maps for both missions were displayed, tacked onto pieces of plywood.

97

Flanking the chairman, on his left, was a three-star air force general. Westland was seated in the center of the second row right behind General Macksey.

Riley was surprised that there were only three people present for the briefback. He had expected a hoard of aides and self-appointed important people. The small number was another fact, added to the events of the last several days, to convince him that somebody was very serious about security for this mission.

Pike went to the wood podium set up in front of the maps. He waited while Macksey ran his eyes over both teams, still standing. Finally, General Macksey introduced his companion. "Gentlemen, this is General Linders. He's the man on my staff who is responsible for Special Operations."

Macksey took his seat and growled at the team members, "Take your seats, gentlemen." He turned to Pike. "Let's get this show on the road."

Pike nodded. "Sir, you'll be receiving an operational briefback from both teams, Eyes One and Eyes Two. Mister Riley is the commander of Eyes One and he'll start."

Riley walked to the front of the room. He had been nervous before the briefing, knowing that the people he was addressing were, as Powers put it, echelons above God from an army perspective. But now that he was about to start, his nervousness abated and he felt confident. They had a good plan and, more importantly, each member of the team had committed the plan to memory. It was just a question of letting Macksey and Linders know that.

"Good morning, General Macksey, General Linders." Riley nodded to the two officers. "I'm Chief Warrant Officer Riley, commander of Eyes One. This briefing is classified top secret. Eyes One's mission is to infiltrate operational area Harkon, located here in the vicinity of Cartagena, Colombia, at 0230 Zulu time, 29 August, and destroy target Nail One, at 0930 Zulu. The purpose of this mission is to verify and designate for destruction a suspected cocaine laboratory located there. We will be exfiltrated at 1038 Zulu time, 29 August."

Riley halted at Macksey's raised finger. "Yes, sir."

"The time zone down there is the same as here, isn't it?"

"Yes, sir. Sierra time zone."

"So we're talking minus five hours from zulu to convert to local."

"Yes, sir."

"So you're talking in at 2130 and out by 0538 local. All in darkness. Good. All right, continue."

Riley gestured toward his split team. "Sir, I'd like to introduce the members of Eyes One and give you a brief operational overview. I'll then be followed by the members of the team, each briefing their own specialized areas.

"Master Sergeant Powers is the team sergeant." Powers rose to attention as he was introduced, as did each succeeding team member. Riley watched the general inspect each man as his name was called.

Riley then stepped out from behind the podium and began his description of the operation. He spoke from memory, without referring to notes, and used a pointer in conjunction with the map to highlight a location or route he described. "The concept of the operation for this mission is as follows: Eyes One will depart Fort Belvoir army airfield tomorrow at 1900 Zulu. The flight . . . "

Riley paused as the air force general, Linders, whispered something to Macksey, who nodded and addressed Riley. "I appreciate your using Zulu time, since that's the proper way to do it, but since everything is in the same time zone, for the purposes of this briefing, let's keep it local. All right, Mister Riley?"

"Yes, sir." Zulu time was used because Special Forces operations usually cut across several time zones, and to prevent confusion and aid coordination, all parties worked off of Greenwich mean time, commonly referred to as Zulu time. But if the general wanted local, the general got local.

"We depart the airfield here at 1400 local. The flight will take approximately seven and a half hours to reach the infiltration point. There will be one in-flight refuel of our C-130 aircraft by a KC-10 tanker en route.

"Our high-altitude release point, or HARP, is here, approximately fifteen kilometers from our primary drop zone, DZ Hatter, which is here. The release point may have to be adjusted depending on weather, most particularly winds aloft. We will coordinate that with the crew before takeoff and en route.

"To get from the high-altitude release point to the drop zone, we will use a technique called HAHO, or high altitude, high opening. Basically, we will fly our free-fall parachutes like hang gliders from our opening at thirty thousand feet to the drop zone. This allows the infiltration aircraft to stay offset from the target over water and should allow us to infiltrate undetected."

Macksey raised another finger and Riley paused. "Won't the six of you get picked up on radar while floating in?"

"No, sir. Our nylon canopies don't reflect radar, and the signature from our bodies will be minimal. Currently, there is only normal air traffic control radar in use in the vicinity of Cartagena. We've jumped into ATC-controlled airspace before and have never been picked up."

Macksey gestured for Riley to continue. Riley slapped his pointer on the map behind him. "Once we land on DZ Hatter we will move to the target and place observation on it to confirm whether or not it is a legitimate target. We will contact the AWACS plane, code-named Moonbeam, that will be orbiting over the Gulf of Mexico. The AWACS will forward our assessment to both the AC-130 Spectre gunship, designated Hammer, that will be en route, and back here to our base of operations at Fort Belvoir, designated Hammer Base.

"If the target's legitimate, Hammer will be on station at 0415. We will highlight the target with laser designators at 0425. At 0430 Hammer will fire. We will then make an on-the-scene assessment of target destruction.

"We will be exfiltrated from this field here—a little over a kilometer from the target—at 0538 by an MH-60 Blackhawk helicopter, designated Stork. Coordination and communication with these aircraft will be done through the AWACS." Riley looked Macksey in the eye. "I'll be followed by Staff Sergeant Marzan, who will cover the terrain, weather, and enemy situation."

Marzan stood up and strode briskly to the map, relieving Riley of the pointer on his way there. This was Marzan's first time briefing the intelligence portion for a mission and Riley silently wished him luck.

"Good morning, sir. The area we will be operating in is bounded by the Gulf of Mexico to the northwest and these mountains to the southeast. Key terrain features in the area include the Caribbean Sea and coastline, the city of Cartagena 14 kilometers to the north of the target, the coastal highway, and, as we close in on the target, this dirt airstrip approximately 1.4 kilometers long that borders the lab site.

"The terrain is mostly swamp, plantation land, or tropical forest. Between the drop zone and the target we will cross what appears to be uninhabited swampland and forest. Since it is the end of the rainy season there, we expect to find the water level at normal or slightly above normal levels.

"Population density throughout the area outside of Cartagena is moderate—approximately one to ten people per square kilometer is the average. The terrain in the immediate vicinity of the target is mostly flat and heavily vegetated. The forest consists mainly of tropical trees with some deciduous. Observation and fields of fire are limited due to the thick vegetation. Concealment is excellent for the same reasons.

"The target itself is partially hidden under the trees. The satellite imagery shows a short airstrip bounding the target on the west side. We have also made out a dirt road leading from the target toward Cartagena and the coast. In the target itself we can see the outlines of three, possibly four, buildings and some metal drums.

"Avenues of approach are basically whatever compass direction we desire to shoot through the swamp. The enemy can also move throughout the area in the same manner and enjoys the advantage of knowing the terrain. There appear to be several small dirt roads in the area and these may be used by the enemy to move by motorized means.

"Possible helicopter pickup zones in the area include the one we are using for exfiltration and our alternate, farther away on the other side of the highway from the target. If necessary, we could use the airstrip next to the lab itself. Other than those, LZs are limited. The beach farther to the west might be a possibility.

"In the area of operations, the weather is expected to be normal for this time of year. Highs during the day are projected to be around ninety-five degrees Fahrenheit, while the lows at night will be in the high seventies. Even though this is the end of the rainy season, the present projected forecast calls for no precipitation. Winds are normally from the north-northwest. Forecast for our infiltration indicates good jumping weather. Winds are expected to be from the north at twenty knots and visibility approximately twelve miles at jump altitude."

Riley looked to his left at Powers and nodded. Marzan was doing a great job.

"Light data is posted here. Of highlight you can see that we will average 10.3 hours of darkness each twenty-four hours. There will be 40 percent illumination on the night of the mission.

"The effect of the weather on either friendly or enemy forces will be minimal. The illumination will aid in our use of night-vision devices and will aid in navigation for our exfiltration aircraft. It is not known whether the enemy has night-vision devices. We are assuming they might have passive devices but it is highly doubtful they have thermal imaging."

If the bad guys have thermal imaging, Riley thought, we might as well kiss our asses good-bye. A thermal imager did away with the concealment offered by both the night and the vegetation by providing a picture of the heat sources in the area. A man's body showed up quite clearly. There were no indications in all their intelligence reports that the drug cartel had yet purchased and utilized the highly expensive and difficult-to-maintain devices.

"The disposition of enemy forces in the immediate area of the target is unknown, but we estimate at least fifteen guards on site. We presume they are armed with automatic weapons with the likely possibility of some crew-served machine guns.

"Colombian military in the area includes elements of the 2d Brigade headquartered in Barranquilla. The closest elements are stationed approximately twenty-three kilometers from our target on the north side of Cartagena. This is an infantry unit, approximately battalion sized, armed with automatic and crew-served weapons. The basic personal weapon of the Colombian Army is the German G-3 automatic rifle. Units also possess their own organic mortars, which we believe are U.S.-manufactured 81 millimeter. State of training and discipline of the army is considered high due to constant operations against the guerrillas.

"There is a rotary wing aviation unit of approximately company size stationed at the Cartagena airport. This unit has four UH-1 lift helicopters and two UH-1s modified with 7.62-millimeter miniguns. We estimate reaction time of this force to range anywhere from thirty minutes to several hours if it is alerted at all. The state of readiness of this unit is expected to be low, as is their maintenance posture. It is estimated that at least half those helicopters are down for repairs. Additionally, the Colombian rotary wing pilots have yet to demonstrate any proficiency at night combat flight operations. They do not conduct flight operations with night-vision goggles.

"The nearest Colombian air force elements are stationed in Cartagena at the airport. Last satellite imagery shows two Mirage jets and one C-126 turboprop transport on the tarmac there. The ability to scramble those jets is unknown."

General Linders interrupted. "Don't worry about any interference from the air. Every night you guys run a mission I'll have air support standing by. If the AWACS spots anything lifting off that could be a threat to you or the aircraft supporting you, we'll take care of it."

Riley was impressed. Somehow, the whole mission had seemed like just a training mission up until now. But the thought of all the support that was being lined up for this mission, and the presence of the chairman of the Joint Chiefs of Staff and an air force three star, made it all seem real. Riley also wondered how the U.S. would explain the interdiction of those Colombian air force jets to the Colombians on the off chance the U.S. air force did have to intervene.

Marzan consulted his notes again. "Overall, we feel that the greatest enemy threats we face are detection during infiltration and exfiltration, discovery by guards during our surveillance of the target, discovery by local population during infiltration and surveillance, and conflict with regular Colombian military forces that might react to the raid."

Macksey raised his finger again. "How long do you plan to be on the ground following your strike, again?"

Marzan answered from memory. "Strike will occur at 0430 and our exfil will be at 0538."

Macksey considered that. "What do you think the chances are of the Colombian forces getting to the target area in that time frame?"

Marzan paused for a second as he thought out his answer. It had been a question the team had spent a lot of time on. "Sir, I think the chances of that are slim. First, they have to know something happened. Our target is pretty isolated, and if we destroy all personnel on the site, that eliminates a possible source of alert.

"Second, even if someone escapes it is unlikely that they will alert the military. There is the possibility some civilian might report the firing, but in Colombia the people have learned to keep their mouths shut about violent acts."

Macksey was satisfied. "All right. If you need to move up that exfil go ahead and do it, but I accept your reasoning for your present time schedule."

Marzan nodded. "Sir, that completes the intelligence portion. I have here our escape and evasion plan, which has been sealed and should be opened only in case of failure of this detachment to make contact with the AWACS or upon receipt of our escape and evasion code word."

Marzan walked over and handed it to General Pike. It was traditional that the escape and evasion (E & E) plan went to the commander taking the briefback, who personally kept it secure until such time as it might be needed. In this case, they gave it to Pike, because he would be the man responsible for the plan's implementation.

The E & E plan was the team's last hope to exfiltrate in case of the failure of exfiltration on the primary or alternate landing zones, and as much time was put into making that plan as the actual operational plan to hit the target. The entire team had been briefed on the plan and had memorized its contents.

Riley watched as Powers rumbled his way up to the front of the room and centered the tip of the pointer on Virginia on the large-scale map.

"Sir, for infiltration we will depart Fort Belvoir army airfield tomorrow at 1400. We will follow this flight route." Powers traced a route traversing the southeastern United States, looping across the Gulf of Mexico to the west of Cuba, and then skimming the coast of Colombia.

"We will fly approximately ten kilometers off the coast of Colombia. The flight route has already been posted as a training mission with air traffic control in Cartagena. Since the aircraft never crosses over Colombian land, we feel it should not raise any suspicions during the brief slowdown the aircraft will have to do for our jump."

Powers paused as General Linders turned to the chairman. "I've had a 130 out of Panama fly that route the last two nights in order to get them used to it. There's been no problem with either one or any indication that the Colombians are suspicious. The AWACS will do enough scrambling of local radar to allow the gunship to remain over the target long enough to do the hit." Macksey acknowledged the information and turned his attention back to Powers.

"Our high-altitude release point is presently pinpointed at this location, fifteen kilometers from our drop zone at an azimuth of 290 degrees. Five minutes from the infil point I will begin giving the jump commands.

"At 2130 we will reach the release point. The team will exit the aircraft in the order depicted here. As jumpmaster, I will lead the jump and Mister Riley will bring up the rear. We will be jumping off the ramp at thirty thousand feet.

"We will assemble in the air, stacked with a hundred-meter vertical interval. I will be the primary navigator, with Sergeant Marzan and Chief Riley backing me up. The azimuth to the DZ will be 110 degrees from the infiltration point and I have several significant terrain features I will be able to see as we descend and get over land that will guide me into the DZ."

Powers paused and Macksey filled the space with a question. "Will you have internal communications on the jump?"

"Yes, sir. We will be wearing built-in helmet radios. The transmitter and receiver are both built into the padding of the helmet."

The air force general was interested. "How does that transmit your voice?"

Powers just cared that it worked. He didn't know how. He gestured for Marzan to supply the information.

Marzan popped to his feet. "The sound is received via an acoustic transducer inside the helmet padding. The antenna is spiraled around the material of the helmet itself. We will be transmitting on low-band VHF with power setting on low."

Powers explained the reason for the equipment. "We can't use boom mikes, because the turbulence on exiting and the opening shock of the canopy could cause you to eat the mike." Riley smiled to himself. Powers always liked the simple answer.

"Mister Riley has responsibility for keeping track of everyone on the way down, since he's the only one who will be able to see all the jumpers. We will land on the DZ one at a time.

"Once all are on the ground, we will move to the target to put surveillance on it. It is approximately 3.4 kilometers on a magnetic azimuth of fifty-four degrees to our observation point. We will have to cross one danger area along the route, the coastal highway running down from Cartagena. We will use our team SOP for linear danger areas to cross that obstacle."

Powers moved over to the mock-up lying on the floor. Holder had put it together using cardboard, strings, and other handy items; it wasn't the most sophisticated representation, but it did the job. Powers pointed at the northwestern end of the simulated dirt runway. "We want to put our observation point here. If we cannot observe the target sufficiently from there, we are prepared to send a recon team of myself and Sergeant Miller around the northern end of the airstrip to get a closer look. The observation point we have chosen will allow us to designate the target yet still have a good enough standoff that we won't be hit by friendly fire."

Riley hoped the air force general wouldn't react to that. Powers had developed a strong distrust of air force aiming capabilities when his A-camp in Vietnam had once been the recipient of some errant air force bombs.

Powers walked back to the podium. "As Mister Riley said, we will radio the results of our recon to the AWACS and then designate the target and verify destruction. Once we have verified destruction, or if the mission is aborted, we will move to our exfiltration pickup zone, which is 1.3 kilometers from the observation site on an azimuth of 312 degrees magnetic. We will be exfiltrated by one lift of an MH-60B helicopter. The exfil—"

Macksey's voice cut in. "What happens if someone gets separated on infiltration? Hold it—don't answer." Macksey turned to the team and pointed at Partusi. "You answer."

Partusi jumped to his feet and assumed the position of attention, staring straight ahead. "If separated during the jump I will still try to make it to the primary drop zone on my own. I have the same checkpoints memorized as Master Sergeant Powers. I will then link up with the team at the DZ. Standard operating procedure for our team is to wait thirty minutes at the DZ if all are not accounted for initially.

"If I cannot make it to the DZ, due to equipment malfunction or weather or whatever, I will try to land as close as possible to the DZ and make it there on foot inside that thirty-minute window. Failing that, our secondary linkup rally point is at the observation point at the target. I will try to link up with the team there up until 0430.

"If I cannot make it to the observation point by that time, my third option is to make the exfiltration pickup zone by 0538. Failing that, my final option is to go into escape and evasion mode as listed out in the E & E packet General Pike has, the contents of which are classified until opened."

Riley could tell that Macksey was impressed with Partusi's answer. Riley and Powers had always insisted that every briefback be given in the simplest terms possible and memorized by all. Each team member had to understand what was going on. One person failing to know a critical part could spell disaster.

Macksey probably didn't realize that the briefback was for the team's benefit also. Every member of the team had to be able to get up and give any portion of the briefback from memory. They'd rehearsed for this briefback by randomly choosing people to give the different portions. Riley knew that if Pike had been the one taking this briefback, he probably would not have allowed the area expert to give his part, but would have randomly chosen people. It was hard to cover all the intricacies of such an operation in a briefing. According to popular movies all it took to accomplish a mission like this was big muscles and a lot of fancy weapons. In reality, it was the detailed planning that determined the success of any difficult mission. The Eyes One team had to outthink the enemy and every mission's constant companion: Murphy's Law. Powers liked to joke that Murphy was

Riley's Irish cousin and that Powers was tired of his team leader bringing his relations along on missions. Over the years both had experienced so many strange things happening on operations, that they tried to anticipate the worst and war-game as many variations of the mission as possible.

The basic plan Powers had just briefed had taken only a couple of hours to put together. It was all the variations and contingencies that had led to the late-night discussions. And after all that, Riley knew something totally unexpected would most likely happen. Then it was the initiative and training of the team members that would make the difference.

Much of the plan was SOP, or standard operating procedure, for the team. The linear danger area crossing Powers had referred to was one of those SOPs. The team's SOP book was almost one hundred twenty pages long and explained damn near any situation they could get into. Everything in the book was in simple detail, with drawings for many of the possible scenarios and reactions to them. For example, each man would pack his rucksack in a standard way so any team member could find needed equipment in another's ruck; another SOP detailed how to break contact with enemy forces coming from any direction. It had taken the men over a year to write their SOP, and after every training exercise it was reevaluated and updated based on lessons learned.

Macksey was obviously satisfied with the answer he had received from Partusi. "All right, go on with the briefing."

Powers put the pointer down on the podium. "That completes my portion, sir. I'll be followed by the medic, Sergeant First Class Partusi."

Partusi briefed the potential medical problems and how the team was prepared to deal with them. He was then followed by Marzan, who was to cover the communications aspect of the mission.

"As already mentioned, sir, our internal communications during the drop and operation will be the helmets. They have an effective range of two kilometers on low power setting. Our external communications will be via satellite communications back to the AWACS. We will make our initial entry report, called an Angler report, upon arriving at the observation point.

"We will radio either confirmation or lack thereof of the target as soon as possible but no later than 0400. We will be able to talk to the gunship and exfiltration helicopter by relay through the satellite and then through the AWACS. All external communications on the SATCOM will be scrambled using Vinson devices.

"It is highly unlikely that any of our SATCOM transmissions will be intercepted, since they are directed transmissions and the antenna is pointing up. However, in the very unlikely event they are intercepted, the scrambling will ensure that they will be unintelligible. I have all codes and frequencies needed. We will refer to all team members and locations by their code names in transmissions.

"All team members are trained in the use of the PSC-3 SATCOM radio and the radio helmets. I will be carrying the primary PSC-3 radio and Chief Riley will be carrying a backup. In the unlikely event both radios fail, we have a visual system coordinated with both the gunship and exfil aircraft. For the gunship, if we have no radio commo, we will signal that the target is legitimate by throwing infrared chem lights onto the airstrip at exactly 0415. We will then designate the target at 0425 with the laser. For the helicopter we will mark the PZ with an infrared strobe for a two-minute window on either side of 0538. If there are no questions, this concludes my portion of the briefback."

Riley now stood up. "Sir, this concludes the briefback for Eyes One, pending your questions."

"I think I've heard enough," said Macksey. "Very impressive, Mister Riley, Sergeant Powers." He turned to General Linders, who simply nodded. Then Macksey addressed Pike: "You going to have the other team brief now?"

"Yes, sir," answered Pike.

Macksey rubbed his chin. "Isn't that a security violation? What if someone from the first team is compromised on the mission? They could give up the information on the second."

Pike looked uncomfortable. "That's true, sir. Unfortunately, we received both targets before we had split up the team, so both teams knew the targets from the start. They've also been exchanging expertise and information during the planning."

Macksey shook his head. "That was a mistake. In the future I want no contact between teams going on different missions."

"Yes, sir." Pike seemed uncertain how far he should go. Riley had no hesitation about jumping in with both feet, however. "Sir, with all due respect, if my team is compromised or even one man is compromised on this mission, it seems unlikely to us that the second mission would still be a go, since the entire security on this thing would be breached."

Macksey seemed lost in thought for a few seconds. "All right. It's too late now to worry about it." He looked at Vaughn. "Go ahead with your briefing, but don't repeat things the first team said."

"Yes, sir." Vaughn made his way to the front. "Good morning, General Macksey, gentlemen. I'm Captain Vaughn, commander of Eyes Two. Our mission is to infiltrate operational area Eaglet, located in the vicinity of Medellin, Colombia, at 2225 local time, 30 August. Our mission statement is to verify, and designate for destruction, a suspected cocaine laboratory located there. We will be exfiltrated at 0300 local time, 31 August."

Riley let his attention wander as Vaughn introduced his team and gave his mission overview. He looked across the room and caught Alexander's eye. Alexander raised his eyebrows slightly and gave a barely perceptible shrug. Riley knew that the senior NCO wasn't too thrilled about being saddled with a brandnew team leader and team going on a live mission. Riley wished him luck.

Vaughn was using note cards to give his brief, which Riley would never have done. If a leader couldn't remember his plan in the quiet of the isolation area, how did he expect to remember it on the ground when things were going to hell all around him? Riley tuned in to the captain's nervous voice.

"We will designate the target at 0230. Once we check out the degree of destruction we will be exfiltrated by an air force HH-53H Pave Low helicopter."

Macksey interrupted, turning to the air force general. "Why an HH-53? Why not a Blackhawk?"

"Range and mountains, sir." The general consulted a notepad. "It would take an in-flight refuel to make the trip down to Medellin and back from Panama. We'd also have to put extra tanks on the Blackhawk. What I've done is moved a navy assault ship, the *Raleigh*, down off the west coast of Panama. An HH-53 from 1st Special Operations Wing is in the process of forward deploying down there today and will operate off the flight deck of the *Raleigh*. Four Apaches are also moving down to the *Raleigh* to provide fire support for southern targets out of the range of those based in Panama.

"Also, this exfiltration point is on the other side of a mountain range. The HH-53H Pave Low has terrain-following radar and other night-flying equipment the Blackhawk doesn't. It's already set for the in-flight refuel if they determine they need it. This is the type of mission the HH-53 was designed for."

Macksey ceded the point. "All right, continue."

Vaughn looked up from his note cards. "I'll be followed by Sergeant Alexander, who will be giving you the intelligence portion." Riley felt sorry for the NCO: not only was he acting as operations sergeant for his split team but intel sergeant as well. A lot for one man.

"Good morning, sir. I'll try to keep this brief. However, the area we will be operating in is quite different terrainwise from what Eyes One is going into. My team, Eyes Two, will be going into mountainous terrain at almost six thousand feet of altitude.

"Key terrain features in our area are the Cordillera Occidental mountains to the west and the Cordillera Central mountains to the east. Medellin is in the foothills of the central mountain range. Our target is approximately thirteen kilometers to the south of the city. Weather is expected to be good for both the drop and mission, with temperatures in the low fifties at night.

"Population density throughout the area is high. Approximately ten to twenty people per square kilometer is the average. This is one of the reasons we are jumping in higher than our target and working down, since the higher slopes will be less inhabited.

"The target itself is cut into the forest on the side of a hill, as you can see on this imagery. There is a helicopter landing pad next to the target and a dirt road leading through the foothills toward the main road to Medellin. For local security, we estimate at least twenty to twenty-five guards on site armed with automatic weapons.

"Colombian military in the area include parts of the 4th Brigade headquartered in Medellin. The closest elements are about twenty-one kilometers from our target. This is an infantry unit, about company sized, armed with automatic and crew-served weapons.

"There is also the possibility of some guerrilla units in the area, since the hills around Medellin are known to have several guerrilla base camps. We feel that the guerrillas would not engage us, but we are prepared for that possibility.

"There are some helicopters at the Medellin airport. Satellite imagery didn't show any, but intel reports list at least two Huey types there. We assume they are hangared out of sight. Some military aircraft are reported at the Medellin airport, but again they must be hangared, since they didn't show up on imagery.

"We have also received intelligence that a Colombian Army Ranger company may be operating against the guerrillas in the vicinity of Medellin. This could cause us some problems, because they might be operating at night and also might investigate any aircraft they hear in the area. Although this possibility is remote, we must be on the alert for the Rangers."

Alexander completed his intelligence portion with a presentation of the escape and evasion plan. He then returned to the podium, figuratively switching hats to do the operational portion.

"Sir, for infiltration we will depart Fort Belvoir army airfield on Friday at 1400. We will follow this flight route." Alexander traced a route similar to the one Powers had shown, except Eyes Two crossed Panama and then flew down the Pacific coast of Colombia.

"We will turn in and head due east into Colombia when we reach this latitude; we will then fly over the Occidental mountains and head for our primary drop zone. We will be jumping T-10 model C parachutes at five hundred feet. This ought to keep us in very tight and keep dispersion to a minimum. We will be jumping automatic CARP, or computed air release point."

Riley shook his head. He wasn't sure which was worse: jumping at thirty thousand feet or jumping at five hundred.

At five hundred feet the men of Eyes Two would barely have time for their canopies to deploy before they hit the ground. Riley had done quite a few CARPs, as the air force called them, or blind drops, as the SF guys called them, out of Talons. Very rarely had he been dropped where he wanted to be. Usually, the air force was anywhere from a few hundred meters to several kilometers off the designated drop zone. Thinking about this brought to mind some equipment Riley thought might be useful to Eyes Two in their assembly on the ground. He made a mental note to tell Alexander about it after the briefback. He tuned back in to the brief.

"Once we have verified destruction we will move to our exfiltration pickup zone, which is the PZ cut into the mountainside next to the lab." Riley wondered if that wasn't too close to the target, but he hadn't looked over the Eyes Two AO to see if there were any other suitable site. The whole area was pretty steep.

Alexander almost seemed to shrug. "That completes my portion, sir. I'd normally be followed by the medic, but his briefing is pretty much the same as the one Sergeant Partusi gave you. The same is true for the commo portion, although we will be using PRC-68 radios for internal commo rather than the radio helmet. I'll be followed by Captain Vaughn."

Vaughn seemed to have gained some confidence as he strode up to the front of the room. "Pending your questions, sir, that concludes our briefback. I want to assure you that this team is ready to go and can successfully accomplish the mission."

Riley gave Powers a sidelong glance. The captain had probably been taught to say that last sentence in the Q-course. Macksey probably wasn't very impressed—it was *his* job to determine if indeed the mission and planning were viable.

Macksey leaned back in his chair and thought for a few minutes, then stood up and walked to the front of the room. "I have to admit I am impressed with the amount of work you've done under a compressed time schedule. Very thorough. I'm going to recommend approval of these first two missions to the secretary of defense and he'll relay that to the president. As of now, assume you're a go." Riley breathed a sigh of relief. He'd been half afraid that the mission would be canceled.

Macksey looked around the room. "I have one minor change I didn't have time to give to General Pike before coming over here." Riley frowned. What change?

"Eyes One will still use Spectre for Hammer One. However, Eyes Two is going to use Apache helicopters. You'll still use the laser designator; just the firing platform will be different. I don't see any problem with that. This way you also get Apaches to fly cover on both exfiltrations.

"The reason for the change is that General Linders tells me that 1st Special Operations Wing wasn't sure they could keep Spectre on target over Medellin without having the Colombian Air Force scramble. We think that Apaches flying off the *Raleigh* in the Pacific can make it in and out without getting spotted."

Riley considered this. The change made sense, but he could also see intraservice politics worming its way into the operation. The army wanted to justify the billions of dollars it was outlaying for the new Apache attack helicopter. However, Apache or Spectre, it didn't really matter. The end result would be the same. Plus, getting the Apaches to fly cover on the exfiltration was something they hadn't thought of. It was a good addition. He had thought Linders's reasons for using the HH-53 for Eyes Two's exfil had been kind of lame. If they could fly Apaches in from the navy ship, then a Blackhawk also could make the distance. But Blackhawk or Pave Low—it didn't matter to Riley as long as the damn thing flew. He glanced over at Captain Vaughn. The captain was accepting the change without comment.

Macksey looked at Riley. "The C-130 for infiltration for Eyes One will be here tonight to give you a chance to coordinate with the crew and set up the aircraft. A KC-10 is scheduled for your in-flight refuel. NSA will set up a base station for the SATCOM radio here. Are you all set on your weapons and personal gear?"

"Yes, sir."

Macksey closed his notebook. "Well, then. I would have to say that you're ready to go."

## 4:00 P.M.

Riley tried to be satisfied. The mission looked good. At first he had thought that taking six people in was a little heavy for what looked like just a reconnaissance and targeting mission, but on reflection he realized it allowed them a bit of flexibility. It also increased their odds of surviving a chance contact with some of the paramilitary folks the drug runners used for security. The plan was a sound one. Nothing overly fancy.

Riley shook his head. It was all too simple. Something was bound to go wrong. They had prepared several contingency plans in the E & E packet, the most extreme being a plan to walk out of Colombia to a U.S. Army post in Panama. The team was carrying a backup laser designator and two PSC-3 radios to up their odds against equipment malfunction.

Riley looked at the members of his team as they packed their gear. All the equipment was supplied by the CIA and was sterile. If captured it could not be traced back to the United States. Unfortunately, Riley mused, the same couldn't be said for the people. They carried no identification and would probably be disowned by the government if captured, but it would still be an ugly international scene.

"Hey, get a load of this!" Riley turned and saw Atwaters holding some glossy paper in his hands. Having gained the team's attention, Atwaters unfolded the paper. "Now who do you suppose put that up in the latrine?"

Riley chuckled to himself. The centerfold from a Playgirl magazine was dangling in the air under Atwaters's fist. Riley had seen the other centerfold one of the team members had put up in the latrine. He'd considered asking them to take it down, in deference to Westland having to use the same bathroom, but he'd decided it was probably better not to make an issue of it. Now he was glad he hadn't. He liked Westland's reply.

Atwaters threw the centerfold in the burn bag, where all the team's paper trash was thrown. Riley held his hand up and pointed at Atwaters. "Take that out and put it back up, or take the other down too and burn it."

Atwaters turned in surprise and sneered. "Why? You want to look at some naked guy, Chief?"

The room fell silent. Atwaters was one of the new guys and had rubbed Riley wrong from the first day he had joined the team. Riley didn't give a damn about the centerfold but he did give a damn about professional respect. Atwaters had just crossed his line. He strode across the room toward Atwaters as Powers quickly moved to intercept him.

Powers put a hand on Riley's shoulder. "Chill out, Chief. I'll handle this pisshead."

Riley stopped and looked at the senior NCO. "Make it good, Top. Because that's his last chance." He turned and left the room.

Powers turned to Atwaters, who had watched the confrontation. He looked at the young soldier and slowly shook his head. "You're probably too dumb to understand that I just saved your ass from a whupping."

"Bullshit, Top. What's the chief got the hots for this CIA bitch that he allows her to put this shit up in our latrine?"

Powers took a deep breath to control himself. "You know, the lady didn't even need to ask you. I could have told her you were better known as asshole than butthole."

He moved his bulk closer to the young soldier. "The chief allowed you to put up your shit, and he only figures turnabout is fair play. And quite frankly, you dumb shit, I don't care about any of that. You open your mouth to the chief or me again like you just did and you're going to be talking out your ass, 'cause that's where I'm going to put your head. You got ten seconds, boy. Either put that back or take the other down like the chief said."

As Powers was talking, the other old members of 055 gathered around him and added their glares to his. The other new members remained where they were, uncommitted. Vaughn stayed at his desk, obviously having enough sense to stay out of NCO business.

Slowly Atwaters was starting to realize that he had screwed up. "Hey! It's no big deal. I was just joking."

"You'd better readjust your sense of humor or it'll get readjusted for you." Powers shook his head. He looked at Atwaters and the other new members of the team. "Let me tell you people something about the chief. He don't talk much, but when he does you'd better listen to him. You also do not want to get into a pissing contest with the man. Size don't mean shit. There ain't three of you in here that could stand against him at the same time. Chief's got a second-degree black belt in tae kwon do and a first-degree in hapkido. Above and beyond that, he's one of the toughest sons of a bitch I've ever met. And I've met a lot of them in my travels. I've seen the chief empty bars when people riled him up enough."

Powers fixed Atwaters with a long, hard stare. "And you, boy, have riled him. You ain't gonna get another chance to walk away."

# BOGOTA
# 5:15 P.M.

The taxi pulled up to the front gate of the American embassy and Stevens got out. As he lifted his bag, he glanced across the street to the Embassy Cafe. He wondered if the bar girl Maria was working tonight. He also wanted a drink real bad. It had been a long, boring flight from Washington.

After tossing his stuff into his room at the embassy quarters and checking in with the deputy ambassador, Stevens went out of the compound and over to the cafe. Going through the swinging doors, he let his eyes adjust to the dimness inside. There she was behind the bar. Just as beautiful as he had remembered. Stevens had planned on eating first, but he passed by all the tables and went up to the bar.

Maria's face was split by a radiant smile as she spotted the DEA man.

"Welcome back, Mister Rich. I missed you."

Stevens blushed and smiled. He hadn't hoped for such a positive reception. "It's just Rich, Maria. Not Mister Rich."

# 8:10 P.M.

Stevens finished another tequila. He knew he shouldn't be drinking so much with an operation coming up the next night, but that was the main reason he was drinking. He knew he wouldn't be able to for the next two days while Operation Hammer was being implemented. Stevens dreaded the thought of two whole days without alcohol.

Maria had been extremely friendly the last three hours. Stevens had enough alcohol in him to work up his nerve. As she came by to give him another round he raised his hand and smiled at her. "Maria, I have something to ask you. Would you like to go out with me?"

The young girl looked at him quizzically. "Go out? Go out where?"

Stevens cursed to himself. He knew she was confused by his terminology, but she had asked a good question nonetheless. Where could he take her? He hadn't thought of that. Grasping at anything, he blurted out: "Come with me over to the embassy quarters. I'll show you some of those books in English you were asking about. They're in my room."

Even as he said it, Stevens realized she was probably thinking he was making a pretty overt pass. But she hadn't said no yet. She stood, regarding him with a half smile on her face. "That sounds like fun. Yes, I would like to see those books. I get off in an hour. We can go then."

It was a long and anxious hour for Stevens. He kept expecting Maria to reconsider and tell him she would not come. But she had remained pleasant and now, at the end of her shift, here she was, ready to go. He couldn't believe he was walking with such a beautiful woman. He didn't dare think of what would happen when they got to his room.

Stevens signed her in at the embassy guard shack, as required, ignoring the curious glances of the two marines on duty there. He took her around to the back of the embassy compound where all the living quarters were and led her to his one-bedroom apartment. He was slightly embarrassed as she took in the normal state of disarray. Even having a maid come in every other day did little to dent the mess he managed to generate in between.

He closed the door and looked at Maria. Somehow she seemed older and more experienced now. She came up to him and looked into his eyes. "Maybe we can look at the books later. There are other things we can do now." He couldn't believe it when she put her arms around his neck and tilted her face up to his.

Stevens managed to survive the rest of the evening without having a heart attack, although a doctor monitoring his pulse rate surely would have compared it to that of a runner battling for the lead in the Olympic marathon.

# THURSDAY, 29 AUGUST

## FORT BELVOIR, VIRGINIA
## 9:00 A.M.

Riley picked at his breakfast as he surveyed the main isolation room. The gear was packed and Eyes One was almost ready to go. At 1300 they would ride over to the airfield. They had done their initial coordination with the aircrew the previous evening. All that was needed was to rig the aircraft prior to takeoff at 1400.

The schedule today called for a few items to be accomplished prior to departure, the major ones being weapons firing and zeroing and a final sterilization check.

Riley had had a hard time falling asleep last night. He'd run the mission through in his mind innumerable times, looking at it from different angles, trying to find a mistake or some possibility they had overlooked. While tossing and turning, he'd also spent some time evaluating himself. He knew his strengths. He was an expert shot with both the pistol and submachine gun. He was proficient in the martial arts and in excellent shape. He was experienced in Special Forces operations. He felt he was a good leader who utilized the strengths of his men effectively and worked around their weaknesses.

Absently rubbing the two pockmarks that adorned his lower right stomach, Riley continued his self-analysis as he sipped his coffee. He considered another advantage that only Powers and he shared: both had been in the heat of combat. Although Riley's combat experience had lasted less than a week, it had impressed upon him the difference between training and the real

120

thing. He hoped the other four members of Eyes One would react well when it occurred.

Riley put away his worries for now. He'd find out soon enough.

Having finished what he could eat of his breakfast, Riley sought out Powers. "Let's do another equipment check. This time you look at the rucks, and I'll do weapons and personal gear."

Powers nodded. They lined up the men and rucksacks in the hallway, leaving the isolation area to Eyes Two. Riley checked the people while Powers went through the rucksacks.

Each man was dressed in unmarked green jungle fatigues, a common enough outfit for paramilitary people throughout Central America. They wore jungle boots—leather boots with canvas sides. For headgear they would wear the radio helmets. This wasn't something they were used to but it shouldn't be a problem. Most carried gloves of one sort or another. Riley used flight gloves, of thin leather and Nomex. Although it would be warm where they were going, the gloves were useful in negotiating the vegetation and handling hot weapons if it came down to that.

Over his fatigues, each man wore a nylon mesh combat vest that fastened in the front with Velcro. Hanging on the vest were two one-quart canteens, ammunition pouches for extra magazines, a strobe light, a knife, a pistol, and a small butt pack that held critical supplies.

Every man carried a knife of his own choosing. Riley had managed to break most of the men of the habit of carrying a big, Rambo-type knife. Such a weapon might be useful if the bearer got into a sword fight with a Roman gladiator but was next to worthless for what most combat knives are used for—silent killing. Riley himself carried a slender, double-edged, six-inch-long commando knife. He maintained the edges in razor-sharp condition. The thinness of the blade allowed it to penetrate between bones—whether in the back, chest, or neck. The double edges meant he could slash in either direction without having to fumble around in the dark.

For a personal side arm each man carried the Beretta 9mm semiautomatic pistol on his combat vest. The Berettas were the same as those being issued in the army but were not engraved with serial numbers, since they had been supplied by the CIA.

Riley, Frank Partusi, and Hosea Marzan each carried the MP5SD3 9mm submachine gun as their primary weapon. The collapsing-stock weapon was equipped with an integral silencer and would be effective at close quarters. Powers carried his favorite weapon—the Soviet-made AK-47 with a folding metal stock. He had carried an AK ever since Vietnam and swore by its reliability under adverse conditions. Holder carried the SAW machine gun. Firing 5.56mm rounds from a hundred-round drum, the weapon was a fine piece of machinery with a range of nine hundred meters. Riley hoped the SAW would keep any bad guys out of arms' reach if they made contact.

Lane carried the heaviest and most unique weapon. The Haskins .50-caliber sniper rifle looked like an overgrown elephant gun. The bolt-action rifle held a five-round magazine and broke into two pieces for jumping and transporting. A ten-power night-vision scope could be mounted on top. The massive bullet, a half inch in diameter, could reach out over two thousand meters and was guaranteed to put its hapless victim down. A .50-caliber round could tear off a man's arm or leg. They were carrying the Haskins for insurance. If Spectre didn't take care of the whole target, or some people escaped, Lane would use the sniper rifle to reach out and touch someone. Trained at the Special Operations Target Interdiction Course, Lane could hit a five-inch circle at one and a half kilometers with the Haskins.

The rucksacks Powers was checking were regular army-issue Alice mediums with external frames. They were in use by various government and guerrilla forces throughout Central and South America. Although the team would be on the ground for less than twelve hours, the rucks were needed to carry the technical equipment.

Riley and Marzan each carried a complete PSC-3 radio along with a Vinson crypto device. This added up to almost thirty pounds of weight per system. Holder was packing some spare batteries for the radios along with extra drum magazines for his SAW machine gun. Powers and Lane each carried a laser designator. Partusi carried an M-5 medical kit along with several different types of IVs in his ruck. Each man also carried a sub-stantial survival kit in his ruck, supplementing the smaller one in the butt pack. Additionally, each ruck contained two Claymore mines and spare ammunition for their weapons.

Having checked the men and their weapons, Riley had Powers look him over. First, Powers checked Riley's weapon. Then he went through Riley's pockets and equipment to ensure that nothing indicated a point of origin—no rings, ID tags, pieces of paper, wallet, and so on. When Powers was done, Riley glanced at his watch—two hours before they were due at the range to test-fire their weapons. Riley sat the team members down and started quizzing them on the mission.

# BOGOTA
# 9:30 A.M.

Stevens lay in bed and stared aimlessly at the ceiling. His eyes couldn't quite focus. Maria was gone physically but she was conspicuously present in his mind. Stevens knew he should be getting up and going to work but he couldn't yet. He wanted to rewind and replay one more time his mental video of the events of the previous night.

Some of the pictures on his mental screen portrayed acts he hadn't known were physically possible. Stevens laughed to himself. Hell, his wife had never even come close to coaxing that kind of reaction out of him.

Not only that, but before Maria had left a half hour ago, she had hinted of even more exotic things to be experienced tonight. Stevens could hardly wait for the dark to come. Then he cursed to himself as his brain kicked in. He couldn't do anything tonight. It was the night of the raid and he was supposed to be on duty in the communication room of the embassy.

# FORT BELVOIR, VIRGINIA
# 10:00 A.M.

The range was set up to accommodate fifty firers at a time. The twelve members of the detachment took up only a small portion of the firing line. The range had zeroing bull's-eyes at twenty-five meters and E-type pop-up silhouettes that simulated the top half of a person ranging out to the far limit of a thousand meters. Each man took his time getting a combat zero on the twenty-five-meter target and then checked his zero at the various ranges.

Riley waited as calmly as he could. His weapons were ready. He could sense the nervous tension in the other members of his six-man team. He watched closely as the last two members of Eyes One finished test-firing their weapons. On the far side of the range, Lane seemed to have just about completed zeroing in the scope on the Haskins, plinking away at pop-up targets ranging from a hundred meters out to the barely visible ones at a thousand meters. To use the night scope during daylight, he had it set on reduced power with a cover that reduced the aperture.

Riley glanced over at Westland, the CIA agent. She seemed visibly impressed with Eyes One's proficiency with their weapons. After zeroing, Riley had led his team through their basic close quarters combat firing drill with both the pistols and the automatic weapons. They had practiced firing on the move and from stationary positions. Firing while doing forward rolls and wilting left and right. Firing when pivoting left and right and 180 degrees. Then they had done the same with the automatic weapons, firing from both the hip and shoulder.

"What do you think?"

Westland shifted her attention to Riley. "It seems like the members of your team are pretty well trained in how to use their weapons. How's everything else going?"

"We're ready. As ready as we can be. You have anything new from your end?"

She shook her head. "Nothing new. Kind of like the calm before the storm, isn't it?"

"Yeah, it is. Nobody likes waiting. I'll be glad once we take off." He looked at the agent. "I thought your little commentary in the latrine was a nice touch. It certainly hit home on a couple of these guys."

Westland laughed. "I thought I'd fight fire with fire. I've always been kind of direct about things."

"It worked, although you and I both know some of these guys are too dumb or ingrained in their ways to change."

"I'm used to it."

Riley considered the woman. This was the most he'd talked to a woman in a long time. He kind of liked it. "How'd you get picked for this assignment anyway? Seems like the CIA would have pulled some guy out of one of their in-country teams down south."

Westland looked at him. Riley knew she was trying to figure out how much to tell him. He had always found that CIA people tended toward the side of paranoia.

"I've been pushing to get a field assignment for a long time. I think this job is a test so they can decide whether or not I deserve it."

Riley snorted. "*Deserve* it. Hell, some of the bozos I've seen running around in the field make the Keystone Kops look good. From what I've seen it's usually the opposite—you've got to prove your ability in order to get stationed over at Langley."

He watched her studying the members of Eyes Two test-firing their weapons. "Are we what you expected Special Forces soldiers to be like?"

"Am I what you expected a CIA agent to be like?"

Riley laughed. She wasn't going to give an inch. "Actually, yes and no."

"That's my answer, too, then. Yes and no."

Riley decided to persist. "I'm basing my answer on having worked with agency types before. I say yes because you strike me as competent and I have found most of them to be reasonably competent, although you have your share of losers just like we do. I say no because you don't have the attitude problem I found in a lot of them. The 'I've-got-a-secret' attitude. The 'I'm-better-than-you' attitude. You seem willing to work with us, rather than in competition with us. More interested in mission goals than agency goals."

He could see that he had her full attention now as she worked out her reply. "To be honest, I've never worked with Special Forces before. I've heard other agents really complain about it. They say you all think you're too good—and they say you're not as good as you'd like to think you are."

"Have you found that to be true with us?"

Westland shook her head. "Overall, no. There's some of that.

More with the captain and the other team than with you and your people."

Riley nodded. He appreciated her honesty, and his ego was boosted by her last comment. It occurred to him that maybe she didn't have the typical macho attitude of most agency types because she was a woman. He silently laughed at himself. Brilliant thinking. He pointed toward the firing line. "Want to fire off some rounds? What kind of piece do you carry?"

Westland reached under her sweatsuit jacket and produced a 9mm Browning Hi-Power. Riley was impressed. A good weapon. He had half expected a snub nose revolver or some other worthless side arm. Riley led her over to the left side of Eyes Two. He could sense his team members watching them. He knew she could sense it, too. He pointed to a silhouette target twenty-five meters downrange. "How about that one?"

Westland nodded and took up a solid firing stance, legs slightly spread, one just in front of the other, a good two-hand grip on the weapon. She raised her pistol and fired nine rounds in rapid succession. Riley smiled. Every round a hit centered on the chest area of the silhouette.

"Good shooting. If I may make a suggestion though?" Westland nodded. "Go for the head. Every person who can afford it is wearing a vest now. Unless you got a hot load, say maybe Teflon slugs in that thing, you aren't going to stop someone wearing body armor. You'll put someone down for sure with a head shot. And if you're gonna shoot someone, you want to put them down. No shooting to wound or any of that crap you see on TV. Shoot to kill and make every shot count."

Westland nodded and reloaded her gun. There was one more thing Riley wanted to know. "I saw you practicing some sort of kata or taegeuk yesterday. Have you had martial arts training?"

"I have a brown belt in aikido."

"That's good. You look like you're in good shape."

Westland's head swiveled around. Riley put his hands up. "Hey, relax. I'm not trying to hit on you. I respect anyone who keeps themselves in shape." He laughed. "Regardless of whether they're a female agent or a woman agent."

Westland visibly relaxed. Riley smiled. "As well trained as you are, you ought to go with us, but I'm sure that wouldn't go over big with the powers-that-be."

Westland looked at him strangely. "That's one of the best compliments anyone has paid me in a long time."

Riley noticed Powers staring intently at the two of them. "Excuse me." He walked over to his team sergeant.

"Your eyeballs are gonna pop out of your head if you look any harder, amigo. What's up?"

Powers presented him with an innocent face. "What do ya mean 'what's up?' "

"I mean why were you staring at me?"

"Hey, come on, partner. I've known you for almost two years now and I haven't seen you spend more than ten minutes talking with any woman. Just kind of curious, is all." He nudged Riley. "She is kind of cute in her own way."

Riley rolled his eyes. "Give me a break. Professional curiosity is the only reason I'm talking with her." He noticed Eyes Two finishing up. "Let's get on back and get ready to go."

## 1:30 P.M.

The inside of the C-130 was spacious enough to hold several cars end to end. The team would have plenty of room for the ride. Sitting in the center of the aircraft was a complex of tanks and hoses that represented the team's oxygen console. Riley walked up to Powers, who was looking over the device.

"Everything hooked up?"

Powers nodded. "The oxygen console checks out fine. I've coordinated with the loadmaster and he's set on our procedures."

Riley looked around the interior of the C-130. The oxygen console squatted in the middle of the cargo bay. The team's rucksacks and parachutes were tied down near the ramp. Riley decided to go up front and do a last check-in with the pilots and navigator prior to takeoff. He made his way past the other members of the team who were lying on the cargo webbing seats hung along the skin of the aircraft, trying to get some rest. It was going to be a long night.

Riley climbed the steep stairs on the left side of the plane into the cockpit. There was only one pilot there and the navigator.

"How you doing? Anything new?"

The pilot, a major, turned in his seat. "The copilot is over at base operations getting an update on weather along the flight route. Everything looks good."

"How's the route in look?"

The navigator looked up from his charts and pointed. "I've got a flight route that basically goes from here to Key West to Panama and then along the northeastern coast of Colombia. The high-altitude release point we were given is here," he pointed on his map, "just outside of Cartagena, still over the ocean."

Riley nodded. "That's it. If we can see the lights of the city we'll be good to go. Our drop zone is southeast of Cartagena, about fifteen kilometers from the city limit. What do you estimate for winds aloft down there?"

The navigator looked at his clipboard. "Presently they've got eighteen knots to the west. I've offset your HARP based on that to right here." He pointed.

Riley pulled out some of the satellite imagery. "I make that right about here on this." The navigator nodded. "All right. Let me get back with my guys and I'll update them on the release point. If you get any changes en route, let me know."

The pilot checked his watch. "We'll be cranking her up in another thirty minutes."

## 2:00 P.M.

The whine of the four turboprop engines peaked. With a slight jolt, the airplane started rolling. Riley looked across the aircraft at Powers, who met his eyes in the dim light let in by the few small, round windows. Powers gave him a thumbs-up. The plane picked up speed and the nose lifted. Wheels up and on the way.

## GULF OF MEXICO
## 8:15 P.M.

A tapping on his shoulder snapped him alert out of an uneasy sleep. Riley peered up at the loadmaster leaning over him. The man pointed at his watch and yelled in his ear. "You told me to wake you at an hour and fifteen out."

Riley checked his watch. Time to get ready. He unbuckled his seat belt and walked across the plane. He grabbed Powers's arm to wake him and then yelled in his ear, "Time to rig."

Powers started rousing the people on his side of the plane. Riley and the loadmaster went to the back of the plane and undid the cargo straps holding their parachutes and rucksacks. They passed out the parachutes, a main and reserve to each. Each man claimed his own ruck.

Riley and Powers buddy-rigged each other. Riley went first, putting on a one-piece thermal suit over his jungle fatigues and combat vest and zipping it up. Then Powers helped him slip the main over his shoulders and settle it on his back. Riley reached down between his legs as Powers passed a leg strap through to him. "Left leg," Powers yelled above the roar of the engines.

"Left leg," Riley acknowledged as he hooked the quick connector snap on the proper side.

"Right leg."

"Right leg." Riley hooked in his other leg strap and then crouched, tightening down both straps as hard as he could. A loose strap could have painful consequences during the shock of the parachute opening.

Powers helped him rig the reserve over his belly, attaching it to D-rings on the front of the harness. Before tying it down, Riley rigged his submachine gun behind the reserve, cinching it in place. His rucksack was hooked underneath the main parachute in the rear so that it dangled behind his legs. It made walking difficult, but it put the ruck in a position where it wouldn't interfere when Riley tried to get stabilized after exiting the aircraft.

Riley tightened the rest of his straps and then turned to Powers, putting his hands on his helmet, signaling he was ready to be jumpmaster inspected.

Swaying in the aircraft, Powers quickly ran his hands over Riley's equipment, starting from his head, working down the front and then going to the back, again working top to bottom. He never let his hands get in front of his eyes as he methodically worked his way around the gear. His tugs and yanks were comforting to Riley. A good jumpmaster made the jumper all the more confident in the reliability and proper rig of his equipment.

Finished, Powers tapped Riley on the rear and gave him a thumbs-up, signaling he was good to go. Riley waddled to the side of the aircraft and with great difficulty sat down on the cargo netting that passed for seats. He watched as Powers inspected the rest of the team one by one.

For jumping, Lane had disassembled the massive Haskins gun into two pieces and placed it in a canvas weapons container. Holder had done the same to the SAW machine gun. Powers rigged the weapons containers on the jumpers' left side.

After finishing with the team, Powers had the loadmaster help him rig. He then checked his own gear as much as possible. He staggered over to Riley and talked him through those checks that he couldn't see for himself.

The entire team now sat, three to a side, with the oxygen console between them. The entire process had taken almost thirty minutes inside the swaying aircraft. Riley checked his watch again. Another forty-five minutes to drop.

## 9:15 P.M.

Powers gestured to the console. Each team member hooked the hose leading to his mask to an outlet. When he saw they were all breathing off the console, Powers gave a thumbs-up to the loadmaster, who had hooked into an outlet in the side of the plane.

They felt their ears pop as the pilot began depressurizing the inside of the aircraft. The temperature dropped as the cargo bay heater struggled against the thin, cold air coming in at altitude.

They'd stay on the console until they stood up for the jump, at which time each man would switch to the small oxygen bottle on his rig. The bottle held only twenty-five minutes' worth of air, so it was best to hold off switching as long as possible.

Even with the thermal coveralls, Riley was shivering. He looked through his clear goggles at the other members of his team. He gave a thumbs-up and received a similar answer from each man. No one was getting woozy from the oxygen.

## 9:25 P.M.

Riley felt his adrenaline start to flow as he watched Powers unhook from the console and hook into his bottle. Party time! At Powers's signal, the rest of the team unhooked from the console and went on their personal supply.

Powers signaled with both hands to stand up. Through the helmet, Riley heard Powers's voice echo the command: "Stand up!"

Riley swayed as the aircraft slowed down to 125 knots. That slowdown meant three minutes out from the release point. He made a conscious effort to control his breathing. This was the worst part of the jump. Waiting. Knowing it's coming but not knowing what will happen.

The roar in the aircraft increased as the ramp cracked opened and the dark night sky appeared. Like massive jaws separating, the upper portion of the ramp disappeared into the roof of the aircraft while the lower section leveled out, forming a platform. The temperature inside dropped as the cold, turbulent outside air swirled in. Riley felt his stomach churn with anxiety. Looking out an open ramp was something he had never grown used to.

The last weather forecast they had received from the navigator had indicated clear skies and winds aloft of nineteen knots at 124 degrees. Almost perfect jumping weather. Riley heard Powers's voice inside his helmet: "All right. Let's tighten it up. Give me a sound check."

"One here." Riley listened as all the members checked off.

"Crack your chem lights." Each man reached up and broke the chem light attached to the back of the helmet of the man in front of him. Riley shuffled in tighter behind the jumper in front of him. They were ready to go.

The loadmaster, breathing oxygen from the aircraft system, held up one finger. "One minute!" Powers relayed over the radio.

Powers led the way to the edge of the ramp and peered out. Looking through the crack where the ramp separated from the main body of the plane, Riley could see the lights of the shoreline of Colombia. Below there was darkness, indicating they were over the ocean. He hated the waiting. He wanted to go.

"Stand by!"

Riley looked up at the red light glowing above the open ramp. Nervously he ran his fingers over his rip cord, making sure that it had not somehow disappeared in the last minute.

Riley would be the trail jumper off and the top man in the formation on the way down, so he would have the added experience of watching the rest of the team leap off in front of him. Any second now. Riley felt himself grow tense as adrenaline coursed through his veins, pushing his senses to their peak. Exhilaration was now taking over, and the fear grew more remote.

The light flashed green. "Go!" Powers yelled as he flung himself out, arms spread wide.

Riley followed the team, throwing himself out into the slipstream. He spread his arms and legs, arching his back, focusing his eyes on the chem lights below him. He had only four seconds to get stable and then pop his canopy, otherwise he'd pass through the team below. He felt his tumbling slow and stop. His mental counting finished and he yanked his rip cord.

The opening shock jerked him upright. His first priority was to gain control of the canopy. Reaching up, he grabbed the control toggles on the risers coming up from each shoulder. He pulled in his air brakes, slowing his descent. Briefly letting go of the toggles, he slid his night-vision goggles down on his helmet visor and rapidly scanned the night sky. He spotted the glow of a chem light below and to his left. He turned and raced after it.

His speaker came alive inside his helmet. "How many you got, Six?"

Looking down through his night-vision goggles he could see five chem lights, indicating the rest of the team staggered below him. "I've got five in sight in a good pattern, One."

As Riley flew through the air, he glanced at the luminous dials on the instrument board on top of his reserve and checked his altitude and direction. He forced himself to relax as much as possible in the harness and control his breathing.

After seven minutes, he was passing through ten thousand feet and heading south. The lights of Cartagena were off to his left rear now. In the reflected and amplified moonlight, Riley could make out the terrain ahead and below. So far, so good, he muttered to himself. They were on course and should reach the drop zone with no problem.

As he descended Riley got warmer. From the freezing temperatures at thirty thousand feet he was descending into steaming, tropical air. They were starting to do S-turns now as Powers had the drop zone in sight. Riley slowed himself and twisted his head, trying to keep the man below him in sight as he banked in a tight right-hand turn. At nine thousand feet, he pulled off his oxygen mask and took a deep breath of the humid night air.

At four thousand feet he risked a quick glance at the ground below. He adjusted his eyes slightly east of a small lake whose location he had memorized, and spotted the postage stamp of lighter green that indicated the drop zone in the middle of the vegetation. In the imagery the drop zone had appeared to be a clearing only forty meters by fifty meters. Because of its small size, the greatest danger would be landing on top of each other. To prevent that, they had decided to stagger the landing interval.

At two thousand feet Riley could see the formation spreading, as each jumper allowed more vertical space between himself and the jumper below. He turned and went into a spiral. His ears crackled as the radio came to life again. "One down. Clear for Two."

Powers was already on the ground. Riley manipulated his toggles and grabbed more air with his canopy, slowing himself further. He wanted to give the other five a chance to completely recover from their landings before he came in.

"Two down. Clear for Three."

"Three down. Clear for Four."

"Four down. Clear for Five."

"Five down. Clear for Six."

Riley released his air brakes and slid down the last two hundred feet. Just above the ground, he pulled in on his toggles and flared to almost a stall, lightly touching his feet to the ground. As his parachute settled around him, Powers was at his side, helping him out of his harness. Riley quickly gathered in his chute and shoved it into his rucksack. The thermal suit followed it. The plan was to carry out their infiltration equipment to avoid leaving any evidence of the raid.

With his gear stowed, Riley readjusted his helmet and goggles. He felt like a creature from a science fiction movie, with the short snouts of the goggles poking out in front of him. The interior eyepieces were lit in a hazy green glow. On the small screens Riley could see almost as well as he could in daylight. The major drawbacks were that everything was a shade of green, his depth perception was distorted, and his field of vision was limited.

Riley adjusted his night-vision goggles as comfortably as he could and motioned for the team to follow him. With every man wearing the light-enhancing goggles, the team moved off in a northeasterly direction. Their target stood 3.4 kilometers away through the tangled vegetation.

Partusi was in the point, with Riley right behind him, navigating. Lane, Marzan, and Holder followed in line, with Powers pulling up the rear. Partusi's job was to keep all his senses attuned to the terrain out front, with Riley directing him with small nudges, keeping the team on azimuth. They moved slowly, taking care to make as little noise as possible.

Partusi eased through the thick vegetation, followed closely by the other five men. Riley counted every right footfall, slowly adding up the distance as they moved. He checked his azimuth every ten steps. After eight hundred meters, according to Riley's pace count, Partusi signaled a halt by holding up his left fist. He drew his fingers across his throat and pointed ahead—danger area. Riley passed the signal back. Riley crawled next to Partusi and peered ahead. Ten meters in front of them was the coastal highway, a two-lane hardtop road.

Riley had been taught in Ranger school to cross a danger area by setting out flank security, sending across far-side security, and then having the main body cross. However, if he followed that method with only six men, he would use up almost the entire element in security and not have a main body left. Riley wanted to spend as little time as possible near the danger area. He turned on his knees, grabbed Lane, and pointed ahead. Lane grabbed Marzan and the two low-crawled to the edge of the road. With their goggles, they would be able to see the glow of headlights from a vehicle long before it came into sight. The two stood up and quickly ran across the road.

Riley waited in the tree line until he spotted a brief flash of the

IR light on a pair of flashlights from the far wood line, indicating that the far side was clear. Riley looked left and right down the road and then tapped Partusi to go. Partusi got to his feet and jogged across the road. Riley then tapped Holder across. Powers slid up next to Riley. Riley was about to tap the team sergeant to go when he spotted a glow in his goggles off to the left. Grabbing Powers, Riley sank down into the grass at the edge of the woods and lay still. A minute later, a car flashed by and roared off to the south. Riley waited a minute for the car to get clear and then got back up to his knees. He checked both directions and then tapped Powers. Once the team sergeant disappeared into the woods on the far side, Riley followed him across the hardtop and slipped into the wood line.

A pair of hands immediately grabbed him. Marzan pointed him in the right direction and he quickly came up next to Partusi. Ensuring that he had all six team members, Riley gave the signal to move out and they continued their trek.

In planning, Riley had allowed the team four hours to reach the target. In actuality it took only three. The team moved steadily and without any further interruptions through the unpopulated swampland until the men finally reached their destination at the observation point on the edge of the small dirt runway.

The team settled into a tight security perimeter. Riley dropped his ruck and lay down next to Lane. He scanned the compound seventy-five meters away on the far side of the airstrip using the special night-vision telescope Lane had carried in for the Haskins sniper rifle. The scope not only enhanced the ambient light like the goggles but also gave him a ten-power magnification. He could see two guards walking about the four ramshackle buildings that made up the laboratory. The sentinels were a good sign. It meant there was still something here to guard. One of their greatest concerns had been that the factory had moved.

Riley could also see barrels stacked around the buildings. Heavy plastic sheeting covered the doors and windows of the largest shed, which, according to their briefing, was where the actual processing was done. Another shack appeared to be a storage area, and the last two were probably living quarters. From what he was seeing, Riley was confident that this was indeed one of the major labs.

The guards were armed with M16s and walked about the camp in a random manner. Riley had a feeling there were probably more than just the two guards on duty. He continued scanning. After thirty minutes, he spotted two more. These two gave themselves away by lighting cigarettes, which showed up in the night-vision scope as if they had fired off a flare. One was just off the airstrip that abutted the compound, only fifty meters from Riley's present location. That guard appeared to be armed with an M60 machine gun. The other was on the far side of the compound, adjacent to the dirt trail that pointed toward Cartagena and the north.

Having seen what he needed to see, Riley handed the scope to Lane, who remounted it on the Haskins. Riley pointed out the four guards and whispered instructions to Lane. Then he slid back farther into the woods, to where the rest of the team was waiting.

Gathering the other four team members around him, Riley proceeded, in a hoarse whisper, to update them on the situation. "We've got four buildings just like the imagery showed. All the signs are there that this is a currently working laboratory—ether in barrels and plastic sheeting around the largest building. So I'm going to call in a go on this target.

"There are four guards—two walking around the camp armed with M16s, one stationary just off the dirt road leading out of the camp. That guy has what looks like an AK-47. Then they have a fourth guy hidden on this side of the camp overwatching the airstrip with an M60. He's only about fifty meters from where I left Lane.

"Here's what I propose." Riley reached out and tapped a team member. "Frank, you lase the target at 0425 as we coordinated. When the first round from Spectre impacts, Dan, you take out the guy closest to us with your AK. Lane will hit the guy on the far side of the camp and keep that way out under surveillance. He'll shoot anyone trying to leave by the road. I'm figuring the two guys on guard in the camp will get wasted by Spectre. If not, then, Dan, you take them down." Riley looked at Powers. "How's that sound?"

The team sergeant gave a ghostly smile in the dark. "Sounds good to me."

"Additionally, the small plane we saw in the imagery isn't there anymore, so we don't have to worry about that. If anything tries to come in during the hit, we'll let Spectre deal with it." He turned to Marzan. "Hosea, go ahead and get the radio set up."

"Right, Chief."

Marzan opened his rucksack and pulled out the PSC-3 satellite communications radio and its small dish antenna. Hooking the two together, he pointed the antenna at the proper azimuth and elevation. Then he hooked the Vinson voice scrambler into the radio. He turned the radio on and checked it by getting a bounce back off the designated satellite. "She's all set."

Riley picked up the handset and pushed the send. "Moonbeam, this is Eyes One. Over."

He waited a second. The signal pulsed from his radio up to the satellite and then was relayed to its target. The radio softly crackled with a reply. "Eyes One, this is Moonbeam. We read you Lima Charlie. How do you read us? Over."

"We read you Lima Charlie. The mission is a go. I say again, the mission is a go as planned. Over."

"Roger. We read mission is a go. Will relay message. Over."

"Roger. Out." Riley broke contact with the AWACS plane that was circling somewhere over the ocean to the north. He looked at the men gathered around. "All right. Let's move on up so we can see what's going on."

## 4:15 A.M.

The Colombians had switched their guards at 0300. The new guards were in the same positions as the old ones. Riley glanced at his watch. Ten minutes till show time. He whispered into the headset: "Hammer, this is Eyes One. Over."

The reply was immediate. "This is Hammer. Over."

"Roger. Everything's still a go. We will illuminate the target in ten mikes. Over."

"Roger. We'll be in position in five mikes. Over."

"Roger. Out."

## 4:20 A.M.

The AC-130 pulled into its counterclockwise racetrack and banked to the left. The modified C-130 cargo plane started circling, with its left side pointing down. Inside, the fire control officer sat looking at a low light level television (LLLTV) screen. Swiveling the external camera, he scanned the countryside. He could make out some vehicles moving along a road far to the south. He wanted to see if he could find the camp without the aid of the laser.

Along the left side of the aircraft the gun crews were prepared. Mostly their job consisted of clearing away the expended brass from the guns. The guns themselves were automatic—aimed and fired by the fire control officer. From front to back, Spectre boasted two 40mm automatic guns, two 20mm automatic cannons, and, poking its snout out farthest back in the cargo bay, a 105mm howitzer. With the five guns, the ship could put out over ten thousand rounds a minute.

The fire control officer adjusted the focus on his night camera and found the small airstrip. He matched it against the imagery clipped to the bulkhead next to his seat. Pushing the intercom button he called up front to the pilot to adjust the racetrack slightly. Leaning forward in his seat, the fire control officer fiddled with his knobs, adjusting the cross hairs on his screen.

The AC-130 Spectre was the most modern in the line of air force gunships, a descendant of the well known Puff the Magic Dragon of Vietnam-era fame. Members of the crew of this particular ship had participated in most of the military actions of the past decade, including the invasions of Grenada and Panama. The gunship was devastating against ground targets but relatively helpless if attacked by air interceptors or by a sophisticated missile defense that could reach up high enough to hit the aircraft. Against the present target it was almost like playing a video game as the fire control officer watched his screen. He reached and flipped open the cover on his arming switch.

"Arming," he warned over the intercom, and after a second delay he threw the switch, sending power to all five guns. He then adjusted the computer program that would fire the guns. The two 20mm Vulcans were fixed and would fire along the path of the aircraft. The two 40mm guns and the howitzer were each separately controlled by the computer. The fire control computer was capable of resolving all inputs on targets to within one milirad, which translated to an accuracy of 1/1,000th of the slant range to the target. The slant range for this mission was seventy-five hundred meters, which was at the far end of the range of the Vulcans; this translated to a ground accuracy of within seven and a half meters of the aiming point for each gun system.

## 4:25 A.M.

"Go ahead and illuminate."

Partusi looked through the sight and zeroed in on the main building. He turned on the designator and the invisible laser beam touched the building. Riley cocked his head to listen. The gunship was so far up he couldn't hear the drone of its engine. He smiled grimly. They'd be hearing it loud and clear soon enough.

Riley grabbed the handset. "Hammer this is Eyes One. Over."

"This is Hammer. Over."

"Have you got the target? Over."

"Roger. We've got it. Give me the dimensions of the target area, since I can't make it all out under the trees. Over."

Riley scanned the target through his goggles as he calculated. "From the point we're designating you've got approximately a hundred meters north, sixty meters south, sixty meters east, and the airstrip as your left limit. The designated point is your main target building. Over."

"We'll put the big one on the designated point. We'll use our other stuff all around the target in a grid pattern, working from the perimeter in, so no bad guys get away. I've got your location on the thermals, so don't be worried if some of the stuff seems kind of close. Over."

"Roger. We're ready when you are. Over."

"We'll commence firing on my count of five. One. Two. Three. Four . . . "

Hearing the five, Riley squeezed Lane's ankle with his free hand. The crack of Lane's .50-caliber sniper rifle and Powers's AK-47 were lost in the roar as four lines of light extended from the sky above and ended in the compound. Each line represented a rope of bullets that tore through the sky and slashed into the earth. Intermingled was the crump of the howitzer pumping out a 105mm artillery shell every two seconds.

During previous training with the air force's 1st Special Operations Wing, Riley had heard the Spectre gunship crews boast they could put a round into every two square inches of a football field in twenty seconds. Now he believed them. The buildings were disintegrating before his eyes as 40mm cannon shells tore through them. The 20mm rounds were puffing up clods of dirt every few inches as they quartered the ground, thirsting for targets. Both walking guards had already gone down. The 105mm shells were blasting the main factory building. Riley winced as the chemicals ignited and a secondary explosion tore the night sky.

After only thirty seconds, Riley found it hard to imagine that anything could still be alive. All four guards were down for sure. It was difficult to make out where the buildings had stood only moments before. Small fires burned and secondary explosions still ripped through the area. Riley leaned over and put his head next to Lane's. "You have any movement?"

"Hell, no. There isn't anything left alive over there. Nobody made it out of the buildings."

Riley nodded. He keyed the handset. "Hammer, we don't have any movement down here. Over."

The calm voice came back. "Roger. We're going to give it another twenty seconds to make sure and then we'll shut down. Your route to your exfiltration pickup zone looks clear. Unless we get some air reaction from the natives, we'll stay up here and cover you until pickup. Moonbeam is tracking your exfil bird inbound only an hour out. Over."

"Roger. Thanks. We're leaving here as soon as you finish. We're breaking down the radio now. Out."

The sudden silence was deafening as the Spectre gunship stopped firing.

## 5:35 A.M.

The pickup zone was an open field only a little over a kilometer away from the target site. They made it there in under thirty minutes and settled in to wait.

Marzan had the radio turned on, with the transmitter and scrambler still in his backpack and the small dish antenna on the ground in front of him. Riley held the handset and peered out into the dark field. Powers was out there in the middle with an infrared strobe light. At exactly 0537 Powers turned on the strobe light and Riley keyed the mike. "Stork, this is Eyes One. Over."

Even through the hiss of the scrambler Riley could hear the muted roar of rotor blades in the background as the immediate reply came back. "Eyes One, this is Stork. Authenticate one seven. Over."

"This is Eyes One. I authenticate one one. Over."

"Roger authentication. We're one minute out. Over."

"Roger. One minute out. Papa Zulu is cold. I say again, Papa Zulu is cold. We've got the IR strobe on. Over."

Riley waited tensely. They could hear the helicopter now, coming in from the north. The beat of the blades sounded louder in the early morning air. Then, suddenly there it was, flaring over the field and settling down. Powers had extinguished the strobe light and was waiting. Marzan gathered up the antenna in his arms and ran with it toward the helicopter along with the rest of the team.

They threw themselves into the cargo compartment through the open right door. Gunners in the crew chief window on each side scanned the tree lines, looking over the barrels of their M60 machine guns with night-vision goggles. As the helicopter lifted, Riley caught the silhouettes of two more helicopters hovering at opposite edges of the field. As the modified Blackhawk picked up speed and headed toward the ocean, Riley pressed his face against the window in the cargo door and looked at their escort. Two Apache helicopter gunships were riding shotgun, one on either side, as they streaked just above the terrain at 130 knots. In a minute they were over ocean and clear of Colombian territory. Riley liked the escort: They were traveling in style for once.

Riley caught Powers's eye across the dimly lit cargo bay. Powers gave him the thumbs-up. First mission a go.

# FRIDAY,
# 30 AUGUST

## FORT BELVOIR, VIRGINIA
## 6:00 A.M.

General Pike let out a sigh of relief and turned away from the radio. "They're on their way back. The mission was successful."

He looked at Westland. "That means Eyes Two goes as planned. We'll give it until this afternoon and then recontact Stevens and see if he has any sort of reaction from the people down there."

Westland smiled as she rubbed her eyes wearily. She was glad things had turned out well. She needed to go over to Langley this morning and update Strom. She looked at the clock on the wall and calculated. She ought to be able to get there and back before the team flew in for the debrief.

## 12:15 P.M.

Riley climbed slowly out of the van. He was exhausted. Pike had been waiting at the airfield to welcome them back as they got off the C-130. Riley had immediately noticed that Westland was not there and for some reason that had bothered him. He wasn't quite sure why he had expected her to be there.

Returning to the isolation area, Riley and his team were greeted by the members of Eyes Two as they entered the operations room. Pike indicated the hot food and drink laid out on a table. "Why don't you all grab some chow. Westland should be back with the debriefer in a couple of minutes and we can start then. I want the other team to listen in, too, so they can know what to expect."

Riley nodded and walked over to grab himself a cup of coffee. Westland should have already been here, he thought to himself. What did she have that was more important than this debriefing? Her not being at the airfield had bothered him personally, he finally admitted to himself, but her not being here on time for the debriefing bothered him professionally. A debriefing needed to start immediately, before any important information was forgotten.

# CARTAGENA, COLOMBIA
# 12:15 P.M.

Roberto Rameriz, better known as "The Shark," ranted and raved and screamed. His closest advisers stoically weathered the storm. After fifteen minutes he subsided and grew silent. For five minutes he stared straight ahead out of the bay windows of his mansion overlooking the ocean. Then he turned and faced his men.

"I want whoever was behind this. I want a name today!" He turned to his right. "Miquel. I want you to take the plane to Bogota. Go to the Ministry of Defense. Find out if they were behind this.

"Jaime. You check our contacts in Suarez's outfit. See if his people were involved.

"Carlos. Check out that pig who calls himself Ring Man. I wouldn't put it past that scum to try a stunt like this."

The Rameriz patriarch worked his neck to relieve the tension. "It had to be one of those. Whoever it was will pay."

Miquel Rameriz shook his head. It was dangerous to interfere with his father when he was like this, but it was up to him as the second-eldest son to point out some things that might prevent disaster. "Padre. We must worry about our shipments. We have the load down at the docks that will go out this week, but after that we have nothing. We lost our next three months' inventory in the destruction. We cannot afford a war. We must restock, or our customers will turn elsewhere."

Roberto glared at his son. "We cannot afford not to have a war! If we do nothing about this attack, we will be seen as being weak. Then our competitors will be over us like jackals. Also, we add the shipment on the docks with the cache in Miami, and our man there will be able to cover for us up there until we can make up our losses. Your brother Julio was right about us putting that cache in. If I had him here now, he wouldn't be arguing with me. He'd be coming up with solutions." The mention of the eldest son, presently awaiting trial in the United States, quieted the other members of the family for a few seconds.

The youngest son, Carlos, the Harvard MBA, raised his arm. "What bothers me the most, father, is that we received no warning of the attack. That is very ominous. If it was the military, how did they do it without one of the people on our payroll letting us know? Besides, I don't think Alegre would be that stupid. If it was one of the others, Suarez or Ring Man, then why didn't our informants warn us? Such an attack cannot be mounted without preparation, yet we heard nothing."

The Shark stood up, indicating the talking was over and it was time for action. "Whoever failed to warn us will pay the same price as those who did the attack. Get going! I want a name today!"

# FORT BELVOIR, VIRGINIA
## 12:30 P.M.

Riley had just finished a long-overdue breakfast when Westland walked into the operations room with two analysts. "I'm sorry I'm late, but let's get started."

Riley shook his head as they began. He'd approach her after the meeting and find out what was going on. The members of Eyes One settled in around the table with the map of the target on it.

Starting from the moment the C-130 took off from Fort Belvoir, the two analysts barraged the team with questions, tracking the progress of the mission up through their return to the same airfield.

It was an exhausting but necessary process. Riley had often sat on the other side of the table as debriefer during training exercises and he knew that some seemingly unimportant fact could turn out to be extremely important. Although, he had to admit to himself, there wasn't much to report about this mission. It had gone almost like clockwork.

Riley hoped Eyes Two's went as well.

# BOGOTA
## 2:15 P.M.

Alegre allowed himself the luxury of feeling good for a few minutes. The raid the previous night had apparently been a success. At least he hadn't received any negative feedback, nor had his door been busted down and he been shot. In Colombia that was a good sign.

Alegre had had his doubts about the information relayed by the Ring Man, but it seemed that the data had been excellent. His chief aide, Montez, had just informed him that the word on the streets was that the Ramerizes had suffered a major setback. Alegre fervently hoped that the next targeting information Montez had relayed to the CIA contact was also valid.

The vote in the United Nations had also gone well. By one vote, the UN General Council had approved Colombia's claim for the mineral and oil rights on a third of the floor of the Gulf of Venezuela. The Venezuelans, naturally, were protesting the decision, but Alegre felt that the claim had a good chance of standing up to the appeal, especially since the Venezuelans had initiated the UN process in the first place. With those rights, he felt Colombia finally had a chance to get rid of the drug cartel.

Alegre knew that there were still many uncertainties, but at least things had started well.

# FORT BELVOIR, VIRGINIA
## 2:33 P.M.

The debriefing took over two hours. By the time it was done, Pike had received the message from Stevens on the scheduled contact. In summary, it indicated that there had been no apparent reaction in Bogota yet. The key part of the message was that the word from DEA informants on the street was that the lab attacked had been a major one, under the control of the Rameriz family.

"It will be coming," Riley warned. "Remember, Stevens told us the guy who ran the lab we hit last night operates out of Cartagena. It's probably going to take him a while to react to the situation and also to track down all his contacts to see if he can find out who's behind this."

Pike nodded. "I know. But that's not for us to worry about. The only problem it may cause us is that there may be additional security on the next target."

Riley leaned back in his chair. He was beat. Between last night and today it had been a long twenty-four hours. The members of Eyes Two were upstairs trying to catch a last-minute nap before departing on their mission later this evening.

Riley had sent the rest of his team to bed. He had been holding off himself until Stevens's message came in to confirm whether or not the target had been legitimate and high level. He was ready to catch some z's himself now. But first, there was one more thing he needed to do. He walked over to Westland, who was reviewing the notes from the debriefing. "Could I have a word with you privately?"

She nodded and followed him into the hallway. Riley turned and faced her. "Why weren't you ready for the debrief when we got back today?"

Westland looked uneasy. "I apologize for that. I got caught up at Langley and didn't leave early enough to get here in time."

Riley knew she was reporting everything that happened back to her boss at Langley. That was the way the game was played.

He didn't like playing for the CIA or trusting their intelligence. He still didn't feel comfortable with the whole framework of this operation. The fact that someone down in Colombia with detailed knowledge of the drug cartel was passing information on lab locations didn't sit too well with him. That someone must have a pretty extensive net of intelligence to be able to get information on different branches of the cartel. That someone's motives were also open to speculation.

Riley could have understood a single turncoat in one gang, but they were getting countrywide information. Something big was going on down there, and he just hoped that when the storm hit, his people would weather it safely.

He had to admit that Westland had played straight with them as much as she could. They could have been saddled with a real asshole in a three-piece suit. Besides, he had developed a respect and liking for Westland over the last several days. He wondered about it, since he was normally someone who warmed to people very slowly. He hadn't had the time to think about it and he was too damn tired to do that now. He decided to let the whole thing slide and move on. "Do you have our next targets?"

Westland appeared relieved to get off the subject of Langley. "We've got another two. They came in this morning. One is up near Bogota and the other is on the coast near Barranquilla. The general has already broken them down. You get Nail Three, which will be the one near Barranquilla. Captain Vaughn's team gets the other one, Nail Four. The general also wants to run the two concurrently. He thinks it will improve security for the team by doing them on the same night."

Riley considered this. "When do Three and Four go?"

"Monday night."

Damn, that was cutting it tight, Riley thought. Especially for the other team. Only two days of preparation. In reality, though, there wasn't that much to plan other than infiltration and exfiltration. He was tired and all this thinking and worrying was giving him a headache. He turned for the stairs. "I'm going to rack out. I'll see you later."

He stopped as he felt Westland's hand on his arm. She

looked into his eyes. "Get some good sleep. Let me do the worrying for a little while, OK?"

Riley replied without thinking. "As long as it's my men's lives on the line, I'll be worrying."

Seeing the hurt reaction in her eyes, he realized he'd been too abrupt. He lightly touched her hand on his arm. "Hey, I'm sorry, Kate. I didn't mean that I didn't trust you. I'm too tired to think straight. Let's talk when we're both up to working speed."

Westland let go of his arm and nodded wearily. "All right."

# BOGOTA
## 4:34 P.M.

Stevens was exhausted. Even his newly rejuvenated libido couldn't keep him going. Just a quick stop across the street to say hi to Maria and then he would try to get some more sleep before having to monitor the radio tonight.

He shuffled across the street to the Embassy Cafe. He peered around the darkened interior looking for the girl. He spotted her uncle behind the bar. Stevens hoped the uncle didn't know about what was going on between the two of them. If he was like most of the greasers around here, he wouldn't approve of her being with a gringo. Stevens tentatively walked over to the bar. "Is Maria around?"

Maria's uncle spared him a neutral glance. "Are you drinking or are you only asking questions?"

Stevens cursed to himself. He glanced around the bar to see if anyone who knew him from the embassy was present. There was no one. "I'll have a beer and shot of tequila."

The barman placed the drinks in front of the American and then stepped back and regarded him. "Maria does not come to work tonight until six. Who should I say is asking for her?"

Stevens savored his beer. "Tell her Rich."

"Rich? As in has a lot of money?"

A beaner smart ass, Stevens thought to himself. "No. Rich as in Rich Stevens. That's my name. Tell Maria I'll give her a call tonight here at the bar."

The barman regarded the American distrustfully. "If I remember, I tell her."

"Thanks," Stevens said. For nothing, he thought. He finished his tequila and turned for the door. Time for a few hours of rack time before having to be bored to death sitting in front of the radio in the comm room. As he walked out the door, he saw Maria coming down the street. He waited for her under the awning in front of the cafe.

When she caught sight of him her face lit up with a wide smile. "Rich! How are you?"

"I'm fine. Well, actually I'm a little tired. I was up all night."

Maria looked concerned. "You are working too hard. I was sad we could not be together last night." She smiled coyly. "We can make up for that tonight."

Stevens shook his head reluctantly. "I have to work tonight, too."

"What is all this work! It is not right. You work much too hard. Will you be working all night? No time off at all to see me?"

Stevens calculated in his mind. "Pretty much the whole night. I should be done around three in the morning, but that's too late for you."

Maria shook her head. "No, it isn't. I can be there."

"But I can't get you in the gate that late."

Maria smiled. "Then I'll go in now and wait in your room."

Stevens protested weakly. "I thought you had to be at work at six."

"My uncle will understand. I'll tell him I'm not feeling well."

# AIRSPACE OVER THE PACIFIC OCEAN, THIRTY KILOMETERS WEST OF POINT SAN FRANCISCO SOLANO, COLOMBIA 9:57 P.M.

The MC-130E banked steeply to the left and headed due east toward the shore of Colombia.

The aircraft, designated as the Combat Talon, was a modified Lockheed C-130. From the outside some of the modifications were obvious. The nose of the airplane had a large bulbous protrusion under the cockpit where many of the additional navigational devices were housed. Another noticeable feature was the extra fuel pods slung under the wings, which increased the aircraft's range.

Two eight-foot prongs scissored out from the bottom of the nose, forming an inverted V along the direction of flight. These snares were for the Fulton recovery system. A cable, pulled up by a balloon, was snatched between the prongs; the cable was clamped in the center and then the speed of the aircraft drew the cable up along the belly of the plane. Hanging off the open ramp in the rear another clamp caught the cable and rotated it into a winch inside the aircraft. Once the winch was activated the cable was pulled into the aircraft, reeling in whatever had been on the ground end of the balloon cable. That whatever could range from a bundle to one or two personnel. It made for an interesting ride.

Inside the aircraft, the members of Eyes Two were pressed deeper into their seats as the aircraft turned and headed for the Colombian coast. The interior of the aircraft was the same size as the one that had infiltrated Eyes One, except that the front half of the cargo area was taken up with banks of electronic equipment, which was constantly being monitored by several air force officers. A black curtain separated the team in the rear half of the cargo bay from the electronic warfare people in the front half.

The most significant changes to the aircraft were not visible except to the electronic warfare personnel and the pilots. The pilots' greatest allies were terrain-following radar and precision ground-mapping radar. These two combined presented the pilots with a visual display of the terrain ahead regardless of the weather and outside light conditions. It was sort of like flying by television. Flying low to the terrain enabled the Talon to avoid radar.

In the complex modern world of radar and sophisticated air defense systems, the Talon's ability to defeat electronic detection was its key. To aid in that battle the electronic warfare specialists in the cargo bay manned a variety of electronic countermeasures designed to foil enemy radars. The Talon crews thought it was ironic that the air force was willing to spend billions on the Stealth bomber while continually trying to cut funds for the ungainly transport plane that had already proved it could beat radar systems and had led the way in every American military operation since the end of the Vietnam war. The big joke among the Talon drivers was that they could up their funding by loading a few nukes in the cargo bay and redesignating their aircraft the B-130.

At the present moment the aircraft was skimming barely fifty feet above the tops of the waves. A darker line on the horizon indicated the Colombian coast coming up. The Talon hit the coast at a hundred feet and the pilot gradually raised the altitude to two hundred fifty feet as they headed into the foothills of the Cordillera Occidental mountains, a small range of the Andes.

The loadmaster turned to Alexander and held up both hands, fingers extended. Alexander nodded, stood up, and turned to the team. Raising both hands, he screamed: "Ten minutes!"

Alexander quickly lowered himself into the safety of his seat. The plane was jerking from side to side and bouncing up and down as the pilots skimmed the margin of safety that kept them from splattering into a mountainside. The plane crested over the mountains and started heading down, flying so low that the pilots could look up out of the cockpit at the ridgelines on either side of the aircraft.

Getting another signal, Alexander stood for the last time

and hooked up his static line. He held six fingers aloft. "Six minutes!" he shouted into the roar of the aircraft. He extended both hands, palms out. "Get ready!" The team members unbuckled their safety straps.

With both arms, Alexander pointed at the team seated along the outside of the aircraft. Then he pointed up. "Outboard personnel stand up." The members of Eyes Two staggered to their feet in the wildly swaying aircraft, using the static line cable and side of the aircraft for support.

Curling his index fingers over his head, representing hooks, Alexander pumped his arms up and down. "Hook up!" He watched as each man connected his static line, snap hook gate toward the skin of the aircraft, into the static line cable, and secured the gate shut with a safety wire.

The loadmaster held onto Alexander's static line and tried to keep him from falling over while he used both hands to pantomime the jump commands. "Check static lines!"

Each jumper checked his snap hook and traced the static line from the snap hook to where it disappeared over his shoulder. He then checked the static line of the man in front, from where it came over his shoulder to where it disappeared into his parachute. The last man, Captain Vaughn, turned and allowed the man in front to check him.

"Check equipment!" Each man made sure one last time that all his equipment was secured and the connections made fast on his parachute harness.

Alexander cupped his hands over his ears. "Sound off for equipment check!" The last man slapped the man in front on his rear and yelled "OK," then the yell and slap were passed from man to man until the second jumper, just behind Alexander, yelled, "All OK, Jumpmaster," giving the thumbs-up.

With all his jump commands done except the final "Go," Alexander gained control of his static line from the loadmaster and turned toward the rear of the aircraft. He waited for the ramp to open, ready to lead the team off into the dark night. He swayed to the front as the aircraft slowed down from 250 knots to 125 knots. Three minutes out.

The noise level increased abruptly as a crack appeared in the ramp and widened into a gaping mouth. As the ramp leveled off, Alexander stared out into the dark. Fighting the rucksack hanging in front of his legs, he got to his knees and, grabbing the hydraulic arm on the right side of the ramp, peered around the edge of the aircraft looking forward. He blinked in the wind. It took a few seconds to get oriented.

He could see the lights of Medellin off to the left under the aircraft. The Cauca River was passing underneath. Alexander at least knew that they were in the right neighborhood, and that was as good as it got with a blind drop.

The loadmaster leaned over Alexander's shoulder and stuck an index finger in his face. Alexander clambered awkwardly to his feet, looked over his shoulder at the team, and screamed, "One minute!"

Ten seconds later his knees buckled as the plane rapidly climbed the 250 feet to the 500-foot drop altitude. Glancing out, Alexander could see the lights of Medellin passing by off to the left. He yelled over his shoulder as he shuffled out to within three feet of the edge of the ramp. "Stand by!"

Alexander stared at the red light above the top of the ramp; as soon as it turned green, he'd go. He moved a few inches closer to the edge.

The green light flashed. "GO!" Alexander was gone. The rest of Eyes Two followed.

In less than three seconds these things happened to Alexander and his equipment: His fifteen-foot static line uncoiled off the back of his parachute, tearing open the pack-closing tie on the chute itself and pulling out the pack-opening loop. The parachute, encased in a deployment bag, pulled free from Alexander's body. The nylon of the parachute was connected to the harness around his body by four risers extending into numerous suspension lines. Reaching the limit of the suspension line, the weight of Alexander's falling body broke the loops of eighty-pound test webbing that connected the apex of the canopy with the deployment bag and static line. The static line, with deployment bag attached, was left trailing behind the Talon still attached to the static line cable, twirling in the prop blast. The parachute, freed of the deployment bag, exploded open and Alexander went from a forward speed of 125 knots and a downward free fall to a zero forward speed and a sixteen-foot-per-second descent.

Feeling the opening shock try to jar his chin through his chest, Alexander quickly looked up and checked in the moonlight to see if he had a good canopy. He reached up on his risers to gain a modicum of control. Steering the T-10 canopy consisted simply of reaching high on the risers, grabbing as much as possible, and hauling it in; this tilted the canopy, and it would slip in the direction of pull.

Satisfied with his canopy, Alexander quickly took a look below. All he could see was a great darkness rapidly approaching. He reached down below the reserve that covered his stomach and searched for the handles to his eighteen-inch attaching straps. He fumbled briefly, cursing to himself. The two straps held the rucksack, which was hanging from the reserve down to his knees. Landing with a ruck still attached was a good way to break a leg. He located one strap and held that tight in his left hand while he forced his right hand between the ruck and reserve searching for the other strap. Finding it, he quickly jerked both straps at the same time. The ruck sprang free and dropped to the end of a fifteen-foot lowering line, where it dangled beneath him.

All that effort had cost him his remaining time in the air. The ground was rushing up. Less than twenty seconds after leaving the aircraft, Alexander reached up, grabbed his risers, rotated his arms in front of his face, bent his knees with his feet together, and said a brief prayer. The prayer turned to curses as his feet hit branches.

Alexander crashed through the branches of a small tree and slammed into the ground. He lay still for a second, mentally inventorying his body and giving thanks that he was alive. There was no evident pain, and everything still seemed to be attached and working. He unhooked the releases for his harness and slid his rifle off his shoulder. He checked to make sure his weapon was functioning and then quickly reeled in his parachute, cutting it out of the branches where it had been stuck. He stuffed the chute and his Kevlar helmet in his ruck.

Upslope from him Alexander could hear someone else wrestling with a parachute. Putting his ruck on his back, he clambered up the hill toward the sound. After two minutes he came upon Atwaters between two trees, rolling up his chute in the dark.

"You all right?"

Atwaters nodded. "Yeah. But this sure don't look like no DZ."

Alexander nodded. He was glad he had followed Riley's advice. He pushed a button on the large watchlike device on his wrist. The two-inch face lit up and a small light started flashing at a point along the edge. Alexander rotated his arm but the light stayed in the same direction, uphill and to the south.

"The captain's thataway," he whispered to Atwaters. "You got all your stuff? All right, let's go." The wrist device could be used as either a homing instrument or a means to home in on another similar device. Only the captain's was set to transmit; the rest of the team's were set to receive. The plan was that they would all converge on the captain. Vaughn had activated his homing device just prior to jumping so it would be the first on, once they hit the ground.

Alexander led the way. He knew that the captain shouldn't be too far away, only a few hundred meters at best. They had jumped too low to be very spread out, unless someone had hesitated going off the ramp.

Glancing at his wrist again, Alexander was dismayed to see another light come on, slightly to the left of the first one. That could mean only one thing: Someone had gotten hurt or hung up and couldn't make it to the captain. Alexander adjusted his path and headed toward the second light. In less than a minute of scrambling up the hillside and breaking brush, he came upon the source of the second light.

Through his night-vision goggles Alexander could make out the dark pattern of a parachute hung up in a tree. Coming closer he found the jumper lying beneath it. It was Paulson, the weapons man. To make sure he wouldn't be fired on, Alexander called out softly, "Eyes Two," as he approached.

Alexander knelt next to the jumper. "What's the matter?"

Paulson shook his head. "I think I busted my ankle. I hit the trees and thought I was hung up, and then the chute popped free and I hit the ground. I can't stand on it. I tried and it hurt too much. That's when I turned on the transmitter."

Alexander turned to Atwaters. "Leave your ruck here and go to the captain. Tell him to turn off his transmitter and bring everyone here." Atwaters nodded and, checking his direction on his wrist, turned and headed off to get the team leader.

Alexander quickly did a primary survey of Paulson to make sure there was nothing else wrong with him. Sometimes the pain of one injury masked the warning signs from another more dangerous one. Satisfied that nothing else was seriously wrong, he checked out the ankle.

Hearing someone coming through the brush, Alexander swung around with his silenced MP5, pointing it in the direction of the intruders. He watched as four men broke out into the small clearing at the foot of the tree.

"Eyes Two," one of the figures hissed. Alexander relaxed. The rest of the team was here. Vaughn and Colden, the medic, came over while the other two men settled in as security, pointing upslope and down. Alexander quietly briefed the captain while Colden worked on Paulson.

After a few minutes Colden rendered his report. "It's a broken ankle, all right. We'll have to carry him."

Alexander reached for the captain's ruck. "Let's see where we are." Digging through the parachute inside, he pulled out a piece of electronics that looked similar in size and makeup to the SATCOM radio. The machine was called MANPADS, for man portable position azimuth distance system. Alexander had relied on it several times before and thought it was one of the most useful pieces of equipment he had ever used.

Opening a cover on the machine, he typed in a brief code by feel. The small LED display dimly lit up with eight numbers, which stood for the grid coordinates of their present location. Then he punched in a second set of numbers that he had memorized—the grid coordinates for the lab site. The display lit up with a second set of two numbers: 282-2.13. Alexander shook his head in amazement. Didn't even need to do a map check. He wasn't sure how the damn thing worked, although he knew it had something to do with satellites. The machine had calculated the azimuth and distance from their present location to the target. Without the machine, they'd probably have spent half the night fumbling around in the dark—a frustrating and time-expensive exercise. According to the information, they had been dropped only about twelve hundred meters from where they had wanted to be.

Alexander looked up at Vaughn. "Just over two k's to the target." He checked his compass. "Thataway."

Vaughn nodded and turned to Colden, who was splinting Paulson's leg and foot. "What's his status?"

"Simple break of the ankle. I'm extending the splint below his foot so he can limp along on it in an emergency, but I don't recommend that unless absolutely necessary."

Alexander pulled a poncho from the outside pocket of his ruck. "I'll make up a travois. We'll pull him. It's downhill most of the way."

# FORT BELVOIR, VIRGINIA
## 11:12 P.M.

Riley woke with a start. Reaching over, he pulled his watch off the nightstand. 2312. Damn, he hadn't meant to sleep so late. Eyes Two was already long gone and on the ground in Colombia. Riley lay his head back on the pillow and silently wished them luck.

# SATURDAY,
# 31 AUGUST

## VICINITY OF MEDELLIN, COLOMBIA
## 12:15 A.M.

Alexander looked up in surprise. Four hundred meters downslope from his location, the dark night sky was split as arc lights clicked on at the lab site. He glanced over at Vaughn, who returned his puzzled look. They watched for a few minutes as activity burgeoned in the camp, then Alexander edged away from the recon site and slid into some bushes where the radio was set up. Colden was there watching over Paulson. The sliding ride down the mountainside from the drop zone to the recon site had entailed a few spills for the unfortunate weapons man, and Colden was monitoring Paulson to make sure shock didn't set in.

Vaughn slid in behind Alexander, having left Atwaters and Haley continuing the surveillance. The captain looked uncertain. "What do you think is going on down there?"

Alexander looked at the young team leader in the darkness. "I think they're either moving or getting a shipment ready to go."

"What do you think we should do?"

Alexander picked up the handset for the SATCOM. "Let's see if we can get the Hammer down here a little earlier. Not much else we can do by ourselves."

## 1:30 A.M.

Suarez swore to himself as the jeep lurched along the unpaved mountain road. The lights from the truck following him wavered crazily in the cool night air as the truck negotiated the trail. Suarez was tired and hung over, but he was also very angry. Angry that he had received word so late.

Only an hour ago one of his informers had reported receiving the warning phone call. The caller claimed that Rameriz's people were going to raid Suarez's main lab in the mountains outside Medellin the next morning.

Unable to confirm the report with his own sources, Suarez had reacted. He couldn't afford not to. He had quickly gathered together all the guards he could find and, after radioing the camp to warn it, had led them out on the narrow trail through the mountains to where the lab was located. Suarez had a well-earned reputation as a man who led his men by example, always putting himself in the middle of any activity.

Suarez blinked as a figure stepped out of the dark in front of him onto the dirt road. He relaxed as he recognized one of the lab's guards. The man waved at him.

"*Buenos días*, Señor Suarez."

Suarez ignored the greeting. "Is the camp prepared?"

"Sí, señor. We have two machine guns here guarding the road. It is the only way someone can get in. We have mountains on all other sides. If someone comes we will kill them before they realize the mistake they have made."

Suarez looked around. It was a good location for an ambush. Good fields of fire on a narrow bend of the road. The camp was another three kilometers away, higher up on the mountainside. But the guard was right. The road was the only way someone could come and attack. Unless of course they used helicopters, but Suarez knew that The Shark didn't have access to enough helicopters to get a sizable force up here, unless he used the military's—in which case Suarez's informants in the air force would have given him ample warning. Besides, the military wouldn't dare. Furthermore, there was still more than enough firepower up at the lab to beat off an airmobile assault. There was only one cleared place flat enough for a helicopter to land within two kilometers of the lab, and that was the lab's own pad. A helicopter attempting to land there would be easily destroyed by ground fire.

"Good. I will leave the men in the truck here. I am going up to the main camp." Suarez signaled his driver to keep going.

In fifteen minutes they pulled into the lab cut into the side of the mountain. Arc lights blazed as men labored to load processed cocaine into three panel vans. Cocaine worth over $800 million in street value was presently in this camp. Enough to keep Suarez's operation going for the next four months. He also had his best lab equipment and technicians at this site. If the location of this lab was no longer secret, as the anonymous phone call had clearly indicated, then it was time to move everything.

## 1:50 A.M.

Alexander glanced up as Atwaters squirmed into their little base camp.

"There's a jeep pulling into the camp. Looks like they're done loading all that stuff into the vans."

Alexander looked at his watch and swore. All they needed was a little more time.

## 1:56 A.M.

Suarez glanced at his watch. Another five minutes and they'd be ready to roll.

One of the men came out of the barracks. "Señor Suarez! A radio call for you."

Suarez swaggered across the clearing to the shack, where the radio operator handed him the mike.

"Suarez here."

"This is Jesus. We found your pilot. He just took off and should be there in five minutes."

"Good. I will meet him at the landing field."

Suarez smiled for the first time that evening. He'd been furious when they couldn't track down the pilot for the brand-new helicopter he had bought last month. With the helicopter now en route, things were changed. Suarez wouldn't have to entrust all his wealth to the vans. He'd take some of the cocaine to the landing zone next to the lab and fly it out with him. Saved time and trouble. The chances of the convoy getting ambushed and all the cocaine lost had now disappeared. In a better mood, Suarez walked out of the shack to give the new orders.

## 1:59 A.M.

"We've got a lot of activity here. Definitely looks like they're packing up to move out. Over."

Chief Warrant Officer Straker curled his finger over the front of his cyclic and pressed his send button. "Roger. I've got your laser designator on the screen. Wait one while I check with upstairs. Break." The last word indicated that Straker was going to talk to another station on the net. "Moonbeam, this is Viper One. Over."

"This is Moonbeam. You've got a slow-mover inbound your location out of Medellin. Looks like it might be a helicopter by the way it's flying. ETA two minutes. Over."

Damn! Straker thought rapidly. They weren't paying him enough to make these decisions. The orders had said blast everything. If that was so, then the helicopter was fair game, too. Whoever was flying at two in the morning wasn't on a mission of mercy. Probably coming in to help outload the lab below.

The entire mission time sequence had been rushed ever since the ground surveillance had initially reported the activity at the lab. They were already forty-five minutes ahead of planned schedule.

"Eyes Two, this is Viper One. We've got an unknown helicopter inbound. I'm going to let it touch down and then start the Hammer. Over."

"This is Eyes Two. We copied Moonbeam. Roger."

Straker had a headache. That wasn't unusual. He had a headache every time he flew the Apache. The advanced attack helicopter was almost too much machine for the pilot to handle. The main source of his headache was flying with his right eye and simultaneously reading the essential telemetry off the tiny display flipped down over his left eye. The need to focus each eye independently caused a spike of pain to bisect his forehead.

Straker occupied the rear seat of the two-seat helicopter. From that position he flew the bird. Directly in front of and offset below him, the gunner, Martin, controlled the gunship's firepower: eight Hellfire missiles, a 30mm chain gun, and thirty-eight 2.5-inch rockets. Martin wore a helmet that had the sighting system for the 30mm gun built in; wherever Martin turned his head, the barrel of the gun, nestled under the nose of the helicopter, followed.

The Hellfires and rockets were mounted on pods that hung below pylons protruding from the side of the aircraft. The rockets were aimed by maneuvering the entire aircraft. The Hellfire was a fire-and-forget weapon designed to destroy tanks. Fire-and-forget meant that the missile was locked onto the target with a laser designator by the gunner. He then transferred the lock-on to the missile's own internal guidance system and fired it. The missile's computer kept it on track with the target and guided it in, even if the target was moving. This was a tremendous advantage over the old TOW system, which had required the gunner to keep the target in his sights the entire flight time of the missile.

Straker keyed his external radio. "Viper Two, Three, and Four, this is One. Move when I do. Remember to stick to your fields of fire. I'll take out the helicopter. Also remember that those friendly grunts are upslope when you open up. You should have their location on IR. Over."

"Two here. Roger. Over."

"Three here. Roger. Over."

"Four here. Why do you get all the fun? Over."

Straker smiled briefly at the gibe. He could see the inbound helicopter now through his night-vision equipment. It was also displayed on his forward-looking infrared radar, coming out of the northwest, to his left front. The Apaches were hovering in a valley five kilometers to the south of the target. Straker's was peaking just over the edge; the other three were below the crest of the ridgeline. Not that anyone from the camp could see or hear them at this distance, but it didn't pay to be careless.

He watched the collision lights of the inbound helicopter settle down into the lit landing field. They could have easily spotted this camp without the aid of the ground surveillance. But it was a good thing the surveillance had been there or else they would have hit the camp too late.

The four attack helicopters had lifted off on schedule from the *Raleigh* thirty kilometers off the west coast of Colombia. But when the ground surveillance had called Moonbeam—the AWACS surveillance plane circling off the coast—with the report of unusual activity, they had opened their throttles wide. Straker had pushed the Apaches in his strike force to almost maximum speed, arriving only three minutes ago. Just in time it now appeared.

Whatever and whomever the Colombians were going to load onto the helicopter were probably on board, Straker decided. Time to party. He pulled in collective and leaned the cyclic forward. The other three Apaches spread out on either side of him.

Straker talked over his intercom to his gunner in the front seat. "Like I told the other guys, Martin: You take out the chopper first, then our designated sector."

"Roger that. This is working out real well. That bird will cover up the noise of us approaching."

Straker nodded to himself and concentrated on flying. They were less than three kilometers away. He keyed the mike. "Open up on my firing. I'm waiting till one klick."

The formation spread farther apart as each gunship gave itself room to fire and maneuver. At a thousand meters from the camp, Straker flared his aircraft into a hover just over the treetops. The helicopter from the camp was just lifting off. "Now," he hissed over the intercom.

A flame exploded on the right side of the gunship as a Hellfire missile leapt forward. Martin had locked in the Apache's laser target designator, and the beam of invisible light was automatically tracking the helicopter, aiming the Hellfire. As the missile roared away, the 30mm cannon under the nose of the helicopter started spitting death into the camp.

The Hellfire impacted on the hapless helicopter, tearing halfway through the aircraft's turbine engine before exploding. The charge, designed to penetrate a tank's armor, devastated the fragile helicopter. Flaming pieces littered the trees below.

Straker rocked in his seat as the aircraft shuddered with the recoil of the automatic cannon. Pencils of light streaked from the pods on the side of the helicopter. Martin had started firing the 2.5-inch rockets.

Flanking Viper One, the other three Apaches were releasing their loads. Through his optics, Straker could see bodies littering the camp, and the buildings in ruin. An explosion sent a tongue of flame curling into the night sky. That explosion initiated a rapid sequence of smaller, secondary detonations. Straker blinked for a second as his night-vision equipment strained to adjust to the light differences.

Death reigned in the camp. Straker knew that the Special Forces team was somewhere off to the east watching this destruction. He heard the radio crackle. "Viper One, this is Eyes Two. Over."

"Viper One. Over."

"You've got everything in the camp as far as we can see. One of the vans made it to the road and is heading south. We think it's carrying some of the cocaine. We're ready to move forward and verify the kill and get picked up. Over."

"Roger that, Eyes Two. Break. Viper Three and Four, go after that van and take it out. Two, move forward with me and cover the pickup zone. Break. Moonbeam, did you copy Eyes Two? Over."

"This is Moonbeam. Roger that." The voice continued. "Stork is two minutes out coming in from the west, to your left front."

Straker edged his aircraft forward as he watched Three and Four break off his right and head for the trail out of the camp. Straker took up a position covering the camp from the northwest, while Two covered it from the northeast. He watched as an infrared strobe light started flashing in his night sight.

"One, you got Eyes Two in sight? Over."

"Roger that. Over."

"Eyes Two, this is Viper One. We have you in sight." Straker could see five men moving through the wreckage of the camp. They appeared to be carrying a sixth man on some sort of stretcher. As Straker watched, one man turned and fired into a body lying on the ground. Straker spotted a seventh figure skulking toward the tree line. Apparently, Martin spotted the target at the same time: The 30mm cannon erupted and the figure was obliterated. A burst of light to the immediate south caught Straker's attention.

"This is Three. Scratch one van full of scum. Over."

Straker reoriented as the HH-53 Pave Low passed between his aircraft and Viper Two, settling into the landing zone. The five men ran on board the ramp with their stretcher. The Pave Low lifted.

Straker pulled in cyclic and keyed his mike. "Let's circle round the wagon, guys."

With the lift helicopter safely in the center, the five aircraft sped northwest just a hundred feet above the terrain at 130 knots.

# BOGOTA
## 3:15 A.M.

Stevens put down the headset. The helicopters were long gone out of Colombian airspace, heading north over the Pacific Ocean toward Panama. The night's mission was complete. Stevens rolled his head back and let out a deep breath. He was exhausted. The thought of Maria waiting back at the room failed to excite him for the first time. She had worn him out before he'd come on duty tonight. He'd almost been late coming up on the radio net. Stevens had reluctantly pried himself out of her arms in order to get here to monitor Eyes Two's activities only an hour and forty-five minutes prior to the actual attack.

# FORT BELVOIR, VIRGINIA
## 10:23 A.M.

"I don't like it one bit." Riley shook his head. Eyes Two's debriefing had just finished, and Stevens had called up with the latest information from his informants regarding the events of the early morning. Paulson was still on the *Raleigh* in the ship's infirmary. The rest of Eyes Two had just left to go upstairs and catch some sleep after their long night. Riley and Pike had gotten together with Westland in Pike's office and were now reviewing the information that had come out in the debrief.

Riley explained his concern. "I don't think Suarez would have tried to move his lab that quickly based on the fact that one of Rameriz's labs had been hit the night before. How the hell did Suarez find out about the first hit? Rameriz has kept it real quiet. Or at least that's what Stevens tells us. And second, why the rush to move it in the middle of the night, almost as if he was expecting to be hit right then?"

Westland shook her head. "I agree it doesn't make sense. If there's a leak, then why didn't Eyes One's target get warned?"

General Pike swung his head around. "Let's look at it logically. Let's also worst case it and assume a leak, although most likely it was just a coincidence.

"The where of Eyes One and Two was known to several people. People here in the Eyes teams, people in the Hammer task forces, those people across the river in Washington whom I had to brief. Also, it was known by the CIA contact who took the information, and, backing up from him, by the person who gave that contact the information in the first place. If there is a leak that's the place I think we should look."

Westland shook her head. "Even if the source told other people what it told our contact, there's no way the source could know on which nights we were going to hit."

Pike considered that. "We're also getting extremely paranoid here. The odds are it was just a coincidence. But I don't like coincidences, so from here on out we're going to be more secure. No one other than the people in this building will know the exact day or time of the hit."

Riley concurred. "Sounds good to me, sir."

They both turned and looked at Westland. The unspoken question was whether she would go against her instructions from the CIA and not report back to her supervisor the timing of the hits. She didn't hesitate. "I agree. The timing stays with us."

Pike glanced at Riley. Riley nodded to his boss. He felt they could trust her.

Pike continued. "I'm going to have the Hammer task forces on alert status starting now, and they go only on the radio call from the team on the ground. That way if the leak came out of the Hammer force, we can prevent them knowing which night the hit actually goes down until they're on their way to the target. I'm sure they'll bitch about that at the Pentagon, but I'll brief the chairman personally on why we're doing it. I'm sure he'll agree and support us."

Riley nodded. "That'll help, sir, but I think the leak, if there is one, is elsewhere." He turned to Westland. "You need to do some hard checking on the contact agent down there and the source. From the beginning I thought it was screwed up getting intelligence from an unknown source. You need to find out as much as you can about the source."

If Westland resented being told what to do by Riley, she didn't show it. "I'll see what I can find out."

# BOGOTA
## 11:00 A.M.

Alegre watched as the chief of his presidential bodyguard sat down across from him. Pasquel Montez was his closest adviser and friend. They had grown up in the same suburb of Bogota and attended the university together. Montez was the only man in Bogota that Alegre would trust totally. He was also the only man in Bogota who knew the complete extent of the plan Alegre had implemented. "What is the report from Medellin?"

Montez smiled. "Most interesting. The raid, of course, was a success. There is nothing left up there. The interesting part, my President, is that Suarez was killed in the raid."

Alegre looked up in surprise. "What was Suarez doing at his laboratory in the middle of the night?"

"I don't know yet. I have some people making discreet inquiries."

Alegre digested this new information. "Certainly I am not going to cry over the death of that pig. With Suarez out of the way, the Medellin gang will be out of circulation for a while. I imagine the Ring Man and Rameriz will fight like wolves over what's left."

Montez seemed noncommittal. "Certainly Suarez's death furthers your cause, but I am worried about why he was there in the middle of the night. Could he have been set up? And if he was set up, by whom? The answer to the last question would seem to be quite obvious. There is only one other man in the country besides you and I who knows about the attacks."

Alegre shook his head. "The Ring Man may know where, since he was the one feeding the information to us, but he doesn't know when. Even we don't know the when until the DEA man at the embassy calls me after it's already completed. How could the Ring Man know what time the attack would go last night in order to set up Suarez? Besides, it doesn't matter. If they want to kill each other off, then so much the better. Less for us to do."

Montez appeared disturbed. "I have to again warn you, my President, that this is a dangerous course you are charting. If you fail to completely break the back of the drug cartel, they will come and break your back when they find out what you have done."

Alegre was bothered by his friend's lack of conviction and sought to reassure him. "We already have won several major victories. The United Nations' vote has gone our way. Suarez is dead and his organization on the verge of destruction. Rameriz has been badly hurt. The power of the cartel has been significantly reduced."

Montez disagreed. "I don't think so, my friend. Rather I

would say that the balance of power has shifted. Ring Man will be moving in to take over the power vacuum these attacks have opened. He is well prepared."

Alegre held up his hand to forestall the doomsaying. "Then we will have to have the Ring Man taken care of."

Montez stared at Alegre in disbelief. "We have no one who would be foolish enough to try that."

"I know we don't." Alegre smiled grimly. "But maybe the Americans do. They are too committed now to back out of the present course of action. We can always claim that we didn't know anything about these attacks and put the heat on Washington by threatening to disclose what has happened. After the Panama invasion they couldn't afford that. It would destroy whatever diplomatic relations they have down here in Latin America."

# FORT BELVOIR, VIRGINIA
## 1:45 P.M.

Riley watched as Pike considered his proposal. The two were seated in the general's office, where Riley had laid out his idea in five minutes. Pike was obviously sorting out the pieces in his mind. When they clicked in place the senior officer looked up. "It's a good idea. Even before you came in, I had decided we weren't going to send both teams concurrently on the next mission. If there is a leak, then I want only one team to be compromised. Your idea does that and also reduces the chance of someone knowing when the mission will go."

Riley nodded. The proposal to mount Eyes Three the next evening rather than on Monday night made sense to him. Right now, everyone involved believed that the next mission would occur in two nights. If they moved it up and ran it tomorrow night the chances of compromise were greatly reduced. Then they would delay Four until Tuesday night. That would give the other half of the team more time to prepare and also give them an edge if their old date had been compromised.

Pike considered the ramifications out loud. "I like your idea for infiltration. Should be no problem getting a regular slick

UH-60 in Panama. I very much doubt that there's any leak in the Special Ops aircrews or that they are being watched, but if there is, this will circumvent that. I can get everything rolling tonight without tipping off anyone.

"As far as the Hammer is concerned, we can go either way. The Apaches are on alert status off the coast and in Panama, and I'm going to have 1st SOW forward deploy an AC-130 to Panama for quicker reaction. Whichever one we use won't have to know what's happening until you give the go from on the ground. The only person I have to brief here is the chairman of the Joint Chiefs, and I don't think that will be a problem." Pike paused. "What about Stevens?"

Riley shook his head. "We don't tell him either until we're on the ground."

"All right. You brief your people and I'll get a hold of the chairman and get his blessing."

## LANGLEY, VIRGINIA
## 4:00 P.M.

" . . . and that's why we believe there is a leak." Westland paused and waited for Strom's reaction. The senior agent was dressed in his golfing clothes and did not appear thrilled with being called in on a weekend to meet with her. There were important people out on the course that he needed to rub elbows with.

Strom shook his head. "That's pretty flimsy. There's a lot of reasons why the camp may have been moving. Hell, they could just have been reacting to the first attack. If there had been a leak, don't you think they would have been better prepared for an attack or have moved earlier? I don't buy it."

Strom looked at her condescendingly. "My dear girl, you have to understand that sometimes in these field operations the unexpected occurs, and the reason it occurs is not due to some dark, monstrous plot but rather just simply the fates weaving their web."

Westland tried hard not to roll her eyes or get angry. She didn't need the patronizing bullshit and she also didn't like being treated like an idiot. She felt she had come here with a legitimate concern and she knew she was getting blown off. "Can you at least give me an idea of how the intelligence on the target sites is getting to us?"

Strom inspected his manicured hands. "My dear girl, you really don't have a need to know that. There's nothing you can do about it anyway. That's my responsibility, and I can assure you there isn't a problem on that end."

Westland decided to push things. If he called her "my dear girl" one more time she didn't think she could control herself. "How can you be sure there isn't a leak on that end? How can you be sure the Colombian source is legitimate?"

He looked up at her in anger, and she was afraid for a second that she'd gone too far. But she really didn't care. She was doing her job, and she had an obligation to the men doing the mission to check on things as much as she could.

Strom had obviously decided enough was enough. "You can be sure because I'm bloody well sure, that's why!" He took a few seconds to gain visible control of himself. "When you've been in this business as long as I, then you will understand."

Strom stood up. Discussion over, thought Westland. He escorted her to the door. "I appreciate your concerns, but I really think you and your Special Forces friends are overreacting. The task force has been a success so far. I think it will continue. However, if you do come across any solid evidence you think points to a leak, let me know right away."

Westland fumed as she watched the door shut in her face. As she walked to her car she considered what she'd just been told. And not told. And where the hell did Strom get that stupid British accent? she wondered illogically to herself.

Westland shook her head angrily as she drove her white Camaro out the gates and headed toward Fort Belvoir. There were obviously a lot of things going on that she didn't have knowledge of. Games within games. She'd seen it at Langley during the past seven years. She wasn't foolish enough to believe that Task Force Hammer was the only operation going on in Colombia, but she had thought that at least she would be informed of any others that might affect her mission, and that she would have high enough clearance to be told about the source of her intelligence. She slammed her fist into the steering wheel in frustration. Maybe she was just overreacting, but a small knot in the pit of her stomach refused to untie.

# FORT BELVOIR, VIRGINIA
# 7:30 P.M.

There'd been no audience for the Eyes Three briefback other than Westland and General Pike. Apparently the powers-that-be had been satisfied with the results of the first two missions and didn't feel the need to keep a scrutinous eye on the actual proceedings. Besides, Riley knew, it would be Pike's ass on the line if anything went wrong. Pike would be the one recommending to the chairman that the plan was good and the mission should be approved. By distancing himself, General Macksey was placing the entire responsibility on Pike's shoulders.

As with the previous two missions, the plan for Eyes Three was straightforward. The means of infiltration was a little different, but other than that it was business as usual.

Riley wondered whether it would be the same. His bad feeling about the intelligence was still there. Westland's angry recounting of how she had been treated by Strom did little to reassure him. Some CIA bureaucrat says don't worry and I'm supposed to buy off on that, Riley thought. Right.

He tightened a strap on his ruck and threw it on the floor, then took its place on his bunk. Powers glanced up from his bunk, where he was perusing a superspy, international espionage novel someone on the team had lent him. "Hey, partner, what's the matter? You still ain't worried about the intel stuff, are you?"

"Hell, yeah, compadre, I'm still worried about that. We could get our asses shot off if there is a leak."

Powers shook his head. "Listen, bud. Let me tell you a few rules I've learned in the college of hard knocks. First off, don't worry about things you can't control. Second, you can't trust them CIA dinks as far as you can throw them, but you also can't do nothing about them either. Third, if you was as good as the hero in this novel I'm reading, you'd be able to use your ninja sixth sense and figure everything out. Did you miss the class on being able to read the future in all those martial arts courses you took? The guy in this book has an inner sense that tells him when danger is near."

Riley laughed. "Yeah, I must have missed that day."

Powers turned serious for a moment. "Listen. This mission tomorrow night is a good one. We'll be coming in a direction they won't expect, and that no one except the people in this building know about. Even if there is a leak, we still have that on our side. I feel pretty good about it. Let it go and relax. Whatever's going to happen is going to happen. All we can do is make sure we got our shit in one tight little bag."

Riley nodded. "Yeah, you're right. You know me, though. I'm not happy unless I'm worrying. The more worrying—" He paused as he heard a knock on the door. "Come in."

He sat up on his bunk as he saw Westland edge her way into the room. "What's up? Some new intel?"

Westland shook her head. "No. Just thought I'd stop by. Say hello."

Riley smiled. She seemed a little nervous, and he wasn't sure how to put her at ease. He wasn't very experienced at small talk. His philosophy was that either you had something to say or you didn't, and he wasted little time talking about things he didn't think were important. It didn't help that Powers was sitting on his bunk watching the two of them, his eyeballs flicking back and forth, as though he was watching a tennis match.

Riley gestured at the small army-issue desk near the window. "Grab a seat. We were just talking about the mission tomorrow."

Powers groaned. "I don't want to talk about the mission tomorrow. I'm tired of talking about army crap."

Riley snorted. "For you that sure doesn't leave much to talk about, other than guns and beer drinking."

Powers put on his hurt expression. "Hey, I'm a cultured person. I can talk about a lot of other things." He stood up. "But seeing as you two don't quite make it up to my high standards of the art of conversation, I think I'll seek company elsewhere." Powers starting easing the door shut behind him.

"I'll knock before I come back in." He made a great show of looking at his watch. "Say in about a half hour. That ought to give you enough time." Riley threw a pillow at the door with a yell.

Westland looked at him and grinned. "I think he likes you."

Riley crossed his legs and sat in a yoga position on the bed. "Yeah, we get along pretty good. In the last year we've spent more time together than most married couples." He turned serious. "Dan's wife left him just after I got to the team, and he went through a rough time. He didn't miss his wife too much, but not having his two kids around tore him up. He started—"

Riley paused. He had just been about to tell Westland things that he had kept between Powers and him. It wasn't his place to disclose something told in friendship. Why had he been so ready to tell Westland, especially after knowing her for only about a week?

"Anyway, if you have a good team all the guys tend to get kind of tight. But it's funny in a way, too. You spend most of your time bullshitting with each other and not being serious too often, and you definitely don't get into someone's personal life. Not unless they want you to."

Riley decided to change the subject. "What about you? How do you find life over at Langley?"

Westland put her feet up on the desk. "I'm not really close to anyone over there. There's a weird mentality in the air. Everything you do is pretty much classified so you can never talk about work, and most like leaving the place behind when they go home at the end of the day. And those who don't I really don't like being around." Westland laughed self-consciously. "I guess I never thought about it much."

Riley contemplated her words. "Sometimes I think we end up living a life-style that we really don't think about too much. Kind of just flow with the stream and never do much steering."

"Are you a soldier-philosopher?"

Riley shrugged. "Sometimes. Sometimes when you're out in the woods in the middle of the night, waiting, your mind can really travel." He smiled. "I'm good at asking questions but I don't have too many answers."

"Neither do I."

Riley's thoughts flickered back to the upcoming mission. "Hopefully we won't get any bad answers to our questions about the security of the mission when we go in tomorrow night."

"I don't think there's anything to worry about. At least I hope there isn't," Westland amended.

"Well, as Powers was just telling me before you came in, we'll find out soon enough."

# SUNDAY,
# 1 SEPTEMBER

## CARTAGENA
## 8:12 A.M.

Roberto Rameriz was frustrated and mad. Events were swiftly moving against him but he didn't know who to strike out against. Despite his ranting and raving Friday, his sons had been able to come up with few answers. He looked up as Carlos, his youngest son and business manager, came in the door and sat in front of his desk. "What is it?"

Carlos looked worried. "Suarez was attacked last night in a manner similar to the attack on us."

Roberto's aged forehead wrinkled as he considered this new development. "That gives us one negative answer at least. We know now that Suarez wasn't behind it."

"There's more, Padre. Suarez was killed in the attack on his main lab outside Medellin."

The Shark was surprised. "Why was Suarez up there in the middle of the night? What is going on? First us and now Suarez. Is the Ring Man waging war?"

Carlos shook his head negatively. "Our informants indicate that the Ring Man's people here have been inactive the last several days. If he is behind it then he has brought in outsiders who have managed to stay well hidden."

"But what about his moves on the markets in the United States that we are getting reports on? It seems as if he knew what was going to happen. He is moving quickly."

His son leaned forward. "I have another theory."

The Shark waved his hand. "What is it?"

"The Americans."

"What! Impossible. How could they do it? How could they have found out where our main lab was? They wouldn't dare attack into Colombia without government approval."

Carlos offered his theory. "Maybe it is the CIA acting alone or through mercenaries. I don't know. But some of the facts point to the Americans. Although there were no survivors from the attack on our camp, the evidence points to heavy-caliber weapons being fired from the air and artillery being used. Perhaps helicopter gunships and artillery at the same time. We know our military didn't do it. Who else could? Who else could move such weapons so quickly?

"There were some survivors at a roadblock near Suarez's camp and they report that helicopters were used in the attack. Since we know they weren't Colombian, that points to American involvement. Maybe they are reacting to the slaying of Santia."

Roberto considered this. "Maybe. But that still leaves us with unanswered questions. How are the Americans getting their information? How did they manage to get Suarez at his lab? Our informants are telling us nothing. And how is the Ring Man involved? His moves on the distributors in the United States are too quick not to have been preplanned."

Roberto rubbed his chin. "We need to find out if the Americans are indeed behind all this. See what you can do about that. Also, contact our people in Medellin and see what we can salvage out of Suarez's operation. We cannot allow the Ring Man to get too strong."

# BOGOTA
# 9:45 A.M.

The Ring Man was satisfied with the way things were going. Suarez's organization was crumbling. Already the man's former lieutenants were fighting like jackals over the carcass of the organization left in Medellin. Ring Man would let them fight each other. He was going to cut them out at both ends. His people were prepared to outbid them on the supply end for the coca paste, and at the distribution end he was already gathering in the major East and West Coast American buyers. He expected more of Suarez's and Rameriz's American buyers and distributors to come around when they realized those sources were no longer able to keep up with the demand.

Ring Man lit a large cigar and leaned back in his chair. All in all a very profitable week. With a few bold strokes he had become the strongest man in Colombia. Now it was time to consolidate his winnings.

# LANGLEY, VIRGINIA
# 11:30 A.M.

Hanks walked with Strom through the executive dining room. "What have you got?"

Strom laid it out in one sentence. "Alegre insists that we terminate the Ring Man for him."

Hanks paused on the way to his table and looked at his subordinate. "You're joking."

"No, sir. Montez contacted Jameson and passed the word. Alegre is threatening to expose the Hammer strikes unless we do it."

"How the hell is he going to do that? Alegre would be cutting his own throat."

Strom wasn't the type to disagree with his boss, but he had to point out the obvious. "We have no proof that Alegre sanctioned the missions and passed us the targeting information. Alegre could probably make it look like we did do this unilaterally, without permission."

Hanks pondered this as he sat at his reserved table in the corner of the room and ordered his meal. He waited until the waiter drifted out of earshot. "Have you contacted anyone over at State or the White House on this?"

"No, sir. I thought I'd better brief you first."

Hanks sighed. He always got the dirty deals. He thought out

loud. "State will shit nails if we tell them about this, and I don't want to hit the president up with it either."

Hanks shook his head. That bastard Alegre had sure put them on the hot spot. Hanks had considered the possibility that they could use the raids as leverage against Alegre, but he hadn't considered the opposite. He hadn't taken the time to think this whole thing through completely and had trusted Strom to handle it. He was a little upset with Strom for not having considered this possibility and getting some hard evidence on Alegre, implicating him in the whole thing. "Did Jameson get any tapes of his exchanges with Montez? Any video or audio?"

"No, sir. Montez always set up the meets and that wasn't possible."

"Jesus Christ!" Hanks exploded. "Who the hell is running this op, Strom? Us or the Colombians?" He focused his glare on his subordinate. "You didn't do a very good job on this. *Always* get leverage material on the other guy."

Hanks paused until after the waiter had put his lunch on the table. "Did Montez give any indication of when they'd like this done?"

Strom was a much different man from the image he presented to Westland. His accent was gone and his confident air with it. "He wants the job done early this week. He's concerned about what will happen when the target finds out he's getting fingered, too."

Hanks considered that. "This is going to be a problem. We could just leave Alegre to take the heat, but the cartel would probably have him for lunch, and our friends across the river wouldn't like that too much." Making his decision, he shifted gears. "We can't have this traced back to us. Do we have any locals we can use down there?"

Strom shook his head. "I'd strongly advise against that, sir. Anyone we use from down there will talk. You know the kind of headlines we'll get out of that. 'CIA Pays Local Assassin.' Plus, you can't trust those beaners."

" 'Those beaners,' " Hanks flared, "outsmarted you pretty damn good on this, Strom." Hanks forced himself to calm down and pondered the situation. "We've got the same problem of being implicated, even worse, if we use one of our people. How about contracting a foreign freelance through a cutout?"

Strom shook his head again. "I've considered that, sir. Not enough time. No freelance worth his weight would take a job like this on such short notice."

Hanks was irritated. "You need to get someone. We can't afford to lose Alegre and we also can't afford to have him go public with the Hammer strikes."

Strom tried to throw some water on the fire. "You really think Alegre would do that? It could raise a lot of nasty questions for him."

Hanks snorted a laugh. "If we don't get the Ring Man off his ass, he isn't going to be alive. Alegre would rather be scorned and alive than noble and dead. That man is going to get desperate soon, once the Ring Man starts figuring out what's going on. Which will probably happen tomorrow night, if things go as planned."

Hanks considered another angle. "You know, if our target in Colombia was behind the Santia killing, we might be able to take him out without too much hassle, even if the cover gets blown. The media wouldn't crucify us then."

Hanks looked up. "Find somebody for the job. I don't want to use one of ours or anybody who can be traced back to the agency. We're going to keep this from the people across the river, so it's got to be kept tight."

# HOWARD AIR FORCE BASE, PANAMA
## 2:03 P.M.

The phone woke Davidson out of the tail end of his recovery sleep. It had been a hell of a night, partying at the officers' club into the morning hours.

Davidson searched for the intruding device under the pile of clothes that littered the floor. Recovering it, he lay back down and put the phone on his chest before answering. "Captain Davidson."

"Captain, this is Colonel Moore."

Shit, thought Davidson. It can't be good news. His battalion commander had never before called him at home just to say hello. "Yes, sir."

"I've got a mission for you to fly today. Are you fit to fly?"

Davidson cracked an eye and looked at the clock. The reg was that a pilot was supposed to have twelve hours after his last alcohol before flying. "What time would I be lifting, sir?"

"Approximately 1800."

Enough time, thought Davidson. "Yes, sir. I'm good to go."

"All right. Here's the deal. I know it sounds kind of strange, but this comes straight from SOUTHCOM headquarters. You're to take either tail number 546 or 907. Make sure you have the external tanks topped off, because the requirement is to be able to fly at least a thousand kilometers."

Christ, thought Davidson. Where the hell was he going to fly? The U.S. mainland? This sure screwed up what remained of his weekend. "Yes, sir."

"There will be a C-130 landing at 1700 at your location. Your cargo will be on that aircraft. You're to do whatever the man in charge says."

That's a bunch of bullshit if I ever heard it, Davidson thought. "What do you mean, do whatever this guy says, sir? Who is this person and what's the cargo?" And where's the destination, while we're at it.

"I know as much as I just told you. This comes straight from the commanding general. Just do what the man says and take him wherever he wants to go. Is that clear?"

"Yes, sir. By the way, sir, who's going to be the other pilot?"

"Chief Hobbes will be PIC."

Fuck, Davidson wanted to scream, not Hobbes. "Yes, sir."

"You'd better get your ass in gear and get whichever bird you're going to use preflighted."

"Yes, sir." The phone went dead and Davidson stared at it. What a bunch of bullshit.

## 3:20 P.M.

Davidson drove up next to the ramp where the Blackhawks were parked. He scanned the line of aircraft as he grabbed his flight vest and helmet out of the trunk. He could see Chief Warrant Officer Hobbes already preflighting one of the two aircraft the colonel had specified. He smiled to himself as he wandered over. Although the colonel had said to get over to the flight line in a hurry, Davidson had deliberately taken a leisurely shower and grabbed some lunch before arriving. He knew that Hobbes would get here first and do the preflight. Davidson was damned if he would do it when a warrant officer could.

Hobbes looked up as Davidson approached. "Afternoon, sir."

"Afternoon." Davidson opened the door to the copilot's seat and collapsed into it. He waited while Hobbes completed the preflight. Besides having to work on a Sunday, the idea of flying with Hobbes really set his teeth on edge. He wondered if the battalion commander had done it to him deliberately.

Despite outranking the warrant officer, Davidson would be only the copilot. Hobbes had over seven hundred more hours in Blackhawks than Davidson and thus would be the PIC, or pilot in command, for the mission. Davidson didn't think it was right for a subordinate to ever be in charge. The killer though, as far as he was concerned, was that Hobbes was a woman.

Hobbes stuck her head in the door. "It looks good to go. I already looked at 546 and this one is in better shape and has a better maintenance record."

Davidson nodded glumly. Having to let a woman be in command of the flight irritated the hell out of him. He hated women in the army and he hated the idea of flying with one. They just didn't belong, in his opinion. Just looking at Hobbes in her uniform made him mad. At five foot four, she was just barely over the minimum height requirement to be a pilot, and she was so skinny she seemed to disappear in the flight suit. It further annoyed him that Hobbes had been here during the invasion of Panama a year and a half ago and had flown combat missions, whereas Davidson had flown back to the States on Christmas leave the day before the invasion and missed the whole thing.

Every time he saw the combat patch on her right shoulder he saw red.

Hobbes had climbed into the cargo compartment in the back and was perusing flight charts. "Any idea where we're going, sir?"

"Nope."

Hobbes scratched her head. "This is the strangest thing I've ever heard. What did the colonel tell you, sir?"

"Be here. Load up on fuel. Wait for a C-130 at 1700. Take whoever gets off wherever they want to go." Davidson wasn't going to make any effort to be friendly.

"The Old Man told me to be ready to fly a thousand klicks." Hobbes shook her head. "We've got the fuel but it's going to be a long ride if we have to go that far. Over five hours in the air."

Davidson decided to ignore her. If she thought she was such hot shit as a Blackhawk PIC, he'd let her worry about things.

"Sir, are you all right?" Hobbes was looking at him strangely.

Davidson couldn't believe she had asked that. The bitch probably thought he was still drunk. He turned in his seat. "Listen. You let me worry about me, OK?" He realized he'd pushed her too far as she slowly put down the maps.

"Sir, with all due respect, I'm in charge of this aircraft and responsible for it and everyone who will be in it. That includes you. If you are under the time limit for alcohol, you need to let me know and I'll ask the colonel to get another pilot out here. It's nothing to be embarrassed about."

Davidson wanted to scream at her and put her in her place. Unfortunately, he knew she was within her rights as PIC to ground him if she thought that was best.

"I'm fine. I'm outside the twelve-hour window. There's nothing we can do until that 130 gets here, so I'm just relaxing. Is that all right with you?" Are you happy, bitch? he thought.

Hobbes nodded. "All right, sir. I'll take your word on it."

Davidson rolled his eyes. Oh, thank you so much.


## 5:00 P.M.

Riley felt the wheels touch down. The plane did a short bounce and then rolled to the end of the runway. The pilot turned the plane as the loadmaster began to open the ramp. Looking out, Riley could see a Blackhawk sitting on the tarmac about a hundred meters away. The plane jerked to a halt and the ramp went down all the way. Powers stood up. "Let's go. Rucks first, then the boat."

Each member of Eyes Three grabbed his rucksack and jogged off the ramp toward the helicopter. Riley could see two pilots waiting by the aircraft. He threw his ruck in front of the nose of the helicopter and went up to the two figures in flight suits. He looked them over quickly. A captain and a female warrant. They were looking at him strangely. He knew his appearance wasn't exactly what they were used to. Each member of the team wore a black wet suit with a combat vest over it. There was nothing to identify who they were, which Riley hoped wouldn't cause any trouble with the pilots.

He stuck out his hand to the captain and then the warrant. "Dave Riley. You all ready to go?"

"Captain Davidson." The captain seemed pissed off about something, but Riley didn't have time to worry about it.

The tiny woman draped in a flight suit took his hand briefly. "Chief Hobbes. We're topped off. Once you all get loaded, and tell us where we're going, we'll be ready."

"What the fuck is that?"

Riley looked over his shoulder at the object of the captain's remark. The other five members of the team were carrying the Zodiac off the ramp. They had already inflated the ten-man craft at Belvoir to save time down here. The black boat measured fifteen feet five inches long and over six feet wide and weighed 265 pounds. Adding the outboard motor and fuel bladders, which were tied down inside, boosted the weight to over 400 pounds. The men were glad to drop it on the ground in front of the bird.

"That's a Zodiac, a rubber boat."

"I can see that," the captain replied snippishly. "What I want to know is where you think you're going to put it. It won't fit into the aircraft. And we're not going to fly a thousand miles with it sling-loaded. We'll lose too much speed and fuel."

"We're going to put it under your aircraft."

The female pilot seemed interested. "How're you going to do that?"

Riley pointed as Powers began directing the movement of the boat between the two front wheels of the Blackhawk. "We've got something called a Boltz rig."

"Never heard of it," the captain snapped.

Riley decided to ignore him. "The rig is a series of straps that go around the entire boat, both directions. We run the straps through the cargo bay and crank down on them. The rubber boat kind of melds along the bottom of the aircraft."

Hobbes walked over closer to watch what they were doing to her aircraft. "How do we release it if we have to, or when we get wherever it is you're going?"

Riley pointed. "Single point release inside the aircraft. Just like a sling load but the boat will almost seem like part of the airframe and won't slow you down or eat fuel. You can fly with the cargo doors closed. The engine will be inside the boat."

Davidson was shaking his head. "I've never heard of this here Boltz rig."

"It was invented by, and named after, a team sergeant in 5th Special Forces Group." Riley decided he'd better reassure the pilots. "It's already been evaluated and tested by the aviation board. It's been approved by them for use. The 5th Group pilots have flown quite a bit like this."

Hobbes looked at Riley. "I'll have to take your word on that. Can you tell me where we're going?"

"You got a chart of the Caribbean?" She nodded and pulled one out of her map case. Riley pointed. "Right there."

The captain exploded upon seeing the location. "Bullshit! What the hell is this? You guys come waltzing off this plane like you own the goddamn place. No uniforms. You introduce yourself without any rank. You're carrying weapons and equipment I've never seen before. You start rigging up our aircraft with some piece of shit I've never heard of. And now you want us to fly you to just off the coast of Colombia? No way. I'm not going to fly with that thing under the bird. Something will go wrong with it and it'll kill us all. I'm going to call the colonel and tell him what's going on."

Powers had wandered over during the exchange, leaving Partusi in charge of the rigging. Riley looked at the team sergeant, who shook his head slightly. Riley stepped in front of the captain. "I'm sorry. For security reasons we can't let you talk to anyone now. I believe your orders were to do what I said. I understand that this is very unusual, but all you have to do is fly us to that point and drop us off."

Riley sighed when he saw that reason wasn't going to work with this officer. That was all he needed right now—some asshole to get stupid. The captain grabbed his hat from out of the aircraft and turned for the base ops building, only to find Powers standing in front of him.

"You ain't going nowhere."

Hobbes quickly tried to defuse the situation. "Everyone calm down." She looked at Powers. "It takes two of us to fly and if you hurt him we aren't going anywhere."

Powers shrugged. "I didn't say anything about hurting him. I just said he wasn't going anywhere—and he isn't."

She turned to Davidson. "Sir, the colonel told us to do what these men say. As PIC I'm willing to give it a shot, flying with the boat." She turned to Riley. "Would it be all right if we tried lifting here, so we can check out how the aircraft feels and reacts with that thing under it?"

Riley was willing to be reasonable. "Sure. You're the pilot."

Hobbes went over to the captain and Riley smiled when he overheard what she whispered to him. At least she had some common sense. "Sir, in case you haven't noticed, these guys have magazines in their weapons and they don't have any blank adapters. Those are live grenades on their harnesses. This is the real thing and I for one don't want to stand here arguing with them."

Davidson gave in. "Fine. Fine. Let's get the show on the road."

Hobbes came back over to Riley. "There will be no trouble."

Riley gestured at the captain. "What's his problem?"

Hobbes leaned closer so Davidson wouldn't overhear. "His dick gets shorter when he has to fly with a woman. He loses an inch or so of his manliness. Makes him irritable."

## BOGOTA
## 6:00 P.M.

Maria was in the shower getting ready to leave for work and Rich Stevens was relaxing, lying on his bed, when the noise of someone knocking on the door disturbed his reverie. Stevens was irritated. Who the hell could that be? Tonight was his night off. He had told everyone on the staff that he didn't want to be disturbed today because he needed to rest after all the night work he'd been doing.

Stevens glanced toward the partly open bathroom door. The knocking came again, more insistent. He jumped up and closed the bathroom door all the way. He grimaced as he realized the noise of the shower still came through. He threw on a robe and went over to his door and opened it a crack. "Yeah?"

One of the staffers from the embassy communications room stood there. "You got a call from the States."

"So what? I left word not to be disturbed. I've been busting my ass working all these nights and you wake me up to tell me I got a phone call? Couldn't you have just taken a message?"

The man was trying to see past him and was obviously confused by the sound of the shower in the background. Stevens had tried to be as careful as possible about having Maria in his room, although the fact that he had to sign her in and out of the embassy compound precluded him from being totally discreet. He didn't need someone prying into his personal life. He knew Washington would take a dim view of a married agent sleeping around, although Stevens found that superior attitude ridiculously hypocritical based on his observations of the marital merry-go-round in Washington.

The office clerk rolled his eyes. "Hey, don't get on my case. No, I couldn't just take a message. Not on a Flash priority call over the STU-III. The caller is still on hold, waiting for you, so you'd better get your ass in gear." The man turned and walked away.

Stevens shut the door and quickly put his pants on, his mind working as he tried to figure out why he'd be getting a Flash call today on the secure phone. It had to be about the hit the next night. He hadn't even told Maria that he would have to work the next evening. He had been waiting until she got ready to go to work this evening. As he finished dressing, she came out of the bathroom, drying herself. As always the sight of her naked took his breath away. He couldn't believe his luck in finding her.

"What is it?"

Stevens strode over to the door. "I've got to take a priority call from the States. I'll be right back." He opened the door and left.

Five minutes later he was back and in an even worse mood. Maria was dressed and ready to leave. She nuzzled up to him as he came in. "I must go to work now but I will be back early, say at eleven tonight?"

Stevens shook his head. "I'm sorry. Something just came up. I won't be able to see you tonight."

Maria looked surprised. "Why not?"

"I have to work again. Just like last night."

Maria seemed confused. "But I thought you were done with that."

Stevens glanced up in surprise. Why would she say a thing like that? "Why did you think I was done working at night?"

Maria seemed flustered. "Well, I, well, you did not tell me that you work at night again, so I thought you not work anymore at night." She looked concerned. "You not going to do anything dangerous are you? Not like on 'Miami Vice' show. What do you call it—undercover?"

Stevens laughed. "No. I'm not going undercover. All I do is sit right here in the embassy and listen to radios. Just like I've done the last two nights I worked."

Stevens appreciated Maria's concern. He was edgy about having the schedule moved up one night and being notified at the last minute. They must have known about the change all day, yet they had held off on calling him until now. He was trying to sort out the reasons for that as he said good-bye to Maria.

Once she was gone, Stevens went back into the main embassy building to the communications room. The NSA communications specialist acting as duty officer spoke up as Stevens came in. "Don't tell me you're going to be here all night again."

Stevens nodded glumly. "Yep." He handed the comm man a

list. "Could you punch me up that frequency and azimuth and direction on the SATCOM? Hook it into booth one. I'll work out of there again."

The man twirled the dials on one of the many machines set up in the room. He looked up. "You got the KAK?"

Stevens pulled out of his pocket the small metal plug holding the encryption and decryption codes that he had just retrieved from the embassy vault and handed it to the man. The comm specialist took it and checked to see that it was labeled for the proper time period. Then he plugged it into a small black scrambler. He pushed a button and the machine hummed. He pulled the KAK back out and handed it to Stevens. "All right. You're all set to go. Freq'd on the radio and coded on the scrambler. Have fun."

Stevens went into booth one and turned on the terminal. He put on his headset and keyed the mike. "Hammer Base, this is Lantern. Over." He waited a few seconds and then the answer came.

"This is Hammer Base. Over." Stevens recognized Westland's voice. Damn bitch was probably the one who cut me out, he thought. Goddamn Clowns In Action and their paranoia.

"I'm ready down at this end. Could you fill me in on what the hell is going on? Why the move up?" Stevens released the send button and waited. When no answer was forthcoming he remembered that he had forgotten to give the obligatory "over." Goddamn military and their radio games. He keyed the mike again. "Over."

The answer came back. "It's for security reasons. We've been concerned about a leak so we thought it best to keep it in tight and move things forward. Over."

Figures, Stevens thought. Goddamn paranoia. He keyed the mike again. "Is the target still the same or am I not authorized to know that either? Over."

"Target's the same and hit time is the same, just twenty-four hours earlier. Just relax. We've got a long night ahead. Out."

Just great, Stevens muttered to himself.

## HOWARD AIR FORCE BASE, PANAMA
### 6:23 P.M.

The trial run with the boat attached had gone well. Hobbes and Davidson had topped off the tanks again and then planned their flight route. Since the majority of the route would be over water, they would use the Doppler internal navigational device to direct them, in combination with following an azimuth and monitoring their speed. Hobbes had been frank with Riley about her lack of faith in the Doppler's accuracy, especially over water.

Riley had told her that all she had to do was get them within thirty kilometers of the indicated drop-off point, which was sixty kilometers due east of Barranquilla. She said she could do that. The whine of the turbine engines increased. Hobbes pulled in collective and the aircraft shuddered as it picked up.

The six members of Eyes Three sat on the floor inside the cargo bay and watched the ground fall away below them as the Blackhawk lifted and turned east, flitting over the Panamanian jungle toward the Caribbean. They were on their way.

## OUTSKIRTS OF BOGOTA
### 6:40 P.M.

Ring Man looked up from the pool table, where he had just been ready to make a shot. "What line?"

His chief aide and bodyguard, Ponte, indicated the phone near the door. "Line two."

Ring Man went over and picked up the phone. Ponte noted that the Ring Man's body became rigid as he talked into the phone. Not a good sign. He listened to his boss's end of the conversation.

"Talk."

"Just like the other two?"

"Tonight?"

"How long ago?"

"Do you know when?"

"Stay there. I'll get back to you."

Ring Man hung up the phone. He looked across at Ponte. His eyes seemed clouded over. Ponte waited patiently. He'd seen that look before. It meant his boss was thinking. Finally he seemed to come down to earth.

Ring Man looked at his watch and then at Ponte. "There's a job you have to do. It must be done quickly. Time is of the essence. Here is what I want done. Get a hold of . . . "

## BOGOTA
## 7:57 P.M.

Stevens was a quarter of the way through the book he had brought with him to help the night pass, when he was interrupted by the duty officer rapping on the door of the booth he was in. He cracked the door open. "Yeah, what's up?"

"You got a local phone call."

Stevens frowned. Who would be calling him? He got up, left the booth, and went to the phone on the wall.

"Stevens here."

"Rich, this is Maria."

Shit, she wasn't ever supposed to call him at work. Stevens glanced around nervously. The duty man was playing games on his desk computer. Stevens hissed into the phone. "I can't talk now. I'm busy."

"Don't hang up, Rich. I'm in trouble. I need your help right away."

Christ! Stevens thought. Women. "I'm on duty. I'll see you tomorrow."

"It cannot wait until tomorrow. Only for five minutes. That's all I need you for."

She sounded like she really was in trouble. Like she had just been crying. "What's the matter? What do you need me for?"

"I cannot tell you on the phone. Just come to my uncle's bar. Around back. I will be waiting for you there. It will only take five minutes. I need your help very much."

Stevens calculated. The team hadn't even infiltrated yet. Hell, no one would miss him. On the last two missions no one had even talked to him until it was over. At that time it had only been Westland calling to verify that he had copied the team's final report on target destruction so he could relay it to Alegre. He could have had a heart attack and no one would have noticed. He pictured Maria without clothes on. "All right. I'll be there in a couple of minutes. But I can't stay longer than five minutes, then I have to get back."

"Oh, thank you, Rich. Thank you."

Stevens hung up the phone and went over to the duty officer. "I need you to cover for me for a little while. I have to go take care of something."

The duty officer winked knowingly. "Yeah, sure. You want me to monitor your net?"

Stevens shook his head. The man wasn't cleared for it. "No. Nothing's going to be happening in there for a while. I'll be back before then."

Stevens left the embassy and went across the street. He looked in the front door of the cafe. Everything looked all right. He wondered what the hell was the matter with Maria. Goddamn women. They got upset at the stupidest things. He hoped she wasn't going to pull some sort of "marry me" bullshit. Christ, he thought suddenly, she'd better not be pregnant. He'd be damned if he would take responsibility for that. She'd told him she was on the pill.

Stevens headed around to the back and stopped as another thought hit him. Maybe her uncle had found out about the two of them and was waiting back there to beat the crap out of the Yankee who was porking his niece. Stevens smiled grimly to himself. If that was the case then the guy had another thing coming. He loosened his snub nose revolver in his waist holster and strode around the corner. He peered into the dark trying to see.

He started as a figure came out of the shadows. It was Maria. She looked very anxious. Stevens relaxed a little.

"Rich! I am happy you come. Follow me."

"Whoa! Where're we going and what's the problem?"

"Just come here and I will tell you."

Stevens allowed her to lead him farther into the alley. Suddenly he had the feeling they weren't alone. His worries about her uncle resurfaced. He wheeled. Two men stood there holding nasty-looking submachine guns.

Jesus Christ, thought Stevens. That's a hell of a lot of fire-power to bring to bear on a guy just for going out with a girl. He forgot any thought he might have had about pulling his revolver. He turned to Maria. "What's going on? Who are these guys?"

She stepped forward, reached calmly under his jacket, and removed his revolver. "Shut up, gringo, and come this way."

# COAST OF COLOMBIA
# 8:50 P.M.

Riley heard Hobbes through the headset. "This is it. As close as I can figure to where you want."

"Roger. Get down to ten and ten. Drop on my thumbs-up. Thanks." Riley liked that this target was just in from the coast, so they could infiltrate and exfiltrate by water. He felt it was much safer than either parachuting or going in direct with helicopters. Plus, by using the regular Blackhawk with no advance warning for infiltration, they had cut out a lot of people knowing where the target was or even that an operation was being mounted.

The two pilots would know the general area, but they had an almost three-hour flight back to Panama and they would be met by military police when they landed. Pike had arranged with the SOUTHCOM commander for the MPs to hold the two pilots for the night. Riley felt sorry for the warrant but he wished the cap-tain could be held for a couple extra days.

"Roger. Good luck," Hobbes offered. The captain said noth-ing.

Riley took off the headset. The helicopter began flying about ten feet above the water, with a forward speed of ten knots. Riley slid open the right cargo door while Powers opened the left.

The men sat on the edge, three to a side, their waterproofed rucksacks in their laps. Riley turned back toward the pilots. Hobbes was looking at him over her shoulder. Riley gave her a thumbs-up and she hit the release on her cyclic.

The Zodiac dropped away from the aircraft and hit the water. Two at a time, one from each side, the members of Eyes Three quickly followed. The first pair, Partusi and Holder, landed within five meters of the boat. Riley was the last one off the right side. He threw out his ruck and shoved himself off the deck. As he descended he twisted in the air so that his back faced the flight direction. He put his hands behind his neck, interlacing his fingers, and touched his elbows together in front of his face. The ten-knot forward speed and the fall combined to slam him into the water, causing him to lose his breath momentarily. He popped to the surface and looked around. With a last flyby, the Blackhawk disappeared into the night sky, leaving him with the sound of the waves.

Riley put on his fins in the water and then headed for the Zodiac. Reaching it he clambered on board. Partusi, as first man on the raft, had already checked for gas fumes to make sure the fuel bladders had not leaked during the trip or drop.

As soon as everyone was on board, Riley broke out the MANPADS and checked their position.

Powers looked over his shoulder. "How we doing?"

Riley nodded. "Good. We're only about eight klicks west of where we should be." He pulled out a chart and a red-lens flashlight and plotted, confirming the readout from the MANPADS. "We go that way."

While Riley had been plotting, Partusi had locked the engine onto the rear. At Riley's direction, Partusi fired it up. Riley sat on one side of the rear and navigated while Partusi drove. The forty-horsepower short-shaft engine initially lifted the bow of the Zodiac, but as the boat picked up speed it flattened out and planed across the waves.

# OUTSKIRTS OF BOGOTA
# 9:00 P.M.

It didn't take a large leap of imagination on Rich Stevens's part to realize that he was in big trouble. The fact that he had been blindfolded, thrown in the back of a car, and driven for twenty minutes to his present location was only the beginning. Now he was tied to a chair in the middle of a warehouse. His arms were bound flat down on the arms of the chair and his chest was against the back. The chair itself was bolted to the concrete floor. Stevens knew he wasn't going anywhere without permission.

The two men guarding him looked as if they'd like nothing better than to empty their submachine guns into him. The DEA agent had been in some hairy situations in his career but never one where he felt so afraid and helpless.

He heard footsteps behind him, and three people walked around into his field of vision. Stevens stared at Maria, who was trailing two other men. She stared back with the hint of a smile on her face. The lead man stood in front of him. Stevens noted that the man had rings on every finger. Suddenly one of those hands flew out and struck him on the side of the face. Stevens tasted blood.

"Where and when is the raid coming tonight?"

Stevens stared at the man in confusion. How could the man know there was an attack tonight? The man must have interpreted his hesitation as defiance, because he reached forward, grabbed Stevens's face with one hand, and tilted his head up so he looked into his eyes.

"You will talk to me, pig. You will tell me what I want to know. The stupider you act, the more it will hurt, but you will eventually talk. Everyone does."

The man let go of him and nodded to the other man who accompanied him. This man, a short, squat, ugly fellow, pulled a meat cleaver out of the gym bag he had carried in. Stevens watched in confusion and growing fear as the man calmly walked over. He talked to one of the guards in Spanish. The guard grabbed Stevens's left hand and curled in all the fingers except the ring finger. Stevens stared in mesmerized horror as the cleaver flashed down and severed his finger. He was initially too shocked to feel the pain. He watched the blood squirt out of the stump. Then he screamed as the pain hit him.

The man with the rings grabbed his face again. "Where and when will the raid occur?"

Stevens was still too stunned to reply. It was all moving too fast. His mind hadn't caught up to the reality of his predicament. It seemed like a terrible dream, but the pain from his missing finger convinced him that it wasn't. The man with the cleaver moved forward and nodded at the other guard. Stevens futilely tried fighting as the man grabbed his hand and extended the middle finger.

"No!" The man in charge stepped forward. Stevens felt a moment of relief. They had finally come to their senses. "We do not have time to waste. We need the information now."

A soft voice spoke up. "I know what to do."

Stevens watched as Maria stepped forward. "Untie him and hold him up." The two guards did as instructed. She reached forward, undid his belt, and unzipped his pants. She pulled down his pants and underpants and grabbed him between the legs.

Maria smiled at him, a smile full of malice. "Why are you not growing hard like you always did when I grabbed you here before?" She turned to the man who had cut off Stevens's finger. "Give me the cleaver."

Stevens's fear overflowed his dike of professionalism. "Barranquilla! They'll be in position by one in the morning. The attack is supposed to occur at three."

Maria let go of him and stepped back. The two guards threw Stevens back in the chair. The man in apparent command came forward. "I need more information. How many men? How are they coming in and leaving? How will they destroy the lab?"

Stevens slumped down in the chair, staring numbly at his severed finger lying on the floor. "Six men. I don't know how they are getting in and out. Probably helicopter. They'll use either helicopter gunships or an air force gunship to destroy the target."

"How did your people find out the lab's location?"

Stevens shrugged. "Some contact through the CIA."

The man with the rings grabbed Stevens's face again. "That can't be. Don't lie to me."

Stevens protested weakly. "All I know is that someone contacts the CIA through a cutout down here, and they forward the information to Washington. It's been the same for all three missions."

# BOGOTA
# 9:00 P.M.

Peter Dotson, the communications man on watch duty for the embassy, looked at the clock on the wall with growing concern and irritation. Stevens should have been back an hour ago. What the hell happens if someone calls booth one and Stevens isn't there to answer?

Dotson swore to himself. He sure as hell wasn't going to cover for the drunken asshole. The guy was probably out with that local woman from the Embassy Cafe. Dotson had seen the two of them talking in the cafe. He wondered what the hell she saw in the old DEA agent. He pictured the two together. He could easily see what Stevens saw in the woman.

Dotson looked at the clock again. He'd give it another thirty minutes. Then he'd have to do something about the net Stevens was supposed to be monitoring.

# 9:48 P.M.

Dotson looked at the clock again. His self-imposed deadline had passed almost twenty minutes ago and he had done nothing. His stomach was churning. He didn't like the idea of raising the red flag, even if he thought Stevens was a jerk. Leaving a top secret net was a serious violation, especially when it looked as though it had been for unofficial reasons. Dotson didn't like the idea of destroying someone's career. Still . . .

He looked at the clock again. He forced himself to change his nervousness to anger. Stevens knew better. He had put his own ass in the crack and it wasn't Dotson's fault if he had to report him. Hell, it was his job.

Despite his resolution to grow angry, Dotson approached the comm booth reluctantly. The shit was going to hit the fan. He opened the door and sat down, then he put the boom mike on his head and keyed it. "Any station this net, this is Echo Oscar Five. Over."

He waited a few seconds and then repeated. "Any station this net, this is Echo Oscar Five. Over."

"Echo Oscar Five, this is Hammer Base. Am I correct in your call sign? Are you the comm duty officer in Bogota? Where's Lantern? Over."

"Roger on my call sign. This is the duty officer. If by Lantern you mean Stevens, he left here about two hours ago. That's why I'm coming up on this net. It's been left unmonitored for that time period. Over."

# FORT BELVOIR, VIRGINIA
# 9:49 P.M.

Westland looked across the room at Pike. He had heard the last broadcast and the surprised look on his face echoed what Westland was feeling. "Where is Stevens? Over."

"I don't know. He received a phone call just before he left. Said he would be back in a little while. That was almost two hours ago. Over."

Westland keyed the mike. "Wait one. Over." She turned to Pike. "What do we do now?"

The general rubbed his hand over his chin. "I don't know. We can abort, but I'd hate to do that right now. They're already on their way in and have left the helicopter by now." A thought seemed to strike him. "Shit! We can't even contact them now anyway. They're in the water and won't come up on the SATCOM until they cross the beach and radio in their initial entry report."

Westland nodded. "Let's see if we can track down Stevens before then." She turned to the radio. "Echo Oscar Five, this is Hammer Base. Get Jameson. I want him on this net in five mikes. Over."

"Roger that. Jameson in five mikes. Over."

Pike grabbed his STU-III classified phone. "I'm going to get the gunship in the air now," he said as he dialed Panama.

# BARRANQUILLA, COLOMBIA
# 10:02 P.M.

Holding his rucksack, Riley fell backward off the side of the low-lying boat. Once in the water, he let go of the ruck and allowed it to float behind him on a six-foot line. Five of the members of Eyes Three gathered in the water and hooked together using a safety line and snap links. Powers was still on board. He turned all the valves in the boat to open, allowing air to pass between the five chambers. He then opened up a one-way bleed valve. Air rushed out of the boat as Powers slid overboard and joined the rest of the team.

The boat settled lower and lower in the water; finally the engine pulled it under and it sank. The only thing that remained where the boat had been was a small black float. It was attached to the Zodiac with a length of line and marked the boat's grave on the bottom, fifteen feet below the surface.

The safety line tied around Riley's waist tugged gently as the rest of the team floated behind him. Riley turned back seaward and tapped the man next to him, gesturing toward the shore. Holder nodded and, with Lane, unhooked from the safety line and started finning toward the shore, two hundred meters away.

Riley lost sight of the two men when they were only ten meters away. With just their masked heads above the surface of the water, the swimmers were virtually invisible. Riley patiently finned in place, using the silhouettes of the mountains behind the beach to judge his relative position. The run in had gone faster than expected. After the two-man security team had reconnoitered the landing site, they could move in.

Finally, after ten minutes, Riley spotted the brief flash of a green chem light coming from the wood line across from the beach. All clear. He tugged on the safety line and the remaining four members of Eyes Three started finning in toward the light.

Fifty meters from shore Riley turned over and started swimming slowly on his stomach, careful not to allow his fins to break the surface. Despite the security team's safe signal he was still cautious. When he felt the sand of the bottom come up he allowed the waves to slide him as far forward as they could onto the beach. The other three members beached themselves to his right. Riley slid back into the water and removed the fins from the man to his right, slipping the back loops over his wrist. He crawled forward and let that man do the same for him. Then Riley put his ruck on his back.

Carefully, Riley slid the hood down from around his head and listened to the night air. Nothing but the sounds of surf and the night creatures in the wood line ahead. Three hundred meters off to his left, he could see the small wooden dock that was the reference point. They had landed in the proper spot.

Riley received a nudge from the right telling him all were ready. With a careful glance each way down the beach, he stood up quickly and sprinted across the sand toward the wood line. The rest of the team followed. He broke into the trees and was immediately grabbed by Lane, one of the two security men who had swum in earlier. "We're clear to fifty meters. No sign of anything."

Riley nodded and quickly stuffed the fins into his backpack. He removed the night-vision goggles and his MP5 submachine gun from their waterproof wrappings, strapped on a shoulder holster, and replaced the .45 Colt automatic he had been carrying in his hand. He waited patiently as each man prepared his weapon. Powers was still carrying his trademark AK-47. Lane bolted together the massive Haskins .50-caliber sniper rifle. While they were doing this, the two security men had gone back out on the beach and obscured the trail across the sand.

All was ready. Riley checked the glowing dial of his watch: 2223. Another hour to target.


# FORT BELVOIR, VIRGINIA
## 10:30 P.M.

"I've got marines in civvies checking all the local places where Stevens could be. We're getting nothing out of the bartender from the Embassy Cafe where the girl Stevens was with works. He's saying nothing and we really can't put too much heat on him considering we're in his country. Over."

Westland stared at the radio in frustration. Jameson's words only reinforced the growing bad feeling she had in her stomach. "Where do you think Stevens is then? Over."

Westland could almost see Jameson shrug as the reply came back. "He probably went out to catch a quick snort and maybe a quick piece of ass, if you'll pardon the expression. Never should have had a goddamn alcoholic on this mission in the first place. Over."

Westland shook her head. She looked at Pike, who angrily gestured at the radio. "Tell them to find him."

She keyed the mike again. "Keep looking. We need to find him. You stay on this net and monitor for him. Out." She turned to Pike. "What do you suggest, General?"

Pike sighed. "I don't like it. We all knew Stevens had problems but I didn't think he'd do something like this. We abort. If it's nothing, we can try again later, but if it isn't, they're in big trouble."

Westland was relieved to find that Pike was thinking the same way she was. "I agree. As soon as we get their initial entry report, we'll tell them to abort."

# BARRANQUILLA
## 11:24 P.M.

Riley slowly edged forward through the dense vegetation, moving one stealthy step at a time toward the target, which should be just over the next piece of slightly higher ground. Since leaving the beach, their route had taken them through swampland interspersed with small areas of higher dry ground.

They moved another two hundred meters inland. Powers, acting as the point man, signaled a halt, and Riley crept forward to the team sergeant. In the glow of arc lights he could see their target. "Shit!" he muttered.

Activity and lots of it. Riley scanned the compound and felt worse the more he saw. At least thirty personnel were up and moving around. They were off-loading weapons from trucks and on-loading cocaine. Riley didn't need to be clairvoyant to realize what this meant.

"Keep an eye on it," he whispered to Powers as he slid back to where the rest of the team waited.

He crawled next to Marzan, who had just set out the SATCOM satellite minidisk antenna. "You set?" he whispered. Marzan nodded. Riley turned down the volume on the radio to minimum and picked up the handset.

"Hammer Base, this is Eyes Three. Over."

The answer was almost instantaneous. "Eyes Three, this is Hammer Base. Over."

At least they were awake up there. "We've got a shitload of activity down here. They're moving weapons in and cocaine out. What's the status of Hammer? Over."

"Hammer is en route. Listen closely. The mission is an abort. I say again, the mission is an abort. Hammer will be on station in forty-five minutes. Use only if needed to cover your exfiltration. Over."

Shit, Riley cursed again. "What happened? Over."

Riley heard Pike's voice come on, replacing Westland's. "Don't worry about that right now, just get the hell out of there. Over."

"Roger." Riley handed the headset back to Marzan. He quickly considered their options. Hell, there were no options. They had to go back the way they came. Riley's thoughts were interrupted by Powers inching back from the tree line.

"We got company coming. About ten sicarios are coming in this direction from the camp and they're loaded for bear. They got patrols heading out in all directions. It's like they were expecting us. I also spotted two Redeye missiles getting off-loaded."

Riley thought rapidly. If they were unloading antiaircraft missiles up there, the sicarios were definitely expecting something. It wouldn't do any good to wait for Hammer's covering fire. Plus they'd probably be found by then. He turned to the team and hissed, "Time to vamoose. Pike just gave me an abort. Let's go!"

Marzan was packing up the primary radio. Riley had the backup SATCOM in his ruck. He pulled out one of the Claymores in there and hung its carrying bag around his neck, as did the other members of the team. Once everyone was ready, Riley started to lead the team back toward the shore. He could hear the sicarios breaking brush behind them.

Riley's mind raced with various thoughts: wondering how the mission could have been compromised; judging the distance to the shore and how long it would take; considering how they would get across the beach; hoping it wasn't guarded.

Despite Riley's night-vision goggles, the dense vegetation cut visibility down to only a few feet. It was probably that, plus his lack of concentration, that allowed Riley to almost walk on top of the Colombian sicarios coming in from the north.

The surprised sicarios' point man called out as he practically collided with Riley. It was hard to say who was the more startled, but Riley's reactions were swifter. He swung up his MP5, firing a silenced burst into the sicario. The man flew back, screaming. Instantly all hell broke loose as tracers split the night.

The man Riley had killed was obviously the point man for a larger party. His partners in crime were now firing blindly into the dark. Riley tore off his goggles, which had blanked out from the light of the muzzle flashes.

"Break left! Break left!" Riley screamed as he blindly gave covering fire. He could hear Powers yelling as the team sergeant led the rest of the men off ninety degrees to the left in an attempt to break contact.

Riley followed in that direction, occasionally firing a quick burst to the rear. He changed magazines as he ran, branches slapping him in the face. He couldn't see well, since his eyes were still adjusting from the goggles to the moonlight. Strings of tracers flying through the trees let him know the sicarios were still following. Riley could hear yelling in Spanish from other sides as more patrols closed in.

Riley sprinted in the direction the team had gone. As he circumvented a dense thicket of thornbushes, a hand reached out and grabbed his upper right arm. Riley swung the muzzle of his weapon in that direction but halted a split second before firing as he heard Powers's voice. "I got a Claymore on a wire in front of you."

Powers guided Riley over the trip wire he had just strung out across the path. The wire ran to a Claymore mine the team sergeant had quickly attached with a few wraps of electrical tape to a small tree at chest height. Riley followed his team sergeant.

Riley knew that the other four team members were not too far ahead. The SOP was for the team to go 300 meters in the break direction, then turn back on the original azimuth they had been on prior to contact. Riley estimated they had already gone 250 meters, although he sure as hell hadn't been keeping a pace count.

The crash of the rigged Claymore behind them was followed by screams from those not killed outright. As it exploded, the mine sprayed the jungle with thousands of tiny ball bearings.

Riley stepped out behind Powers into a sparsely treed area. Twenty meters ahead, the rest of the team was just about to go into the far wood line.

Riley dove for cover as the roar of automatic weapons seared the night. He heard Marzan cry out, screaming for Partusi, the medic. Riley poked his head up. The four other members of the team had gone to ground just short of the wood line. They were taking fire from their right front. Riley could see muzzle flashes in the far trees. He fired off a sustained burst in that direction, giving the men some covering fire. Powers, lying next to him, also emptied a magazine.

Riley glanced over at his four teammates as he changed magazines. Partusi was the only one moving, still trying to drag Marzan back toward the tree line that Powers and Riley had just exited. Lane and Holder were giving them covering fire. Even as he watched, Riley saw Partusi punched down with the impact of rounds. The medic didn't move again. An explosion seared the night in the vicinity of Lane and Holder. When Riley's eyes cleared, he could barely make out those men's crumpled forms.

A group of sicarios burst from the wood line, firing wildly. Riley and Powers raked the group in concert, mowing them down. Riley attempted to move forward to check out his men but was grabbed by Powers and slammed into the ground. A line of tracers reached out at an angle from the far tree line and probed the ground, running over the prone bodies of Riley's men.

"They're all dead!" Powers yelled at him over the sound of the firing. "We got to get out of here."

Riley was torn. He didn't want to leave his men, even if they were dead. He fired another burst toward the source of the tracers. He was rewarded by the deadly stream of bullets turning his way, joined by several others.

Powers grabbed him by the arm and started pulling him away. "Let's go! You can't do anything for them."

Riley allowed himself to be led away. Initially the crackle of rounds in the air around them diminished, but Riley knew it wouldn't be long before the chase would be on again. He calculated rapidly as Powers led him on a northwest course, directly toward the ocean. They were probably only three hundred meters from the water. If they could get there and get in the water without being seen, they could make it. He felt the sweat pouring down his body underneath the rubber of his wet suit. Not far now.

Riley could hear the sound of pursuit pick up behind them. All he could hope was that they didn't run into anyone on their way to the beach. As if in answer to that thought, Riley heard voices off to their left front. The Colombians were yelling to each other, trying to coordinate their search.

Riley contented himself with following Powers, as the veteran wove his way toward the coast, using the noise the patrols were making to avoid them. Faintly, and then growing stronger, the pounding of the surf could be heard. Powers came to a halt at the edge of the tree line and peered out.

"Fuck," Powers muttered. A group of five sicarios stood on the beach looking toward the tree line, weapons at the ready. Powers turned to Riley. "Here's what we do—and I don't want any bullshit arguments from you. I'm going to head south, away from the city. Give me two minutes to move and then I'm going to blow a grenade and pop some tracers across the beach. That ought to draw these guys down my way. You hit the water and head for the boat.

"I'll keep running to the south and stay about four hundred meters from the shore. You get to the boat, bring it up, and then come up on the spare SATCOM. Get Hammer to circle. I'll tie an infrared chem light to my hood and they can track me with that, and the bad guys using thermals. With Hammer giving me covering fire I can make it to the beach, and Hammer can guide you in to pick me up."

Riley's brain spun as he listened to this desperate plan. The situation called for extreme measures, but he'd be damned if he was going to leave his team sergeant holding the bag. "Sounds good, but I'll run the diversion and you swim out."

Powers grabbed Riley by the shoulders and looked into his eyes. "Listen, asshole, we ain't got no time to argue. It will take me twice as long as you to swim out to the boat. Also, I'm a hell of a lot better at surviving in the woods than you are. GO!" With that, Powers turned and disappeared into the darkness.

# MONDAY,
# 2 SEPTEMBER

## BARRANQUILLA
## 12:14 A.M.

Riley forced himself to remain calm. He stopped finning and looked over his shoulder back toward shore. From the curve of the beach, he knew he was very close to the buoy marking the Zodiac's watery grave. He needed to relax and search the area slowly. It wouldn't do him any good to splash around and miss the buoy by ten meters. Every so often, as he topped a swell, he would turn over onto his stomach and scan the area, trying to spot the low-lying marker.

A sense of urgency tightened its icy grip around his heart. It had already been over twenty minutes since he had heard Powers's diversion. He'd made the dash across the beach as soon as the sicarios had taken off toward the sound of the firing. Shortly after he started swimming, he'd heard another burst of fire and some explosions that sounded like grenades. He was afraid that Powers had made contact again. Since then Riley hadn't heard anything. He prayed his team sergeant was still alive.

## FORT BELVOIR, VIRGINIA
## 12:18 A.M.

"This is Hammer. I say again, I have negative radio contact with Eyes Three element. Over."

208

Westland stared at the radio, her brow furrowed in thought as Pike talked into the mike.

"Can you make contact with the *Garcia*? Over."

"Wait one."

Pike took a deep breath as he sat back in the chair and endured the pause. He'd much rather be out there in the action than sitting here on his ass talking on a radio.

"Roger. We have contact with the *Garcia*. Over."

"Order its captain to move in closer, to within forty-five kilometers. Over."

"Roger, will relay your order. Over."

Pike waited a minute and then keyed the mike again. "What about IR chem lights or strobes on the shore? Do you have anything on your screens? Over."

"Negative on that. Through the thermals we can see a lot of people running around near the target, but no indication of friendlies. Over."

Westland suddenly leaned forward. "Ask Hammer to use its thermals over the water, between the boats and shore. Maybe they're in the water, trying to swim out."

Pike nodded. "I didn't think of that." He keyed the mike. "Hammer, this is Hammer Base. Scan the water near the shore for any swimmers. Our people may be trying to swim out to the boat. Over."

The disembodied voice from the Spectre gunship rogered the message and Westland sat back in her chair as she waited for the result.

She rubbed her eyes wearily. What a screwup. Still no word on Stevens. No word from the team. This had the potential for disaster written all over it. Always before when she'd heard about something like this it had seemed kind of distant. Like watching a TV show or reading a spy novel. But now that the men in danger were flesh and blood people she was working with, it all seemed so different. Not glamorous or thrilling, the way it sounded when field agents recounted stories of their missions.

The worst part for Westland was the realization that Dave Riley had predicted this very occurrence. She hadn't been convinced there was a leak. Now she was. The story of Stevens cavorting with a local woman had surfaced as Jameson tried tracking down the missing DEA agent. Westland was upset with Jameson for not having reported it earlier. It was a little late now to do us much good, she thought bitterly. Riley had pointed to Stevens as a weak link from the start. Unfortunately, he'd been proven correct.

She started as she heard the gunship come back on the air.

"Hammer Base, I've got a heat source in the water approximately four hundred meters from shore. Over."

# BARRANQUILLA
# 12:20 A.M.

Riley rode the swell and finned hard, rising up out of the water to his midchest. He scanned the immediate area. Out of the corner of his eye he spotted a black dot—the buoy. He swam over to it and grabbed the line. He released his ruck from its buddy line and attached the snap link to the buoy line. Taking a deep breath, he pulled himself down on the line to the boat. The line was tied directly into a large carbon dioxide-charged bottle strapped to the boat's floorboards. Riley fumbled along the bottle until he felt the valve. He pulled the release, let go of the boat, and swam to the surface.

He had barely taken his second breath of air when the Zodiac popped up almost underneath him. The carbon dioxide was still inflating the boat as Riley clambered over the side. He pulled in his ruck. When the gas stopped hissing, he closed the inlet valve and the compartmental valves. Then he tore through the waterproof bags in his pack and pulled out the SATCOM radio.

He didn't bother with a bounce-back test, just keyed the mike and spoke. "Hammer, this is Nail Three Five. Do you have an IR chem light on shore, moving south along the coast, about four hundred meters in? Over."

"Nail Three Five, this is Hammer. That's a negative. We've scanned the whole area for ten klicks each direction over the past ten minutes and have found nothing. Hammer Base is patched into this net and wants to talk to you. Over."

Riley slumped down in the boat. He was too late. Powers was either dead or captured; otherwise his IR light would still be on. Riley slammed his fist into the side of the boat. His team wiped out. He'd known from the beginning that the whole mission was flaky.

"Nail Three Five, this is Hammer Base. Over."

He stared at the radio. Westland's voice drifted away over the waves. Riley shook his head. He needed a few minutes to sort things out. He ignored the radio.

He considered heading in toward shore, but he knew that would be futile, since he had no way to contact Powers. His team sergeant would be doing something to gain the attention of the gunship, even if his IR chem light wasn't working. The lack of any signal was a very bad sign.

Riley wondered what brilliant cover story was going to be concocted to explain the deaths. He was sure the CIA or DEA had one ready. Which led him to the thought of what the Colombians were going to do with the bodies. Another Desert One scenario with American bodies being displayed to make a political point? And how was the American government going to explain away the bodies in the hands of the Colombian drug cartel? Probably claim there was an aircraft crash during training.

Riley drew a deep breath. It didn't matter to him what the government did. His men were dead. He had other more important questions swirling through his mind. Was Powers really dead or had he been wounded and captured? Who and where was the leak? What was going to happen to the task force now?

Riley knew that the CIA—hell, even the Department of Defense—considered him and his men expendable, just dumb GIs who didn't need to know the whys and the wherefores but just what to do. Well, Riley had a somewhat higher opinion of himself.

He picked up the mike.

# FORT BELVOIR, VIRGINIA
# 12:30 A.M.

Westland stared at the radio in exasperation. Why wasn't Riley answering? She'd recognized his voice even as he gave his call sign. His asking about the IR light meant he had probably left someone alive back on the beach. Maybe the whole team was hiding somewhere and Riley had swum out to bring in the boat.

She jumped as the radio came alive.

"Hammer Base, this is Nail Three Five. Over."

She grabbed the mike before Pike could get to it. "Give us a situation report. Over."

"Four dead. One missing. They were waiting for us. Over."

Oh, God! Westland closed her eyes. Pike took the mike from her limp hand.

"What's the status of the one missing and how do you know the other four are dead? Over."

"I saw the four bodies. I left Eyes Three Six on the shore. He provided a diversion for me so I could swim out. He was supposed to break an IR chem and move south along the coast. Hammer hasn't picked up his light, so he's either dead or captured. Over."

Pike nodded and took a deep breath. He did some quick tactical calculations and made the hard but correct decision. "All right. Bring it on home. There's nothing more you can do. I'm having your pickup ship come in to you. Head on the old azimuth and you should run into the *Garcia*. Moonbeam will direct you if you need it. I'll have Hammer hang around to see if it picks up anything. Over."

"Roger. Break. Hammer, be advised that the bad guys have Redeyes, at least two that we saw. Over."

"This is Hammer. Roger. Thanks for the info. We're too high for them anyway. Out."

Riley reached back and primed the engine. The waterproofing of the engine was perhaps the most amazing feature of the submersible Zodiac. The engine cranked on his second pull. He turned the nose of the boat away from shore and, with a last lingering look over his shoulder, headed out to sea.

# LANGLEY, VIRGINIA
## 7:20 A.M.

Hanks looked up from the paperwork scattered across his desk as Strom walked in. His senior aide looked much the worse for wear after having gotten the alert call from Westland in the middle of the night. Hanks gestured toward the coffeepot. "Grab a mug."

He waited until Strom had his coffee and had settled in the chair across from his desk before jumping him. "What the hell is going on?"

Strom ran a hand through his carefully managed hair. "Nail Three was compromised last night. Of the six Green Beanies, we've got one back over at Belvoir getting debriefed, four dead, bodies not recovered, and one missing."

"Shit." Hanks slammed his mug down on the desk. "I thought the next mission wasn't getting run until tomorrow night. Why weren't we informed of the move up?"

Strom protested weakly. "I didn't know either, sir. Westland didn't bother to keep me updated."

Hanks shook his head. "What the hell was she thinking of?"

"She says the army general in charge, that guy Pike, told her to keep the timing in tight and not let us know, based on their concern about a leak."

"Bullshit! I want her ass! I briefed her myself to keep us up to date. Who the hell does she think she works for?" Hanks fumed for a few seconds, considering the ramifications.

Strom took the opportunity to throw the blame elsewhere, trying to minimize the heat heading his way. "Those SF guys could fuck up a wet dream. I've been working on damage control. We're implementing a cover for the bodies. I already had that worked out." Strom paused in thought. "Hell, I guess we can extend that cover to the missing guy even if the cartel has managed to capture him. As long as he doesn't talk."

Hanks looked at Strom as though his subordinate had two heads. "You know as well as I do that they'll make him talk if they've got him. I don't like saying it, but hopefully he got blown away and his body is lying in the jungle somewhere. How'd they screw this thing up?"

Strom talked quickly, trying to further diffuse the responsibility. "It wasn't all the Special Forces guys' screwup. That DEA guy Stevens was grabbed by the cartel and probably made to talk. He must have given up the time and location. We haven't been able to locate him either."

"Christ." What now? Hanks thought. He considered all the information Strom had given him. The loss of the Special Forces team really wasn't that important right now. It was history. Hanks's job was to look to the future.

What was important was hitting the Ring Man. In fact, it was even more important now that the Ring Man's lab hadn't been hit. And Hanks was no closer to having an answer to that problem. He knew the shit was going to hit the fan in Colombia today. The cartel probably already knew about the role of the U.S. if they had grabbed Stevens, and it wouldn't take them long to trace the plan back to Alegre, especially if they had captured one of the Special Forces team members. There was going to be blood flowing in the streets in a couple of days.

Hanks looked up at Strom, who had waited nervously while his boss sorted things out. "What about the Ring Man hit? Come up with any ideas on how to handle that?"

Strom answered tentatively, not sure what his boss's reaction would be. "Maybe we should talk to the survivor from the Special Forces team, sir."

Hanks looked up, interested. "Get Westland over here."

# FORT BELVOIR, VIRGINIA
# 8:40 A.M.

Riley was tired, depressed, and irritated. He had made it to the navy destroyer *Garcia* without any problem and had been hoisted on board. Two marines had hustled him, without a word, right onto a helicopter waiting on the fantail. He'd been flown to Panama and cross-loaded again onto a C-130 for the trip back to Virginia. Sitting alone in the back of the C-130 for six hours had slammed home to him the realization that the rest of the team wasn't coming back. Unable to rest during the flight, Riley had alternated between pacing the cargo bay and sitting. He had reviewed his actions during the firefight innumerable times, in a pitiless self-flagellation.

He hoped the powers-that-be wouldn't ignore the possibility that Powers might still be alive. He knew they probably wished the team sergeant was dead. That would make everything simpler for everyone, Riley thought angrily. Less ass-covering to do. The thought of Powers being still alive and abandoned triggered an impotent rage in Riley.

He had not been disappointed in Pike's reaction after the debrief. Pike was over at the Pentagon right now pleading his case to the chairman for efforts to be made to find out what had happened to Powers.

Westland had briefed Riley on Stevens during the debrief, then she had taken off for Langley. Riley should have known that the DEA man had been the source of the leak. Everyone was also writing Stevens off, assuming he was dead. If he ever saw Stevens again the man would wish he was dead.

With nothing to do, and instructed to stay in the isolation building, Riley figured he might as well try to get some sleep. Maybe that would clear away the visions of the rounds impacting into Partusi as he tried to drag Marzan to safety.

Riley hadn't been able to figure out Westland's reaction. She had seemed a little dazed by the whole thing. Welcome to the real world, lady, he mused bitterly. He sighed as he trudged up the stairs to his room. He really shouldn't take it out on Westland. It wasn't her fault.

The members of Eyes Four were studiously avoiding him. They hadn't been told what had happened and hadn't been asked to sit in on the debriefing. All they knew was that the rest of the team wasn't coming back.

Riley was at a loss as to what to do next. He was overcome with a feeling of complete helplessness—a pawn on a chessboard who couldn't see far enough to make out the next square.

He opened the door to his room and walked in. The first thing that greeted him was the sight of the other bunk with a duffel bag on top of it: Powers's gear. Riley felt a stab of grief tear through him, quickly overcome by a blanket of weariness. Too much adrenaline, exertion, and grief in the last twelve hours had taken its toll. He collapsed on his bunk fully clothed and quickly dropped off into an uneasy sleep.

# BOGOTA
## 8:45 A.M.

Alegre looked across the presidential limousine at Montez. "Why did they not tell us that they were moving up the strike?"

Montez smiled bitterly. "They were concerned about security. The fewer people who knew, the less the risk."

Alegre's voice dripped irony. "Obviously that worked very well. The mission was compromised and they have a missing DEA agent. It won't take Ring Man long to figure out what is going on, especially if he is the one who kidnapped Stevens."

The limousine pulled up in front of the building housing the presidential offices. Alegre waited until the head security officer outside indicated it was safe for him to leave the vehicle. As Alegre stepped out, he was greeted by the roar of an explosion. He dove to the ground as his security men wheeled about, automatic weapons at the ready. As he lay on the sidewalk, Alegre heard the distant crump of other explosions ripping through the air.

Tentatively, he raised his head and was greeted by the sight of dust settling across the street where one of the most important and progressive newspapers in Colombia had its offices. The facade of the building was ripped away and people were tearing through the wreckage trying to rescue those trapped inside.

Alegre allowed Montez to help him to his feet. Montez pointed at the destruction. "I think the Ring Man has already figured things out and is giving us his answer."

# LANGLEY, VIRGINIA
# 9:04 A.M.

"Late yesterday evening, at approximately 11 P.M. eastern time, a U.S. army helicopter on a training mission over the Gulf of Mexico crashed. The general location of the crash was here," the Pentagon briefer slapped a pointer on the map blowup behind him and held it there so the reporters could get a good shot, "just off the coast of Colombia. We have rescued one survivor but the other five personnel that were on board are still missing. We will continue our search and have asked the government of Colombia for assistance.

"The helicopter was on a routine training mission from a base in Panama at the time of the accident. At present we have no idea of the cause of the accident."

The voice of the reporter cut in. "This news was announced only an hour ago at the Pentagon. There is still no . . . "

Strom turned off CNN and faced Westland. "That ties up some of the loose ends."

Westland disagreed. Despite the ass-chewing she'd received over not keeping Strom updated on moving up the strike, she had stuck to her guns. "What about Powers? And Stevens? Either or both could still be alive."

"We have a report that five bodies have been recovered by the people at the target site. As far as Stevens goes, we have no word but have to assume he's dead."

Westland was surprised. How had Strom received word so fast about bodies? Did he have an agent on the inside of the drug cartel? That could explain the intelligence they had been receiving pinpointing target sites. But if Strom did have an agent on the inside, how come they hadn't gotten any warning of the compromise? Or was Strom just putting up a smokescreen? "How do you know about the bodies?"

Strom looked at her sharply. "Suffice it to say that we have sources down there that keep us up to date. Powers is dead, so you can stop worrying about him. There are other things we need to concentrate on right now. The task force may be compromised but that doesn't mean the war on the drug cartel is over. Just the first battle. And I think we can safely say that we won the first round."

Westland stared at Strom in amazement. He calls four men dead and one captured a victory? And what does he mean "first round"? What's next?

Strom sensed her puzzlement. "I know we took some losses but you also have to look at the big picture, my dear girl. We've managed to destroy two major processing labs and in doing so seriously hurt two of the three major drug lords down there. In fact one of them, Suarez, is dead as a result of the raid on his lab. President Alegre is ready to declare martial law and really crack down on the cartel while they are still in the throes of confusion. With a little help he may be able to succeed.

"Unfortunately, even under martial law there is a limit to what he can do. As long as the leadership of the cartel is intact it's going to be an uphill fight for him. If we can cripple the leadership, Alegre stands a chance of winning."

Alarm bells were sounding in Westland's mind. What the hell did he mean by "we"? She had the feeling she was listening to a well-rehearsed speech. And how are we going to cripple the leadership? she thought.

Strom plowed on. "The primary problem is the drug lord called Ring Man. His lab was the one that Eyes Three was going up against. Ring Man's people are the ones who killed the members of your task force. Already he's trying to consolidate his power down south in Colombia and up here on the distribution end in the United States. We also have reason to believe that he was behind the Springfield massacre. President Alegre has asked our assistance in handling this man."

Westland stared her boss in the eyes. "Why can't Alegre simply arrest Ring Man? What kind of assistance is he asking for?"

"Like I said, even under martial law Alegre's powers are limited. The Ring Man has so many layers and cutouts in his organization that arresting him and prosecuting him would be extremely difficult.

"Even more importantly, though, is the fact that seizing Ring Man would only escalate the violence in the country as his people tried to get him back. After what they did here in the United States against Santia, you can well imagine what they would try against Alegre if he had Ring Man arrested.

"As far as what we're going to do, that is basically up to us as long as we remove the Ring Man as a problem. The simplest way to do that is termination."

Westland sat back in her chair. Her mind swirled with the implications of what Strom had just said. Termination. Why was Strom telling her this? She knew he had to have a reason. Surely he didn't expect her to do the mission. She wasn't trained for that sort of thing. And she wasn't sure she wanted to be involved in it anyway.

"Isn't that illegal, sir?"

Strom snorted. "Grow up, woman! This is the big leagues. You've wanted to be out in the field. Well, here's your chance." He held up a hand as she started to protest. "No, no. We don't expect you to do the actual job. You're going to be the handler for the action agent."

"Who's the action agent?"

"That's why we've picked you. Because you've already worked with him. Your lone survivor, Mister Riley, is going to be the man."

# BOGOTA
## 10:23 A.M.

"The bombs were good for a start, but I want Alegre's head!"

Ponte disagreed. The Ring Man was very upset and it wasn't smart to go against him right now, but Ponte knew he had to be the voice of reason during this crisis.

"I do not think that would be a wise move right now. The

president is very well guarded. We would lose many men trying to attack him. Also, the reaction of the people and the army to such a move is uncertain. Without Alegre the government would fall apart within a week."

"That is good. I will then be the government."

Again Ponte shook his head. "I do not want to disagree with you, but we are not ready for that yet. We still have to take care of Rameriz and also the rest of Suarez's operation. Maybe then we will be ready."

The Ring Man slumped down into a chair. He was silent for a few minutes. More than being angry he was humiliated. Alegre had tricked him, and it was hard for Ring Man to admit that he had been bested, even temporarily. It had been a close thing. If it had not been for Maria, Alegre's plan would have succeeded and the Ring Man would now be in the same situation as Rameriz.

He looked up at his assistant and grimaced wearily. "As always, you are right, my friend. I do not like being betrayed and that is what that scum in the palace has done to me. We will eventually catch up with him. Have you brought in our informant yet?"

"Yes. As you thought, he knew nothing of more information being passed to the CIA. It was obviously the president or perhaps his aide, Montez, who gave the Americans our lab location."

"Kill the informant anyway. I want no one else to know what went on between Alegre and me."

"Yes, sir." Ponte wasn't surprised. He'd figured that was what the Ring Man would do. "What about the DEA agent? What should we do with him? We've gotten all the information we can out of him."

"Let Maria keep him. She deserves it. She did a good job. Tell her to take her time."

The Ring Man stood up. "Continue the bombings. Let the government know they cannot act with impunity. Also make a videotape of the bodies of the American soldiers and the one we have captured. I will write a letter to go with the video, then we will release it. We will let the world know what is happening down here and what will happen if the United

States and Alegre continue their foolish actions against us."

Again Ponte dared to disagree. "Señor, I suggest we leave the live American off the video. I think that will only give the American government more incentive to involve themselves down here. We may be able to use the man as leverage at some time in the future, but only if we keep it quiet. We need to stay out of the media up there. A hostage would be the wrong tack to take.

"Showing the dead ones will get our point across. The bodies will show what the Americans have done, and later we can make a show of turning the bodies over to their embassy while at the same time publicly deploring the attack."

Ring Man considered this and then inclined his head, indicating assent, before leaving the room.

# FORT BELVOIR, VIRGINIA
## 1:20 P.M.

Riley's time sense was confused. Having spent the previous night awake and now having napped for five hours, he was somewhat rested but felt as though it should be morning.

The building was also too quiet. No noise from the members of Eyes Four. He got up, padded out into the hallway, and started checking rooms. There was no sign of anyone else—even their gear was gone. It was as if no one else had ever been there, except for the room where he had slept. There, the half-empty duffel bag lying on Powers's bunk was a meager monument to the missing team sergeant.

Riley pulled on his boots and laced them up. Finished, he slumped back into the chair at a loss for what to do next. He didn't want to allow himself to dwell on what had happened. When he probed his feelings, he felt a long, jagged cut tearing through his stomach and into his heart. He needed to do something to help heal it.

Hearing a car pull into the lot outside, he rose from the chair and glanced out the window. He saw Westland being waved through the gate by the MPs on duty.

Riley walked slowly down the stairs, arriving at the bottom at the same time Westland entered the hallway. "Where's the rest of the team and Pike?" Riley wasted no time on pleasantries.

"The team went back to Bragg. The task force has been disbanded." Westland gestured for Riley to follow her into the isolation planning room.

Riley gently but firmly grabbed her shoulder and turned her around. "What about Powers? We just going to write him off?"

Riley saw a flash of anger, replaced quickly by sorrow, in Westland's eyes as she replied. "Powers is listed as dead. I just found out over at Langley."

Riley wasn't going to give up that easily. "And how do the geniuses over at Langley know that?"

Riley could see his own doubt reflected in Westland's eyes. Even in the midst of his anger he felt an affinity for her. The disaster with the mission had affected her also, beyond just the realm of professional loss.

She shook her head. "They wouldn't tell, but I have it straight from the director that they have confirmation of his death." She sighed. "Listen, Dave, I tried pushing Strom on it. It's like talking to a damn wall. I know how you feel and I feel crappy about this whole thing, too. You were right from the beginning about the mission being kind of flaky, and you were also right about Stevens."

Riley released her shoulders and followed her into the isolation area. She sat down on a metal folding chair and Riley sat on the edge of one of the large tables, facing her. "What about Stevens? Any word on him?"

Westland shook her head again. "Nothing."

"Well, what now? Do I get to go back to Bragg and face the widows and the kids?" Riley asked bitterly. He dreaded the thought of seeing Gina Partusi and not being able to tell her the truth about how Frank had died.

He watched Westland carefully. She had something on her mind. He had a feeling there was a reason why he hadn't been awakened and sent back with the others. Maybe another, more extensive debriefing was coming up over at Langley. He waited while she chose her words carefully.

"Although Task Force Hammer has been disbanded, there's still a great deal of concern about Colombia and the drug cartel. A lot has happened in Colombia in the last couple of hours. Alegre has declared martial law. There have been several bombings and assassinations in Bogota and Medellin. It looks like it's starting to shape up into an all-out war between the government and the cartel.

"The man whose lab you were about to hit last night, Ring Man, has tried consolidating his power base by moving into the vacuum caused by the first two Hammer strikes. The feeling seems to be that if Ring Man was out of the picture, then Alegre would have a good chance of actually beating the cartel."

"This is all very interesting, but what does any of it have to do with me?" Riley stretched out his legs on the table.

Westland continued slowly. "Even under martial law, Alegre isn't able to touch the Ring Man, legally. There's also the fear that if he does try something against the man personally, it could backfire and bring even more bloodshed."

Riley was getting tired of her beating around the bush. He had a feeling where all this was leading. "What are you trying to tell me?"

Westland looked him in the eyes. "They want you to terminate the Ring Man."

Riley lay back on the table and contemplated the ceiling. Clowns In Action has *got* to be what CIA stands for, he thought. These people can't be for real.

Riley spoke as if to the ceiling. "The last time some Special Forces people 'terminated,' as you say, someone on orders of the CIA, at least the last time it was publicly noticed, was at a place called Nha Trang in Vietnam. Your agency gave some of our people evidence that one of their local indigenous agents was a double. Your people also gave some not-so-subtle instructions on how to deal with the double.

"Unfortunately, someone squealed after the deed. The Special Forces people involved, all the way up to the highest ranking Green Beret in country, the 5th Group commander, were investigated and almost court-martialed for murder."

Riley rolled his head toward Westland. "Your fearless colleagues all of a sudden had collective amnesia. They knew nothing about a double agent and certainly nothing about orders to kill anyone. The Special Forces men were left out on their own." Riley sat up suddenly. "So why should I do this? Give me one good reason."

Westland faced him. "Revenge."

Riley snorted. "By the way, who the hell is this *they* who want me to kill—and that's the proper word, not 'terminate'—Ring Man?"

"I got this straight from the deputy director."

" . . . who will swear on his mother's grave that he never said anything of the kind if I get caught and my head is blown off." Riley shook his head in wonder. "Have you thought about why they want me to do this and not one of their own superspy, Joe-ninja assassins? You guys employ a bunch of ex-Special Forces and ex-SEALs just for stuff like this. Any of them could do the job. I mean why me?"

Westland seemed confused. "I really didn't think about it too much. I guess I just assumed it was because you had already been working in Colombia and could be ready to go quickly, rather than bringing in someone new. It just seemed to be an extension of the task force."

Riley shook his head. "Maybe I'm cynical but I think there's another reason why I'm the man of the hour. It's because if this does leak or blow up, then your fine organization is in the clear and Special Forces is left holding the bag. I can see the headlines now: 'Crazed Special Forces Soldier Goes on One-Man Rampage in Foreign Country.' "

Another thought struck Riley. "By the way, does DOD know that you all want to borrow me for this?"

"You've been released to us for special duty for an unlimited time period."

"Yes, but do they know what you all want me to do?" Riley held up a hand. "Don't bother answering. That's a stupid question. Of course they don't."

Riley got up and walked around the room. He knew he should say "screw you" and walk away from this mess. It stunk bad. *BUT*. Maybe he could turn this to his advantage and use the mission to do some things he wanted to do. He considered it. His head and common sense told him not to touch this with a ten-foot pole. He checked his gut to see what it had to say. Then he turned back to Westland. "I know the what and the who. Kill Ring Man. Give me the rest of the mission statement: when and where and how."

He could see Westland's eyes widen in surprise. She didn't think I'd do it, Riley thought to himself. She has a lot to learn. He felt some of the pain from the loss of the previous night being twisted around inside of him. It was wrapping around his heart and hardening in place. Riley knew that if he was going to follow through on this, he would have to be stone-cold. He would have to enter another world and another reality with its own set of rules. And he would have to live by those rules. He felt sorry for Westland. She really didn't understand what they were getting into. This was a no-win situation whichever way it went.

Westland put her briefcase on top of the table and opened it. She pulled out a 1:250,000 map of Colombia. "Everything will be verbal and I'm going to be your point of contact for this operation. When is Thursday evening. Where is in Bogota. How is up to you."

Riley laughed at the sheer craziness of the situation. He couldn't help it. "Oh, that's real good. You're giving me seventy-two hours to go to a foreign country, assassinate one of the most guarded men there, and you can't even give me a head start on a way to accomplish it."

He looked at Westland. She seemed so earnest he almost laughed again. This was beyond the point of being ridiculous and was rapidly approaching the absurd. "Come on, Kate, give me a break. You've got more common sense than this. What's going on? Why the big rush?"

Westland shook her head. "I'm leveling with you, Dave. You know as much as I do. I agree this whole thing is screwed up, but I don't think we have much choice."

Riley put his hands on her shoulders and made her look him in the eyes. "That's where you're wrong. Don't ever believe that. You always have a choice. It's just that you have to pay the price that goes along with your choice." He let go of her and started pacing around the room. He would find out in a few days if she was willing to pay the price.

"The problem is not killing the Ring Man. You can kill anyone in the world. The problem is killing the Ring Man and coming home alive. There're some other factors involved here, too."

He considered Westland, trying to decide how much he could trust her. Throughout his life, Riley had never really trusted anyone. He'd always had what he called situational trust. He trusted certain people up to certain points in certain areas. But he had never trusted anyone completely.

Here he had to trust Westland with his life. He liked what he'd seen of her in the past week, but that was too short a time to really judge someone. Also, he had an almost pathological distrust of the organization she represented. Riley decided on a compromise. He'd trust her to the extent he had to, but he'd also ensure that she had a stake in things.

"What about contacts in country? Weapons? Safe houses? Travel arrangements?"

Westland nodded. "I've got you tickets for a flight tonight and a reservation under your cover name at a hotel in Bogota that the agency uses. There's a man in the office down there who you're supposed to meet for local intelligence. We can go over to Langley now and get the latest they've got there.

"If there's any equipment you think you'll need, give me a list and I'll forward it to our logistics section when we get to Langley. They'll either forward the stuff down on a hop or get it out of local supplies."

Riley reached over and grabbed a notepad from Westland's briefcase. He thought for a minute, then started writing. He listed several items and tore off the top piece of paper. "Here's what I need." He handed it to her.

As she stood up to go he spoke out. "There's one other thing I need that's not on the list."

"What's that?"

"You."

Westland stared at him in surprise. Riley smiled grimly. "I need you to go with me to Colombia as part of my cover. If I try going in alone I'll be spotted in a minute, but if we go together as a couple, with a good cover story that's backstopped, I'll have a much better chance of success."

He walked over and punched her lightly on the arm. "What the hell. Here's the big chance you've been waiting for."

# BOGOTA
# 2:05 P.M.

Montez sat at the side of the president's desk and warily watched the American as he approached his boss. Montez was not happy at all with the present situation. The Americans had gotten Alegre into a real mess and for the past several days had been skittish about following through on their commitments. Montez's right hand caressed the handle of the Walther PPK that was tucked into his waistband.

He also didn't like this meeting with Alegre present. Always before Montez had managed to control the meeting place. But this time Jameson had insisted the president be here. Montez had advised Alegre not to agree, but Alegre felt they had to go through with it. They needed the Americans now more than ever before.

For a change, Jameson was smiling, which disturbed Montez even more. He didn't trust this American.

Jameson took the seat across the desk from Alegre. "We will take care of the Ring Man as you asked."

Alegre raised his eyebrows. "Why the sudden turnaround?"

"Let's just say we've found the right tool to do the job."

Alegre nodded. "Get rid of Ring Man and I can deal with the scum that are left."

Montez shook his head silently. His old friend did not know what he had gotten himself into.

Jameson stood up. "I hope you appreciate the expense my country has paid to run those missions for you this past week. Five dead men is a high price."

Montez narrowed his eyes. Why was Jameson bringing this up now?

Alegre answered solemnly. "I do appreciate it. But it is a

war that both our countries are in. Your country must shoulder its part of the burden."

Jameson nodded. "That's true, but I must tell you that certain parties up north were not amused by your threat of disowning your role in the Hammer missions."

"I use whatever tools I have."

Jameson picked up his briefcase. "It has been a pleasure doing business with you, Mister President. I hope everything turns out all right for both of us."

"I hope so too, Mister Jameson."

Montez watched the American leave the room. Something had just happened, but he wasn't sure what it was.

# PENTAGON
# 2:30 P.M.

Pike stalked through the hallways. He knew the way from his travels of the past week. He made it through the first three echelons deployed around the chairman's office before anyone even dared to question his presence. A fresh-faced major jumped up from his desk and moved to intercept Pike as he homed in on the door leading to the inner sanctum.

"Excuse me, sir, but the chairman is in a meeting."

Pike turned his glare on the unfortunate officer. "I have the chairman's permission to see him at any time. I'm exercising that right."

The major wasn't even close to being a match for the scarred veteran. Pike twisted the knob, stepped into the office, and shut the door behind him. The several generals who were clustered around the chairman's desk glanced up in confusion, wondering who dared barge into the chairman's office unannounced.

Pike stopped and stared at Macksey. He was willing to be somewhat tactful about things. The room grew quiet as the other occupants watched the silent confrontation. Finally Macksey gestured abruptly. "Everyone out." The other generals scattered like geese.

When the door shut behind the last one, Macksey shook his head. "This is stupid, whatever you think you're doing."

"I just want to hear it from you and not the CIA."

"Hear what from me?"

"That the Hammer Task Force is disbanded."

"All right, you're hearing it from me. It's disbanded. That comes straight from the president. You all did a fine job while it lasted."

Pike felt the strength drain out of him. He knew he was about to butt his head against the wall again, but there were some things he would not compromise. He limped his way to the massive desk and leaned both gnarled hands on it. "You're just going to forget the chance one of those men may be alive? And leave those bodies there?"

Macksey shook his head. "That man is dead. We've received intelligence to that effect."

"From whom? Those assholes up the road at Langley? Why should they give a shit? They left our people to hang in Vietnam and Cambodia and Laos when they had confirmed sightings. Why the hell should they change now?" Pike laughed bitterly. "Shit. We left our own hanging, too. We're not any better than they are, but at least I thought we might have learned."

Macksey leaned slightly forward. "Watch your tone with me, Pike. Remember who you're talking to. I can bust you in a heartbeat."

Pike laughed mirthlessly. "Bust me! Bust me into what? I was busted when I hit those trees twenty-one years ago. I was busted every time I didn't roll over and kiss ass, and spoke what I felt was the truth regardless of who it pissed off."

Pike put his face as close to Macksey's as the desk would allow. "Let me tell you something, General. While you were brown-nosing on a general's staff during your one tour in 'Nam, I was watching buddies of mine get their asses shot off for three years in the bush. I took a round through my gut and busted my back. While you were playing politics here in Washington, kissing politicians' asses, I was traveling around the world going places you pretty play soldiers never go. Doing the job you couldn't and wouldn't do.

"You don't scare me. Let me tell you one last thing. There aren't many things I believed in in the army. But one of them was taking care of my men and I always did that. And when the army has gotten to a point where the head man doesn't do that, then you don't have to bother busting me. I quit!" Pike turned and headed for the door.

Behind him Macksey's tone had changed. "Listen, goddamnit. There's nothing I can do. The president doesn't want the incident down there to get any worse. He's specifically—"

Pike slammed the door on Macksey's explanations and his army career.

# LANGLEY, VIRGINIA
# 3:00 P.M.

Riley didn't bother standing up as did Westland when Strom walked in the door. There was only so much of the game that he'd play. He eyeballed the deputy director taking his place at the table across from him. Strom dominated the spare briefing room with his air of confidence and control. This was his turf and he wanted Riley to know it. Riley found it interesting that Strom chose to sit as far away from him as possible, leaving Westland at the head of the table, figuratively in the role of mediator.

On the drive over from Belvoir Riley had pumped Westland for more details, but the results had been lean. Strom was the man with the hard information, and just how much of it he would divulge was questionable. Riley knew Strom would give up only enough for Riley to do what they wanted him to, if killing Ring Man was indeed the purpose of the mission.

Strom slid two folders and two large envelopes to Westland, who passed one of each on to Riley. "That's all we've got on Ring Man, plus a listing of some information on our operations down there that you're going to need. In the envelopes you'll also find your cover documentation." Strom sat back in his chair and watched as Riley slowly opened his folder.

The top item was a five-by-eight photo of a man entering a limousine. "That's the latest photo we have of the Ring Man, taken a week ago in Bogota."

Riley examined the picture. The figure labeled as Ring Man

would be easy to recognize. Riley scanned the rest of the picture. The limousine was obviously armored. In the background of the photo he caught glimpses of other figures, apparently security. "How big is Ring Man's normal guard detail?"

Strom shrugged. "Anywhere from three to ten. You can be sure he's upped it since he's started this war against the government and the other cartel leaders. In fact he hasn't been seen out and about for the past week, since that photo was taken."

"Where's he holed up?"

Strom gestured at the file folder. "The next picture is a ground shot of his villa outside Bogota. You've also got overhead imagery in there of the grounds and four kilometers around them, plus a one-to-fifteen thousand geo map of the area. We haven't had time to get any blueprints or details on security and alarms, but our man in Bogota is working on that and might have something for you tomorrow after you get there."

Riley examined what he could see of Ring Man's villa. Fortress would probably be a more appropriate term, he figured, as he took in the obvious security details. A ten-foot stone wall completely enclosed the grounds. He could make out guards at the main gate. The overhead imagery showed several more guards scattered around the grounds on the inside. Riley spotted some smaller shadows. "Looks like he's got dogs in there. Do you know what kind?"

"No info on that, old boy."

Riley glanced up in irritation. Strom was sitting there unperturbed with the hint of a smile on his face. Riley decided he was through fooling around. "Why don't you tell me what the hell you *do* know."

The smile grew slightly larger. "It's all in the folder. You'll know as much as I do after you read that."

"What about a name, or did that yo-yo's mother name him Ring Man?"

"All we have is Ring Man."

Riley glanced over at Westland and back to Strom. All right, he thought, fine. That's the way it's going to be. For the next thirty minutes, Riley carefully read through the rest of the folder, commiting the important parts to memory.

There wasn't much there. Obviously someone had done a rush job on parts of the intelligence packet, although that was contradicted by the dating on some of the photos and imagery. That made Riley wonder when this mission had first been authorized.

Getting the high-resolution imagery of the villa required someone with a lot of power in the intelligence community. Riley didn't think there were too many spy satellites with orbits over Colombia, although for all he knew there might be. Besides, he knew they could always run a U-2 overhead for imagery if needed. The dates on the photos indicated an extensive surveillance had been in place as early as two days ago.

Finishing his studying he looked up. "Thursday night's too soon. With this amount of intelligence I can't move that fast. I'm going to need to put some surveillance on that villa, and I won't be able to do that tonight. If I'm able to eyeball it all night tomorrow night, I'll still need some time to plan. Friday night's the earliest I could hope to do anything, and that's only if I spot a weakness I can exploit."

Strom considered this for a few seconds, then shook his head. "Thursday night. We can't go any further than that."

Westland spoke for the first time. "Why not?"

Strom swung his imperious gaze over to her. "My dear girl, there are more things going on than this simple operation." He turned back to Riley. "However, the main reason is that Alegre is under intense pressure from Ring Man. We're afraid there may be a counterplot by Ring Man to assassinate President Alegre. We can't afford to have that happen. The sooner Ring Man is out of the picture, the better."

That's all fine and good, thought Riley, except for the fact that a half-assed attempt to hit Ring Man was more likely to end with himself dead rather than Ring Man. "What about backup or equipment? Can I get some more bodies if I need them?"

Strom showed his sly smile again. "We've decided to go along with your request and send Westland with you as your liaison and to help with your cover. If you need equipment or information, she'll be your contact with our local agent down there. She's already been briefed on how to make that contact."

Riley pressed. "What about extra people?"

"My dear boy, she is your extra people."

Which meant, Riley knew, that the CIA had a cover story in the event she was exposed. By keeping the in-country team to Riley and her, the CIA could cut its losses if the whole thing blew up.

He looked through the folder one more time. There wasn't much there, and he realized he wasn't going to get anything worthwhile out of this smiling bureaucrat. He was also getting real tired of the "dear boy" crap. Riley scooped up the envelope with his new identity and opened it.

His new name was Roberto Gonzalo. He was a cabdriver from New York City. His union card was there along with a driver's license, social security card, credit card, and photos of his wife. Riley looked over at his new wife. "Who are you?"

"Catherine Gonzalo. I'm a secretary at Misericordia Hospital in New York and we live in the Bronx."

Riley nodded. He wasn't sure how much Kate knew about her background, but he was very familiar with it. "Yeah. We live at 1846 Arnow Avenue. I know that neighborhood. Not too bad. Hopefully, we won't run into anyone who knows New York better than me. I'll tell you about it on the way to the airport." He gathered his documents and stood up. "Let's get going."

Kate halted. "Wait a second. What's our cover for being there? I mean, why are two New Yorkers going down to Bogota?"

Strom shrugged. "Up to you, dear girl. Tourists is the easiest."

Riley shook his head. "No. We're going there for a baby."

Westland stared in surprise. "A baby?"

"Yeah, a baby. Cocaine's not the only thing you can buy on the black market down there. And since my beautiful wife is unable to have a baby, we're going shopping for one."

# KENNEDY AIRPORT, NEW YORK
## 6:27 P.M.

Riley found himself sinking lower into the hard plastic box that masqueraded as a seat in the foreign departures waiting area. Five hours' sleep just wasn't enough after the recent events. Just twenty-four hours ago he'd been bouncing around on the Gulf of Mexico with the rest of his team. Now four were dead and Powers was missing.

Riley felt only a shadow of the pain he had felt this morning when he thought of that. There was no time for it now. The grieving could come later. Right now he had a job to do. He glanced over at Westland. She looked exhausted also. Her eyes were half closed and her head was playing the bobbing game.

Riley sat up and tapped her. "We'll miss our flight if both of us fall asleep. We'll have five hours to sleep on the plane."

Westland yawned and got up. "Want some coffee? We've got probably fifteen minutes before they call our flight." Riley nodded and followed her toward the concourse.

They'd added forty minutes to their flight time by catching the shuttle up to New York from D.C., but it made sense for them to arrive in Colombia on a flight from New York. It fit their cover.

Riley was impressed with the thought and energy that had gone into their covers. Someone had actually taken the time to review both his and Westland's backgrounds to find a location in which they had both spent some time. It turned out that Westland had gone to college at New York University in Greenwich Village and thus was familiar with the city. Riley hoped all that information wouldn't be needed.

After grabbing a cup of coffee, they headed back to the waiting area. As they passed the bar Riley halted and peered in at the television. The logo for CNN had just flashed across the screen. He glanced at his watch. It was almost the half hour.

"Let's see if there's anything more in the news on Colombia or the accident."

They stood outside the entrance, sipping their coffee, waiting through a few commercials. Riley edged closer when the announcer came on with an outline of Colombia highlighted behind him. Riley strained to catch the words.

"Late today a videotape was delivered to *El Tiempo*, a Colombian newspaper, showing the bodies of four men wearing scuba diving dry suits. A letter delivered with the video claims that the four men were members of the U.S. military and had been killed attacking Colombian nationals near the city of Barranquilla. The video is in the possession of the Colombian government and has not yet been released. We have a report from Bogota that the U.S. ambassador is meeting with Colombian officials to discuss the matter.

"There are rumors that the tape and letter were made by members of the Colombian drug cartel and delivered to the newspaper as a warning against a recent crackdown by the government.

"We switch you now to Henry Lowell, our correspondent at the Pentagon, for more on this story."

The picture now showed a reporter standing with the Pentagon in the background.

"Jim, the Pentagon has declined to comment on the report. However, earlier today, the Pentagon issued a news bulletin indicating that five U.S. servicemen had been killed in a helicopter crash in the Gulf of Mexico near the coast of Colombia during what the Pentagon described as routine training. Whether these men are the same as the ones in the video remains unclear. The names of the men involved are still being held pending notification of next of kin; however, I have been informed by an undisclosed source that the men were from Fort Bragg, North Carolina.

"Fort Bragg is the home of the elite antiterrorist Delta Force. The possibility exists that these men may indeed have been from this unit and may have been involved in some sort of antidrug operation near Colombia. Even if it was just an accident during training, as the Pentagon claims, how their bodies ended up in the hands of the drug cartel is unknown at this time."

The scene shifted back to the studio.

"Thank you, Henry. CNN will keep you updated on this story as more information becomes available.

"Colombia is also in the headlines tonight as violence continues to escalate in that country. Three bombs exploded in the city of Medellin today and four people were killed, including one policeman.

"This violence is the reaction of the drug cartel against measures imposed by the government to crack down on their lucrative business. This brings to twelve the number of people who have been killed there in the last two days.

"On other fronts, in the Soviet Republic of . . . "

Riley grabbed Westland and hustled her away from the screen back to their chairs. Riley scanned the waiting area. There was no one within twenty feet. He lowered his voice and put his head close to hers. "Looks like Ring Man is making a point. Wonder how your boss is going to explain the bodies having little bullet holes in them and being on Colombian land rather than in the ocean?"

Westland shrugged. "Did you notice that they mentioned only four bodies, not five?"

"Yeah, I noticed." Riley looked her in the eyes. "I think Powers is still alive. When we get down there I want you to get a copy of that tape. We need to see if his is one of the bodies."

If Westland wondered what that had to do with hitting the Ring Man, she didn't mention it, for which Riley was grateful. Maybe she would go along with what he had planned. He stood up. "I have to go to the bathroom. I'll be right back."

Westland nodded wearily. "We board in ten minutes."

Riley walked down the curving corridor until he was out of sight of Westland. Then he went up to the first pay phone he saw. He rapidly punched in eleven numbers and waited for the operator. "I'd like to make a collect call. The name's Riley."

While he waited for the operator to make the connection, he prayed that someone would be home on the other end. Finally he heard the receiver lift and the answerer accept the charges. Riley was quick and to the point. "I can't talk long. I'm about to take a flight down south."

"Down south? Where you just were?"

"Roger that. Did you see the story about the video on the news?"

"Yes."

"I think he's alive."

"I agree."

"Do you know what my status is right now?"

"No. You're not going down there on your own, are you?"

"No. It's worse than that. I'm being sponsored by you know who. You need to check on what Department of the Army has to say about my status. I think I'm going to need your help. This thing is really flaky."

"Whatever you need, you got. I'll check on my end. If you have to talk to me can get to it. The army military attaché may be able to help you—he's a good man."

Riley prepared to hang up. "I've got to go. I'll be in contact."

"Hold on a second! Just one thing. What do they want you to do?"

"Terminate the Ring Man."

"Jesus! You're going to need help. I'll see what I can work on up here."

"Thanks. But make it quick. I only have till Thursday night." Riley hung up.

# TUESDAY,
# 3 SEPTEMBER

## BOGOTA
## 1:12 A.M.

The hotel was three blocks away from the American embassy. American travelers did like to have the embassy close by, but Riley still felt that the close location showed some laziness on the part of the CIA. It did put Westland close enough to make contact with Jameson without much difficulty. She was set up to meet him later this morning at a nearby restaurant. At the meeting, hopefully, she'd coordinate pickup of the equipment Riley had requested.

At the moment she was unpacking her bag and storing the few clothes she had brought, while Riley stalked about the room, inspecting it. A queen-sized bed took up the middle of the room, and an old, stuffed armchair stood near the sliding, glass doors that opened onto their second-floor balcony. Riley glanced around the curtains. The balcony itself held two chairs and a tiny table. Their window looked out onto an alley rather than the main street. A drab modern office building dominated the view.

Riley turned back to face the room. Westland was perched on the edge of the bed. Riley didn't need to read minds to see that she obviously had something on hers.

"What do you want to do about sleeping arrangements?" she asked.

Riley smiled. That was by far the least of his worries right now. "Personally I prefer sleeping. Unfortunately that's not in the cards tonight for me. You get some z's. I've got some things I've got to do."

Westland stood up. "Are you going to let me in on your plan? I am supposed to be your partner here."

Riley slid open the balcony door. "See you before dawn." Before she could get to the balcony he had swung over the railing and dropped to the deserted alley below.

He glanced back once before he turned the corner and saw her silhouetted against the light from the room. I'll have to talk to her about that, Riley mused, as he moved through the streets. He counted corners, following the directions he had memorized from the street map on the flight down.

It was cool in Bogota. Over eight thousand feet in altitude made for a significant drop in the temperature compared to the coastal plain. Riley zipped his black windbreaker up to his neck. He wore an old pair of loose-fitting jeans, a gray New York Knicks T-shirt, and a pair of beat-up work boots. The boots were a special design custom-made for him during a tour of duty in Korea. The toes were pointed and reinforced with steel. Thin steel reinforcing ridges were placed under the rubber sole along the outside edges. They weren't the most comfortable things to wear but were quiet and devastating when used as weapons, amplifying the effects of his kicks.

Riley felt as though he was back home in the South Bronx, running the streets. In the South Bronx, late at night, the police didn't respond to trouble and those who went out were on their own. Bogota had that same feeling of lawlessness. People did what they had to do to survive—the strong ruled at night and the weak hid. Riley planned on being one of the former.

Turning a final corner, Riley spotted his destination. He had considered various plans of action, but realizing that time was short, he decided on the direct approach. He went up to the doors of the Embassy Cafe and pushed them open.

An aging Colombian man, one side of his face lined with an old scar, looked up from where he was mopping the floor. "I'm closed," he said in Spanish.

Riley took in the rest of the bar. Perfect. It was just the two of them. He replied in the same language. "That's all right. I'm not thirsty."

The man looked up at the strange accent. "You are not from here. Are you a gringo?"

"I'm from New York. I have business down here."

The man's interest went back to the floor. Another goddamn gringo— probably from the embassy, although he spoke pretty good Spanish and looked native. The old man filed the information away for possible future use. "I am still closed."

Riley walked over to the bar and took a stool. "I'm looking for someone and thought you might be able to help."

The man continued his work and spoke in a weary monotone. "I am not open. I cannot serve you. There is nothing else I can do for you."

Riley placed $50 U.S. on the bar.

The man glanced up but didn't stop his listless mopping. "I do not work for Americans. Go back across the street to your little hole."

"I am not from the embassy. I just flew in tonight from my home in New York. The name's Martinez. I heard you might be able to put me in contact with someone who can give me the information I need."

The man hung the mop on the wall and trudged behind the bar. With a swipe of his rag the $50 disappeared. "Who?"

"A woman named Maria."

The old man regarded him for a few seconds. "What can she tell you?"

"I need information on babies."

"Babies?" The old man raised his eyebrows in surprise.

"Babies."

The old man shook his head. The Ring Man didn't deal in babies and he surely would not like an American asking about Maria. These gringos were crazy. "Come back tomorrow at one in the afternoon."

Riley nodded his appreciation and headed for the door. It wasn't likely that the old man knew what Maria had been doing there, but Riley was sure of one thing. The word that a strange American was looking for Maria would be forwarded to somebody. With any luck he'd find out who tomorrow.

## 6:25 A.M.

Westland practically stepped on Riley as she slid out of bed. He was lying on the floor on the bathroom side of the bed, covered by a light blanket. She looked at him sleeping there for a few seconds. She hadn't heard him come in. It was a scary feeling knowing that someone could enter the room without her even knowing it.

She threw on her robe and padded quietly into the bathroom. When she came back out, Riley was dressed and seated at the small table on the balcony.

"I've already ordered from room service. Left the little card on the door. Should be here in about five minutes."

"What time did you get in?"

"About two thirty."

"Where did you go?"

"Checking on some things."

Westland took a deep, exasperated breath. "Are we going to play twenty questions? Are you going to let me in on the plan? We are—"

She was interrupted by a knock on the door. Riley got up and squeezed past her. "Excuse me."

He opened the door and relieved the bellboy of his tray. He carried it past her and laid it on the table. Westland stared at him while he prepared his coffee and took a satisfying sip. "Ah. I'm not worth a damn until I get some coffee in me." He waved at the other chair. "Care to join me?"

Westland gave up. She slumped down into the chair and poured herself a cup.

Riley took another drink and then turned to her. "All right. I'll tell you as much as you need to know. First off, like I told you last night, I don't think Powers is dead. Finding him is my number one priority. I wouldn't even be telling you that if I didn't think I could trust you not to squeal on me.

"Second, I'm going to have a hell of a time trying to take out the Ring Man the way things stand right now. He's sitting in a defensive position. I have to go attack him. In military terms it's considered appropriate to have a force superiority of three to one when attacking someone in an established defensive position. In case you haven't noticed, we don't quite have that, so I figure we have to try another approach."

"What's the plan?"

Riley shrugged. "Haven't quite figured that out yet. Depends on what happens. We're going to have to play this by ear and react quickly when we get an opening. There's a lot of forces in motion down here and we have to try to arrange them in our favor as much as possible. I'm going to do some pushing and see what pushes back.

"I pushed the first button last night, and we'll see today if there's any reaction. The information you can hopefully get from your contact this morning will be a big help and fill in some of the missing pieces. That should give us some more buttons to push.

"As far as agenda goes, all I know right now is that you go to a meet in a half hour. I go to another meeting at one today with someone who might give us a link to the woman Stevens was seeing. Tonight I head into the hills to take a look at Ring Man's villa."

Riley took another sip of his coffee. "By the way, you look pretty good early in the morning."

# RING MAN'S VILLA, OUTSKIRTS OF BOGOTA 8:20 A.M.

Ponte acted as chief of staff for Ring Man. Everything going in and out went through him. In performing this role he also accrued a certain degree of power in that he could, within limits set by the Ring Man's volatile temper, screen that information as he saw fit and take action in the name of the Ring Man.

The story of the strange American in the Embassy Cafe was just one of many intelligence reports forwarded to Ponte's desk by a network of informants this morning. Ponte puzzled over it for a few seconds. He decided that the Ring Man had more important things to worry about. Ponte would take care of it himself.

He called in one of Ring Man's sicarios. Pablo was a little smarter than the average gunman and Ponte felt he could trust him with some simple instructions on how to deal with the American. The Americans had started the war by attacking them. It was time for some more payback.

# BOGOTA
# 10:00 A.M.

Kate threw her bag in the corner of the room and dropped into the armchair with a sigh. Riley raised an eyebrow from where he was reclining on the bed. "Get anything good from the contact?"

She nodded. "He didn't have answers for all your questions, but he did give me some information."

"Were you stopped or followed?"

"No."

"You sure?"

Westland gave him a hard look. Riley raised his hands in surrender. "OK, OK. I believe you."

Westland began to relate the events of the morning. "The contact was the local embassy rep, Jameson. I knew him up in Virginia when he was stationed there."

"Shit!" Riley cursed. "That's great. I'm willing to bet better than even money that he was followed."

"He said he wasn't. From what I could see we weren't being watched. Also, if he was followed, it would make sense that they would try to follow me from the meet, and I'm sure I wasn't."

Riley waved at her to go on. "All right, I get the picture and I trust your judgment."

"Anyway. We met at the restaurant near the cemetery and all the safe signals were in place. Jameson said the area was secure. He also complimented me on my legs."

"Well, they are nice legs," Riley confirmed playfully.

Westland rolled her eyes. "He's an asshole. He tried hitting on me when we were stationed together in Virginia and I was still married. Not that any of that matters now.

"He said they had no leads on Stevens. They presume he's dead and the body was sunk out in the ocean somewhere or buried deep in the jungle. As for the video of the bodies, he says it's going to be released to the local media this afternoon and we can watch it just as well on TV as his getting us a copy. Plus there is a certain lack of a VCR in this room," Westland pointed out. "Local news comes on at six.

"As for Powers, Jameson said that his body was not shown on the video but they're pretty certain he was killed that same night."

"Oh, now it's 'pretty certain,' " Riley snorted. "Sounds like the story is changing. And they're up the creek without a paddle if he shows up alive. Sort of blows their cover story, which probably isn't doing too well now anyway."

Westland threw a copy of a local paper on the bed. "The official reply by Washington has been that your guys were killed in an aircraft crash, but obviously it was over land instead of water and that's how the bodies were recovered. Apparently the aircraft mistakenly strayed over land while on a training flight."

Riley rubbed his eyes. The government still wouldn't change their story and admit the truth. He wasn't sure what they were afraid of. Probably admitting they had lied. The media would jump all over that. There could be no such thing as a covert operation in the United States. The freedom of the press to keep the people informed guaranteed that. Of course, Riley always wondered why there was never any mention of the need for the press and media to make money by getting a scoop. Newspeople rarely talked about money and ratings, but that was the bottom line for them.

"What about the hit? Any further intel?"

Westland shook her head. "Nothing other than the fact that Ring Man is still holed up in his villa."

"What about the guerrillas? Any information on how I can contact them?"

"Jameson thought that was the craziest idea he ever heard."

"I don't care what Jameson thinks. I want to know if there's any way I can make contact with them."

Westland shook her head. "He said he didn't know of any."

Riley didn't believe it. "You're telling me the CIA has no way to contact the guerrillas in a country? I'd think they'd be bosom buddies."

Westland got as sarcastic as Riley. "I think in this country the U.S. party line is to support the government. The guerrillas are somewhat communistic at times here."

Riley scratched his head. That avenue wasn't looking too promising. "Did you get the car?"

"It's out back in the hotel lot, fueled and ready to go."

"Good. Anything else?"

She reached inside her shirt and produced a piece of paper. "I've got the location of the cache with the equipment you wanted," she said, handing the paper to Riley.

"When did you put it in there?"

"I had to go to the bathroom. I can't make much sense out of it but I'm sure someone else might be able to. Figured it would be safer there if I was stopped."

Riley took the paper and looked at it, with Westland peering over his shoulder. "What does it say?"

"It's a cache report. Should contain the stuff I requested. I hope they didn't decide to delete anything."

Westland shook her head. "I doubt that. I gave it direct to the logistics branch at Langley before we left and didn't go through Strom. As far as log branch was concerned it was a priority request for one of our own agents. They sure were damn fast in putting it in though."

Riley nodded. It must have been emplaced overnight. He was surprised that the CIA was capable of such a feat. The equipment must have already been in country or flown in from Panama. "Did Jameson say whether he or someone else emplaced this?"

"He said the army military attaché did it. I got the impression that he didn't want to be too involved in this whole thing. He said the army guy was gone all night taking care of it."

Riley was relieved. Not only might Jameson have been

followed, but he could have screwed up the emplacement. Hopefully the army man had done a good job.

"What do all those lines mean?"

Riley translated for her. "It's an UNDER report format. The fact that it's in this format tells me that the army attaché has some Special Forces experience or has worked with SF before. We use formats like this for all our radio messages because it keeps them shorter."

Westland nodded. "I've met the attaché during a couple of my coordination trips to the embassy over the past year. Lieutenant Colonel Turrel. Seemed like a pretty efficient man. He certainly has been forwarding good intel copy on the Colombian military."

Upon reflection, Riley realized it wasn't unusual for an attaché to have SF experience. Special Forces and also military intelligence officers had the language and intelligence training necessary for foreign service jobs. Riley also remembered Pike mentioning the army military attaché in Colombia as a good man.

Riley pointed to each line as he translated:

BBB—submersion: "That means the cache is underwater. It's faster than digging if you're in a rush. I just hope it's waterproofed well enough."

CCC—as req: "That means it contains what I requested."

DDD—one: "Means there's one container."

FFF—IRP = tgt Villa. 1.3 k. AZ 14 mag: "This gives the immediate reference point. Obviously he used Ring Man's villa, so he must have gotten some idea from Jameson of where I'll be operating. The direction to the final reference point is 1.3 kilometers on a magnetic azimuth of fourteen degrees." Riley pulled out the geo map he had brought with him. He traced a line from the location of Ring Man's villa.

GGG—FRP = waterfall, rock in center: "The final reference point is a waterfall." He pointed. "Must be right here, where this stream crosses these contour lines. Rock in center indicates the final checkpoint. Must be the pool at the base of the waterfall."

HHH—N side: "I'm supposed to check the north side of the rock."

III—2 meters: "The cache is two meters under the water. I hope the water's not too cold."

KKK—3 Sept: "This last line indicates when it was put in."

LLL—knife: "This means that I'm going to need a knife to recover the cache."

Riley memorized the location. Then he went into the bathroom and burned the note, flushing the remains down the toilet. He knew that even having the geo map was a risk but he felt he could cover for that. Many campers and nature lovers carried such maps when they went out into the field, and being a nature lover was going to be his cover if he went near the Ring Man's villa during the day. At night it would be a different situation.

Time for him to be heading out to put some surveillance on the cafe. He turned to Westland. "I've got to be going. Here's what we in the army call a contingency plan. I'm going to be gone until about three this afternoon. If I'm not back by five, consider me compromised. Get your ass out of this place and go over to the embassy."

Westland nodded. "I don't suppose you're going to tell me where you're going?"

"You don't want to know."

## 12:45 P.M.

Riley closed the paper and laid it on the bench next to him. The old newspaper-on-a-park-bench routine was one of the oldest methods to survey a location and it seemed kind of hokey. Yet it allowed Riley to blend in with other people in the area and not arouse suspicion. Riley had learned the rudiments of surveillance in the Special Forces operations and intelligence course and he realized that perception played a key role in any covert operation. People tended to see what they were expecting to see.

Riley had been watching the Embassy Cafe for the last hour and fifteen minutes. In that time he had seen numerous Americans and a smaller number of Colombians enter and leave. He had yet to see anyone or any group of people that might pass as a reception party waiting to greet the foolish American.

Riley had hoped to get some reaction out of the Ring Man's people with his questioning of the worker in the bar earlier this morning. He knew, from the CIA intelligence reports, that the girl who worked there, Maria, was most likely the person who had set up Stevens. The fact that she had not been seen since Stevens's disappearance supported that suspicion. If he could get a handle on her she might lead him to Stevens. And Stevens might lead him to Powers. It was a tenuous chain at best, but it was the only thing he had. With the clock running down to Thursday night, Riley felt he had to try anything that held even the slightest chance of working.

Riley left the paper on the bench and meandered over to the cafe. Passing through the swinging doors he quickly scanned the dim interior. Some embassy workers finishing their lunch. A Colombian couple seated at a booth in a corner.

Riley walked up to the bar and took a seat that allowed him to watch both the front door and the entrance to the kitchen. The old man he had talked to the previous night was nowhere in sight. A teenage boy was tending the bar and acting as waiter. Riley ordered a local beer from the boy and settled in to wait.

## 1:12 P.M.

Riley figured he'd give it another ten minutes and then leave. The cafe was practically deserted. The Colombian couple had already left and the last Americans were paying for their meal and leaving. No one else had come in.

Hearing the door open, Riley didn't need a program to tell him the two men coming in were the emissaries from the Ring Man. The way the boy behind the bar quickly departed through the kitchen door told him that these men were trouble. Riley guessed the boy was going around front to make sure no one came in during the meeting.

Riley sized up the two men as they swaggered across the room toward him. The way the one on the left held himself told Riley that he was in charge. He was big, almost six foot two, and he showed off his muscles with a sleeveless sweatshirt. He seemed disappointed that Riley was so small. Riley spotted the bulge of a pistol under the man's sweatshirt, tucked into his front right waistband.

The second man wore a loose-fitting shirt over old army fatigue pants. Riley figured he was probably a knife man. His forearms and face were covered with the telltale tracing of old knife scars. The way he held his arms in close and kept his right hand near his side reminded Riley of some of the knife fighters he'd known in the South Bronx, plus there was no telltale bulge indicating a firearm. Riley knew a knife was harder to spot and at close ranges more effective than a gun. A good knife man could clear his sheath and gut a gunman standing less than five feet away before the other cleared his holster.

Riley turned to face the newcomers as they came up close, standing within a foot, flanking him in front. "Good day," Riley greeted in English.

The big man showed a gap-toothed smile and spoke in accented English. "Good day, gringo. I hear you ask too many questions. That is a bad habit."

"I did not mean to upset anyone. I am just looking for someone."

"It is not good for strangers to come here looking for someone. Especially American strangers. We do not like Americans here."

Riley saw the barely perceptible signal go from the big man to the other, yet he didn't react to it. They grabbed his arms and bent him backward over the bar. The knife Riley had anticipated was there at his throat.

"Stand still, gringo, or my friend's hand may slip."

The big man released his hold and quickly patted Riley down. Finding no weapons, he pulled Riley's wallet out of his pocket. He flipped through the contents.

"Gonzalo, heh? Who you work for, Gonzalo?"

"I'm a cabdriver in New York. My wife and I are down here looking for a baby to adopt. I didn't mean to cause any trouble."

The big man looked at Riley quizzically and then at the wallet. The contents bore out Riley's story. The man struggled to read the English on Riley's taxi union card. This wasn't what he'd been told to expect. The American didn't act like any of the DEA or other American agents who ran around the city.

The big man signaled his partner to put the knife away, then stepped back, pondering the situation. His instructions had been to hurt the American. Kill him if he put up a fight. He hadn't been told to think or make a decision. "You are stupid. You have a very good story but I know you work for the DEA."

"I don't work for the DEA. I'm here on my own. What about Maria? I was told she might be able to get me in contact with someone who could help us." Riley looked at the man beseechingly. "You understand, my friend. It is my wife. She is unable to have children and she wants to have a child so badly."

The big man shook his head. "There is nothing Maria can do for you. Who gave you her name?"

"An American marine who used to be stationed at the embassy told my brother, who is also in the marines."

The big man laughed. "You tell a good story. I am going to feel sorry to hurt such a good storyteller. Maybe we cut out your tongue so you not tell any more stories."

The big man turned to his partner. "Do you want to take care of him or should I? Ah, he is too small for me. He's yours."

The knife man smiled. "Thanks." He reached back under his shirt to retrieve his knife.

Riley's crescent kick caught the man on the side of the head before the knife had even cleared the shirt. He dropped with a loud thump onto a table and rolled to the floor, unconscious. The big man was still in the process of reaching for his gun when Riley's side kick caught him in the ribs. Riley heard the crack as two of the man's ribs splintered under his steel-edged boots.

Riley stepped up and watched as the big man painfully straightened and tried for his gun again. He snapped a front kick into the man's crotch, and as it doubled him over, caught the man's face on its downward motion with his opposite knee. A satisfying splat told him he'd broken the man's nose.

Riley rolled the big man onto his back and pulled the gun from under his sweatshirt. A Colt Python revolver. Riley tucked the gun under his own shirt. Then he placed his boot on the big man's neck. He spoke in Spanish. "If you carry a gun you should put it someplace where you can get to it more quickly. That's free advice. You should also learn to be more friendly. I am going to ask you some questions and I want answers. It will make everything much nicer for all involved if you answer with the truth."

"Fuck you!" The big man spat. Blood was seeping from his nose, covering his face.

Riley removed his foot from the man's neck and jabbed it straight into his side, nudging the broken ribs. The man groaned and rolled, trying to protect himself.

Riley glanced at the door. Even if the kid didn't check in, he knew he was running out of time. He went over to the unconscious sicario and removed the knife from under the man's shirt. It was a Randall hunting knife with an eight-inch blade. Only one cutting edge but honed razor sharp.

The big man was making an attempt to get to his feet. Riley stomped the inside of his boot onto the outside of the man's knee. He screamed as the cartilage gave way and crumpled onto the floor.

"I need to find Maria." Riley held the knife to the man's throat.

"Fuck you!" The big man tried spitting at him.

Rather limited vocabulary, Riley thought. He also knew the kid outside had undoubtedly heard the yell. He just hoped the boy would assume it was the American doing the screaming as the sicarios worked him over.

Riley pressed the knife harder into the big man's throat, drawing blood. "I need to find Maria. I'll kill you if you don't tell me where she is."

"Fuck you, gringo. I know you won't kill me. You're one of those motherfucking drug enforcement scum. You'd better catch a flight for home before I kill you."

Big words for a bleeding man, Riley thought. Playtime's over. Riley turned and strode across to the unconscious man. He placed the knife under the man's jaw, pointing up. "Hey!" he called to the big man. Waiting until the sicario had focused on him, Riley put the weight of his body on the handle and shoved the blade up through the unconscious man's jaw into his brain. The body twitched violently for a second and then was still.

The big man's eyes bulged. "You're crazy, you fucker!"

Riley pulled the knife back out and wiped it clean on the dead man's shirt. He cut the dead man's belt and relieved the body of the knife scabbard. The pungent odor of the corpse's released bowels filled the cafe.

Riley stepped back in front of the big man. He stomped down, breaking the man's right hand. The sicario backed himself into a corner and put his arms up, right hand dangling, to defend himself.

"Maria!" Riley hissed. He pulled out the gun and pointed it.

The big man was frantic in his attempt to talk. "I don't know where she is. I swear!"

Riley tried another tack. "What about the DEA man, Stevens?"

"I don't know. I swear on my mother!"

"Too bad. Sucks being shot by your own gun. Kind of adds embarrassment to the whole thing. Besides being dead, of course." Riley cocked the pistol.

"Try the warehouse!"

Riley uncocked the gun. "What warehouse?"

"About two maybe three kilometers out of the city on the north mountain road—route 46. It says International Coffee Shipping and Receiving on the outside. It's a big brown building. You cannot miss it. It's off to the right, about a hundred meters from the road."

Riley put the gun in his waistband and the sicario breathed a deep sigh of relief. Riley reached down and grabbed the top of the big man's head with one hand, placing his other forearm under the man's neck and tilting the head so he could look into his eyes. "One last question, my friend, and then I go.

Do you know anything about the American soldier who was captured?"

The man rolled his eyes, obviously confused. "American soldier? I know nothing of that. Please, I have told you everything."

Riley nodded. He rotated his forearm upward from the elbow, levering the big man's jaw while keeping a tight grip with his other hand on the top of the man's head. The man's eyes showed a moment of panic before the crack of his neck caused them to lose their focus.

Riley stood up to leave. To his surprise he found he was trembling.

## 2:47 P.M.

Riley slid the key into the lock and swung the door open. Westland looked up from the bed where she was reading one of the local papers. "What's the matter? You don't look so good."

Riley shut the door and went over to the armchair, sinking down into its comfort. He drew the Colt Python out from under his shirt and tossed it on the bed. "You keep that."

Westland picked up the revolver and checked the load. "Am I going to need it?"

Riley shrugged. "Might. Might not. It's started."

"What's started?"

"The fun and games. I ran into two of Ring Man's thugs. They're the ones who donated the gun and this knife," he said, pulling up his shirt to show the scabbard.

"Where are they now?"

"They're dead."

"Dead?"

"Yeah, dead," Riley snapped. "I killed them."

Westland stared at him, not quite sure what to say. "What happened?"

Riley took a deep breath. He knew he needed to level with her, particularly since he had realized, while on the way back to the room, that he had made a mistake. A mistake that might lead the Ring Man's thugs right to this room.

"Let me start from the beginning. Last night I went to the Embassy Cafe and told the man working there that I was looking for Maria. Since Maria obviously works for Ring Man, I figured this would get some sort of reaction from his people. Something that might help me find either her or Stevens.

"The man told me to be there today at one. That's when and where I ran into the two goons. They thought I was DEA, and they were probably under orders to rough me up. I preempted them. In the process of that, and trying to get some information, I had to kill them both.

"Shit!" Riley slammed his fist into the arm of the chair. "That's not the whole truth. I didn't have to kill them in the fight. I killed the first one to let the second know I meant business to make him talk. I killed the second one because I didn't want him going back and reporting what he'd told me. I got a lead on Maria and I need to follow it up tonight before they can react." Killing two men still didn't sit right with Riley, even though they would just as easily have killed him and had obviously planned on at least hurting him badly.

Westland sensed his distress. She came over and put her hand on his shoulder. "Remember what you told me on the plane? This is war. We've got to be as hard as they are."

"Yeah, I know. It's just that I'm not used to killing people in cold blood."

"I hope you never get used to it. That's what separates you from them."

Riley looked up at her. He appreciated her concern and support. "You know, Kate, I hope when this is all over, you and I have some time to get to know each other."

She smiled and gave his shoulder a squeeze. "I hope so too."

"I'll take you up to the Bronx and show you the part of the city you didn't see at NYU. I'll also introduce you to my Mom. I think you'd like each other."

But, Riley thought, we don't have time to even talk much right now. "There's something else you should know. When I talked to the guy in the bar last night I made a mistake. I told him I had just flown in from New York and that I was with my wife. I gave him a false name but that still might be enough for Ring Man's people to get a line on us. That's one of the reasons I want you to have the gun."

"Do you think we should move?"

Riley shook his head. "If they're going to track us off the airline manifest, looking for a man and his wife from New York, they'll check all the hotels. This is as good as any. We'd have to use our cover names off the passports in order to check in anyplace else too. We just need to be more careful. We only have two more days."

## PENTAGON
## 2:57 P.M.

Pike's office in the Pentagon was buried in the basement, indicating that his position as head army staff officer for DCSOP-SO didn't rank very high. The best offices were on the main floor and on the outermost, or E-ring, of the building. Being in the basement near the heating plant wasn't the place for on-the-go officers.

Pike took a break from making calls on his secure STU-III phone and contemplated the marvels of military bureaucracy for a few moments. Despite the fact that a little over twenty-four hours ago he had basically told the chairman of the Joint Chiefs of Staff to go screw himself, here he was still sitting in his office and still wearing his star on each shoulder.

Pike knew the reason for this wasn't that the chairman had had a change of heart. The reason was that nothing in the Pentagon, or the army for that matter, worked quickly and everything was compartmentalized. Somewhere over his head, Pike was sure, was a note from the chairman stating that one Col. Michael Pike (temporarily breveted to brigadier general) was to retire as soon as it could be expedited. Pike was just as sure that the memo made no mention of the events of the last several days.

From his twenty-nine years of wrestling with military paper-work, Pike estimated he had about two weeks before that memo was translated into retirement orders. In the meantime, Pike was considered by his colleagues to be in the same position, and still breveted to Flag rank.

Pike was utilizing this situation to his advantage. He had already found out more information than he'd thought he could. The mention that a general was on the phone personally and wanted some information often got results. Plus, Pike had an extensive network of old acquaintances throughout the military and intelligence communities who owed him favors.

He had already traced the orders placing Riley under the operational control of the Central Intelligence Agency. The CIA's Pentagon liaison had gotten the deputy chief of staff for intelligence, G-2, to hack off on the request and then had one of the G-1 (personnel) people hand carry it over to military personnel headquartered down the road in Alexandria to get the classified orders cut. Pike figured that the G-2 had owed the CIA representative a favor, or now one was owed the other way, but he was sure that no one in the army knew the reason for Riley's transfer of control.

The orders themselves were classified and Pike had not been able to get a copy. He could well guess what was written on them, since he had seen those types of orders several times in his service with Delta Force. Basically they would say nothing about the reason for the transfer and would consist only of a start date, with the ending date left blank.

Pike also had found out the present location of Ring Man. A few calls to old friends in the Defense Intelligence Agency had produced the information about the CIA's request for satellite surveillance on the Ring Man's villa. Pike had called in a big favor and had had copies of the imagery faxed to him over the secure line from Fort Meade, where the National Security Agency had its headquarters.

Pike looked at the pictures laid out across his desk. If the CIA expected Riley to hit the Ring Man at that location, they were stupider than he had always thought they were. One man going against that place was suicide.

Of course, Pike smiled to himself, it wasn't just one man. His inquiries with some retired Special Forces men working at the agency indicated that Westland was with Riley. Pike had been impressed with the young woman during the time they worked together. He hoped she got out of this mess all right.

Pike had also watched the tapdancing by the Department of Defense and Department of State on the issue of the bodies on the video, which had still not been released. Pike didn't relish the idea of seeing those young fellows he had commanded being paraded like meat. He'd seen too much death in his time. The fact that there were only four bodies wasn't lost on him either. Powers really might be alive.

Putting all the pieces together told Pike one thing: Riley was in a bad situation and it wasn't likely to get any better. Pike wasn't sure what he could do to help, but he knew he had to try. He took out a notepad and started war-gaming options.

## RING MAN'S VILLA
## 3:20 P.M.

Ponte took the phone call about Pablo's and his partner's deaths. The news was disturbing, not because two of their men had been killed but because the identity of the killer was unknown. The kid tending the bar had given a poor description of the man Pablo and his sidekick had met. It might or might not be the American who had approached the worker the previous night.

Ponte decided it was time to bring the boss up to speed. He knocked on the door of the office adjacent to his.

"Come in."

Ponte entered and walked over to the Ring Man, who was talking on the phone to the man who was leading their war in Medellin against what remained of Suarez's operation. The Ring Man's latest attraction, a slight girl of fifteen, was sitting on the corner of the desk while the Ring Man's free hand absently fondled her.

Ponte waited nervously until the conversation was over. The Ring Man never liked bad news, and the report about Pablo wasn't exactly the best.

Ring Man hung up and turned to his aide with a small smile on his face. At least it looked like he was in a good mood to start with. "We are doing well in Medellin. Many of Suarez's people are seeing the light and switching over. I think in another week we will have firm control there."

The Ring Man rubbed his hands together, oblivious of Ponte's discomfort. "Soon I will be able to focus on the government and the Ramerizes. Have you heard any word from Ariel in Cartagena? Will he be able to get to the Ramerizes?"

Ponte shook his head. "He has not called back yet. I talked to him this morning, and he said he had some ideas. He was going to see how feasible they were this afternoon. We should hear something tonight."

Ring Man nodded. "Good. Ariel is a good man even though he is a foreigner. What would we do without our Israeli friends, eh? They teach us how to kill so much better." Ring Man laughed and pulled the girl onto his lap.

Ponte agreed that the handful of former Israeli military men who were in Colombia advising the various gangs were a valuable asset. The Israeli government formally denied their presence and privately abhorred the fact that these men were there. But there were always a certain number of military men, no matter what the nationality, who were willing to sell their skills to the highest bidder.

Ariel had been a paratroop commander in the Israeli Army. In coming to Colombia he'd given up his right to go back to Israel, but he had exchanged his citizenship for money and the opportunity to exercise his "talents." The fact that Ring Man trusted him with the war against the Ramerizes spoke volumes about his ability.

Ponte knew that if the Ring Man grew any more fond of the Israeli, Ariel might well end up sitting in Ponte's office next to the Ring Man. That did little to dispel the unease Ponte felt about having to relay the news about Pablo.

"What else is new, my friend? Anything I need to know about?"

Ponte nodded. "There is a strange American here in Bogota. He's been asking questions about Maria."

Ring Man shrugged. "Kill him."

Ponte licked his lips. "I sent Pablo to take care of him this afternoon."

"Good. Then we don't have to worry about the strange American anymore."

"Pablo is dead."

The Ring Man's humor vanished and he abruptly stood up, letting the girl fall off his lap. "The American killed him?"

"I'm not sure."

"What the hell do you mean you're not sure?" the Ring Man yelled.

Ponte backed up slightly. "I mean, I think it was the American. Pablo went to the Embassy Cafe to meet the American. There was a man there. Apparently they fought and Pablo was killed."

"You have no witnesses?"

"The barboy saw the man, but his description is not good enough to tell if it was the American. The American who asked about Maria looked like a Latino and was short. That is the same description of the man who killed Pablo. Since the description is the same and the American was supposed to be there at that time and place, I think it must have been him."

The Ring Man sat back down, his anger changing to thoughtfulness. "Was Pablo alone?"

Ponte sighed. He'd hoped he could keep the second man out of it. "No. He took one man with him. He was killed also."

The Ring Man raised an eyebrow. "This American killed Pablo and another man? How were they killed?"

"The backup had a knife shoved into his jaw going up into the brain. Pablo's neck was broken. It looks like Pablo was in a pretty bad fight before he was killed, so maybe he hurt the American."

The Ring Man looked even more impressed. He'd expected his men had been shot. But whoever this stranger was, he used his hands well, taking out two armed men.

The Ring Man pulled the girl back onto his lap and pondered the information. The whole thing was strange. The Americans had always been reluctant to use force. In fact, the Ring Man despised the American people as a whole for their failure to use the power they had. The DEA had always been a joke in Colombia. Any aggressive agent was usually transferred back to the United States. They were more concerned with image than with results.

Ring Man stared straight ahead. His eyes grew vacant and Ponte stirred uncomfortably. That meant the Ring Man was plotting. Ponte waited for almost five minutes while the Ring Man's internal computer worked. Finally his boss's eyes refocused.

"I don't think this American was DEA. This isn't their style. What about CIA?"

Ponte shook his head. "I have had no reports on any new actions by the CIA. It's possible, though."

"Whoever this man is, he wants Maria. That means he probably knows about the connection between Maria and Stevens. Is he trying to find Stevens?" Ring Man didn't wait for an answer as a new thought struck him. "He might be after the American we captured. They must know by now that there were only four bodies on the video. So maybe they figure there is one left alive."

Ponte shook his head. "But just one man? Wouldn't they be sending more down here if that's what they are after?"

Ring Man didn't know. "The Americans are funny people. They do strange things. Maybe this man is just here to get information. Whatever the case, I want the American prisoner moved. Bring him here. They will never be able to get at him here."

"What about Maria?"

"She knows nothing about the American prisoner. She's all right where she is. Warn her, though, to be careful."

"What should I do about the American in the city?"

"Find him and kill him."


# PENTAGON
## 3:50 P.M.

Pike had done as much as he could over the phone. It was time now to do some face-to-face talking and get the wheels moving. He took the elevator to the first floor and strode to the outer corridor. The offices here had become familiar to him over the past week during his mission coordination. Right now Pike was going to find out how far down the chairman had passed word of the termination of the Hammer missions and Pike's own loss of stature.

He turned in under a sign that read DCSOP-SO and pulled up in front of the secretary who guarded the inner sanctum. "Is your boss busy, Jean?"

The secretary smiled at Pike. "Let me buzz him, Mike."

Pike licked his lips as he waited. Throughout the Hammer missions he'd been the one coordinating all the various parts. The DCSOP-SO, Lieutenant General Linders, had been one of his key points of contact, in charge of all support from the Special Operations Forces of the different services. The only time, as far as Pike knew, that Linders had had direct contact with Macksey was the initiating phone call and his attendance at the first briefback. All other contact had been through Pike.

"The general says go in, Mike." Pike nodded his thanks and entered.

Linders stood up to greet him. "Hey, Mike, I'm sorry about those guys you lost. It's a hell of a mess. I've had a bunch of calls from 1st SOW and SOCOM about it. I did what you asked and referred them to the Public Affairs Office but I'm not sure they're buying it. Slaight down at Bragg is being a particular pain in the butt trying to find out what the hell happened."

Pike shook his head as he sat in the offered seat. "Yes, sir. It's a problem all around. The video those assholes are releasing is screwing up the cover story. The chairman's doing a lot of tapdancing on it. I guess he's under pressure from State and the White House to keep everything under wraps, trying to protect President Alegre's involvement."

Linders cursed. "I don't know why they don't just come out and put everything aboveboard. Let us go down and kick some ass and not have to do all this sneaky stuff. Plus it's a disgrace to those men who died not to have their accomplishments noted."

Pike was relaxing. It was obvious from his comments that Linders didn't know Pike had been fired. He decided to go for broke. "Well, that's kind of what I'm here to talk to you about."

Linders looked interested. "You going to run Hammer Four on that same target?"

Pike shook his head. "No, that target has been compromised. We're moving on to Hammer Five."

# BOGOTA
# 6:00 P.M.

Riley and Westland sat on the edge of the bed watching the Spanish broadcast of the Colombian news on the small TV in their room. The video of the American bodies made the lead story.

Riley watched the screen fill with a slow pan of the bodies of Partusi, Marzan, Holder, and Lane. The camera was obviously hand-held and the video was of poor quality, yet there was no denying the identity of the dead. Nor would there be any denying that the four men had been shot up pretty badly. The back half of Lane's head was missing where a round had torn through. The video was about twenty seconds long and showed only the bodies. No sign of Powers, dead or alive.

Riley listened to the comments of the newscaster:

"This video was delivered to *El Tiempo* yesterday evening. It was accompanied by a letter signed 'Protector of the People.' The text of the letter is:

" 'People of Colombia, see what your president has allowed in your country. American soldiers come here and attack our citizens. And President Alegre knew about it! He allows Yankee imperialists to invade our sovereign territory and kill our people. These Americans were killed attacking farmers in the Barranquilla province.

" 'Take these bodies as our warning that we will not accept this situation.'"

The newscaster came back on.

"The office of the president has denied the report that the American soldiers were in Colombian territory at the request of President Alegre.

"The American government claims that the soldiers were killed in a helicopter crash flying out of Panama. The American military maintains that the aircraft was misoriented in flight and the crash in Colombian territory was a result of this navigational error. Washington denies that American forces have been conducting any sort of operations in our country."

Riley turned off the TV as the story shifted. He didn't feel quite so bad about the sicarios he had killed this afternoon.

## 8:30 P.M.

"Nice wheels." Riley took a walk around the beat-up Ford Pinto. "Your man definitely worked hard to get us something with a lot of power. At least it will fit in with all the other cars we've seen around here, except of course the BMWs and Mercedeses owned by the drug people. I've never seen so many fancy cars in one place before."

Westland laughed as she got in the driver's side. "I think there've been something like ten thousand new millionaires in Colombia over the past ten years, and they all want the good stuff."

Kate cranked the engine. Riley was relieved to hear that the engine sounded in good shape. "Do you know the way?"

"Sí, Señor Gonzalo."

As Kate drove, Riley went to work disconnecting the interior dome light. She wound their way out of the city. By the time she cleared the northern limits of Bogota the sun was almost all the way down and night was beginning to blanket the sky. She turned to the north along a highway with the mountains looming in close on the right side.

Riley was sleeping on the passenger side. The lack of sleep and tremendous amounts of adrenaline he'd gone through in the last forty-eight hours had finally caught up with him.

Westland drove slowly along the two-lane road, allowing Riley as much sleep as possible. After twenty minutes she reached over and gently tapped him on the shoulder.

"What's up?" he asked groggily.

Westland pointed up ahead and to the right. "See those lights on the mountainside?"

"Yeah."

"According to the plot on the map, my odometer says that's got to be Ring Man's villa." She pointed as they passed a tar access road on their right. "That must be his driveway. From here it's about three klicks up that road along the mountainside to his place."

Riley watched as the lights grew closer. He rolled down his window and peered out as they passed the site. He could see very little, since the house was almost eight hundred feet above the highway. The glow indicated that the Ring Man probably had the entire grounds illuminated. Riley wasn't sure yet whether that would be an advantage or a disadvantage.

Westland was watching the odometer carefully in the dim dashboard light. She jumped as a vehicle flashed its lights in her rearview mirror and then roared around her. A truck load of drunk farm workers leaned over the railing of the truck bed, screaming at them for going too slow.

Riley reached out and put a hand on her shoulder. "Relax, Kate."

She nodded, still keeping her attention on the odometer. "Anywhere along in here." She pulled over and slowed even further.

He cracked open his door and turned to her. "See you soon." Then he rolled out, throwing the door shut as he went.

Riley hit the ground and rolled into the drainage ditch on the side of the road. He landed in the cold water at the bottom, which seeped into his clothes. Crouching in the ditch, he allowed himself a few seconds to get oriented. Looking to the east, in the dim starlight, he could make out the notch in the mountains ahead that indicated the top of the draw. Down that draw ran the stream he was looking for. He figured the stream must be somewhere off to his left, since they had not crossed it in the car prior to his jumping out.

He took out his compass and shot an azimuth to the notch, rotating the glowing lines in the base of the compass to match the illuminated north arrow on that setting. Then he offset that slightly to the north. He wanted to intersect the stream prior to the waterfall.

Counting every right footfall, Riley headed up the draw. He estimated it was 1.2 kilometers to the waterfall. He knew that his pace count, normally sixty right steps for every hundred meters, would be inaccurate due to the steep terrain. But the pace count and azimuth were really backups. He was counting on running into the left limit of the stream and following that, or hitting the front limit of the steep shelf from which the waterfall dropped, and following that to the left.

It felt good to be back out in the open again. Riley took a deep breath of the cool night air as he strode along. Being alone in the dark might be a terrifying experience for some, but it gave Riley a sense of freedom. There were no distractions, and he was accountable to no one. He always enjoyed the feeling of being out in nature, even if it was during a mission.

After fifteen minutes the noise of falling water became perceptible. He turned his course a little more to the left, hitting thicker vegetation the closer he got to the water. Suddenly he broke through to a slightly overgrown path next to the stream. Riley knelt down and ran his fingers over the dirt at the base of the path, searching for recent footprints. In the dark he couldn't see anything, and his fingers yielded no information. Drawing the knife he had taken from the sicario, he headed up the path.

Riley knew the attaché had most likely used this same path to put in the cache. He just hoped no one else would be on it tonight. He made much better time on the path than he had in the thick brush and was quickly rewarded with the sound of water crashing into a pool ahead. Riley stepped out into the moonlit clearing at the base of the waterfall.

The rock mentioned in the cache report was easy to spot. It stood on the south side of the pool a short hop from the shore. Riley bounded over to the rock and knelt down. He felt along the north edge for a fishing line or anything else that might be connected to the cache. Nothing.

Riley sighed and took his clothes off, shivering in the chill night air. Gripping the knife in his teeth, he held onto the rock with his hands. Damn. He hated cold water. The icy mountain pool made his skin crawl as he slowly lowered himself in, sliding his feet along the side of the rock. Totally immersed, except for his head, he took a deep breath and pushed himself under the water. When his feet hit something, he turned upside down, and swam down the few feet to the bundle. Quickly feeling around, he determined that the cache was buoyant and held in place with an anchor cable. At that point he ran out of breath and headed back up.

Riley broke the surface and took a few deep breaths. His body was shaking from the cold. He hoped the cable was cutable. It should be, since the cache report had said to bring a knife. Gripping the knife in his hand, he dove again. Working his way around the bundle, he finally found the anchor cable. To his numbed fingers it felt like rope. Probably attached to a heavy rock the attaché had found somewhere close by to use as an anchor. Riley sawed at the rope with the knife until he couldn't stay down any longer.

It took Riley two more trips before the rope parted and the cache popped to the surface. Hanging onto the cache with his numbed fingers, Riley pulled it to shore. Beaching the bundle, he dragged himself out of the water. He was shivering so badly it took a tremendous amount of willpower to rouse himself. He grabbed his clothes and, after inadequately drying himself with his sweatshirt, he pulled them on. Riley wanted to kick himself for forgetting to bring a towel.

He glanced at his watch. He had forty-five minutes before Kate did her first pass by on the road below. After that it would be once every hour. He knew there was much to be done tonight and decided to get going immediately. Besides, the walk down would warm him up.

He inspected the cache more carefully. It was a box about two feet by five wrapped in plastic sheets. An unwieldy package at best. Riley picked it up and carefully balanced it on his shoulder. He estimated it weighed about fifty pounds. He took off down the path, determined to follow it all the way to the road rather than beating cross-country through the brush. If he ran into someone that would be that person's tough luck, because Riley was in no mood to mess around.

As he walked, he felt his body warm up from the exercise. The box dug into his shoulder and slipped a few times as he descended. Finally, about ten meters ahead he saw the dark line of the road. He checked his watch. Five minutes to eleven. He edged up to the road and quickly crossed. Settling in behind some bushes he waited.

Finally he heard the muted rumble of a car heading his way from the north. He peered up the road and watched. Two headlights came into view. Riley smiled in relief as he saw the brights flash on and off three times in rapid succession. Looking back to make sure no cars were coming from the opposite direction, he stepped out into the road and lit his lighter. The car swung off the road next to him and stopped. Riley opened the back door and slid in the bundle. He crammed himself in next to it.

Westland pulled back out into the road and continued heading south. "How'd it go?"

"Could you turn the heat on, please? I had to take a swim. I hate cold water. That attaché did a good job putting it in. I just hope it has everything."

As Westland drove, Riley tore through the protective wrapping with his knife, uncovering a plastic case sealed with duct tape. He cut the tape and opened the lid. The contents had been individually waterproofed. Riley unwrapped each item carefully.

The largest was a rifle: an M21 sniper rifle. Riley still wasn't sure how he would hit the Ring Man, but he wanted to have the capability to do it from a distance if the opportunity presented itself. The M21 was a match grade M14 rifle with the upper receiver glazed into the lower with fiberglass to prevent any movement between those parts. With the rifle were two magazines of ten rounds each of national match 7.62mm ammunition and an ART2 scope already mounted. Riley had asked that the scope be zeroed in and he hoped it hadn't been jostled out of alignment during the emplacement and recovery of the cache. Riley felt confident he could hit the Ring Man out to a kilometer, maybe more, with this system if he got the chance. He placed the rifle on the floor.

Next, he unwrapped the second-largest package. A short, bulky muzzle soon appeared, attached to a collapsing-stock submachine gun. It was an MP5SD3 mounted with a silencer, just like the one he had carried on the missions. There were twenty thirty-round magazines of 9mm ammunition in the box. Ten of those magazines were already in the pockets of an assault vest. Riley slapped a magazine into the weapon and loaded it. He placed it next to himself on the seat and put on the vest.

Next he pulled out two similar small packages. Unwrapping them disclosed two canvas bags, each holding a Claymore mine with time pencil, remote clacker, and trip wire. Riley wasn't sure how he would use the mines but they opened up possibilities. A plastic case contained a set of PVS-5s with four spare batteries. Riley unscrewed the battery cover and put one of the batteries in the goggles.

The last two packages were also identical. Each contained a Beretta 9mm pistol in a shoulder holster. There were six fifteen-round magazines with each weapon. Riley strapped his on, put the rifle and Claymores back into the plastic case, and climbed over the passenger seat into the front. He placed the other pistol on the seat next to Westland. "Got you a gift. Don't ever say I never gave you anything. You can take that Colt out of your pants now. Must be kind of uncomfortable."

Westland smiled as she negotiated the road. "Thanks. Maybe I'll get you something for Christmas."

Riley had been so busy unwrapping his toys, he had lost track of their whereabouts. "Where are we?"

"We made the turn onto route 46 about a minute ago. You're done just in time. Another two klicks and we should be at the turnoff for the warehouse."

Riley looked around. This road was more heavily traveled than the one to Ring Man's villa. "Go past the turnoff and see if you can find a place to pull over."

Riley spotted the driveway the same time as Westland did. He could make out lights and the edge of the warehouse the sicario had described to him. Westland went about four hundred meters past the turnoff and then pulled off the road, edging the car between the asphalt and the drainage ditch.

Riley grabbed the MP5 and one of the Claymore bags. "Let's go." He slipped the night-vision goggles over his head and turned them on.

Westland locked the doors and then followed, strapping on her Beretta. She kept the Colt tucked into the waist of her jeans. Riley led the way through the trees, slowing his pace for Westland, who kept her hand on his back and blindly followed him.

# WEDNESDAY, 4 SEPTEMBER

## OUTSKIRTS OF BOGOTA
## 12:02 A.M.

Riley pulled off his goggles and peered at the warehouse. He blinked for a few seconds to allow his eyes to adjust to the dimmer light. Westland stood beside him in the shadows, her shoulder touching his.

"What now?" she whispered in his ear.

Riley spent a few moments surveying the scene. The warehouse was a squat building measuring approximately fifty meters by seventy-five. A loading dock with two large bay doors encompassed the side they faced. Two tractor trailers were backed up to the loading dock, which was dimly lit by several light bulbs. The tail ends of two cars were visible parked on the left side of the building where the road to the highway came in. Riley imagined that the office and personnel door were over there. The building had no windows that he could see on this side.

All Riley knew was that Maria might be in this warehouse. The whole setup could even be a trap. Any plan was going to have to be an improvisation at best. "All right. We got two cars and two trailers. Two cars means there might be anywhere from two to eight people in there. We don't know if they're all bad guys or if this is a legitimate business or what the hell is inside. We're going to play this by ear. We'll try going around the right side and see if there are any windows or doors we can gain entry through. I don't like the idea of going in the front door.

270

"Once inside we'll move as a team. I'll go first and you cover. If we run into someone, I'll do the talking and I want you to stay out of sight. You're my ace in the hole if the shit hits the fan."

He turned and looked into Kate's eyes. "If shooting starts, remember to shoot to kill. If it's only one person, I'll try taking them out with the silenced submachine gun. If you have to fire, then we go for broke. Let people run away but take out anyone who fights. If you see a woman who matches the description of Maria, try to take her alive."

Riley smiled grimly. "I know it isn't much of a plan, but it's the best I can come up with under the circumstances. You ready?" Kate nodded.

Riley followed the trees to the right until they got around the edge of the building. The side of the building stretched to the next corner without a break. Riley continued on around until he could see the fourth side. Another solid blank.

"All right. Let's try the doors where the trailers are."

He retraced his steps. Checking to make sure no one was around, Riley led the way out of the safety of the forest and across the open area up to one of the trailers. Sidling along the vehicle, he came up to the loading dock. He clambered up onto it and then turned and helped Westland up.

Checking the loading doors, he found both of them locked. Shit, Riley thought. "We're going in the front. Be prepared to start shooting."

Westland pulled out her Beretta and chambered a round, slipping off the safety. Riley crept up to the corner of the building, then lay on his stomach and peered around. The door was between the two cars about ten feet away. Riley hoped that it was at least unlocked. He stood up and edged his way around the corner and up to the door. Westland was behind him, keeping an eye on the driveway for any cars that might be coming.

Riley slid his hand over the doorknob and turned it. The knob rotated all the way. Slowly he tugged and the door opened with a creak. As quickly as he could, he slipped inside to the right of the door, submachine gun at the ready. Westland followed him in, moving to the inside left of the door.

They were in what looked like a small waiting room or reception area. The room was unoccupied and a dim bulb was the only illumination. Plywood walls defined the room, but there was no ceiling and the warehouse roof loomed overhead. There was one door straight ahead, another one to the left, and two to the right.

Riley could hear voices echoing from the warehouse. The two doors on the right led to bathrooms, judging from the signs on the doors. He figured, based on the setup, that the door to the left probably led to another office. The door straight ahead had to lead into the main warehouse area. Signaling Westland to cover the door to the warehouse, Riley quickly checked out the left door. The room behind it was empty.

Riley rejoined Westland. Glancing around he spotted a couch. He gestured to Westland, and the two of them picked up the couch to move it to the inner wall. He could stand on it and look over the wall before going in.

They froze as a long, drawn-out scream split the air. Westland looked at Riley; someone wasn't having a good time. They put the couch against the inner wall; Riley stood precariously on the back of it and peered over the wall.

The warehouse had stacks of shipping crates as far as he could see. From his vantage point he couldn't see the source of the screaming. Pathways large enough for small forklifts wove through the stacks at right angles.

There was another scream, followed by whimpering. Riley clambered off the couch and pointed at the door. Westland raised her pistol and nodded. Riley swung the door open and stepped through.

As he entered the warehouse, Riley sensed movement to his right. He dropped to his left knee as he turned to his right, swinging around the muzzle of the MP5. His eyes focused on a man trying to pull a gun out of a shoulder holster. As the stubby muzzle of Riley's sub centered on the target, he smoothly drew back on the trigger.

The sound of the bolt chugging back and forth as the rounds spewed out was startlingly loud to Riley. The guard grunted and slammed back against a crate as Riley stitched a pattern of five rounds from the man's chest up to his head. The expended brass casings tinkled to the floor.

Riley whirled and faced down the pathway between the crates that led to the center of the warehouse. The entire place had gone silent except for the continued sound of someone crying. Westland materialized at Riley's side, took in the sight of the body, and then turned her attention to the pathway.

Riley gestured for Westland to cover him as he started moving forward. He halted as a male voice called out, "Roberto? Roberto?" Riley pressed himself back into the shadows as he heard footsteps coming his way.

Another guard appeared, weapon still in his holster. Riley resisted the temptation to fire. Letting the sub drop on its sling along his side, he drew the knife. He waited until the man was practically upon him and then, in one powerfully smooth movement, stepped out and attacked. One hand buried the knife in the man's throat and then slashed the carotid arteries and windpipe, while the other hand applied opposite pressure against the man's head.

The guard stared at Riley in shock as his hands went to his throat. Blood bubbled over his fingers and his breath wheezed out the new opening. He dropped to his knees and fell over onto his face. Riley put the knife back in its sheath and rotated up his submachine gun. He took a deep breath and continued on his way, Westland trailing him by about fifteen feet.

The light grew stronger and the sobbing louder as they got closer to the center of the room. Reaching the end of the aisle, Riley dropped to his knees and edged forward. He could hear the voices more clearly now, raised in argument. He could make out the voices of at least two men and one woman.

Riley took a quick peek around the corner and then drew back. He examined the image imprinted in his mind. A chair in the middle of an open area. A naked man tied to the chair, his back to Riley. Two men and a woman gathered around the chair with a table next to them, discussing whether someone should go after the man Riley had just killed. One of the men called out. "Pablo!"

Riley turned and pointed, directing Westland to take a position in the shadows on the far side of the aisle. Then he stood up and took a few deep breaths to calm himself. He knew he had about twenty-five rounds left in his submachine gun magazine. He quietly released the lock and extended the telescoping stock. He placed the butt deep into his shoulder. Melding his cheek to the steel stock, with his right eye over the weapon, he peered down the barrel.

Riley stepped out from behind the crates. He fired two three-round bursts in the space of half a second. The two men flew backward, fatally hit, while they were still registering his appearance. The woman reached for an automatic rifle on the table.

"Freeze!" Riley screamed in Spanish as he started to move forward, the weapon still tight in against his cheek. The woman ignored him and grabbed the rifle. Riley fired a five-round burst, aiming low. The 9mm steel-jacketed rounds tore into the woman's legs, blowing them out from underneath her.

The crack of a pistol being fired from behind caused Riley to go into a diving spin to his left. As he brought his weapon up to bear he was treated to the sight of Westland firing a second round into the head of a guard who must have circled around the warehouse and come up the same aisle Riley had. Half the guard's face was missing as he slid to the ground. Westland gave Riley a quick nod, indicating all clear.

Riley returned his gaze to the wounded woman. She was reaching for the rifle she had dropped when she'd been shot. Riley jumped to his feet and ran to her, kicking the rifle away. She glared at him from where she lay in a puddle of blood.

He looked up as Westland joined him. She kept her pistol pointed at Maria and gestured over her shoulder. "Is it Stevens?"

Riley turned his attention to the man in the chair. It was Stevens. Riley felt conflicting emotions as he stared at the bound figure. This was the man who had betrayed his team and caused the death of four of his friends. The Colombians had been doing quite a job on the DEA man. A car battery was on the table and electrodes were attached to Stevens's scrotum. A flick of a switch and current would flow. It also looked as though they had spent some time pounding him about the head and shoulders. From the droop, Riley guessed that both his collarbones were broken.

"Yeah, it's him. Keep her covered. Shoot her in the legs again if she tries moving."

"She's bleeding pretty bad. If we don't stop it she'll be dead soon."

Riley ignored the last comment and moved over in front of Stevens. The man looked up but without recognition. He was too far gone. They hadn't been torturing him for information, Riley realized. They'd been torturing him for vengeance. Riley could see where one of Stevens's fingers had been cut off.

Riley pulled his knife and cut the straps that bound Stevens to the solid wood chair. He was just starting to pull Stevens up when he realized he had made a mistake. "Get down!" he screamed as he dove for the ground, letting go of Stevens in the process.

The blast stunned Riley. He lay on the ground for a few seconds and did a mental scan of his body as debris clattered down about him. His ears were ringing and he could hear nothing. He slowly sat up and looked around. Westland was dragging herself to her knees from where the blast had knocked her down. Riley could see blood spattered on her shirt. He looked down at himself. He was covered in blood also.

Then he saw the source of the blood. A piece of gnarled meat was all that was left of Stevens. Riley suddenly remembered Maria. He got to his feet. The Colombian woman was trying to crawl away. Riley admired her guts. He tried yelling at Westland but could barely hear himself, and it was obvious that she was still too deaf and dazed from the explosion to hear him. He ran after Maria and blocked her way. She had left a copious trail of blood behind her. Weakly lifting her head, she glared at Riley.

She was trying to work up the saliva to spit at him when she died. Riley looked down on her for a few seconds. A link gone, along with Stevens. He went back to tend to Westland.

Kate had regained her senses, except for the ringing in her ears. She was staring, mesmerized by the remains of Stevens. Riley took a quick look around to see if there was anything they could use, then grabbed Kate's arm and led her out.

## 12:33 A.M.

Riley swung up his MP5. He could hear noises ahead where they had left the car. Signaling Westland to stay behind, he crept forward.

As he got closer he could hear what sounded like two people in the vicinity of the car. He slid forward and peered out from the tree line. A pickup truck was pulled up behind the Pinto and two men were trying to pry open the hood.

Riley shook his head in amazement. After all he'd been through, he couldn't believe that these guys were trying to rip off his car. This country was worse than the South Bronx.

He pulled off the goggles and gave his eyes a few seconds to adjust, then put down the submachine gun and pulled out his Beretta. As he broke through the brush, the two men swung around to face him, one pulling a knife, the other brandishing the tire iron they had impolitely been using on the hood.

"You have three seconds, then I blow your heads off, my friends."

The pair were in their truck in two and gone in less than ten. Riley called for Westland to join him as he retrieved his sub.

"What was that?"

"Two assholes were trying to rip off our car. You believe this place?" Riley looked at Kate with concern. "Are you all right to drive?"

She nodded weakly and got behind the wheel. Riley jumped in the other side and they headed back the way they had come. As she drove, Westland asked the question that had been disturbing her. "What happened back there in the warehouse with Stevens?"

Riley sighed. "I fucked up. One of the rules of rescuing hostages is to make sure they aren't booby-trapped before moving them. I forgot all about that when I cut Stevens free. They must have wired him up. The charge was probably a stick of dynamite shoved up his ass, because I didn't see anything. I'm lucky I heard the fuse release when I started lifting him and that there was about a second delay on the charge. His body contained most of the force of the blast. We're also lucky it was a simple wood chair and there wasn't much, other than Stevens, to turn into shrapnel when it blew, otherwise we'd both probably be dead."

Westland shook her head. "What the hell are we going up against here? Why did they still have Stevens? What were they hoping to get from him? If he compromised the mission he must have told them everything they wanted to know by now."

From what he had seen of Stevens before the explosion, Riley knew that the Colombians had wrung the DEA man dry well before this night. "I think they were letting Maria work on him for fun. Maybe that was her payment for having screwed Stevens to get the timing and locations on the missions. Just remember that these people are working with a different set of values than we are. You need to keep that in mind. Don't hesitate because of sympathy or doubt. If you do you'll be dead."

Westland glanced over at him. "I think you had that in your mind when we came down here. What you did in that bar didn't leave much room for sympathy or the possibility that you might have been making a mistake."

Riley met her gaze. "When you're in hell you play by the devil's rules."

## 1:26 A.M.

They flashed by the turnoff for the Ring Man's villa again. Riley rechecked the magazine in the submachine gun and placed the empty magazine in his vest. He waited until Westland pulled up next to the stream. "Don't pick up any strangers."

"Be careful, Dave."

Riley got out of the car and strode off up the hard-to-find trail next to the stream. He draped his night-vision goggles over his eyes and switched them on.

After fifteen minutes of walking he turned off the trail and beat his way cross-country to the southeast toward a knoll he had located on the map. The glow of the security lights from the Ring Man's villa lit the sky to the south. Riley clambered up the slope until he got to the tree-covered knoll, designated by its elevation on the map as 8548, that looked down on the villa's grounds about five hundred meters to the south.

Riley climbed one of the taller trees and settled himself down on a forked limb. It wasn't comfortable but would have to do. He scanned the grounds.

He could easily see over the ten-foot stone wall into the interior. The house was well lit with floodlights pointing down from along the edge of the roof. The main house was two stories tall with one-story wings on either side. A large oval swimming pool was behind the house. The driveway and circular parking area in the front were bordered by an extensive garden that stretched out to the walls on the front third of the grounds. The helipad was barely in sight over the east wing of the house.

Riley carefully watched the grounds and gradually started locating the guards. They moved in seemingly random patterns about the grounds. Whoever set up the pattern obviously had more of a security than military background. It would have been more effective to have hidden the guards in good defensive positions. There were six in the outer grounds that Riley could spot. Four were assigned one to each side of the compound; the other two roved the entire perimeter, one in each direction. It was a good system in that these two could quickly spot whether any side guard was no longer at his post.

Riley couldn't see down into the parking circle in the front so it was impossible to tell how many vehicles were parked there. From what he could see of the house, it was hard to ascertain whether or not there were interior guards. After an hour and a half of observation, Riley deduced that there had to be some sort of security command post inside the house. He had watched several of the guards talk into shoulder-mounted mikes attached to radios on their belts. He'd been unable to see any of the other outside guards reply. It would make sense to have them report to someone inside, and Riley also figured it would make sense to have a reaction force of at least the off-duty guards inside sleeping. He estimated that there were probably several more guards awake inside as a second line of defense and also as an immediate reaction force if an attack came.

The apparent lack of a roadblock or antiarmor weapons led Riley to assume that probably at least one ambush was set up along the one-lane drive that came up from the highway to the villa. No worthwhile security man would fail to defend that obvious avenue of approach.

Riley gave it another hour of watching and then climbed stiffly out of the tree. He waited a few minutes to let the blood circulate back into his legs and then set off downslope to link up with Kate.

# BOGOTA
## 5:46 A.M.

Kate handed Riley another cup of coffee. "What do you think?"

Riley rubbed his eyes wearily. "I don't know. I've ruled out going into that place. I wouldn't last five minutes. If the Ring Man goes outside during the day to either the pool or elsewhere in the back, I could get a good shot at him from the knoll where I was doing the surveillance. Even then I'm not sure I could escape, since I imagine they'd react pretty swiftly. I'd have to make it from the firing point down to the road, and they would beat me there."

"What about hiding in the mountains after you shoot?"

Riley shook his head. "This is their territory. They'd have a better chance of finding me, or having one of the locals turn me in, than I would of being able to evade."

"What about using Spectre or the gunships? I could probably get a hold of Pike through the attaché in the embassy."

Riley shook his head dubiously. "It's worth a shot, but I doubt that either our government or the Colombians would be too willing to try anything like that after Nail Three and the video being released. I'm also not sure what Pike's status is right now. You said the task force had been disbanded. They've probably shoveled the colonel off into his old job, although if I know him as well as I think I do, he probably made quite a ruckus about Powers getting abandoned. Hell, he may even be out of the army by now." Riley didn't add the information about the phone call he had made prior to their flight departing from New York.

He got up, went over to the bed, and flopped on it. "I'm too tired to think straight right now." He wanted to let himself drift off, but his mind was still swirling, trying to find an answer. Plus, he still had no line on Powers.

He cracked an eye open at Westland, who was slumped wearily in the armchair. "It might be worthwhile for you to talk to the attaché later today. Let's grab a couple hours of rack time and then you can head over to the embassy."

Riley patted the bed next to him. "Come on over. I don't bite. I'm too damn tired to do anything more than sleep anyway."

Westland got up and slid into the bed, still wearing her outfit from the previous evening. Within five minutes she was breathing gently and rolled over with her back to Riley, knees tucked up into her stomach. Just before Riley succumbed to the weights on his eyelids he curled up around Westland's warmth.

# RING MAN'S VILLA
# 6:00 A.M.

The attack at the warehouse wasn't discovered until 5:10 A.M., when a new shift of guards showed up for duty. Ponte had taken the report with a certain degree of regret. He wished he hadn't gotten up so early and been present when the phone rang. The Ring Man wasn't going to like the bearer of these tidings.

Ponte ran the information through his mind one more time, summarizing it so he could be prepared for his boss's questions. The Ring Man normally swam laps in the pool at six in the morning but had been talked out of that routine by Ponte, based on the increased threat of attack. So now Ponte went down into the west wing, where a complete set of Nautilus equipment was set up. The Ring Man was already halfway through his first iteration. Ponte walked over to the biceps machine, where the Ring Man was working out. The ever-present young girl was wiping his forehead with a towel. Ring Man waved her off when he saw Ponte. "What is it?"

"The warehouse on route 46 was attacked last night."

Ring Man dropped the weights with a loud clang. "Tell me what happened."

"Someone must have hit it between ten last night and this morning. It was just discovered by the new shift of guards. All five guards were killed. Four were shot and one had his throat cut out."

"Maria?"

"She was killed also. Shot."

"What about the American DEA agent?"

"He's dead too. At least we think it was him." Ponte hastily explained as Ring Man frowned at him. "Maria had him booby-trapped in case something like this happened. There's the remains of a body that the guard who called in says is Stevens."

The Ring Man threw his towel across the room and stalked out. Ponte meekly followed him to his office along with the girl. The Ring Man sat behind his desk and for almost five minutes stared out the bulletproof windows at the mountains stretching off to the north. Finally he turned to Ponte. "We must find this American. Do you have anything further on him?"

"The man from the Embassy Cafe who originally met him says that the American told him he was from New York City and that he had just flown in on Tuesday night with his wife. He gave the name Martinez."

"Have you checked the manifests from all flights from New York that night?"

"There was only one flight. There was no Martinez listed."

The Ring Man looked up in disgust. "You idiot! Did you check every couple that flew in? Do you think the man would be stupid enough to tell you the right name? Did the man say anything else?"

Ponte was shaken. "He said he was looking for a child to adopt. He said his wife couldn't have children and that's why they were down here. He also said that he'd heard about Maria from his brother, who had been told by a marine from the embassy that she could help."

Ring Man shook his head. "Maria never dealt in babies." He slammed his desktop and stared hard at Ponte. "I want you to go through the manifest of that flight from New York and track down every couple that came and find out where they are. Hell, track down every man on the plane, in case the story of a wife was a hoax too. Get the man at the bar to give you a better description and also keep a hold of him to identify the people when you find them. There can't be that many off that flight."

Ring Man stood up and went over to Ponte, grabbing his face between his fingers. "You'd better not fuck this up, my friend. You have already done too much with your incompetence."

# CARTAGENA
## 6:40 A.M.

Ariel felt alive. The thought of upcoming action sent the adrenaline flowing and dried out his throat. In his opinion this was better than being with a beautiful woman knowing you would soon bed her. Much better.

He peered once more through his tripod-mounted binoculars from his aerie on top of the Citizens Bank office building. The twenty-four story building, tallest in this section of the city, afforded him a superb view. Most importantly it gave him a lengthwise view of the main road that ran down the center of the city.

Still no sign. Ariel pulled his eyes from the binoculars and scanned the rooftop, ensuring that his local security was in place. He felt confident that their presence had not been leaked, even though Rameriz effectively controlled the city. His men had broken into the building two hours ago and covered any signs of the intrusion. Ariel had ten sicarios on the roof, four deployed guarding the staircase entrance, and one on each corner scanning the adjacent roofs and sides of the building.

The last two were next to him. One had a U.S.-made Redeye antiaircraft missile in the unlikely event they were spotted from the air and attacked from that direction. The other was the gunner for the bulky weapon they had hauled to the roof with great effort.

The Hughes BGM-71 TOW was designated as a heavy antitank weapon manufactured for use by the U.S. Army. TOW stood for tube launched, optically guided, wire command linked missile. The entire system had five parts and totaled 172 pounds without the missile. Each rocket weighed 42 pounds. Set up, the system consisted of a tripod with a fiberglass tube into which the missile was inserted. An optical sight with clamp was on the left side of the tube. A missile guidance system, MGS, in the form of a large black box was connected to the sight by a heavy black cable. Having been fielded since 1970, the TOW was the most widely used antitank weapon in the world. Ariel had purchased this system and two missiles from a source that had dealings with various governments in the Middle East.

Ariel was somewhat concerned because he wasn't sure of the shelf life of the two missiles he had. The little indicator window on them still showed blue, meaning the warhead was good, but Ariel's experience in Israel had taught him that missiles that sat in the depot too long sometimes developed faults without tripping the indicator.

He was also concerned with his gunner. The man had never fired the weapon before. In some ways, firing the TOW made video games seem difficult. Basically, the firer centered the cross hairs of his sight on the target. He pulled a trigger and the missile used a quad boost motor for a recoilless launch. The missile coasted briefly, then a rocket kicked in and flew the missile to its target. The key was that the gunner had to continue tracking his target, keeping it in the cross hairs. If the cross hairs were on the target when the missile arrived, the result was devastating. The warhead held 5.3 pounds of high-explosive shaped charge. It would be more than sufficient for the target Ariel had in mind.

His surveillance of the last two days had revealed a pattern. Patterns were dangerous things for men with enemies. His target left his strongly defended seaside home every morning and drove into the city to meet with his subordinates in the city infrastructure.

The target's security chief wasn't totally foolish, however. Although the timing was the same every day, the route varied. This had led Ariel to throw out the idea of an ambush or mining one of the roads with a command-detonated charge.

The bottom line, however, was that the target left one place and went to another at the same time of day. With those three constants in mind, Ariel had come up with his present plan. He checked his watch one more time. Any minute now.

The earphone running from the radio on his belt crackled. "Target is moving. Taking route B."

Ariel twisted his binoculars in the indicated direction. There they were. Two limousines trailed by a van. Ariel knew that the two limousines was another trick thrown in by the target's security chief. The main target was in one of the two, but because of the dark windshields it was impossible to tell which. An attacker might destroy one and miss his intended victim. Ariel felt a passing moment of respect for his adversary. Supposedly the target had hired a former West German commando officer to serve as his security chief.

Ariel thought that was amusing in a way. An Israeli against a German in a South American country. What a twisted world, he laughed to himself. He reached over and grabbed the shoulder of his gunner. The man had shown the steadiest hands in Ariel's testing. Now he would have a chance to put them to use. "Do you have them?"

"Sí, señor."

"Good. Wait till I tell you." Ariel wanted to make sure his gunner didn't fire when the vehicles might be in a position to go out of sight before the missile completed its flight. The missile flew at about 620 miles per hour once it got up to speed but, including the launch time, it would still take almost five seconds from leaving the tube to impact. The missile was connected to the launcher by a thin metal wire that relayed instructions from the guidance system to the warhead and fired small maneuvering rockets that changed the missile's course to keep it on target. If the target went behind a building or power lines crossed the missile's path in that flight time, the shot was wasted.

Ariel watched the convoy a few seconds. He knew that the van contained a contingent of guards with heavy weapons. One of the two cars held the primary target. Ariel waited. He made his first decision. "The lead car."

The gunner nodded and pressed the rubber eyepiece of the sight deeper into his eye socket.

Ariel swung his binos from the convoy up along the street they were on. He made a quick calculation. "When they reach the middle of the next block. Do you see the gas station?"

"Sí, señor."

Ariel waited, feeling his excitement rise. "Steady. Steady. Fire!"

There was a blast and a roar. The missile leapt out the end of the firing tube and screamed toward the target. It made an ear-piercing noise as it picked up speed and roared downrange.

Ariel was torn between watching the target and watching his gunner to make sure the man didn't screw up. He decided to keep his eye on the target. In two seconds the missile appeared in his binos as a ball of flame flying away.

"Yes!" Ariel yelled as the missile impacted in the lead car and the warhead exploded with a roar. He turned and helped the gunner as they unlatched the clamp, pulled the empty missile case out of the tube, and slapped the second missile in. By cranking down on the clamp, Ariel engaged the tracking system wires. He slapped the gunner on his back. "Up."

He peered through his binoculars as the gunner gained his next target. The second limousine had pulled off to the side of the street and stopped. That was a mistake. Guards were pouring out of the van, quartering the immediate area, looking for the source of the explosion. Ariel wanted to laugh from his perch over two kilometers away. The TOW belched and screamed as the second missile roared off.

The gunner cursed and Ariel pulled his eyes away from the binoculars in dismay. Instead of flying true, the second missile had curved and now flew almost straight up into the air.

"Keep tracking," Ariel yelled, in the vain hope the missile might turn. His military mind already knew it was too late.

The missile was already too far off course to be able to correct. Something had gone wrong in its guidance system.

The 3,750-meter spool of guidance wire reached its end and snapped. The missile was a dim ball of flame that suddenly winked out, its fuel expended. Ariel was unconcerned with where it would land now.

He took a last view through his binoculars. The guards were pulling bodies out of the first limousine. It was impossible to tell who they were at this distance.

Ariel turned to his men. "Let's go." As they headed for the stairs, he pulled the pin on a thermite grenade and laid it on top of the missile guidance system nestled underneath the tripod. He turned and leapt for the stairwell. Oh well, he reasoned. It was a fifty-fifty chance they had gotten Roberto Rameriz.

# BOGOTA
# 7:20 A.M.

Kate Westland stirred. She had a strange feeling of warmth along her back. As consciousness grew she realized that warmth was Riley curled up behind her. The realization caused her no discomfort. On the contrary, she felt quite secure in his arms. She lay still for a few minutes, relaxing and enjoying the sensation.

Finally, she slipped out of his arms and stole quietly to the bathroom. Coming back out she regarded the sleeping form for a few seconds. Riley's normally intense face was relaxed. The lines in his forehead were smooth. She stood there, hesitating to wake him.

"Makes me nervous to be stared at," Riley drawled as he cracked open one eye. "You ready for another exciting day?"

Westland shook her head. "I don't think I could take any more excitement. Especially on an hour and a half of sleep. What's on the agenda?"

Riley sat up. "First you take me out to the villa site again. I want to check it out during the daytime. Then you go and get a hold of the military attaché and try to make contact with Pike. I've got his STU-III number. Then you come back out and meet up with me sometime this evening to let me know what you've learned. Sound good?"

Westland nodded. "Ready when you are."

# RING MAN'S VILLA
# 7:45 A.M.

Ponte stiffened as he heard the Ring Man call for him from the adjacent office. Today had not been a good one so far and it was still early in the morning. Ponte went through the connecting door into his boss's office.

The Ring Man was on the phone. He gestured for Ponte to take a seat across from his desk and paused in his conversation. "I want you to listen in. This is the type of information I like hearing." The Ring Man punched the intercom on his phone and put the receiver down. "Tell me again what you have done, my friend."

"About an hour ago I assassinated Roberto Rameriz." Ponte cringed as he heard Ariel's accent come out of the speaker.

"How did you do that?"

"I hit his limousine with an antitank missile. Completely destroyed it. From what I've been able to find out, it killed not only Roberto but his second-oldest son, Miquel."

Ring Man laughed out loud. "The Shark is fish bait now." He turned to Ponte. "Miquel was the next in line, wasn't he?"

Ponte nodded glumly. Ariel's good work made his own involvement with the mysterious American seem all that more incompetent. "The eldest, Julio, is still in the States facing trial. He's looking at a life term. That leaves the third son, Jaimé, and the youngest, Carlos. I'd say the younger is the more dangerous of the two left."

The Ring Man had already turned his attention back to the phone. "What are things like there? How are Rameriz's people reacting?"

Ariel's disembodied voice floated in the room. "There hasn't been time for them to do much of anything. They've recovered the bodies and pulled back to his house on the ocean and are fortifying themselves. In my opinion they're scared. I think the time is ripe for us to move into the city here and take over. The Ramerizes will be too busy trying to protect themselves to come out and try to stop us."

The Ring Man was all smiles. "Good. Very good. I want you to come back up here. Hold on a minute." He turned to Ponte. "Is my helicopter flying yet?"

Ponte glanced at his watch. "The repairs were just completed. It will be taking off from the airport in about forty-five minutes to go up to Barranquilla."

"Have it also pick up Ariel at the airfield in Cartagena. I want him down here."

As Ponte listened to Ring Man relay this information to Ariel, he realized that Ariel wasn't coming down here just to get a pat on the back. Job security wasn't exactly the highlight of Ponte's position. Ring Man himself had sat in Ponte's office prior to assassinating Ahate. Although Ponte knew that the Ring Man didn't consider him a threat, his boss might consider Ariel to be even less of a threat. Ariel, as a foreigner, could never rule in the cartel in Colombia.

The Ring Man startled Ponte out of his self-absorbed thinking. "Do I have to tell you again? Get moving on the call to the pilot."

Ponte scurried out of the office, half of his mind on what he had to do and the other half on what he needed to do to survive.

# BARRANQUILLA
## 9:23 A.M.

Ariel enjoyed flying in helicopters. He'd had the pilot fly low over the coast on the short run from Cartagena to Barranquilla. He could see the bulk of the city farther up the coast as the aircraft banked right and headed down onto a dirt runway. Ariel had heard about the aborted attack by the Americans on this lab site. He wished he had been there. The thought of meeting one of these American commandos piqued his military interest.

The pilot didn't want to shut down his engines so he had radioed ahead for the guards to have the prisoner waiting. As the skids of the Bell Jet Ranger touched down, four guards rushed forward, dragging a hooded and shackled figure. Ariel opened the back door and helped them position the man inside and lash him into the seat with the safety straps. The helicopter lifted and turned to the south.

Ariel reached over and removed the hood from the American. The prisoner blinked as his eyes adjusted to the light. Ariel could see that although the man's face was unmarked he was in some degree of pain. Ariel assumed that the sicarios had amused themselves with beatings while keeping in mind the Ring Man's instructions not to mark the face. Also, Ariel knew that the man had been knocked unconscious by a grenade blast during the firefight—but not before he had killed several of Ring Man's men. Ariel wanted to talk to this man who had shown such bravery and military prowess.

The Israeli grabbed the extra headset and plunked it down over the American's ears, positioning the boom mike in front of his lips. The prisoner regarded him with dark, angry eyes. Ariel knew he would have his hands full if this bear of a man got loose. There was little chance of that, though: The Colombians had shackled his wrists with two sets of steel handcuffs, and his feet were held with two rings welded to an iron bar that was tied into the floor of the helicopter.

"Can you hear me?"

The man's gaze swung around.

"What is your name?"

The man shook his head.

"You can talk. You have a hot mike. I'm interested in what you thought you were doing when you tried to attack this facility."

The man just glared.

"My name is Ben Ariel. I might be able to help you. I'm a professional military man just like you."

That brought a reaction. "You call yourself a professional, working for these scum? You're a hired killer. You're lower than whale shit."

"Ah, I see you can talk." Ariel smiled. "Yes, I do call myself a professional. I am just like you. I get paid to provide military services. I just do it for an individual instead of a government. I don't see much difference between the two."

The American shook his head. "You work for the money. I do it for my country. I would think you'd understand that, seeing where you come from if I read your name right."

Ariel shook his head. "I don't do this for the money. I do this because I am good at it. Just this morning I set up a beautiful ambush. You would have been impressed. Destroyed an enemy vehicle at almost two thousand meters. Do you have a name?"

The man shook his head. "You get no information out of me."

Ariel laughed. "If we wanted it, we'd get it. No one is immune. Everyone breaks. There isn't anything you could tell us that we don't know already. We're just keeping you alive in case we need you as a chip on the table later on. How does that make you feel? Just a bargaining piece, and not a very valuable one, I might add, since your government is still denying it did anything and is sticking to its air crash story."

"My feelings don't matter."

Ariel considered the man. He felt a certain empathy for him. From the report he had received the American had been captured by sheer luck. He'd been moving south along the coast when he'd run into one of the patrols Ring Man had ordered out after he'd received word from Maria on the impending raid.

"It is a shame that we have to waste your talents. The Americans have at least admitted that the dead men were from the 7th Special Forces Group. I'm impressed. I have heard good things about you Green Berets. Not as good as our commandos in Israel but still a potent force."

The man didn't rise to the barb. Ariel tried another tack. "Maybe I can talk to my boss about you. Would you be interested in working with me?"

The man turned and carefully spit into Ariel's face. In a fit of fury the Israeli pulled out his pistol and cocked it. The copilot in the right front seat had been following the conversation and now yelled, "Put that away! What do you think you're doing?

You can't fire that in here. Besides, the Ring Man wants the American alive."

Ariel slowly regained control of his temper. He pushed the muzzle of the pistol into the man's temple. "You will pay for that. Maybe not now, but later."

The American looked at Ariel and smiled. "Fuck you. Fuck your mother. Fuck your father. Fuck your—" The rest of the tirade was lost as Ariel tore the headset off the man. That didn't stop the American, though. He rocked in the web seat as much as the restraints would let him and shouted profanities at the top of his lungs.

Ariel spent the rest of the flight pressed up against the door, as far as he could get from the crazy American, thinking of things he would do to him if the Ring Man let him.

## UNITED STATES EMBASSY, BOGOTA
### 10:05 A.M.

Westland looked across the desk at Lieutenant Colonel Turrel, the army military attaché to Colombia. Turrel returned her stare with a look that ranged somewhere between amusement and concern.

His amusement came from having watched Westland fight off Jameson. The CIA man had nearly had a fit when Westland appeared in the Marine Corps' guard post in the embassy, demanding to see the army military attaché. Jameson had hustled her into the embassy and tried to steer her into his office. Westland had sabotaged that plan by the simple tactic of not getting on the elevator with Jameson and watching the door shut in his surprised face. She'd then climbed the stairs to the second floor and presented herself to Turrel. Before she could talk to him, Jameson had stormed into the room, ordering her to his office. Westland had stubbornly refused, and Jameson had just left in a huff, threatening her, telling her he was going to call Virginia and ship her ass back on the first thing flying.

Turrel's concern stemmed from his knowledge that something fishy was going on. Putting the cache in three nights ago had alerted him to that fact. This young woman seated across from him must be involved somehow.

Westland sighed deeply and tried to figure out how to begin. Riley had told her to be up front with Turrel. She decided to be as truthful as she could without giving away any classified information on the mission. She was already in enough trouble.

"My name's Kate Westland. As you can tell from the last couple of minutes, I work for the agency. I'm down here on an operation and I need to use your STU-III line to call someone in Washington."

Turrel leaned back in his chair. "Why don't you use Jameson's? He's got an even higher priority line than I do."

"He wouldn't let me. I'm not supposed to even be here."

"I gathered that much. If you're operating with a cover you've probably blown it."

"I had no choice. I have to get in contact with someone in the Pentagon."

Turrel raised his eyebrows. "Anybody I might know?"

"Do you know General Pike?"

"Mike Pike?" Westland nodded. "I didn't know he'd been promoted. I know him by reputation. Anybody wearing these crossed arrows on their collar from Special Forces branch knows about him." Turrel seemed to consider this for a few seconds. "I assume you want to talk to him privately?"

Westland nodded. "It's highly classified."

"Does this have anything to do with the cache I put in the other night?"

"I can't answer that." Westland looked him in the eyes. "Please, I need to make this call."

Turrel relented. "All right. I'll stand guard outside. Do you know how to work that thing?" He pointed at the bulky phone with a line of buttons over the normal telephone keypad.

She nodded. Turrel removed the activating key from the string around his neck, turned on the phone, and left the room.

Westland punched in the number Riley had given her. She'd feel really stupid if no one answered, after going through all this trouble. She waited anxiously as the phone buzzed twice on the other end. She let out a deep breath when it was picked up and a familiar voice came on.

"Pike here. This line is unsecured."

Westland didn't give her name, hoping her voice would be recognized. "We need to go secure."

"Roger. You ready on your end?"

"Yes."

"All right. I'm on now."

Westland punched two numbers on the top row of buttons. She heard a beep and then a hiss. A red light came on her set. "I'm showing red."

Pike's voice came back. "I've got red too. I assume that's you, Kate."

"It's me, General. Riley told me to call you. I'm in Colombia with him."

"I know that."

Westland looked at the phone in surprise. How did Pike know that? "Do you know why we're here?"

"Yeah. Some bozo from your outfit figured that Riley could take out the Ring Man."

How the hell did he know all this? Supposedly the only people in on the whole thing were at Langley or down here. Was there a leak in Langley? Then it occurred to her. "Riley called you from the airport, didn't he?"

"Of course. He figured he might need some help and he thought I was the one who might be able to do that for him. What did he tell you to relay to me?"

The son of a bitch, she thought to herself. I wonder what the hell else he's done that I don't know about. Westland shook off her surprise and proceeded to relate the information Riley had given her. She concluded by asking about the possibility of a Hammer strike on the villa.

Pike's bitter laugh wasn't distorted by the phone. "Hell, no. You got a better chance of the Ring Man having a heart attack than you do of this government taking any action. The video has caused people to head for the hills. They're still denying everything at State and here at the Pentagon.

"If Alegre falls there's going to be some hard questioning. This most recent wave of assassinations and bombings has people here running scared. The feeling is that the drug cartel is going to make a big push against the government and that the Hammer missions may have been the spark. And no one wants to admit publicly that they were part of that."

Then what am I doing talking to you then? Westland thought. "Is there anything you can do?"

"I'm working on something. I'm flying down to Bragg in an hour for the memorial service for those guys. If I come up with something useful, how can I get a hold of you?"

"I don't know."

"Whose office are you calling from?"

"The army attaché's."

"What's Riley doing?"

"He's got surveillance on the Ring Man's villa."

"Good. Tell him not to take any action before midnight tomorrow night. I know he'll be keeping pretty tight surveillance on the target. If I can do anything, I'll get back to him somehow."

Westland was confused. How the hell could Pike contact Riley? And it was obvious that Pike also knew the deadline for the hit. "How will you contact him?"

"I'll get a hold of the attaché down there and relay a message through him to you, and you pass it on. If he's letting you use his phone he should be willing to pass a message. Will that work?"

"Yes. The attaché here is a Lieutenant Colonel Turrel."

"I know. I'll talk to him later today. Is there anything else?"

"No."

"Good luck."

Westland heard the click on the other end. She hung up and turned off the phone. When she opened the door Turrel was standing there with Jameson in front of him and an air force full colonel next to him. They all turned at her appearance in the doorway.

"What were you doing in there?" Jameson demanded.

"Nothing." Westland sidled up next to Turrel.

"Bullshit." Jameson turned to the air force officer, who was probably the ranking attaché. "Your man here has made contact with this woman despite my protests. I demand that you discipline him."

Westland could see that Jameson had taken the wrong approach with the military man. He confronted the CIA man. "I don't appreciate you telling me what to do. You can demand all you want. From what Colonel Turrel has told me, your person approached him. I don't see where he did anything wrong. If you can't control your own people that's your problem." With that the colonel turned and stalked away.

Jameson tried another approach. "Did you make a call?"

Westland played innocent. "Who would I call?"

Jameson bullied past them and looked into the office at the phone. "Where's your STU-III key?"

Turrel pulled out the key Westland had slipped him. "It's been right here the whole time she was in my office." He put away the key. "You know I'm really getting tired of the two of you. Go work out your problems elsewhere." With that the army officer went into his office, slamming the door behind him.

Jameson faced Westland. "What are you doing? What's going on?"

Westland shrugged. "I just wanted to check on some things about the cache the colonel put in for us."

Jameson was totally lost. "I gave you the information on that."

Westland nodded. "I know." She started heading for the stairs. "Well, I'll see you later."

"Wait!" Jameson cried out. "I have a call in to Langley. Strom's supposed to be getting back to me any minute now—I'll find out then what they want me to do about you."

Westland was already halfway down the stairs. "Sorry. Have to go."

As she slipped out the gate of the embassy and headed for the hotel, Westland failed to notice the man shadowing her from a discreet distance. Her mind was on the confrontations in the embassy, not on making sure she didn't have a tail. Prior to entering the hotel, she did a cursory check but noticed nothing unusual.

# KNOLL 8548, COLOMBIA
# 10:46 A.M.

In the daylight Riley had managed to find a tree with a slightly better view and a more comfortable branch. He had the M21 rifle with him and was observing the target through the ART 2 scope. He had yet to see any sign of the Ring Man in the grounds. All the windows were polarized, which prevented a clear look inside, and Riley had no doubt they were also bulletproof. Even if they weren't, the odds of getting a good shot through glass at long range were low. The first-floor windows were also covered with bars to prevent anyone going in that way.

Riley had spent the morning watching the guards, trying to determine their patterns. He shook his head. If the Ring Man didn't come out, he wasn't even going to be able to use the sniper option. His ears perked up as he heard the snap of rotor blades coming from the north. He tracked a Bell Jet Ranger swinging in through the valley, heading for the Ring Man's mansion.

Riley chambered a round. If the Ring Man came out and got on that bird, he'd take it out when it took off. It would be an excellent way of doing the job. They wouldn't figure out what had happened to the helicopter until he was long gone.

Riley started considering where the best place would be for his shot. If he got a frontal shot, he'd try penetrating the windshield in the vicinity of the pilot. He had ten rounds in this magazine. He figured he could put all ten into the cockpit in about five seconds. If he didn't get a frontal shot, he'd go for the transmission and engine to crash the bird.

The helicopter flew past Riley's position barely four hundred meters away. He kept the scope on it as it settled down onto the helipad in the front yard. The blades started slowing and three men approached the aircraft. Riley zoomed in on them. None was the Ring Man.

He watched as the doors opened. A man got out from the left side and scooted around the front of the aircraft to the right door. Riley focused on that man's face. An Anglo. Riley wondered who he was. The right door opened and the guards seemed to be helping someone out.

Riley's hands gripped tight on the rifle as he recognized the man they were lifting out. He took a deep breath to calm himself and thought furiously as he watched them drag Powers toward the villa. His finger curled around the trigger and he sighted in on the Anglo who'd gotten off the bird.

"Fuck," Riley muttered to himself as he forced his arm muscles to relax. Blowing away the man, whoever he was, wouldn't help anything and would probably get Powers killed in retaliation. Riley watched as the party disappeared behind the rise of the house. The helicopter picked up and winged away in the direction of Bogota.

Riley leaned back against the trunk of the tree and considered the situation. He'd been right all along. Now he knew not only that Powers was alive but where he was.

Gradually, Riley's initial surprise and elation at seeing Powers dimmed as he realized he still had the same problem. In fact it was even worse now. His first priority was to rescue Powers. Killing the Ring Man wouldn't accomplish that.

If Powers didn't come back out of the villa, Riley knew that meant one thing. He was going to have to go in.

# FORT BRAGG, NORTH CAROLINA
# 11:54 A.M.

The man in civilian clothes looked up from the piece of paper in his hands and rubbed his chin thoughtfully. "I'm going to have to verify this with DCSOP-SO, you know."

Pike nodded. "Of course."

For the tenth time in the last five minutes, the man looked

over the satellite imagery Pike had brought. "Goddamn, Mike. You sure have tossed a live grenade in my lap with a damn short fuse."

"Can you do it?"

The man equivocated. "I don't know. It's chancy. We could take a big hit trying to pull this off with such little heads-up. You got the aircraft lined up?"

Pike nodded. "All set. You guys had the warning order to plan contingencies for this last week. Why all the fuss?"

The man relented a little. "Well, we did the area study and some basic plans, but we didn't have anything specific to work from. You're not giving us much time to actually plan the details." The man gave Pike a hard stare. "This isn't any bullshit exercise you assholes in the Pentagon have thought up, is it?"

Pike spread his hands placatingly. "Listen, Jim. We've known each other for a long time. Would I do that to you?" If they wanted to think it was an exercise so much the better, Pike thought. It wouldn't change the way they planned or prepared.

The man thought for a few more moments, then grinned. "Guess I'd better get the ball rolling, then. About goddamn time we did something like this."

# RING MAN'S VILLA
## 12:10 P.M.

The Ring Man enjoyed watching Ponte squirm. The man had fucked up too much lately. Both Ponte and Ariel had been sitting across from his desk for ten minutes now, in complete silence. The Ring Man let it drag on. Give them both time to do some thinking. He liked toying with people mentally and physically. He was feeling good watching the two men and caressing his young girl's thigh as she sat on the corner of his desk.

Finally he gestured toward the Israeli. "You did very good in Cartagena. There will be a bonus for you."

The Israeli nodded. "Thank you, sir."

Ring Man turned his gaze on Ponte and his face hardened. "I hope you have some information on the strange American."

Ponte licked his lips. This was his chance. "I do. One of our men trailed a woman from the American embassy to a hotel nearby. She's registered under the name of Gonzalo along with her husband. We have a Gonzalo couple listed on the manifest for the flight on Monday night."

Ring Man considered that. "Did you get an identification on the man?"

Ponte shook his head. "There's no sign of the man. The desk man says he left early this morning and has not returned. His description matches the one the man at the bar gave. The woman is still in the room. I'm having it watched."

"What do you plan on doing?"

Ponte licked his lips again. "Keep the hotel under surveillance until the man shows up and then grab him."

The Ring Man turned to the other occupant of the room. "Are you familiar with the situation with this mysterious American?"

Ariel nodded. "Ponte briefed me."

"What would you do now?"

The Israeli leaned forward in his seat. "We must seize the initiative. I would take the woman now. Find out where the man is from her. If you wait, you leave the initiative up to the opponent. That is unacceptable in war. This man has killed quite a few of our people. Who knows what he is up to at this very minute. There is a purpose to his actions but we don't know what that purpose is. Maybe it has something to do with the American soldier we hold prisoner here."

Ring Man agreed. "I like your reasoning. I do not like letting this American lead us in a foolish chase." He turned to Ponte. "Get the woman and bring her here. From her we will find out where her man is and then get him too."

Ponte nodded weakly and stood up, dismissed. As he headed for the door he was stopped by Ring Man's cold voice. "This is your last chance, my friend. Do not fail."

# PRESIDENTIAL PALACE, BOGOTA
## 12:15 P.M.

Alegre looked up as two distant booms rattled the windows of his office. A few minutes later the door swung open and Montez strode in. "What was that?"

Montez sighed. "Two bombs went off at the Supreme Court building. We're not sure yet how many were killed. It is bad, my President."

Alegre closed his eyes and said a brief prayer for the dead and wounded. "Bring in additional troops."

"My President, we have already brought in three battalions. They cannot guard everything and be everywhere. There is suspicion that some of the troops have been planting the bombs. The commander of the army just called and said he could not afford to remove any more troops from fighting the rebels."

Alegre stood up. "I must go and see what has happened. I must make my presence known to the people and give them confidence that we will win this war."

Montez put out a hand and grabbed his old friend. "You will die if you leave here. That is what they are waiting for. You must stay inside. This is the only place you are safe."

Alegre threw the hand off angrily. "Am I prisoner in my own home? In my own country? The president is unable to leave his palace because he will be killed if he does?"

"I am sorry, my friend. That is the way things are unless something happens soon in our favor."

# KNOLL 8548
## 12:25 P.M.

Riley watched the car roll down the driveway and pass through the gates of the grounds. He tracked it through the scope to where it pulled onto the main road and headed toward downtown Bogota. He wondered who was in the car and where they were going.

He checked his watch. Another four hours until he started down the hill to meet up with Westland.

## LANGLEY, VIRGINIA
## 12:35 P.M.

Hanks slammed his desktop. "What the hell is she doing?"

Strom shook his head. The news that Westland was a loose cannon running around Colombia wasn't going over very well.

The director fumed. "She's finished. You get on the horn and tell Jameson to reel her in."

Strom protested weakly. "But she's handling Riley."

"Correction. She *was* handling Riley. I want her ass up here tonight. Jameson can take over."

Strom didn't want to, but he felt he needed to point things out. "I'm not sure Riley will still do the mission if we yank Westland."

Hanks considered that for a few moments as he let his temper cool. "All right. She stays until it's over. But I want Jameson with her from here on out. Call him and tell him to get his ass over to where she is and stay with her. He's not to let her out of his sight."

## BOGOTA
## 1:10 P.M.

Westland stirred in her sleep. She cracked open her eyes as she tried to focus on what had awakened her. There it was again. Someone trying the doorknob. Westland's eyes flew wide open as she rolled off the bed, pulling the Beretta out from underneath the pillow as she went. Her heart was pounding as she centered the sights on the door.

She released the safety and curled her finger around the trigger, applying pressure. She tried to slow her rapid breathing. The lock turned and the door started to swing open. She was halfway through the five pounds of pressure needed to fire the gun when she recognized the figure in the door.

Jameson stopped in surprise at the sight of the muzzle aimed at his forehead. "Whoa! I'm one of the good guys."

Westland stood up, putting the pistol down on the bed. "Jesus Christ. Don't you believe in knocking? How the hell did you open that lock?"

Jameson dangled a key from his hand. "I made the arrangements, remember? Don't you think I'd have an extra key?" He shut the door behind him, strolled over to the balcony doors, and peered out. Then he turned back to the room. He winked at her. "You and Riley pretty cozy here?"

Westland was still frazzled from the near shooting and in no mood for his intimations. "What the hell do you want?"

Jameson was enjoying himself. "You are screwing up big time, girl. Your little escapade at the embassy has pissed off some very important people. The only reason you're not getting on a plane back to the States is because they're not sure Riley would still do the job without you and your, uh, shall we say assets? But from here on out I've been ordered to baby-sit you." He grinned. "Kind of a ménage à trois, eh?"

He was still grinning as the door burst open. Jameson's reactions were slow but his presence was enough to distract the men coming in. They hadn't expected anyone other than the woman.

Westland dove for the floor, putting the bed between herself and the intruders. As she hit the ground she remembered that the Beretta was still lying on top of the bed. Near the window, Jameson was belatedly reaching for his gun, inconveniently located in a holster in the small of his back. He was still reaching as the first man through the door blew the agent out the balcony doors and over the railing with a sustained burst from his Ingram MAC-10.

Westland slid underneath the bed. Looking to her right she saw the legs of three men enter the room. One of them called to her. "Come out, little lady. You left your gun on the bed. We just want to talk to you."

The man who had blown away Jameson kneeled down and peered under the bed. His eyes opened wide momentarily as he saw the black hole of the muzzle of the Colt Python pointing right at his forehead. Westland's round blew off the top half of his head.

The other two men stared in surprise. That gave Westland the time to roll back out from under the bed on the far side. The two men angrily emptied their magazines into the bed, sending feathers flying. As soon as she heard the clicks of their bolts sliding forward onto an empty chamber, Kate rose up to a kneeling position. The two sicarios stared slack jawed at this apparition of death.

She fired one round through each man's forehead.

## PENTAGON
## 1:35 P.M.

Linders nodded as he spoke into the phone. "Yes, that's right. I verify the orders General Pike showed you. He's working on direct vocal orders from the chairman."

"What about the comm link?"

"Didn't Pike give you one?"

"No."

"I guess I'll have the normal setup prepped here, then. I'll have the comm channel opened up starting at 0600 tomorrow morning. Will that give you plenty of time for your checks?"

"It ought to. Who's the verifier?"

Linders frowned. "I imagine it's the chairman. Didn't Pike give you that?"

"He said it was operating according to something he called the Hammer strikes."

Linders paused in thought. "All right. I guess they'll be picking you up over at Belvoir then for the comm link. I was wondering why he hadn't given you that. Is Pike still around down there?"

"Yeah, he's over at the memorial service. He said he'd stop by later."

"Check with him then on that. He should be able to square you away on everything."

"Roger that. Anything else I need to know, sir?"

"No. Good luck."

Linders turned off his STU-III and swiveled his chair around. Something didn't sit right with this whole situation. He'd understood the need to keep the Hammer strikes in real tight for security reasons, but this thing was almost getting out of hand.

Linders considered calling the chairman with his misgivings. He thought about it for a few seconds, then picked up the phone and punched in an internal number for the Pentagon.

"Chairman's office. Colonel Cross here, sir."

"This is General Linders. Is the chairman available?"

"No, sir. He's across the river testifying on the B-2. Do you have a message?"

"When will he be back?"

"He left word that he'd be heading straight home to Fort Myers after finishing there, sir. Would you like me to forward a message to him over at the hill?"

Linders sighed. "No. That's all right. I'll get a hold of him tomorrow."

# FORT BRAGG, NORTH CAROLINA
## 2:00 P.M.

The chaplain stood in the shadow of the famous Iron Mike statue of a Green Beret soldier that stood outside the Special Forces Museum at Fort Bragg, across the street from the 1st Special Operations Command headquarters. His words drifted out over the crowd gathered for the service.

"We are gathered here together to honor the memory of our fallen comrades. Ours is a profession that is fraught with dangers, even during the apparent safety of peacetime. We all know the risks involved in training hard and we all . . . "

Pike tuned out the 7th Group chaplain. He hated the hypocrisy of the whole thing. Partusi, Marzan, Holder, and Lane had all died in combat fighting. Yet, that reality would never be acknowledged.

Pike turned his weathered gaze on the people seated in the front row facing the statue. Two of the four men had been married and both had children. The weeping families sitting in that front row had paid a high price, and they would never know how their husbands and fathers had really died.

Pike knew he could still stop the wheels he had set in motion. But looking at those crying faces steeled his heart. There'd been too much backing off and too much running away. He was going to push this to the limit. He'd probably be found out and fail, but he'd go down trying.

# LANGLEY, VIRGINIA
# 2:18 P.M.

"I'm scrapping this whole thing."

Strom looked up in surprise at his boss's reaction to the news on Jameson. "But they don't know if Riley or Westland were compromised."

Hanks shook his head. "This thing's turning to shit. What did the local authorities say?"

Strom looked up from his briefing notes. "They say Jameson was killed during a robbery attempt."

"Bullshit!" Hanks exploded. "A chest full of 9-millimeter? Anything on Westland?"

"No."

"Think they got her?"

Strom paused for a second. "I don't know. Somebody had to waste those three cartel guys."

"You think Westland did that?"

"The report I've got says that Jameson's weapon was still in his holster and unfired. Since the bodies were still there when the police arrived, I'd have to assume that nobody was left alive from their side to retrieve the dead. Otherwise you can pretty much figure they'd have tried to cover things up."

"Where is she then?" asked Hanks. "Why didn't she show up at the embassy?"

"I don't know. It only happened about an hour ago. She could be anywhere."

Hanks considered the situation. "You think they'll still try and go ahead with the Ring Man hit?"

"My best guess is that Riley and Westland have gone into hiding. Maybe they have aborted and are on their way back. They've got to know their cover is blown."

The director made his decision. "I've already stuck my neck out too far on this one. I want you to fly to Bogota immediately on my jet and lay down the law to Alegre. Tell him he can do all the talking he wants about the Hammer strikes, but we're done doing his dirty work. I'm going over to State and brief the secretary, then take him over to the White House to let the Old Man know what's going on. It's time to cut our losses."

"What about Riley?"

"Try to use the local people to track him down and call him off if he's still on the mission, which I doubt anyway." Hanks shook his head. "I don't know why I authorized this thing in the first place." He pointed a finger at Strom. "You tell Alegre to cool this stuff with the cartel. We did what the president wanted and we've pushed it as far as it's going to go without losing Alegre. I think State will back me up on this."

# EGLIN AIR FORCE BASE, FLORIDA
## 2:20 P.M.

The operations officer for the 1st Special Operations Wing reread the message flimsy. He looked up at his assistant. "What the hell is this?"

The major shrugged. "Got that about twenty minutes ago."

"Did you verify?"

"Yes, sir. It's genuine."

The ops officer scratched his head in irritation. "Shit. How the hell are we supposed to plan a mission off this piece of crap? I'm getting real tired of this bullshit. I hope this isn't another one of DCSOP's no-notice tests."

The major smiled. "Can't be one of those. They're giving us eighteen hours of advance warning."

The operations officer chuckled. "Keep it up, smart ass." He turned his chair and looked at the status board behind his desk. "Hotel Six is already in place. Alert Tango Three for the lift. Tell them to be prepared for whatever the hell they think those yahoos up at Bragg can dream of. Tell 'em to also make sure they can talk SATCOM to Hotel Six, and get"—the ops checked a clipboard to see who was the pilot in command of Hotel Six—"Mackelroy up to speed once they find out what's going on."

The assistant operations officer presented his superior with a mock salute. "Aye, aye, sir."

# FORT BRAGG, NORTH CAROLINA
## 2:53 P.M.

Pike poked his head around the doorway. "What's up, Jim? Pete said you wanted to see me before I left."

"Hell, yeah. I just talked to Linders a little while ago. He verified the operations order but he didn't know shit about commo or verifying. You know I got to have a comm link and a final verifier."

Pike eased around the doorway and into the office. He'd been half afraid to find the whole thing blown. He was getting too old for this stuff. His heart couldn't take much more. "I'm sorry. I guess I was just too caught up with this memorial thing. I knew those guys who were killed. They used to work for me."

"Yeah, that was a real shame."

"Anyway." Pike reached into his pocket and produced a piece of paper. "Here's the call signs and comm instructions. You'll be talking back to me at Fort Belvoir and I'll have a link direct to the chairman of the Joint Chiefs." Pike chuckled. "Who the hell *he'll* be talking to I don't know, but I'll be relaying the verification from the chairman if it's a go. Is that good enough?"

The other man relaxed. "Yeah, that will be fine. By the

way, 1st SOW just called all pissed off about not getting any operational info. I told that piss-head ops officer to go pound sand and just get me a bird up here." He shook his head. "Fucking air force thinks the world revolves around them. How the hell can I give them any operational info when I don't even know how it's going to go down yet?"

Pike nodded in sympathy. "You know how the air force is. Try to treat them good. It's a long walk without them. Got any ideas yet?"

The man smiled. "Yeah. We've run some scenarios like this in training. The troop commander is working it out with his people right now."

## VICINITY OF KNOLL 8548
## 4:36 P.M.

Riley crouched in the drainage ditch on the side of the road and watched the occasional car flash by. He checked his watch again. She was late. There were few things he hated more than someone being late. Especially with him sitting here exposed. He'd cached the rifle in his tree, and the submachine gun and other equipment were in a sack by his feet.

Riley glanced at his watch one more time. Another minute. He slid down lower in the ditch as a truck full of workers roared by. In doing so, he knocked the bag from its perch and it splashed into a puddle.

Riley cursed as he picked it up. Now he'd have to clean everything in there and recheck the functioning. He hoped the goggles hadn't gotten wet. He took another look down the road and spotted the Pinto rolling toward him. Gathering his gear, he stood up and waited by the edge of the road.

Westland rolled up and stopped briefly. Riley hopped in, throwing his sack in the backseat. "Where the hell you been?"

He looked behind to make sure no one was following. The lack of a reply caused him to look at Westland more closely. Her hands were gripping the steering wheel so tightly the whites of the knuckles showed. She was staring straight ahead as she drove unevenly down the road.

"Hey. You all right?" When she said nothing Riley tapped her on the shoulder. "What the hell is the matter, Kate? Hey, pull over."

She pulled the car over to the edge of the road. Riley waited until she shut the engine down before reaching over and grabbing both her shoulders. He turned her so she had to look at him. "What happened? Take a deep breath and then just tell me."

Kate took the breath and leaned back against the seat as Riley released her. "I went to the embassy like we agreed this morning. I talked to Turrel and he let me call Pike."

Riley watched her carefully as she related the events of the morning and afternoon. When she told him what happened in the hotel room he reached out again and held her shoulder. "What did you do after you took out the three guys?"

Westland shook her head. "I wasn't sure what to do. I couldn't go to the embassy. They must have followed me from there. Plus, with Jameson getting blown away they'd probably have held me, and I knew you needed me to pick you up. So I grabbed our stuff and left."

"Didn't the cops or anyone else react to all that shooting?"

Westland shook her head. "Most everyone seemed glad to get the hell out of the way when I came out. I went down the stairs, grabbed the car, and took off out of town. I parked on a trail about ten kilometers south of here until it was time to come get you."

Riley squeezed her shoulder. "You done good, Kate. You used your brain."

"I killed three men."

"Four, if you count last night." Riley shook her slightly. "Hey, listen. I know it isn't fun to kill someone, but remember what you said to me our first night here after I killed those guys in the bar? As long as you still feel bad about it, that means there's a difference between you and them. You didn't have any choice. You did what you had to."

Westland straightened up. "What do we do now?"

"We can't go back into town. Looks like we camp out tonight. We'll park the car about three or four klicks past the stream path, then walk back to there and head up the knoll.

We'll go to my surveillance point and spend the night there."

For the first time Westland thought to ask what had happened to Riley. "Did you spot anything? Any way to get the Ring Man?"

Riley shook his head. "Ring Man's not the issue anymore. Something else happened."

"What?"

"I saw Powers alive at the villa."

# RING MAN'S VILLA
# 7:20 P.M.

Ring Man stared at Ariel. "The only fortunate thing out of the incident this afternoon is that Ponte managed to get himself killed. He saved me the trouble of having to do it. I want you to find and kill this American and his woman. They have been a source of great trouble."

Ariel nodded and popped off with a hearty "Yes, sir," while at the same time wondering how the hell he would find the two Americans. The trail of the woman from the hotel had gone cold. For all he knew they were both on a flight back to the United States. That would be the smart thing to do and what Ariel would have done in their place. They were good, whoever these strangers were, but they would run out of luck sooner or later if they stayed in this country. Ariel figured that his best shot was to have the pressure on the street increased. Someone would see them eventually if they were still here.

Ring Man had another thought of even more importance. "What do you think of taking out Alegre?"

Ariel considered his answer carefully. He knew that Ponte had advised against it and that the Ring Man hadn't been pleased with that answer. On the other hand Ariel was smart enough to realize that the Ring Man's ambitions of running the country were a little too lofty for the present circumstances; nor did he understand them. Wasn't becoming the head of the multibillion-dollar-a-year drug cartel enough for the man?

"That is a very difficult target, sir. The presidential guard is a good unit and we have been unable to penetrate it with one of our men. Alegre has not left the palace since this started."

Ring Man wanted action, not talk. "I know all that. I want you to find a way to get to him."

# PRESIDENTIAL PALACE, BOGOTA
## 10:56 P.M.

Alegre was fuming after the brief meeting with Strom. As the door shut behind the American he turned to Montez. "Do you believe that American pig has the balls to come in here and threaten me?"

Montez shook his head. He didn't like it either, but he knew it was time to face reality. They'd taken their chances and been burned. With the audiotapes of the last meeting Jameson had had with Alegre, the Americans stood a good chance of making Alegre out to be a liar if he tried to use the Hammer missions as blackmail. Montez had sensed something funny about the meeting on Monday with the American agent. Now he knew that Jameson had insisted on the meeting in order to get Alegre on tape authorizing the killing. The Americans were using that as counter blackmail, effectively neutralizing Alegre's threat of exposure.

Alegre was feeling the growing pressure from the cartel, but he wasn't ready to quit. "We must stop Ring Man. He's the main threat now, especially since Rameriz was killed this morning. If the Americans will not do it, I will do it directly. I am going to upgrade from a state of emergency to a state of siege."

Montez knew that was the next logical step for the president if he wanted to truly fight the cartel. Unfortunately, it also ignored the reality of what would happen. Under the official title of state of siege, Alegre could suspend civil law. It gave the president more power than the present state of emergency. But they also had to consider the unwritten law of Colombian politics. For every action Alegre took, the cartel would react with increasing violence.

Between the cartel, the guerrillas, and a government crackdown, Montez could envision a return to the days of *la violencia*, the period during the 1940s and 1950s when Colombia was almost torn apart by a vicious, undeclared civil war. The numbers of casualties from this violence ranged anywhere from 100,000 to 300,000, depending on who was doing the estimating. The specter of that happening again was enough to chill the heart of any thinking person.

Montez decided to make another attempt to talk some reason into the president. "If you announce a state of siege, we cannot be sure how the people will react. There is already a great amount of discontent. We have pushed this war with the cartel to its limit now. If we push farther we run the risk of alienating the people.

"We must give the development of our sea bottom rights in the Gulf of Venezuela time to mature. You won a great victory there. We must allow time for the people to see that we have an alternative to the drug business. Time for that project to help the economy. If you go to a state of siege, the cartel and guerrillas will tear this country apart."

Alegre stared at his top adviser. "What do you suggest I do? Give in?"

Montez tried placating his friend. "Not give in. But we must play for time. You tried to defeat the cartel and—"

Alegre pounded his desk. "We still can defeat them. I will use the army under the state of siege provisions."

It was time for the president to crash on the harsh rocks of reality. "The army will not fight the cartel," Montez argued. "Not all the way. They'll do police work and fight some of the lesser dealers, but they will not go against the main body of the cartel. Not until we have an alternative for the people, and not until we can solve the guerrilla problem."

Alegre stared at his old friend. "Are you saying you will not support me on this?"

"You are my friend and my president, but I must do what is right for the country. If you pursue this course of action, I believe you doom this country to a period like *la violencia*. I do not want to see that again. I cannot support you on this."

Alegre's shoulders slumped. If even his friend Montez would

not support him, he knew he stood little chance with the army. "What do you suggest we do?"

# KNOLL 8548
# 11:23 P.M.

Since darkness had settled over the countryside, the temperature had fallen. Riley estimated it now hovered around fifty degrees. He took another look through the ART 2 scope at the lit villa compound. No change from last night. He still had no viable plan. The best he could come up with was trying to go in over the wall at night. He figured that plan ranked somewhere up near Custer's at Little Big Horn in tactical soundness.

Westland was curled up at the base of the tree. Riley hoped she was sleeping, but he imagined she was shivering. She'd told him about her conversation with Pike. The general's admonition not to do anything before midnight on Thursday was the only thing keeping Riley from going in tonight and trying to get Powers out. He had no idea if Pike could come up with something but he'd follow the instructions. Plus, he wasn't too keen on dying tonight. He figured that if they'd kept Powers alive so far, they'd keep him alive at least another day or so.

Riley decided there wasn't much else he could see tonight that he hadn't seen last night. Even if the Ring Man showed up in the backyard with a spotlight on himself, there was nothing Riley would do. His first priority was getting Powers out.

Riley climbed down the tree and squatted next to Westland's reclining figure. "You awake?"

"No. Of course I am. It's too damn cold to sleep."

Riley chuckled and slid down beside her. "Two's warmer than one. When we used to go on winter warfare training, the guys on the team would always buddy up against the cold. Same thing in Ranger school. I think on some of those cold nights in the mountains at Dahlonega I was closer to my Ranger buddy than any woman I've ever been with."

Kate pressed her body back against his. "Want to test that last thought?"

# THURSDAY,
# 5 SEPTEMBER

## FORT BELVOIR, VIRGINIA
## 2:43 A.M.

The buzzing of the phone woke Pike out of an exhausted sleep. His hand shot out and grabbed the receiver. "Pike here."

"Go secure." Pike obliged the caller. "Where'd you get that information on the guards and their shifts and the helicopter? Do you have a source on the ground down there?"

Pike relaxed as he recognized the voice on the other end. "I've got a man pulling surveillance on the target."

"Do you have commo with him?"

Pike reflected on his conversation with Turrel late the previous evening. He was just guessing that Riley and Westland had gone into hiding at the surveillance site near the villa. But he figured it was a good guess, since the two hadn't shown up at the embassy or used their escape route back to the States. Unfortunately, their going into hiding had severed his communications link through Turrel at the embassy. "No," he responded.

"Shit." The voice on the other end paused for a second. "I guess that's not a problem. We already have our own surveillance en route. I just hope the two don't bump heads. Is there any way my people can identify him?"

"There should actually be two people there. A man and a woman. The man's a guy from 7th Group named Dave Riley. The woman's name is Kate Westland."

314

"Is this Riley the same guy as the finger card in the file you gave me?"

"Yes."

"I'll assume they are there for the same reason we're going in. That's all I need for now. I'll get back to you if we need anything else."

Pike forestalled the quick hang-up. "How're things looking?"

"Well, we're refining a couple of ideas and we've coordinated with the aircraft we're going to need. It's cutting it tight but we'll have something ready." The voice paused briefly. "Hey, I got to go, Mike. I'll keep in touch when you come up on the SATCOM later this morning."

"All right. Thanks."

Pike hung up and slumped back on the couch in the office. The emptiness of the building reminded him of the loss of the men of Eyes Three even more than the memorial service had the previous day.

The forces he had set in motion were now rumbling and moving. Pike just hoped they made it through the day without someone getting wind of what was going on and questioning it.

# KNOLL 8548
## 5:42 A.M.

Riley was disoriented for a few seconds as he awoke. He felt cold on one side and warm on the other. The comforting feeling of a woman nestled alongside him contrasted with the harshness of the hard ground. He stared up at the branches above his head, dimly lit in the approaching dawn.

The reality of his situation hit him with a rush. He sat up and peered around in the dark. The lights from Ring Man's villa lit the sky to the southwest, slowly being overwhelmed by the rising sun.

Riley looked over at Westland, who was still sleeping peacefully. For a moment he wished they could simply leave this all behind. If it was just the Ring Man mission, Riley would have been willing to. True, Ring Man had been responsible for the killing of his teammates, but they had all known the risks when they signed on for the mission. He'd kill Ring Man if he had a chance, but he wouldn't throw away his, or Kate's, life on it.

The anchor that held him on this knoll in the mountains of Colombia was the presence of Powers in the villa below. Riley wasn't going anywhere until he gave rescuing his old friend the best possible shot. He still didn't have much of a plan, but he was going to wait until this evening and see if anything developed.

Of course, Riley knew, Westland didn't have the same commitment, and she was crazy if she still believed in the Ring Man mission. Riley was determined to lay it on the line when she woke up. He would tell her that the Ring Man hit was off. He didn't want her here. He wanted her safely back in the U.S. embassy or even better on a flight back to the States. Riley didn't know what the next twenty-four hours would hold, but he was certain it would be dangerous.

He sat back against his lookout tree and let his eyes adjust to the growing light. As he waited for Westland to wake, he broke down his weapons one by one and cleaned them. Using his sweatshirt as a rag he wiped the morning moisture off all the parts. He carefully reloaded the magazines, bullet by bullet, and checked the functioning of the weapons' actions. He put the M21 back in the plastic case. The Berreta was strapped back under his left shoulder. The MP5 he placed on his lap.

Finished with his morning priorities, Riley turned his gaze back on Kate's relaxed face. He realized he'd never had such strong feelings for a woman. He'd lived with a girl for a while at Bragg several years ago, but like all his other short-term relationships, he'd ended up drifting out of it. All those women had seemed too weak. It was hard for him to put his finger on the reason Kate attracted him, but it had a lot to do with her personal strength and self-confidence. She didn't need him but she wanted to be with him. That made a lot of difference. He felt they were on an equal footing.

Riley switched his thoughts to the mission at hand. Sitting

in the lotus position, he relaxed his breathing and contemplated the villa below. There had to be a way in. Riley took it one step at a time. He had all day to think.

# RING MAN'S VILLA
# 7:20 A.M.

Ariel knocked on the door to the Ring Man's bedroom with caution. The Ring Man's moods in the morning were known to vary widely. Waking him was considered a move fraught with danger. Ariel felt that the information he had just received was worth the risk. The boss would want to know.

"Enter."

Ariel opened the door and peered into the darkened room. He shut the door and walked to the foot of the bed. The Ring Man was sitting up, back against the headboard. The young girl was looking out from the other side of the bed with wide brown eyes.

"I assume you would not be disturbing me if it wasn't important."

Ariel nodded. The Ring Man considered him for a few seconds, then pushed the girl's head underneath the covers toward his crotch and leaned back. The man's a pig, Ariel thought.

"What is it?"

Ariel tried to ignore the movement under the covers. "I just had a talk with the president's aide, Montez. Alegre is looking for a truce."

The Ring Man's face cracked in a wide smile. "A truce?" He laughed. "That is very good. A truce. They must be running scared. It figures Montez would be the one to call. He is the more sensible one. What kind of truce did he have in mind?"

"He says Alegre will stand down from the state of emergency and pull the troops off our operations in the cities if we stop the war."

"What about the extradition treaty?"

"It will be suspended indefinitely."

Ariel was somewhat surprised at the Ring Man's initial

reaction. He had thought Alegre's betrayal was something his boss would never forgive. He had expected the Ring Man to explode in anger that Alegre dared propose a truce. His boss's next words confirmed his thoughts.

"I will never agree to anything with that pig. The fact that he wants a truce and is also willing to anger the Americans by reneging on the extradition treaty means he must really be in a bad position. Also the Americans are probably not supporting him as much. Maybe their loss at Barranquilla took the wind out of their sails. If Alegre wants a truce we must increase the pressure on him and break him. That pig betrayed me and he must pay for that."

Ariel wasn't sure he agreed with the Ring Man's reasoning. If Alegre fell, then someone else would take over. He knew the Ring Man was not yet in a position to assume that role and doubted whether he ever would be. They were having enough trouble right now consolidating their grip on the cartel. It was not working as smoothly as the Ring Man seemed to think it was. Ariel felt they would be better off accepting the government's offer. However, he also knew that was what his predecessor had recommended. His very dead predecessor.

"What do you want me to do?"

"Have you come up with a way to kill Alegre?"

Ariel had anticipated that question. "I think there may be a way to do that using this new offer and the American we have prisoner."

The Ring Man was intrigued. "Wait a minute outside."

Ariel nodded and exited the room. About two minutes later the Ring Man came out, slipping on his robe, with a satisfied look on his face. He headed for the dining room, where his breakfast was being laid out. "Join me for breakfast and tell me more."

## VICINITY OF KNOLL 8548
## 7:46 A.M.

"I'll guard while you wash off and then we'll switch."

Kate gave Riley a sidelong glance as she stripped down.

Riley was scanning the trail down to the road. As she slipped her foot into the water he casually mentioned, "By the way the water's real cold."

Kate pulled her foot out and gave him an accusing glare. He was pretending to look down the trail. "Thanks for the warning." She took a deep breath and dove into the water. The shock of the cold caused her to lose her breath and splutter to the surface. She wondered if feeling clean was worth this.

After a freezing two minutes she clambered out. Shaking off as much water as she could, she quickly dressed, slipping the Beretta back into its place under her shoulder. They'd thrown the Colt into the bottom of the pool on the way up yesterday, since it was out of ammunition.

"Your turn."

Riley shook his head. "No thanks. I've already had my share of that mountain water. I hope you feel better and that it was worth coming here."

"What happened to 'I'll guard and then we'll switch'?"

Riley came over and put his arms around her. "That was just a ploy to get you naked."

She looked at him and smiled without humor. "Well, it worked. What now?"

Riley let go of her. "Now we talk about getting you out of here."

Kate's smile disappeared. "What do you mean 'get me out of here'?"

"Exactly what I said. Either to the embassy or preferably out of the country."

She squared off and faced him, her face set into those determined lines Riley had seen before. "Why should I leave?"

"Because the Ring Man hit is off. I'm not here for that."

It was her turn to surprise him. "I knew that yesterday."

"What?"

She shook her head. He still didn't know the first thing about her. "I knew that as soon as you told me about Powers. I knew you'd make him your first priority."

"Then why did you come up here with me?"

She couldn't believe his obtuseness. "To help you, of course. You told me early on that rescuing Powers was your number one priority, and I went along with you and helped you. I'm not going to quit now."

"I don't have a plan, and whatever I do is going to be dangerous," Riley argued. "I can't ask you to take that risk."

Westland was starting to get angry. "Don't take that attitude with me. I'm capable of making my own decisions and I'm also capable of taking care of myself. In case you've forgotten, I've managed to do that pretty well so far. It's not up to you whether I stay here or leave. It's up to me."

Riley tried another line of reasoning. "I'm not trying to tell you what to do. You have no responsibility toward Powers. He's my friend and that's why I'm doing this. You ought to get while the getting's good."

Westland put her hand on Riley's shoulder. "Let me tell you a few things. First off, don't ever try to tell me what to do. You can ask and suggest, but don't order me. Second, I do feel some responsibility toward Powers. Third, I also feel some sense of responsibility toward you, and I'm not going to let you get your head blown off by doing something stupid. And last, I do what I want and I want to stay here."

Riley was staring at her. He'd expected her to be obstinate but he hadn't realized the depth of her feelings. He was at a loss for words.

Westland let go of his shoulder. "So what's the plan?"

Riley gave in. "Your guess is as good as mine. We go back up and continue surveillance. I don't know if Pike has come up with anything, and even if he has there's no way we can contact him. Whatever he may have done he'll probably have to cancel now. We have to assume we're on our own. Between the two of us we have to come up with a way to get into that villa, rescue Powers, and get out again—hopefully keeping all of us alive."

Westland nodded. "We'd best get back on up the hill then and put our thinking caps on."

# PRESIDENTIAL PALACE, BOGOTA
## 1:25 P.M.

Montez had seriously considered not passing on the message from the Ring Man's aide. The whole thing stunk and Montez didn't trust the Israeli. The problem was that this was the only way to get things back to normal. They would have to take a chance that the offer was legitimate.

Montez had waited patiently while Alegre finished a meeting with the mayor of Bogota. The mayor was complaining about the increasing toll the revenge of the cartel was exacting on the city. Montez found the whole thing darkly amusing, considering it was well known that the mayor was on the payroll of the Ring Man. Appearances were important, though.

After ushering out the still-protesting mayor, Montez joined his old friend at his desk. Alegre poured them both a stiff shot of brandy, then waited until Montez had swallowed his before querying him. "Any news?"

Montez put his glass down. "I have heard from the Ring Man's representative. He says they agree to the truce but they cannot speak for the other members of the cartel."

The news didn't make Alegre feel any better. He felt as if he had sold a part of his soul. "They agree to stop the bombings and killings?"

"The representative, one of those Israeli mercenaries named Ariel, said that they would stop any attacks against what he called 'civilian targets,' but that the fighting in Cartagena and Medellin would go on as long as there was opposition to the Ring Man's rule. He promised peace here in Bogota but said they could not be held responsible for any attacks instigated by other families."

Alegre nodded. That was the best they could expect. The problem was that this truce assisted the Ring Man more than it did him. It allowed the Ring Man to concentrate on the war against his fellow drug dealers, with no interference from the government. Alegre's main concern was that the Ring Man would once more turn his attention to toppling the government when he had secured his power base within the cartel.

Montez poured them both another brandy. Handing one to the president he added, "The Israeli also added something to the terms of the truce."

"What?"

"As a sign of good faith he says they are willing to turn over an American soldier they captured during the raid on the Ring Man's lab."

Alegre looked up in surprise. "Another secret the Americans did not tell us. Do you think they really have a prisoner?"

"I don't think they have any reason to lie about that."

Alegre couldn't follow the logic of the offer. "Why didn't they put him on the video, and why are they giving him to us?"

"I think they didn't put him on the video because it would have given the Americans an excuse to come down here and intervene. As to why they are giving him to us," Montez shrugged, "your guess is as good as mine. I am concerned, though, by the conditions this Israeli set for the turnover." He looked Alegre in the eye. "They want you present when they give him to us."

"Why?"

Montez could make a good guess. "I think it is a ploy to get you out into the open."

"What do you recommend?"

Montez finished his brandy with a swig. "I recommend we accept the offer. However, I will insist that the Ring Man also attend the turnover."

Alegre smiled as he realized his aide's cunning. "When and where is this scheduled?"

"I will call the Israeli back to set up the timing and see if we can work out a mutually acceptable site. I imagine we could do this tomorrow."

# KNOLL 8548
## 2:34 P.M.

Riley sat on the opposite side of the tree trunk from Westland. They were perched on branches, almost twenty-five feet over the top of the knoll. He pointed while he briefed her on the plan he had devised. As he spoke, he realized how bad the plan was.

"An hour before the guards change at 0300, if they do it the same time they did it the night before last, is when I'll go in over the east wall where the wing of the house comes closest. The way we'll do it is that you stay up here with the M21. You should be able to see the guards through the scope because they keep the place illuminated all night. I'll have on the PVS-5s and the MP5.

"I'll go down to the wall and wait. When you see that the guard on that side is out of sight of the place where I'll be going over, or walking away with his back to it, you light a match. You only need to light it and blow it out—it'll be like a flare in the goggles. I'll go over at your signal. I'll only have to make it from the wall to the building. I can do that in a few seconds." He didn't add that he had no idea whether there were sensors on the wall that would pick up his intrusion.

"The windows are barred and maybe even rigged with alarms, but I think I can climb up to the roof of the wing and make it over to the second floor of the main building. I'll have a better chance of getting in there.

"Once I'm in . . . " Riley paused. Something wasn't right.

Westland was startled by the pause. "What's the—" Riley held up his hand, signaling her to stay still. He scanned the immediate area, first with his naked eyes. Seeing nothing unusual, he surveyed the area using the sight mounted on the M21. He could sense Westland becoming restless as the minutes stretched out.

Powers had always told him to trust his sixth sense. The experienced NCO had explained his theory of sixth sense one evening at Fort Bragg, and his reasoning had seemed logical. Powers told him that people took in much more input with their senses than their minds could handle. The mind filtered out many of the things a person's eyes actually saw and their ears actually heard or any of the other senses were picking up. The sixth sense was some part of the mind alerting you to something seen or heard or smelled or felt that the active mind wasn't focusing on.

Riley was trying to find whatever it was that had caused him to alert. Finally he picked it out. The noise of the birds and other small creatures on the hillside had altered. Riley knew patience was important now. Whatever, or whoever, had disturbed the wildlife would either make its presence known or go away. Riley was willing to wait it out.

He scanned the sides of the knoll in small arcs, noting the plant life, looking for any disturbances. Finally he was rewarded. He spotted a branch sway, its movements contrary to the direction of the wind. Riley focused in on the spot, about one hundred twenty meters away on the west side of the knoll.

After five minutes a man materialized at that spot, standing up and stretching. The man turned and spoke to someone still concealed by the undergrowth. Riley inspected the person he could see. About six feet tall, well muscled, wearing a pair of jeans and a flannel shirt. The man was dark haired and sported a large mustache. In a sheath tied off on his backpack, he carried a machete. What really caught Riley's attention was the weapon slung over his shoulder. A Mossberg Model 500 Bullpup shotgun nestled against the man's hip, ready for action. Not a typical sicario's weapon, Riley thought. Although the twelve-gauge automatic shotgun was a devastating weapon at short range, Riley knew he held the advantage at this distance with the M21.

That advantage of weapon range disappeared as the second man stood up. This one was blond haired with a full beard and stood even taller than his partner, at almost six and a half feet. He had a long-barreled rifle slung over his back and an Uzi submachine gun on a sling hung over his belly.

The two men were obviously discussing their position. The taller man was gesturing up the hill toward Riley's location. If the man intended to use that rifle against the villa, or cover the villa from attack, Riley knew the top of knoll 8548, where he and Westland were sitting, was the place. He wondered who the two men were. He figured either they were extra security placed out by the Ring Man to cover his villa or they were enemies of the Ring Man and were up here for some of the same reasons Riley was. Although not Colombian, the two could be foreign mercenaries. The tall man looked as though he might be German. The two had apparently reached a decision. They headed upslope.

Riley focused his cross hairs on the chest of the man with the long-barreled weapon. He debated firing. If they were enemies it was best to kill them now, while he still had the range. Every step they took up the hill decreased his odds of successful engagement. However, his firing would also be heard down in the villa and would undoubtedly bring a reaction force. It was this last thought that stilled Riley's finger.

He pulled away from the eyepiece and glanced over at Westland. She had spotted the two men and had drawn her pistol. Riley gestured for her to take no action. He quietly put the rifle down in the crook of the branch and took hold of his submachine gun.

The two men moved with evident field experience. The lead man had the shotgun at hip level and swung it back and forth in concert with his head as he scanned their way up. The second man carried the Uzi, folding stock extended, and was trailing the first, allowing a good tactical separation of almost twenty meters. The mistake they were making was one that even the most experienced soldier can make: They were focusing on the ground and not checking up in the trees. It was a universal bad habit. There was a good chance the two would pass right beneath his and Westland's position without noticing them. But Riley knew he couldn't afford to take that chance.

He got Westland's attention and pointed at the lead man, indicating that he was hers. She nodded. Riley centered his sights on the second man. He waited until the lead man was within ten meters of the base of their tree. "Freeze, I've got you covered," he yelled out in Spanish.

They froze. The lead man slowly lifted his head until he could see into the tree. He took in the two people crouched up there and their weapons. The odds were against him. He called out to his partner in Spanish. "There's two in the tree. Man and a woman. They've got a sub on you and a pistol on me."

"Shut up," Riley yelled. Now that he had frozen the action he wasn't sure how to proceed. The trail man was easing himself over toward a tree trunk, trying to get its cover. "Move another step and you're dead."

The man stopped. The lead man was still looking up at them. "Perhaps we should talk."

"Who are you?" Riley called out.

The lead man seemed rather confident for someone who had a pistol pointing at him. "That's a good question. One we might ask you. But I think I might know more about you than you know about us. Your name Riley?"

Riley studied the man. Who the hell would know his name?

The man switched to English. "And the lady there is Westland, I presume. Only a goddamn Green Beanie would take a woman into a tree on a date."

Riley was confused. "Who the hell are you?"

"Let me ask you something first. If you answer right we can do all the talking you want. What was your first car?"

Riley recognized the question. It was from his finger card— the card every member of the team had filled out prior to the mission and placed inside the escape and evasion packet that had been given to Pike. Each man's card had his fingerprints and photograph, plus three questions only he would know the answers to. The purpose of the questions was to verify identity in case a link had to be made with an unknown party. The person asking had access to the information in the E & E packet, which meant he was legitimate; the person being asked established his identity by answering the obscure question correctly.

"A '64 Plymouth Valiant," Riley answered. The man lowered his shotgun. Riley sighed. He turned to Westland, who had followed the exchange in confusion. "They're friendlies."

He led the way down out of the tree. By the time they got to the bottom the two men were waiting there. The shorter one gestured and the tall blond man climbed up to take their place. Getting to the branch, he rested his rifle on it and started scanning the compound.

The other man stuck out his hand. "Andy Thompson. That's Ron Tremont up there."

Riley shook his hand. "Dave Riley. This is Kate Westland."

Thompson nodded. "I know. We were told you all might be hanging around here."

Westland took the offered hand. "Where you from?"

The man shrugged. "I'm not supposed to tell you that, but suffice it to say that I'm from the same place you are, Dave. Used to be in 7th Group myself. We're here to help you all out with your mission."

Riley's suspicions were confirmed. They had to be from Delta Force. "What were you briefed our mission was?"

The man pointed down toward the villa. "From what we were told there's a very bad man living there who isn't supposed to see the sun rise tomorrow. We've got a plan we think will do that."

Riley shook his head. "There's a complication."

Thompson frowned. "What complication?"

"My team sergeant is a prisoner down there."

"What!" The man shook his head. "We weren't told about any hostages. Shit. I'm going to have to call the old man and let him know. Fill me in while I get the radio set up."

As Riley updated him, Thompson slipped the ruck off his back and pulled out a SATCOM radio. He unfolded the tripod legs of the little dish and angled it up to the sky, then hooked in a scrambler and put on a small headset. He did a trial shot and got a successful bounce back from the satellite, indicating he was on the right direction and azimuth.

Satisfied he was set, Thompson keyed his mike. "Eagle Leader, this is Snake Leader. Over."

The reply came back in less than two seconds. "Snake Leader, this is Eagle Six-Kilo. Wait one while I get the Six. Over."

After about thirty seconds another voice came over the radio. "This is Eagle Leader. Go ahead. Over."

"Roger, we've linked up with the surveillance element down here. They're in good health. We've got the compound under surveillance. There's a slight complication. Riley says there's an American hostage in the villa. His team sergeant who was captured during an earlier op. Over."

There was a moment of silence on the other end. "Roger. I'll have to talk that over with the planning cell. I'll let you know what we come up with at the 1800 contact. In the meantime continue on as planned and find out as much of the information we need as possible. Over."

"Roger. Over."

"Out here."

The radio went dead and Thompson switched it off. Riley and Westland looked at him expectantly. They had been able to hear only his end of the conversation. Thompson looked up at them. "Our forward element is down in Panama by now. They're going to work in the hostage. They'll let us know if there are any modifications at our 1800 contact."

Riley nodded. "What's the plan in the meantime?"

"We wait and observe. I've got a whole list of questions we need answered about that place down there."

## 4:32 P.M.

Riley was beginning to feel a bit like Tarzan with all this hanging around in trees. Tremont was on the other side of the trunk, continuing to scan the compound through the scope on the rifle he carried. Riley had never seen that particular sniper rifle. It was bolt action with a bulky covering around the barrel.

Tremont seemed more than happy to explain his weapon. Riley had found that most military men liked talking about the tools of their trade.

"This is an Accuracy International Model PM sniper rifle, made by the Brits. We used to use the M21 like you guys in SF, but this thing is more accurate. Fires 7.62 match ammo. It's single bolt action because the receiver is high-carbon solid steel. Tightens up the whole action. The barrel is free floating and never comes closer than an eighth of an inch to the stock."

Riley pointed at the barrel. He'd never seen an accurate silenced sniper rifle. "That a suppressor?"

"Yeah. It's an integral one, like the one on your MP5."

"What about the round? Don't you get the supersonic crack?"

Tremont enjoyed being the expert. "Nope. I use Lapua subsonic match ammo. I lose some range but I can still hit out to about eight hundred meters and put someone down forever, and no one will hear a thing."

Riley was impressed. "How fast can you reload and fire?"

Tremont looked down at the villa. "At this range, at a man-sized target? I figure I can put a round out every two seconds and hit. The British SAS have . . ."

Tremont paused, swung up the rifle, and looked down the hill. Riley followed suit with his M21. Two cars were rolling down the driveway, heading for the gate. It was impossible to see through the dark windshields. Riley watched until the cars were out of sight, heading down toward the main highway.

Tremont turned and looked at him. "Do you think this Ring Man fellow was in there?"

Riley shrugged. "I really don't care if he was or wasn't. What worries me is that Powers may have been in there. Let's hope not."

## PENTAGON
## 5:15 P.M.

Linders punched in the numbers on his phone and waited. After two buzzes the other end was picked up.

"Pike here."

"This is General Linders. Just checking to see how things are going."

There was a pause on the other end. "Fine, sir. Everything's looking good to go."

Linders still wasn't feeling comfortable with the whole setup. He hadn't been involved in the actual running of the previous Hammer strikes either, but this time, using Delta Force in a selective strike, there was a higher level of compromise. Linders was surprised they were doing this after what had happened to the third Hammer mission.

"Anything else I can do for you, Mike?"

"No, sir. Everything looks good to go."

"I assume this mission goes tonight?"

Another pause. "Yes, sir, but I'd rather not go into too much detail. We're keeping this in extra tight after what happened to the last one."

Linders felt a little put off by that answer. "I understand, Mike. I assume the chairman is on top of things?"

"Yes, sir."

"All right. Out here."

Linders put down the phone and leaned back in the chair. The trend in Special Operations over the past decade had been for fewer and fewer people to be informed and involved in actual operations. The afteraction report on the debacle at Desert One had shown glaring faults in the number of people who were actively involved in the decision-making process, from the president on down. The military had pushed for less outside involvement and more autonomy for the leader on the ground.

Linders himself agreed with this: He believed that the military should get mission statements and then be left alone by the civilians to do the job. But right now he was wondering if that streamlining and canalization of operational information wasn't working against him. Something didn't seem right with this whole operation. In reality, Linders realized, he had only Pike's word that this operation was legitimate. Not that he had any problem with that. Pike did have a letter of authorization from the chairman. It was just that someday, Linders was afraid someone with enough knowledge might be able to circumvent the system. He decided to have one of his staff officers write a staff study examining whether or not that could really happen.

Linders glanced at his watch. He had to attend a formal reception over at Fort Myers this evening. He needed to head on home now if he was going to make it on time. Turning off the light, he left his office.

# KNOLL 8548
# 6:00 P.M.

Tremont was still up in the tree. He hadn't been inactive. With Riley's help, he'd constructed a brace for his rifle, using broken branches and 550 cord he had carried in. The muzzle of his weapon now rested securely in front of him and he could scan the entire compound with ease.

Riley and Westland were on the ground, providing local

security around Thompson as he made his 1800 contact. He was on the air quite a while. Riley had an instinctive distrust of staying on a radio a long time even though he knew his fears were groundless. The Colombians certainly had nothing that could intercept signals from a SATCOM radio. Still, old habits died hard. He gave a sigh of relief as Thompson shut down the radio.

Thompson gestured for Tremont to come down out of the tree. He left the rifle in its cradle and shimmied down. The four gathered in tight as Thompson outlined the plan for the evening. Riley had to admit it was a bit better than the one he had come up with earlier in the morning.

# HOWARD AIR FORCE BASE, PANAMA
# 7:45 P.M.

"Hammer Base, this is Eagle Leader. Over." Lieutenant Colonel Edberg released the transmit button on the radio and waited.

The radio crackled. "This is Hammer Base. Over."

"This is Eagle Leader. I'm calling for final mission authorization. Authenticate please. Over."

Edberg released the send and licked his lips nervously. This was when they would find out whether the mission was a practice dry run or the real thing. Since Edberg had taken command of B Troop, Delta Force, a little over a year ago, his troop had participated in eleven deployments. Six had been in response to real-world alerts but had not progressed further than deployment and planning, because the crises had been resolved in other ways or because the politicians had decided not to commit Delta Force. On the other five deployments, they had been given, just like this one, what looked like a real mission and had forward deployed to a staging area. After completing the planning and being ready to go, these deployments had ended when final authorization was not given; an evaluation team from Delta headquarters then came in and evaluated the plans and preparations. Not knowing if a deployment was real or not kept the men honed to a sharp edge of performance but was also extremely stressful.

The radio hissed. "I authenticate Bold Gambit. I say again, I authenticate Bold Gambit. Over."

Edberg stared at the radio in surprise, then looked at the members of his assault force. It was the real thing.

"Roger, Hammer Base. I copy Bold Gambit. Over."

"Hammer Base, out."

Edberg keyed the mike again. "Tiger Leader, this is Eagle Leader. Did you copy Hammer Base? Over."

From two hundred fifty kilometers to the south the reply came back. "Roger that. I'll get it cranking. Over."

"Good luck. Out."

# FOUR KILOMETERS NORTH OF THE PANAMA-COLOMBIA BORDER
## 7:48 P.M.

Sergeant Major Ed Rabitowski signaled for Griffin to pack up the SATCOM. He looked at the pilot. "Crank her up, Cullen. We lift on time."

The pilot, a rated aviator from Delta, nodded and went over to start his helicopter. The aircraft was an OH-58, the military version of the Bell Jet Ranger. The twin-bladed helicopter could hold only the pilot and the three men of Tiger element.

The four men were dressed similarly, all in black, including black balaclavas pulled over their lower faces. Night-vision goggles hung around their necks, and each man wore a headset for communication among the team and with the other elements. They wore combat vests with the various tools of their trade hanging on them.

The single turbine engine started to whine as Cullen began his start-up procedures. Rabitowski glanced at his watch just before getting in and taking the left front seat, next to the pilot. Since the OH-58 was the slowest aircraft involved in the operation, it would leave first, even though it was two hundred fifty kilometers closer to the target than the Eagle element up at Howard Air Force Base. This whole mission depended on split-second timing from the various elements involved.

As soon as Cullen had sufficient engine speed, the blades started turning and the aircraft began rocking. Rabitowski looked over his shoulder at the two men seated in the back. Jacobs and Griffin both gave him a thumbs-up. Their RPG rocket launchers were between their knees, muzzles pointing down.

Rabitowski nodded calmly. This was going to be a bit hairy and a lot of things could go wrong. But Rabitowski prided himself on not worrying about things he couldn't control. Twenty-nine years in the army had taught him that. He pulled his cut-down SAW machine gun closer to his side. The comforting feel of the weapon's cold metal was what he believed in. The SAW was something he *could* control.

Rabitowski would be retiring in one month, and Colonel Edberg had been against his going on this mission. Sergeant Major Rabitowski had been adamant. He wanted to go in his assigned place with his troop. He wanted one last live mission after twenty-nine years.

He pulled out the acetated map with their flight route on it. Written in grease pencil along the route were the time hacks for the various checkpoints on the way in. A stopwatch was taped to the map. Rabitowski checked his watch. Cullen lifted the aircraft to a three-foot hover. When his second hand swept past the twelve and the watch indicated 7:54, Rabitowski indicated go and clicked the stopwatch. Cullen pushed forward on the cyclic and they were on their way.

## FORT MYERS, VIRGINIA
## 8:20 P.M.

Linders entered the officers' club and immediately headed for the bar. He was over an hour and a half late but he didn't care. He hated these formal functions. This one was being sponsored by Linders's own service, the air force, under some pretext or other. In reality it was a chance to invite some of the politicians from across the river to come rub elbows with the brass. Linders knew the hot topic of the evening would be the B-2 bomber, and the party line would be to support that effort. He couldn't care less about the B-2 bomber. Any aircraft that cost that much was ridiculous, in his opinion, but he didn't dare voice that heresy. He was here because protocol required it.

He circulated through the crowd, nodding to acquaintances. Linders wasn't very popular with his air force cronies because as DCSOP-SO his priorities were somewhat different. He fought his own service for funding for more Combat Talon and Spectre Special Operations aircraft. Linders had a bitter appreciation for where the priorities lay: In the last air force budget, procurement of more Combat Talons was forty-fifth on a fifty-two–item aircraft priority list.

Linders's musings on the skewed sense of priority of the air force were interrupted when he spotted General Macksey holding court on the other side of the room. Why was the chairman here when he was supposed to be overseeing the operation by Delta Force? The only logical answer Linders could come up with was that the general would be returning to the war room of the Pentagon later this evening.

Linders worked his way across the room toward Macksey. He was further surprised to see that Macksey was drinking alcohol. There was no way the general would be drinking with an operation pending later in the evening. Linders elbowed his way through the crowd of sycophants and insinuated himself next to the chairman.

Macksey noticed the intrusion. "General Linders. How are you?"

Linders grabbed the chairman's elbow. "Sir, I need to talk to you privately." Macksey nodded. He led the way out of the main ballroom and into the foyer. Ignoring the people entering, he fixed Linders with a hard gaze. "What's so important?"

Linders figured the direct approach was the best. "Sir, do you know about a Delta strike this evening in Colombia?"

Macksey frowned. "The Hammer strikes have been canceled since the third one was compromised. What are you talking about?"

"Sir, Delta Force was alerted yesterday and elements of it are presently forward deployed in Panama preparing for a strike tonight."

"What!" Macksey grabbed Linders's shoulder. "Who authorized that?"

"Mike Pike came to my office yesterday with the OPORD. He said it was authorized as a continuation of your Hammer order. Since I hadn't heard any cancellation of the Hammer missions, I assumed it was part of the same mission and verified the OPORD."

Macksey closed his eyes briefly as the reality of what Pike had done sank in. He thought rapidly, trying to sort out the pieces. "Do you know when the strike is happening?"

Linders shook his head. "All I know is it's tonight. I called Pike today and asked him what time. He wouldn't tell me. He said security was being tightened."

"Where did you call him?"

"He's at the same STU-III he was for the other missions."

Macksey made up his mind. He called for his aide, who was hovering out of conversation range. "George, get my car around front." He turned to Linders. "You're coming with me."

# HOWARD AIR FORCE BASE, PANAMA
## 8:38 P.M.

The Combat Talon lifted off the runway and its four powerful turboprop engines drilled it into the night sky. Inside the cramped cargo bay, Edberg sat as comfortably as his parachute and equipment would allow on the web seats rigged along the side of the aircraft. He wore a headset connected by a long cord to a SATCOM radio nestled in among the electronics gear in the front half of the bay. The other nine members of his team were spread out in the rear half.

This was Edberg's first live mission. He hadn't expected to get the final go. He'd anticipated another no-go and mission evaluation, especially after the haphazard way General Pike had alerted them and with the tight time limit that had been imposed.

They had an hour-and-fifty-two-minute ride to their infiltration point. The Combat Talon was going to rely on something besides its terrain-following ability for this flight. The electronic warfare people in the front were sending out a transponder signal indicating the Talon was a civilian airliner en route from Panama City to Buenos Aires, Argentina. The aircraft would fit this profile except for the brief one-minute slowdown over the infiltration point for the drop.

Edberg's ears perked up when he heard the radio come alive.

"Eagle, this is Hawk. I have lifted and am en route." Edberg checked his watch. 8:44. The HH-53 Pave Low helicopter had lifted from the USS *Raleigh* off the coast of Colombia on time. All the pieces were moving.

## KNOLL 8548
## 9:05 P.M.

Riley waited at the base of the tree with Westland and Thompson. The Delta Force soldier had on the headset for the SATCOM. Tremont was in the tree continuing surveillance and in place for the role he would play shortly.

Thompson gave a thumbs-up. "Tiger, Hawk, and Eagle forces are all en route."

Riley turned and stared at the lit compound below. His adrenaline was starting to flow. He forced himself to calm down. They still had a while to go before things started happening. Another hour and twenty-five minutes.

Thompson pulled one of the cups of the headset off his ear. He reached into his ruck, took out two small radios with headsets, and handed them to Riley and Westland. "You know how to work that thing? We brought spares in case we found you all."

Riley nodded as he put the radio into a pouch on his vest and rigged the headset. He showed Westland how to work hers.

Thompson waited until Riley was done. "All right. You

and Westland head down at 2200. You'll be able to talk, but remember that those guys coming in are going to shoot anything moving. I don't know why the old man agreed to have you two go in, but he did, so I'm not going to argue with him. I guess he figures he needs all the help he can get, plus you're a backup for Tiger if they don't make it in. The elements have been told you're going in over the wall, but you know how it gets in the dark when bullets are flying."

Thompson pulled a roll of tape from his ruck. He peeled off a long strip and wrapped it completely around Riley's chest, taking care not to seal any of his ammo pouches. With other strips he encircled Riley's wrists and ankles. For a finishing touch he put a strip around Riley's head. "That'll give you better odds of not getting shot. All the good guys will be wearing this IR tape in the same places. It'll show up like a strip of light in the goggles. Shoot anyone who doesn't have it."

Thompson removed his combat vest and gave it to Westland, who put it on. He then taped her with the IR chemical tape. Reluctantly he handed his Mossberg Bullpup to Westland. The squat weapon was only thirty and a half inches long. Thompson ran her through a quick overview of the weapon. "You got eight rounds in the tube under the barrel. As you can see, the sights are on top of the handle so it aims high. If you're going to fire from the shoulder, aim about half a foot low."

Westland hefted the bulky gun. "What about recoil?"

Thompson smiled. "It's a beauty. You fired shotguns before?" Westland nodded. "It's got less recoil than any shotgun you've ever fired. You can fire it from the hip."

Riley interrupted. "What kind of load you got in there?"

"Alternating slugs and number four buckshot." Riley whistled lightly. That thing could clear out a room. Thompson pointed at Westland's vest. "You got solid slugs on your right side and number four buck on the left. Don't forget that if you reload. It's best to alternate the rounds. The slugs will knock the shit out of someone if you hit. The buckshot gives you some dispersion. Alternate them and you raise hell."

Westland nodded. "I can handle it."

Thompson pointed out one last important feature. "You've

got two safeties. First is a normal cross-bolt safety, right here. See, this is safe and this is fire." Thompson flicked the switch. "The second safety is in the grip, kind of like the .45-caliber pistol. You have to maintain pressure on the pistol grip to fire."

Westland nodded. Thompson slapped her lightly on the back. "Take care of my gun now. Hate to lose it."

Riley had grown to like the gruff commando over the course of the day. He'd been surprised to find out that Thompson was a major and the assistant operations officer for his troop. He certainly had not seemed concerned about rank in dealing with Riley or Tremont. Thompson's role in the upcoming conflict was to be the coordinating point for the attacking elements from his bird's-eye view up here on the hill. With the SATCOM he could talk to the incoming aircraft and with the small FM radio he could talk to the members of the Tiger and Eagle forces along with Tremont up in the tree.

Thompson looked the two of them over. "Looks like you're ready to party."

# FORT BELVOIR, VIRGINIA
## 9:23 P.M.

Pike watched the headlights turn into the parking lot. He counted two cars, one of which was a military police vehicle. Pike looked at his watch and then at the SATCOM set. Since giving the final authentication he had monitored B Troop's traffic. He knew all the elements were in the air and en route.

Unfortunately, he also knew there was still plenty of time for those forces to be recalled. If only he had another hour.

The door to the building swung open and General Macksey strode in, followed by Linders. Pike stood and faced the oncoming storm. He decided he'd open the pleasantries.

"You didn't have to get all dressed to come see me, sir," he said, noting the dress mess uniform in which Macksey was regaled.

Macksey failed to see the humor. "What the hell are you doing, Pike? Is Delta actually on alert in Panama?"

Pike considered several possible stalling replies. The only problem was the SATCOM radio behind him on the table. All Macksey had to do was pick up the mike and he could talk to the B Troop commander himself. "Yes, sir."

Macksey glared at him. "What the hell are you doing?" he repeated.

Pike stopped the general in his tracks with his next statement. "Sir, do you realize that one of the men from that last mission, the one who escaped, has been sent by the CIA down to Colombia to assassinate one of the members of the drug cartel?"

Macksey seemed stunned. "What?"

Since he was being honest, Pike decided he'd overwhelm the general with the bald facts and hopefully forestall him getting on the radio with a recall. "Let me start from the beginning, sir. I think you'll find this all quite interesting. The day that last Hammer mission was compromised, the . . . "

## AIRSPACE OVER COLOMBIA
## 9:44 P.M.

Rabitowski looked at the fuel gauge. They were down to less than a third of a tank. He checked the map as the helicopter whizzed over a single-lane road. "Checkpoint 15, on route and on time."

Cullen nodded but didn't speak. They were flying terrain contour, approximately twenty-five feet above the highest obstacle. Even with the night-vision goggles it was a tiring operation for the pilot.

Rabitowski checked the map again. "Turn left. Stop turn." He peered ahead through his goggles. "The route goes slightly to the left of that hill ahead."

Cullen made the slight adjustment and the aircraft steadied on the new course. Rabitowski checked the time again. Another forty-five minutes to target.

# FORT BELVOIR, VIRGINIA
# 9:46 P.M.

Macksey shook his head as Pike finished his tale. "That's all fine and well, but you had no authority to do what you've done. I'm canceling your party." He gestured toward the SATCOM radio. "Do you have commo with the Delta Force commander down there?"

Pike nodded reluctantly. As Macksey moved toward the radio Pike decided to play his trump card. "Sir, did you also know that the missing man from the Eyes Three mission is alive and being held in the target Delta is heading for?"

That stopped Macksey in his tracks. "I was told he was dead."

Pike drove the nail home with a vengeance. "I told you not to write him off. We have a verified visual sighting of Master Sergeant Powers being held by this Colombian, Ring Man."

Macksey looked Pike in the eye. "You're already in enough trouble as it is. I'm asking you to tell me the truth. Is Powers really alive and being held there?"

Pike glared back. "Sir, one thing I'm not is a liar." He pointed at the radio. "You make the decision. Are you going to abandon the only chance we're going to have to rescue him?"

Macksey seemed torn for a few seconds and then shook his head. "I have to cancel. This whole thing is unsanctioned. We'll never get away with it."

Pike was starting to get angry. "Is that all you care about? Covering your ass?"

Macksey stood firm. "Goddamnit, man. Why didn't you go through channels if you knew Powers was alive?"

"Because the CIA would probably not have allowed verifying, and the bottom line is that there wasn't enough time."

Macksey picked up the handset for the radio. "I'm sorry, Mike. You screwed up and I'm going to have to fix things. What's the call sign for the Delta commander?"

Pike sighed. "Eagle Leader."

Macksey keyed the mike. "Eagle Leader, come in. Over."

The reply was almost instantaneous. "This is Eagle Leader. Please identify yourself. Over."

"Eagle Leader, this is General Macksey. I'm ordering you to abort your mission and return all your elements to friendly territory. Over."

There was a pause on the other end. "This is Eagle Leader. I need verification of abort. Over."

Macksey turned to Pike. "What's the code word for abort?"

Pike didn't answer, but even as he stood there saying nothing he realized he had made a mistake in that area. Macksey glared at him, then keyed the mike again. "This is General Macksey. General Pike has authorized this mission without proper authority and refuses to give up the abort code word. I'm ordering you on my authority to abort. Over."

There was an even longer pause on the other end. "I'm sorry, sir, if this is General Macksey on the other end, but I cannot abort without the proper code word. Over."

A thought struck Macksey. "The code word is Cage Thunder. Over."

The reply was quicker this time. "Roger, I verify Cage Thunder. Over."

## AIRSPACE OVER COLOMBIA
## 9:52 P.M.

Edberg looked up in dismay as he verified the abort code word. The other members of his force were still in their positions. His ops officer was looking at him strangely, wondering what the long conversation was about. Edberg gestured for him to come over. The man waddled over awkwardly and threw himself on the adjacent seat. He yelled in Edberg's ear to be heard over the roar of the engines. "What's up?"

"I just got the abort code word from the chairman of the Joint Chiefs of Staff."

The ops officer rolled his eyes. "Jesus Christ! It's a little too late for that."

Edberg looked at him. "What do you mean?"

"Shit, sir, Tiger element is already past the point of no return. They don't have enough fuel to make it back out."

Edberg winced as he remembered that. The OH-58 had barely enough fuel to make it to the target on a one-way trip. That was the way it had been planned. He decided to hold off on giving the turnaround order until he put this monkey on Macksey's back. He didn't know what the hell was going on up there in Virginia, but it was a little late to be pulling this stuff.

"Hammer Base, this is Eagle Leader. Over."

He heard the chairman's voice come back over the radio. "This is Hammer Base. Over."

"We've got a problem with an abort at this time. One of my elements is on a helicopter that doesn't have enough fuel to make it back out of Colombia. Over."

There was a pause. "What's time on target? Over."

"2230. Over."

"Is there any way you can get those people in the helicopter out? Over."

Edberg considered the options. "My best bet would be to link up the Tiger element with our exfil bird coming in from the coast, but that will be kind of flaky. We don't have a linkup point designated other than the target." Another thought hit Edberg. "I've also got two men on the ground in addition to Pike's two people, pulling surveillance. They were supposed to come out by the HH-53. Over."

The irritation in the chairman's voice was evident. "Do you have a backup plan to get them out? Over."

"Roger, they have an alternate for coming out covertly, but there's no provision in there for Pike's people. Over."

"Wait one. Over."

# FORT BELVOIR, VIRGINIA
## 9:55 P.M.

Macksey put down the mike and looked over at Pike and Linders, who had been following the conversation. He shook his head at Pike. "You sure managed to get things rolling, didn't you?"

"Sir, things are so far in motion that it's just as dangerous to abort at this point as it is to continue the mission," Pike argued. He was still mad at himself for not having changed the abort code word from the other Hammer missions. It only stood to reason that Macksey would remember it.

Macksey turned to Linders. "What do you think?"

Linders carefully weighed his answer and then committed. "Sir, I agree with Pike. The plan is to hit the target, not to abort. I think they can execute the plan better than they can piecework out an abort this late."

Pike wasn't through. "Sir, that's an American soldier being held by those people. An American soldier who went on a mission under your orders. Are you going to quit and not even take a chance at rescuing him? I've heard you speak out at the POW and MIA meetings. Were those just words you were spouting or did you really mean what you said?" Pike was also hoping the tirade he had thrown in Macksey's office earlier in the week was still fresh in the man's mind.

Macksey's next statement indicated he was wavering. "What's the chance of success for this strike? For getting Powers out?"

Pike shook his head. That was a question he expected from a politician, not a military man. "Sir, you know I can't give you that. It's a good plan and they're the best soldiers you have. There's risk involved, but those men are willing to take that risk. Give them a chance."

Macksey turned and stared out the window at the MP car in the parking lot, the car he had brought to take away Pike. He reached over and picked up the mike.

# AIRSPACE OVER COLOMBIA
# 10:00 P.M.

Edberg pressed the headset in tighter as the radio came alive.

"Eagle Leader, this is Hammer Base. Ignore Cage Thunder. I say again, ignore Cage Thunder. Mission continues as planned. Over."

"Roger that, sir. Mission is a go. Over."

"Good luck. Hammer Base out."

Edberg turned to his ops officer with a big grin. "We're going in."

## KNOLL 8548
## 10:02 P.M.

Thompson had monitored the entire exchange between Belvoir and Eagle Leader over the SATCOM but had not said a word to Riley or Westland, who were huddled nearby. His heart had been in his throat listening to the exchange. Like all the men of Delta he wanted action, and the thought of an abort this late made him almost physically ill.

Hearing the last go, Thompson turned to the two. "Time for you all to head on down. Good luck."

Riley gave a thumbs-up and led the way down the hill.

## FORT BELVOIR, VIRGINIA
## 10:03 P.M.

Pike gestured toward the chairs stacked in the corner. "You two might as well grab a seat. We've got a little while to go."

## AIRSPACE OVER COLOMBIA
## 10:16 P.M.

A red light started flashing and a caution segment light appeared on the console of the OH-58. Rabitowski stared at it in concern. "What the hell is that?"

Cullen kept his attention fixed on the terrain ahead. "Fuel warning light."

Rabitowski didn't like that. "I thought you said we'd have enough fuel to make it to the target. Are we going to make it or not?"

"Should."

"Should!" That answer didn't please the old sergeant major. "Listen, kid, I've got thirty years in this here green machine, and I don't want to end it by running out of gas and becoming part of the countryside."

"Relax, Sergeant Major. All that light means is that we're low, not that we're out. We should have about twenty minutes left. We'll make it. And if we don't," Cullen added mischievously, "I'll just autorotate into the trees."

"Just great," Rabitowski muttered to himself as he checked the map. "Checkpoint 24. That's the last one before we hit our final reference point." He looked at the stopwatch. "Right on time. Don't screw this up, kid, by running out of fuel. You done a good job getting us this far."

"No sweat, Sergeant Major."

## VICINITY OF RING MAN'S VILLA 10:25 P.M., EAGLE FORCE

The ramp opened and the air swirled in with a roar. Edberg pushed himself up tight behind the jumper in front of him. One minute out from drop. It was too late now even if they changed their minds back in Virginia. He was no longer hooked into the SATCOM. Once he got closer to the ground he'd be able to talk to Thompson on the FM radio.

Edberg kept his eyes fixed on the glowing red light above the ramp. He took a few deep breaths. The light turned green and the ten men shuffled off the ramp in formation.

Edberg felt the plane's slipstream grab him and buffet him about. He spread his arms and legs and arced his back in an effort to stabilize. He had barely achieved that state when he pulled his ripcord. His chute blossomed above him and he oscillated under the canopy.

Quickly getting his bearings, Edberg spotted the other members of Eagle spread out below him. He dumped air and caught up with them.

## 10:28 P.M., TIGER FORCE

Rabitowski heaved a sigh of relief as the lights from the target popped into view. Cullen raised their altitude for the final approach. The blinking of the fuel warning light for the past twelve minutes had gotten on Rabitowski's nerves. They'd find out in another minute or so if the villa guards would fall for the ruse. The theory was that the guards would not fire on the helicopter since it was the same type aircraft as the one that Ring Man owned.

Rabitowski's headset crackled as he heard Thompson for the first time over the short-range FM radio. "Tiger, this is Snake. I can hear you coming. Situation at target as briefed. LZ clear. Break. Riley, you're clear to go. Over."

Cullen swung the chopper around in a left-hand bank and they approached the villa from the south.

## 10:29 P.M., RILEY AND WESTLAND

The muted buzz of the inbound helicopter reverberated through the air. Riley boosted Westland up on the wall, then reached up and grabbed her hand as she helped him up alongside her.

They lay on top of the thick stone wall getting their bearings. The corner of the wing of the house was only twenty-five feet away. Riley spotted the guard on this side of the wall heading toward the landing pad, just as they had hoped he would. If the guards fired on the helicopter, Tremont would intervene with his suppressed rifle.

Riley slid off the wall and landed on the inside, followed by Westland. He led the way toward the house across the lighted section of lawn. As he did so a dark form leapt out of the shadow of the house. Riley fired a quick burst from his submachine gun and the dog was slammed back into the shade.

# 10:30 P.M., EAGLE FORCE

The inbound helicopter not only drew attention away from the wall, but it covered up the slight noise Eagle Force made as it landed on the main building. The dark forms touched down on the roof like winged vampires.

Edberg was the trail man in the airborne formation. He could see the canopies from the other jumpers draped all over the roof. He braked and felt his knees buckle slightly as he made a perfect landing in the center of the roof. Two of the first jumpers were already at work, prepping a charge on the locked door that barred their way down. Thompson had passed on the warning that the windows were barred, so they had changed their original plan of rappeling off the roof and going in through the windows.

Edberg looked up as the OH-58 swooped in from the south, its bright searchlight blinding the guards on the ground as it settled in toward the landing pad. The man in charge of the demolitions gave Edberg the thumbs-up. Edberg signaled for him to wait.

# SECURITY CENTER, RING MAN'S VILLA

Lopez, the security man in charge of this shift, was confused. He was listening to the radio reports from the guards outside concerning the inbound helicopter. From his room on the back side of the first floor of the main building, Lopez couldn't see anything, but he could hear the aircraft. The guards were reporting that it looked like the Ring Man's helicopter, yet Lopez had not been told that the aircraft was en route or that the Ring Man had called for it.

He didn't even consider ordering his men to fire at it. The Ring Man would have his ass if he shot up the boss's helicopter. He keyed his radio. "Let it land and find out what that idiot of a pilot is doing up here. The boss is going to be pissed if this woke him up."

The guard at the landing pad acknowledged.

## TIGER FORCE

Rabitowski smiled as the skids of the bird settled on the concrete landing pad. Two Colombian guards were moving toward
the aircraft from the front. Cullen suddenly twisted his throttle
to flap the blades. The two guards bent their heads even further
and covered their eyes at the sudden onslaught of wind.

As they did so Griffin and Jacobs leaned out of the open
back doors, one on either side, and gunned down the guards,
using their silenced MP5s.

"Tiger, two down LZ," Rabitowski reported over the radio
as he got out. Griffin and Jacobs started sprinting for the front
gate, their RPG rocket launchers over their shoulders. Cullen
rolled off the throttle and stepped out next to Rabitowski; they
headed for the cars parked in the lot.

## 10:31 P.M., SNAKE FORCE

Tremont started firing. He was slightly off his boast to Riley
of a round every two seconds, but he wanted to be sure he
hit his targets. He fired and worked the bolt like a well-oiled
machine. The rifle puffed as each of the three rounds left the
barrel. They were all out in slightly less than nine seconds.

"Tremont, three down, north, north, and south," he whispered into his mike.

Below him, Thompson was trying to find the last remaining
guard. The man must be somewhere on the west side. He
spoke into his voice-activated mike. "We've still got one on
the outside. I think he's on the west side."

## SECURITY CENTER,
## RING MAN'S VILLA

Lopez heard nothing but the sound of the helicopter winding
down. He keyed his mike. "Hosea? Antonio?" He frowned at

the lack of an answer. He was interrupted by the buzzing of his phone. He sighed as he realized it was the line from the Ring Man's room.

"Yes, sir."

"What is going on? What is my helicopter doing here?"

"I don't know, sir. I'm trying to find out."

"Find out and let me know." The other end slammed down.

An unpleasant, tingling feeling grew in Lopez's stomach as he continued to receive no answer from the men who had been waiting for the aircraft to land. He considered alerting the other guard shift of eight men who were sleeping in the room next to this one. Or perhaps he should go out himself to check on why the helicopter was here. He wished the Israeli was here to handle this. He was still trying to figure out what to do when the guard from the west wall called him.

"Lopez, this is Rene. I'm heading around front. I don't see—" There was a thunk followed by a brief gurgling noise.

## SNAKE FORCE

"Tremont, one down west side." Tremont smiled as he worked the bolt and reloaded. The last guard had shown just enough of his head around the side of the building.

Thompson listened as other reports came in.

"Tiger One in place."

"Eagle going in."

## EAGLE FORCE

Edberg signaled. There was a flash and hiss as the charge ate through the lock. The door swung open and the ten men slipped in, Edberg in the lead. They halted at the foot of the stairs and the team split. Four men headed toward the west wing, while the other six began work on the second floor.

They fanned out on the second floor, moving in a practiced routine. They began clearing, room by room. The first indication that anything unusual was happening in the building finally occurred—the muffled roar of a shotgun echoed up from the east wing.

## RILEY AND WESTLAND

Getting in had been easier than expected. The patio doors at the rear of the wing had carelessly been left unbarred. Riley had pried them open with his knife. Starting from the farthest room out, they had begun working their way down the corridor toward the main building. The first three rooms had been empty.

Riley turned the knob on the fourth door and stepped through to the right while Westland stepped to the left. In the dim light shed by a single lamp, they were greeted by the sight of a man and a woman in a compromising position on the bed.

The man dove for a gun on the nightstand and Riley pinned him against the headboard with a sustained burst from the MP5. The room echoed lightly with the noise of his expended brass tinkling onto the wood floor.

"Stay put and you won't get hurt," Riley hissed at the woman in Spanish. She nodded weakly, holding the sheet up in front of herself with one hand. Riley turned for the door.

The repeated roar of Westland's shotgun reverberated in his ears. Riley turned in surprise to see the girl on the bed crumpling forward, a pistol in her hand, practically disemboweled by the slugs and buckshot from Westland's gun.

"Riley, two down east wing," he whispered into the mike as he and Westland turned for the hallway. He was conscious that he'd made a bad mistake in not shooting the woman to start with. Kate had saved his ass.

## 10:32 P.M., SECURITY CENTER, RING MAN'S VILLA

Lopez screamed for the men in the next room as he grabbed his MAC-10. He yelled into the radio: "Jaime, get your people up here. We're being attacked!"

He waited for the brief acknowledgment from the leader of the four men manning the ambush position down the driveway before he headed for the door.

Lopez swung the door open and stepped into the main foyer. He spotted two black-clad men moving up on the second-floor stairwell. He was preparing to fire when an explosion blew open the locked front double doors. Lopez swung around to see two more dark-clad men stepping through the smoking wreckage. He fired a wild burst at them. In return, a sustained burst of machine-gun fire pummeled him back into his office.

Rabitowski let up on the trigger of the SAW machine gun with a satisfying click. "Tiger, one down first-floor foyer, main building."

He swung the muzzle slightly to the left as another door opened and a half-dressed Colombian stepped out waving a pistol. As he pressed the trigger Rabitowski could see the outlines of other men behind the first. He decided to make a clean sweep of things. Keeping the trigger depressed, he swept the doorway and then stitched a pattern on the walls.

The 5.56mm steel-jacketed rounds tore through the plaster, leaving carnage in the guard room. Rabitowski fired until he expended all one hundred rounds in the drum magazine. When the bolt slid forward and halted for lack of ammo, he expertly pulled another drum out of the bag on his hip and reloaded.

"Tiger, a bunch down, first-floor foyer, main building." Rabitowski smiled contentedly and glanced over at Cullen. The pilot shook his head. Some of these old guys sure were crazy.

Rabitowski swung his barrel to the left as two figures stepped out of the hallway from the east. He relaxed his finger when he saw through his goggles the glowing bands of tape on the newcomers. The old sergeant major's eyes widened as he noticed that one of the newcomers was a woman. Goddamn, he thought. What the hell was the army coming to?

# EAGLE FORCE

Edberg was the second man into Ring Man's bedroom. They were met with the sight of the man, whose picture they had memorized, holding a pistol to the head of a naked young girl whom he held in front of him as a shield.

"I'll kill her if you come any closer," the Ring Man yelled out in Spanish.

Edberg keyed his mike. "Eagle. I've got our target here. Second floor. Center door. He's holding a young girl prisoner. Rest of floor secured."

From the hill Thompson updated the team leader. "Thompson. Sitrep. Compound secure. East and west wings secure. First and second floors main building secure. No sign of the prisoner. You've got the only live one there. Hawk two minutes out."

Edberg considered the situation. The girl was expendable. No one would say anything if they wasted her.

Another figure appeared behind Edberg. "Back out, sir. I'm Riley. I'll handle this."

Edberg didn't question the man and, nodding his head at his partner, he backed out the door around Riley.

Riley glared at the Ring Man. He knew the exfil bird was due shortly and they didn't have time to screw around with this fellow. He dropped his MP5 on its sling and drew his Beretta. He aimed it directly at the Ring Man's forehead.

"Where's the American?"

The Ring Man smiled. "If that is who you came for you are too late. He's not here."

The two cars that had left earlier, Riley realized. That was the only time they could have moved Powers. He took a step closer to the Ring Man.

"I'll kill her!" the Ring Man screamed as he screwed the muzzle of the gun into the side of the girl's head, causing her to cry out.

"Go ahead." Riley fired. The round impacted exactly in the center of the Ring Man's forehead, making a tiny black hole on entry. It exited the rear, blowing off half the back of his head. The pistol slipped out of lifeless fingers. The girl stayed where she was, frozen. Riley drew a bead on her momentarily, then lowered his barrel. He whipped off his belt, tied her hands together, and threw her over his shoulder.

"Riley. Ring Man dead. Has anyone seen any sign of Powers?"

"Thompson. Negative. Building has been cleared. He isn't here. Any idea where he could be?"

Riley felt as though he'd been hit with a sucker punch. All this only to find that Powers had been moved. "Riley. They must have moved him out this afternoon."

Westland appeared at his side as he carried the girl down the stairs. She pulled the mike away from her lips as she spoke to him. "What now? They must have moved Powers in that two-car convoy you saw leave earlier."

Riley nodded. His brain went into overdrive as he ran out into the backyard with his prisoner. The two cars had returned less than an hour after departing. If Powers had been in one of those cars, he had either been transferred to another vehicle or was being held relatively close by, probably in Bogota, Riley thought.

## 10:33 P.M., SNAKE FORCE

Thompson shifted his gaze as Tremont alerted him.

"Tremont. Got a pickup truck coming up the drive. Probably the guards from the road. I can see two men in the back with weapons."

"Thompson. Tiger, you copy that?"

"Tiger, roger."

## TIGER FORCE

Griffin released the safety on the RPG. He glanced over to the other side of the road where Jacobs was crouched, ready with his rocket launcher. Through his goggles he could make out the glow of the headlights coming closer.

Griffin pulled off the goggles and peered into the darkness

through the NSP-2 infrared night sight of the launcher. The headlights appeared around a curve, eighty meters away, coming fast. Griffin centered the cross hairs of the RPG right between the two lights, and tracked. He waited until they were only fifty meters away before firing.

The rocket leapt from the tube. It covered the fifty meters in less than a second. The 85mm projectile tore into the front of the pickup truck and exploded, turning the vehicle into a blazing fireball that rolled off the left side of the road and tumbled down the slope toward the valley.

"Tiger, vehicle destroyed."

"Snake, roger. Hawk one minute out. All elements pull back."

Griffin and Jacobs ran back up the driveway, where they met Rabitowski, who had just lit the fuse running to the charges he and Cullen had rigged on the cars. The old NCO ran over to the OH-58 and threw in a satchel. He patted the side of the aircraft. "You done good," he muttered and then turned back to the other members of his team. "Let's go."

They raced around the building, where they were met by the other members of the strike force heading for the backyard. Edberg was standing next to the elevated diving board, counting heads as people came running up. He could hear the helicopter now, coming in from the west. He spotted Riley with a girl over his shoulder and ran over to him.

"What are you going to do with her? We can't take her with us."

Riley shook his head. "I'll keep her here. I'm not going with you."

"What!" Edberg glanced up as the massive HH-53 chattered in above them. "What are you going to do?"

"I have to find Powers. I'll take one of the cars up front."

Westland stood next to him. "I'm staying with you."

Edberg shook his head. He had no time to argue. "If you don't get on that bird you're not my responsibility anymore. Also, the cars up front are rigged to blow."

"How long a fuse?"

Edberg shrugged. "Five minutes, but I'm not sure how long ago Rabitowski lit it. He's . . . " His next words were lost in the roar as the helicopter settled in. Edberg shook his head as Riley and Westland sprinted off for the front of the villa, Riley still carrying the young Colombian girl.

## 10:34 P.M., HAWK FORCE

The pilot of the Pave Low flared to a hover above the swimming pool and carefully rotated his aircraft around. The pool was the only place large enough, and clear enough, for the massive blades of the helicopter to rotate freely. As the pilot lowered the bird he listened to the instructions of his crew chief, who was leaning out the open back ramp: "Five meters. Four. Three. Little more back. Good. Two. One. Hold it. Hold it." The aft end of the aircraft hit lightly into something solid.

The pilot fixed on the horizon as he tried to steady the aircraft. In the back the members of the strike force were clambering on board, using the three-meter diving board leading to the back ramp. The pilot held the helicopter in place for the twenty seconds it took all the members to get on board.

He heaved a sigh of relief as the radio crackled. "This is Eagle Leader. We've got everyone on board who's coming." Pulling in collective, the pilot lifted and headed for knoll 8548.

In the rear, the two crew chiefs were preparing the hoist with a jungle penetrator. As the pilot brought the aircraft to a hover over the knoll they quickly lowered the penetrator. Tremont and Thompson hooked their vests onto the loop on the penetrator with snap links. "We're on," Thompson called out on the radio.

The pilot didn't wait for them to be reeled in; he lifted and accelerated to the west. They'd be pulled in while the helicopter was moving.

## RING MAN'S VILLA
## 10:35 P.M.

Riley led the way around the corner of the building. The HH-53 was already winging off to pick up the men on the knoll.

He stopped at the first car he found in the lot. A blue BMW. He put the girl down and told Westland to watch her.

He tore the detonating cord off the charges on the car and opened the door. He reached under the dash, hoping his skills from childhood were still good. With his knife he slashed the ignition wires and then crossed them, ignoring the sparks. The engine coughed and then roared to life. Westland swung open the back door and followed the young girl in.

Riley spun the wheel and headed for the gate. He was halfway down the drive when the OH-58 blew. He instinctively ducked as shrapnel pinged off the back of the car. They were just passing through the gates when the charges in the cars went off, turning the parking lot into a roaring inferno.

# FORT BELVOIR, VIRGINIA
## 11:12 P.M.

"Hammer Base, this is Eagle Leader. Over."

Macksey grabbed the microphone. The last report they had had over the SATCOM was from the Snake element, advising that the exfiltration helicopter was retrieving the people from the strike force at the villa and that they were shutting down their radio in anticipation of being picked up.

"Hammer Base here. Give me a sitrep. Over."

"Mission a success. I say again, mission a success. No friendly casualties. Over." Three sighs of relief of varying magnitude could be heard from the generals gathered around the radio.

"What about the target? Over."

"Target completely destroyed and designated individual terminated. Over."

Pike nudged Macksey. "Check on Riley and Westland. And see if they got Powers out, too."

"This is Hammer Base. What about the assets you met down there and the hostage? Over."

There was a lengthy pause. Pike felt his stomach tighten in anticipation of bad news. "The assets chose to remain in country to search for the hostage, who was not present at the target site. Over."

"What!" Macksey exploded at Pike. "What the hell do they think they're doing?" He didn't wait for an answer as he keyed the mike. "What are they going to do? Over."

"Uh, that's unknown. I really didn't have a chance to talk with them. They made the decision as we were loading this bird for exfil, and I had more important things to worry about. Over."

Macksey dropped the mike and turned to face Pike. "What the hell do we do now? I've got to go over and brief the people across the river about what just happened, and we still have those two idiots of yours running around down there."

Pike looked the general straight in the eye. "Don't forget you also have Powers still being held prisoner. If Riley decided to stay there, he must feel there is still a chance to rescue him. Don't forget that when you brief the politicians. Also don't forget to tell them that we finally went and kicked ass, just like they run their mouths off about doing."

# FRIDAY,
# 6 SEPTEMBER

## BOGOTA
## 12:52 A.M.

Riley glanced in the rearview mirror as he negotiated the streets of Bogota. Kate had put her sweatshirt on the young Colombian girl, who was huddled on the left side of the seat, her hands still tied behind her back with Riley's belt.

"Where are we going?"

Riley pulled the car off into an alley. "This is as good as anywhere."

Westland leaned over the seat. "What do we do now?"

In answer, Riley got out of the car and into the backseat, shoving the girl between Westland and himself. He grabbed the girl's face and made her look up at him. "Do you know where the Ring Man moved the American soldier?" he asked her in Spanish.

The girl spoke for the first time. "Are you the crazy American? The one who killed Maria?"

Riley glanced at Westland, then back at the girl. "Yes."

"Why did you save me from the Ring Man? What are you going to do to me now? Are you going to kill me?"

"I need this information. If you tell me where they moved the American, I'll let you go. The Ring Man is dead. He cannot harm you anymore."

Riley sat back against the door and waited as the girl sorted all this out. He didn't want to start hurting her, but he would if he had to. He was startled as Westland spoke to him in English. "Dave, could you leave the two of us alone for a few minutes? Let me talk to her."

Riley shrugged. It was as good a bet as any. He got out and began to check the alley. They were about a mile from the American embassy, according to Riley's calculations. The immediate neighborhood was pretty rundown. The alley entered onto the main road and at the other end led to a series of smaller roads. It was a satisfactory place to hole up until he could figure out their next course of action. If the girl didn't give them anything, Riley wasn't sure what he'd do.

He glanced back down the alley as the car door opened. The girl slipped out and ran in the opposite direction. Riley drew his Beretta as he started in pursuit.

Westland followed the girl out of the car and raised a hand at Riley. "Hold it! Slow down. I'm letting her go."

Riley was torn between chasing the girl and hearing Westland's explanation. He decided to trust her. Holstering his pistol, he sat on the hood of the car and stared at his partner expectantly.

Westland sat down next to him. "Powers was in that convoy that left yesterday. Apparently, President Alegre had asked for a truce with the Ring Man. There's an Israeli named Ariel who works for the Ring Man. He suggested offering to turn over Powers to Alegre as a sign of good faith. In reality, the girl says they were planning to use that meet as an assassination attempt on Alegre."

"That still doesn't tell me where Powers is."

"How about if I drive you there before I forget the directions?"

Riley hopped off the hood. "The keys are in the ignition."

## 1:10 A.M.

Since the word of the attack on the villa and the confirmation of the Ring Man's death, Ariel had watched the sicarios in his detachment slowly melt away. One hour later he was alone in the house with the American prisoner. Ariel knew the sicarios were going into hiding until they found out which way the winds of power were blowing. They'd reappear when they knew who was the strongest and attach their new loyalties there.

Which wasn't too bad an idea, Ariel thought to himself. Without Ring Man he was in a precarious situation. The Rameriz family, or what was left of them, would be after him as long as one of them was alive. The Colombians were as bad as Sicilians when it came to a blood feud.

Ariel was tired of this pigsty of a country anyway, but his options were limited. He couldn't go back to Israel. Africa had plenty of employment opportunities but was an even worse place to live than Colombia, in his opinion. Whatever he did, Ariel knew he had to do it fast, before one of the sicarios made the brilliant deduction that killing the Israeli would be an excellent way to ingratiate himself with the Rameriz family.

Ariel looked at the bound and gagged American soldier lying on the floor. The man was still glaring back at him defiantly. Ariel had never met such a mule-headed man. He had tried taking the gag out of his mouth to let him eat, but the man immediately started into a cursing tirade like the one in the helicopter yesterday. Ariel was tired of dealing with him. He had planned on killing him after hitting Alegre anyway.

Ariel drew his Walther PPK and walked over to the prisoner. The man's eyes followed him until Ariel went behind him and knelt down with a knee in the man's back. "I'm afraid your friends have caused us much trouble. Plans have changed and you are excess baggage I can no longer afford to carry around."

Ariel placed the muzzle of the PPK in the back of the American's head. The man was jerking with all his might, trying to throw Ariel off, but he was too securely bound for that. Ariel released the safety. As his finger started to tighten on the trigger a thought occurred to him.

Ariel stood up and went into the next room. He picked up the phone and asked for the operator.

# UNITED STATES EMBASSY, BOGOTA
## 1:10 A.M.

Strom was still half asleep as he walked over to the phone the duty officer indicated. He didn't appreciate being woken out of a sound sleep to take a phone call from an anonymous person. The duty officer said that the man wanted to talk to someone who knew something about Jameson.

Strom grabbed the phone. "What do you want?"

The voice on the other end had a strange accent. "Are you a person who is able to make decisions?"

Strom rolled his eyes. "Who the hell is this?"

"Are you aware of what really happened this past Sunday night at Barranquilla when your commando team was ambushed trying to destroy a cocaine-processing factory?"

Strom was quickly waking up. "Who is this? What do you want?" He put a hand over the phone and hissed to the duty officer. "Can you trace this?" The man nodded and ran from the room.

"Who I am doesn't matter. What does matter is that I have the fifth man from that team in the house here with me and he's still alive. I want to give him to you in exchange for a little something."

"How do I know you really have him?"

"You don't. But you have nothing to lose. If you don't give me what I want, I will simply blow his brains out and go on my merry way, and neither of us will be very happy. But if you take a chance and come here, we can both be happy."

Strom gripped the phone harder. What the hell was the duty officer doing? "What do you want?"

"An American passport. I know you have spares there in

the embassy for travelers who have lost theirs. I want to go home and I can't get there with my present passport. So you will give me one made out in a new name and appropriately stamped. You have forty-five minutes to be here."

Strom looked at his watch. Getting Powers back would be a nice feather in his hat, especially after all the screwups on this operation over the past week. "What name on the passport?"

"I'm glad you're a reasonable man. The name doesn't matter."

"Where do I meet you?"

"Go down Bolivar Boulevard until you pass the Memorial Park on your right. Turn right on the first street after the park. Go two blocks and turn left. Third house on the right. Come alone. Try anything stupid and the American dies. You can make it in forty-five minutes if you hurry."

The phone went dead. Strom took a second to memorize the directions. The duty officer came running in, followed by another man with a case under his arm. "What line do you want traced?"

Strom sighed. "You bloody fools. You're too damn late." He turned to the duty officer. "Where do you keep the blank passports and official seal?"

# BOGOTA
## 1:33 A.M.

Riley looked through the windshield down the darkened street. "She didn't know which one exactly?"

Westland shook her head. "She said it was either the second or third in."

Riley checked the action on his MP5 one more time. "Shit. I don't want to bust into the wrong house. It'll cause a ruckus and warn the people in the right one."

Westland pulled out her Beretta. "How about we each take one?"

Riley considered that. He didn't like it. The sicarios were sure to have a lot of firepower in whichever house they were holding Powers, especially if they were planning on assassinating the president. Going in alone would be almost suicidal.

He looked at the two houses in question one more time. Both were similar one-story structures surrounded by a low wall with a small gate facing out into the street. "Sure is damn quiet here. You'd think they'd have more cars or something." There were a few cars parked in the street. One was in front of the third house in. He didn't recognize the car from his surveillance at the villa. Still, this Israeli had to have wheels. Neither house had a garage.

"The third one in. We'll both . . . "

He paused as headlights turned the corner behind them. He pressed Westland down into the seat as a car drove past slowly. Riley peeked over the dash. The newcomer parked behind the car Riley had just been watching. "What the hell is going on? That's an American embassy car from the license plate."

Westland popped up next to him and they watched a man get out. "That's Strom," she whispered.

Riley had no idea what was going on, but he knew that it could not be a coincidence. The third house had to be the one. He watched as Strom pushed open the front door of the house and disappeared inside.

"Let's go."

## 1:34 A.M.

Ariel turned on a light in the living room and examined the passport carefully. "Very good."

Strom spoke from his position across the room. "Where's Powers?"

Ariel looked at the American. "Did you record this passport into the log at the embassy?"

Strom nodded. "If I didn't it would be reported as stolen."

"Good." Ariel looked at the passport one more time, then put it into his pocket. Getting a photo would be easy. This passport would at least get him back into Israel. After that he could assume a new identity. He had enough money squirreled away in various world banks to live comfortably for the rest of his life. If he had killed the American that would have just added another group of people who would have been after him. This had worked much better for everyone.

"Your man is in the kitchen. He's tied up on the floor. He's been quite a pain in the ass." Ariel headed for the door. "It's been a pleasure doing business with you."

## 1:36 A.M.

Riley had heard enough. He kicked the door open and drew down on the Israeli. Westland slid in behind him and to his right. The Israeli froze with his pistol halfway up.

Riley spoke. "Don't move an inch."

Strom started to intercede, but Westland shoved him back out of the field of fire. The CIA man put out his hand. "Don't do anything stupid. Powers is alive in the kitchen. Let this man go and Powers is ours."

Riley nodded at Westland. "Check the kitchen." He kept the muzzle on Ariel. "You stay there until we find out if he really is alive."

The tableau stayed frozen for thirty seconds. Then out of the corner of his eye Riley spotted a familiar figure in the doorway to the kitchen. "You all right, compadre?"

"Yeah. Little sore and hungry."

"Who's this I've got under my gun?" Riley was pretty sure it was Ariel, as described by the girl, but he wanted to confirm.

Powers sidled across the room followed by Westland, making sure to keep out of Riley's line of fire. "That's an ex-Israeli scumbag named Ariel. He's the Ring Man's main security man. He was about to kill me when he came up with the brilliant idea of trading me for the passport."

Riley squeezed the trigger. The chugging of the silenced weapon was the only sound in the room as Riley's rounds slammed Ariel into the wall and held him there momentarily. The Israeli slowly slid down the wall, leaving a smear of blood behind him.

Riley looked up at Strom, who was staring at Ariel with a mixture of shock and outrage. Riley reloaded his MP5 and turned for the door. He stopped in front of Strom. "No more deals."

# FRIDAY,
# 20 SEPTEMBER

## BRONX, NEW YORK
## 8:10 A.M.

Riley stared at the old building across the street. Students were streaming toward it from all directions. It was a beautiful fall day with the sun warming away the night's coolness.

He turned and smiled at Kate as she linked her arm through his and gave it a squeeze. They'd driven up to the city yesterday. The previous evening had been taken up with introducing Kate to his family. Riley thought his mom liked her.

"So that's where you went to high school?"

Riley nodded. "Evander Childs. Graduated more professional basketball players than any other high school in the country, although I think some school in Philly says otherwise."

Kate laughed. "That's something to be proud of."

Riley gave her a mock serious frown. "Well, actually it is. You got to have something. For a lot of these kids the future isn't too bright." He tugged her. "Come on. Let's cross."

They dashed across Musholu Parkway and walked past the front of the school. Riley was feeling pretty good. The last couple of weeks had been rough, but things were sorting themselves out. Pike had been forced to retire but nobody was anxious to make waves. There were several reasons for that. The people in power in Washington couldn't argue with success. The Colombian government hadn't done any complaining. Keeping the whole thing quiet seemed to be the best route.

Riley's thoughts were interrupted by two black youths who stepped in front of them. Riley had let go of Kate and was already moving into his ready stance when he realized that it wasn't a rip-off.

The taller of the youths leaned forward. "Yo, man. Want some stuff? Got good stuff and it's cheap."

Riley doubled over the tall one with a side kick. His leg swept the second boy down and he slammed an elbow into the prone youth's stomach, leaving him gasping for air. Riley returned his attention to the first one. He spun the kid over his hip onto the concrete, knocking the wind out of him.

Riley knelt over and did a quick check of the youth's pockets. The search yielded several sandwich bags of various drugs. Riley looked up threateningly at the gathering crowd of students.

Westland grabbed his arm, pulling him to his feet. "Let's go."

Riley paused, then followed her as she pushed her way through the crowd and headed off. When he caught up with her, Westland turned and angrily faced him. "Why did you do that?"

Riley shook his head. "I didn't go through all that shit down south and have my friends killed just to have some punk try to sell me drugs in my own hometown."

"That's great, Dave. What the hell are you going to do? Clean up New York City by yourself? What did you plan to do to those kids? Break a few ribs? Maybe an arm?" Riley paused. He hadn't really been sure what he was going to do.

Westland grabbed him and looked into his eyes. "This isn't Colombia, Dave. You can't go around beating up on people and killing them because they're drug dealers."

Riley felt the energy seep out of his body. "What the hell are we supposed to do, then?"

Westland looked back at the school. "We've done what we can. If they want it they're going to get it from somewhere. It's time you and I spent some time and energy on us."

# CARACAS, VENEZUELA
## 12:10 P.M.

Carlos Rameriz twirled his Harvard ring as he watched the various military and political figures he had invited to the luncheon enjoy themselves. They were all pigs in his opinion. Eating and drinking without a single brain among them. The women he had brought were circulating and Carlos carefully noted as couples disappeared off to the right, where the bedrooms in the house were located. His video cameras would be recording the action in those rooms for posterity.

His attention was distracted as his brother came over and sat down next to him. Jaime grabbed a glass of champagne and offered it to Carlos for a toast. Carlos clinked his glass indulgently. "And to what are we toasting, my brother?"

"The general agreed to let us have the old airfield at Punto Fijo. We can run both aircraft from the airstrip and our boats from the docks. There's plenty of room for the lab." His brother smiled at him. "This was a brilliant idea of yours, moving here to Venezuela. It is a perfect setup."

Carlos smiled back at his brother. They were back in business again.

# ABOUT THE AUTHOR

Bob Mayer is a graduate of West Point who spent several tours of duty with both the Infantry and Special Forces. After leaving the Army, he moved to the Orient to devote his time to writing and studying the martial arts.

Mayer is from New York City and currently lives near Nashville, TN, where he is working on his second novel.

Flung wide across miles of sea, the task force moves across its face with ponderous eagerness; and from each ship, above the antennas and signal lines, streams the red-and-white-striped ensign of impending battle. *The landing has begun....*

# THE MED

## DAVID POYER

"Update *The Caine Mutiny* and *Away All Boats*, move the action to the Mediterranean, throw in some Arab terrorists with American hostages, and you've got *The Med*...a naval thriller at full speed!"      —*St. Louis Post-Dispatch*

"I LOVED IT!"
        —Stephen Coonts, author of *Flight of the Intruder*

It was America's longest, most withering war, as hellish in the air as it was on the ground. But little has been told of the airmen who fought, who died, who lived and dared to remember...until now. Three dozen airmen tell their secret stories of the air war in Vietnam the only way it ought to be told: in their own words. In this brutally accurate picture of brave men fighting a tragic war—a portrait that touches upon every branch of the armed forces—aviation journalist Philip D. Chinnery finally honors the heroes who have been nearly forgotten.

# LIFE ON THE LINE

## TRUE STORIES OF VIETNAM AIR COMBAT TOLD BY THE MEN WHO LIVED IT

### Philip D. Chinnery

"An uncommonly vivid picture of what it's like to wage a modern air war...engrossing!"            —*Kirkus Reviews*

It was first called a "police action." Three years and thousands of casualties later, they called it a war. But it wasn't a glirious war. There were no monuments built to honor the dead. No parades to celebrate the survivors. It was a controversial war in which Americans fought and died bravely, pitted against numbing cold, overwhelming odds, and the horrors of a trench war to rival that of the First World War.

In this stirring oral history, the man who brought the words of World War II vets to life in *Sempre Fi, Mac* lets Marines who served in Korea speak their minds. From machinegunners to radiomen, from Medal-of-Honor winners to Purple-Heart recipients, from Naval doctors to POWs, Henry Berry has assembled a memorable host of soldiers who vividly recount what it's like to be America's "forgotten heroes."

# HEY, MAC, WHERE YA BEEN?
## Living Memories of the U.S. Marines in the Korean War
## HENRY BERRY

### Special foreword for this edition by General Al Gray, Commander, U.S. Marine Corps

"A treasure trove of first-person reminiscences...highly recommended."
—*Booklist*